"SO THIS IS HOW ... CASUALLY ... YOU WOULD STRIP A GIRL OF HER VIRTUE."

He took her face in his hands. "Believe me, Anastacia Herrera, I don't feel casual. Do you know how long I've ... loved you?"

"I know how long you've wanted me."

. . .

But later, content, she was also frightened. "I'm afraid about tomorrow," she whispered. "Sneaking across the border into the huge giant of a country. Illegal. Anything can happen to us ... once we're separated."

"It's got to be, Tacha," he answered. "It's our only chance."

She stilled his lips with a forefinger. "I know, I know. It's the only way out of a dead end. But I'm still scared."

Other Avon Books by
Richard Vasquez

CHICANO

Avon Books are available at special quantity discounts for bulk purchases for sales promotions, premiums, fund raising or educational use. Special books, or book excerpts, can also be created to fit specific needs.

For details write or telephone the office of the Director of Special Markets, Avon books, 959 8th Avenue, New York, New York 10019, 212-262-3361.

ANOTHER LAND

RICHARD VASQUEZ

AVON
PUBLISHERS OF BARD, CAMELOT, DISCUS AND FLARE BOOKS

ANOTHER LAND is an original publication of Avon Books.
This work has never before apeared in book form.

AVON BOOKS
A division of
The Hearst Corporation
959 Eighth Avenue
New York, New York 10019

Copyright © 1982 by Richard Vasquez
Published by arrangement with the author
Library of Congress Catalog Card Number: 81-66464
ISBN: 0-380-79400-4

All rights reserved, which includes the right to
reproduce this book or portions thereof in any form
whatsoever except as provided by the U. S. Copyright Law.
For information address The Associates, 8961 Sunset Boulevard,
Suite B, Los Angeles, California 90069

First Avon Printing, March, 1982

AVON TRADEMARK REG. U. S. PAT. OFF. AND IN
OTHER COUNTRIES, MARCA REGISTRADA, HECHO EN
U. S. A.

Printed in the U. S. A.

WFH 10 9 8 7 6 5 4 3 2 1

This novel is dedicated to
Candace, Holly, and Joey.

Many thanks to the U.S. Immigration and Naturalization Service for the indispensable cooperation in researching this novel—particularly to Immigration Judge Bernard Hornback and INS Public Information Officer Robert Seitz, and INS District Director Joseph Sureck.

R.V.

They came—
From everywhere,

Some walked, some crossed the ocean
Some swam a river—

They came to another land seeking a better life.
                                                R.V.

CHAPTER 1

The fashionable Los Feliz district of the city of Los Angeles did not escape the daily humbling effect of early-morning bumper-to-bumper traffic jams. On this summer day the sun chased the morning chill away quickly, giving fair warning to all of what it had in store. Big luxury sedans and snappy sports cars emptied from the high-security underground parking lots of the plush condominiums, weaving among the countless smaller and older cars clogging the lanes, moving toward the freeway on-ramps.

One large and otherwise nondescript sedan drew attention because of the lettered decal on the door: United States Immigration and Naturalization Service—U.S. Border Patrol Div. The INS was an arm of the government that had made the news a lot in the past few years. And all who read the lettering glanced at least briefly at the driver, some with mild interest, some with sympathy, and some with apprehension. The driver of the official car paid scant attention as he maintained the capricious pace dictated by the signals at each intersection.

Traffic was moving at a grudging pace as Frederick Wilder pulled onto the Golden State Freeway from Los Feliz Boulevard and maneuvered into the "Los Angeles Only" lane.

He checked his watch and knew he was on schedule. He frowned, recalling the slightly unpleasant tone of the conversation he had had with his wife before leaving home for work.

Here he was, an acting assistant district director of the Los Angeles office of the U.S. Immigration and Naturalization Service ("acting" only because they were understaffed and underbudgeted) and in the home of his next-door neighbor, doing housework at this very moment, was a Mexican wetback maid. Wilder and his wife, Thelma, had been dinner guests in their house the previous night, and an awkward situation had developed when Wilder was forced to translate for the hostess. The maid's origin and status were quite obvious and could hardly be ignored, and although it was the duty of every investigator or agent of the immigration service to follow through whenever a suspected illegal alien was encountered, the INS employees realized the madness of attempting to do this every hour of every day.

Wilder slowed to allow another car to enter the lane ahead of him and continued to reconstruct the events that had led to this morning's hostility at the door. When they'd returned home the night before—early, at his request—the argument with Thelma had been over his objecting to being put in such a position.

Wilder had said, "Thelma dearest, can't you *see?* I'm an assistant director for the goddamn INS. My sworn duty is to deport IA's. I can't condone a wetback maid living next door . . ."

But Thelma had accused him of bringing his job home and then dragging it along to their social affairs. "You never object at the carwash when a dozen obvious IA's scrub your Lincoln clean," she retorted in INS jargon.

Wilder's argument had been weak. "I know, but that's different somehow," he had said without conviction.

This morning Thelma was still upset over their leaving the party early. He had seen the only way out of the argument was to forget it for the time being. But he felt better that now, in the unlikely event anything came of their neighbor's live-in maid, he was on record—at least with Thelma—as having objected to the situation. That was the lawyer training in him, he mused, as he pulled off Temple Street onto Los Angeles Street and circled the Federal Building.

He parked and as he walked around to the front of the building he saw the long line of people waiting. He knew what they were there for. The line stretched from the lobby of the first floor, where applicants were initially screened, out the door, and down the block.

Wilder entered the lobby, paused, standing aside, and took in the scene. His job was to send people who were here illegally back to where they came from. That woman changing the baby's diapers on the floor while her husband held their place in the line; that old man with the drooping moustache who wore what had once been a fine smoking jacket; that young handsome man in a sportcoat; the frightened couple with what looked like a newborn baby wrapped in blankets. They all differed from the working-class people he'd seen in Mexico in one respect: They had hope. They had found a way to survive. Yes, and his job, at least part of it, was to shatter that hope. To take away their survival.

But many of those waiting today were here because a federal judge in Chicago had ruled that when the INS had given some 140,000 quota numbers to Cuban refugees, it should not have deducted that number of admissions from the annual quota admissible from other Western Hemisphere nations. The judge had therefore placed a restraining order on the Immigration and Naturalization Service, temporarily stopping the deportation of all illegal aliens (primarily those from Latin American countries) who, after having registered for a legal immigrant quota number, had then chosen not to wait the usual four- or five-year period and had come illegally into the United States. These and only these were affected by the federal court's ruling. But that ruling had stopped deportation proceedings against 60,000 illegal aliens in Los Angeles alone. Now all they were required to do was make contact with the INS—inform the INS they were waiting— and they could not be deported. They lined up by the hundreds each morning.

Well, Wilder thought, that was only one of an indeterminate number of problems the Los Angeles office of the INS tried to deal with every day. He walked by the line of dark waiting people. For an instant he wondered whether, if they knew he was an assistant INS director, they would mob him. It was ironic. They, within a few feet of him, didn't know that every hour he made decisions that affected the lives of people like themselves, whose only real crime was seeking what millions of others had sought: a good job.

He crossed the lobby and waited for the elevator, listening to the babble of those in the line. He considered his Spanish nearly fluent, but he knew those dark faces judged you by appearance. They would be surprised to know that this gringo in the pinstripe suit with an expensive briefcase by his side understood them as they talked of their quasi-underground existence, the daily frauds and conspiracies that allowed them to survive. To judge *them* from appearance, one would think all Latin Americans were smallish, swarthy, and dark-haired, but Wilder knew there were countless thousands of illegal aliens from south of the border who never or rarely came in contact with the INS simply because they were light-skinned and otherwise physically resembled average Americans.

Inside the elevator, he kept an eye on the floor-level indicator. All the floor plans in the Federal Building were the same, and more than once to his chagrin he had gotten off the elevator, turned left, and journeyed past the innumerable government-brown offices with the steel desks and tables and arrived at what should have been his own office only to find himself surrounded by strange and puzzled faces. You could be sure only when you were going to U.S. Customs, as that floor had carpeting. Somebody in Customs must have connections, he guessed.

He entered his outer office and saw his secretary at work at her desk. "Good morning, Jenny," he said.

She looked up, smiled, grabbed a list of names and telephone numbers from her desk, and followed him into his office.

"Oh, Mr. Wilder. You have several . . ."

He cut her off, holding up a hand. "Jenny, please. Let me have a cup of coffee first, will you?"

She smiled, restraining herself, and went to the percolator in the corner.

Wilder looked at her appreciatively. She was somewhat younger than himself—early forties, he thought—and she wore severely tailored suits to discourage any nonbusiness thoughts. But her figure was nice to look at and she had a face to match. Wilder liked her, and regarded her as a misplaced person; she was a secretary out of a Sinclair Lewis novel. When tempers exploded and colorful adjectives modified four-letter nouns, as was not infrequent in INS offices, Jenny simply did not react. She had never in her life reacted to a profane word, much less used one. Her Victorianism was like the armor of a Sherman tank; profanity was like 22-caliber bullets.

He plopped into the upholstered swivel chair, looked at the papers strewn across his desk, and felt tired. There was a folder on a suit being brought against the INS. Happened all the time. That would go down the hall to the legal department. A request for clarification of hearing procedures from a congressional committee. That would go to the immigration trial judges. There was a memo reminding him he had to sit in on an administrative hearing regarding a Border Patrol agent accused of beating illegal aliens. He shook his head, mumbling something about one bad apple. Jenny entered with his cup of coffee. He took it and put it on the desk.

"Okay, what's up?" he asked.

She looked at her list.

"Senator Brand has called twice this morning—you know, he's on the committee . . ."

"I know," Wilder said with quiet emphasis. "Go on."

"He wouldn't say what he wanted."

Wilder closed his eyes as he guessed. "Let's see . . . some rich influential friends of his had their wetback maid picked up by us and he wants special treatment for her."

Jenny smiled. She indulged his little enlivening games.

"Probably. He wants you to get back to him like real soon. Also—get this—T. C. Segal called . . ."

Wilder was surprised. "The big trial attorney?"

"Right. Call him back."

"What else?"

"Jesus Ochoa and Victoria Casimiro will be here momentarily."

"Now let me see. T. C. Segal has a client naming me in a paternity suit. Ochoa and the Casimiro girl want to do an article on why I should be American Citizen of the Year. . . . Is that all?"

Jenny laughed. "Almost. Captain Glade, L.A.P.D. Homicide, wants you to call him."

"Let's see. He wants . . . he wants . . ." Wilder fumbled, then threw up his hands. "I give up. I can't imagine what a homicide captain wants to talk to me about. Okay, get the senator on the phone. I'll deal with him first."

As she left the office, Wilder picked up his coffee and swung it in a toast toward the picture of the smiling President of the United States on the wall. "Jimmy," he said aloud, "do you know what your hint of possible amnesty for illegal aliens is doing to us guys in the field?"

He took a sip of the coffee and let his eyes wander around the office, analyzing how he felt about it at the moment. Wilder believed he was basically an outgoing, optimistic person, but he had to struggle constantly to keep from being dragged into depression by his office surroundings. Who was it, he often wondered, who made the decisions as to how government offices were decorated and furnished? Why was he (it had to be a man, a former Pentagon official) incapable of coming up with a bright, positive color? The walls, the metal filing cabinets, the tall metal locker that served as a storage place and coat closet, his desk and chair, even the copy machine, which he understood was rented from a giant corporation, were all faded aqua, beige, or light dull brown, with either aluminum or stainless-steel trim. Even the carpet was a dull, hard brown. Valiantly he had fought back. The pictures of his wife, Thelma, and his daughter in her graduation attire were framed in rich polished walnut, and he himself had bought and paid for the bright yellow burlap-covered pinup board on the wall next to Jimmy Carter. But the chairs in his office, except for his upholstered swivel chair, were all simply a piece of form-fitting plastic fastened to gray metal legs. And the crowning indignity, reducing everything to a bureaucratic common denominator, the great equalizer, were the overhead fluorescent lamps. He shook his head with resignation and drained his coffee cup.

The phone on his desk buzzed. He picked it up.

"Senator Brand on the line," Jenny said.

"Hello, Senator! What can I do for you?"

"I won't beat around the bush, Fred," Brand said in a businesslike voice. "And far be it from me to throw around what little weight I carry. But . . . yesterday you picked up an illegal alien." The senator paused.

"What do you mean, *an* illegal alien?" he snorted. "Some days we pick up thousands . . ."

"I know, I know, you're overworked," Brand said impatiently. Wilder grimaced as the senator went on. "But this one, her name as I understand it is Ana . . . Anastacia, or something like that, and then the last name I can't pronounce, it looks like Hair . . . hair-air . . . well, anyway, it's spelled *Herrera*. How do you pronounce it?"

Wilder was thinking. "Anastacia Herrera, it's pronounced." Why did it ring a bell? "Anyway, Senator, what about her?"

"Well, I just want to ask . . . would you mind extending

her every courtesy and convenience? A personal favor to me."

"We extend everybody we pick up every courtesy and convenience, Senator," Wilder replied.

"Well, you know what I mean, Fred. I know you can't go easy on her, or bend the law, but, well, if you'll make it clear some one high up is looking out for her, it'll be appreciated."

"Will do, Senator." Yes, he thought, and then Senator Brand will owe *me* one. "Don't worry. I understand perfectly."

"Thanks a million, Fred. I'll get back to you when I have more time to chat."

Wilder hung up and sipped his coffee. The girl's name, Anastacia Herrera. Then he remembered. A man, a Mexican citizen, here on a business visa, had informed on her— "out of good conscience," he said. Yes. What was the businessman's name? Seemed like a nice fellow, no trouble. Huerta, wasn't that it?

And then something else came back to him. He himself, just after being named assistant district director, had gone on the pickup when it had occurred. The name Anastacia Herrera had remained in his memory ever since because she had made the most spectacular escape from INS agents in the history of the U.S. Immigration Service. He laughed at the memory. The story had made the rounds at INS cocktail gatherings for months afterward.

Looking up, he saw Dan Ellison, one of the L.A. office's chief investigators, leading a frightened-looking girl in her early twenties into the room. Ellison, always dressed in a sportcoat and colorful tie and shirt, was the perennial optimist and do-gooder. Although in his middle thirties, his exuberant and at times naïve attitude gave him a personality that seemed a decade younger. He was carrying a case file in one hand. The girl he was with seemed apologetic and anxious to please. Wilder waved him into his office.

"Fred," Ellison said after seating the girl, "I want you to look at this folder. I think maybe we can put Old Lady Masters out of business over in Hollywood. The deputy DA, Rinehart, is on his way up right now. Read this folder and see if we got something this time."

Wilder took the folder, appraising the girl with what he

hoped was not an altogether judgmental attitude. She was slight, dressed in discount-store flashy clothes. She had a quick, self-conscious smile that seemed to apologize for existing. Her white, even teeth contrasted vividly with her dark brown skin and gave a brief unfulfilled promise of beauty. Wilder had become ethnologist enough to recognize a back-country Indian girl who probably spoke her native Indian language better than Spanish.

With misgivings, Wilder read the papers in the folder. He nodded, indicating the girl. "She's perfectly willing to cooperate?" he asked Ellison when he'd finished.

"Absolutely. Rinehart won't have any excuse for not nailing that old battle-ax. Hey! Here he comes now."

Deputy District Attorney Vaughn Rinehart entered Wilder's outer office with the air of an important man who was called upon occasionally to do unimportant things. His manner, the way he cut his hair, even the expensive suit he wore, would all seem perfectly acceptable to a judge on the bench. He saw he was expected and entered with a minimum of flourish. He took in Wilder, Ellison, and the shy girl with a sweeping glance and a nod, and sat down expectantly.

Wilder stood up. "Vaughn. Good to see you. You know Agent Ellison, I believe."

"Sure. Good to see you. All right, Fred, what's up?"

Wilder read from the folder. "This young lady is Eugenia Gomez. We got her at the Fairgrove Nursing Home in Hollywood last week."

"Oh," Rinehart said knowingly, "one of Mrs. Masters' happy employees, eh?"

"Right. And I think we got the old girl this time."

Rinehart shook his head. "Fred, I hate to seem negative, but it's just about impossible . . ."

"Wait till you've heard this. We got something this time. If your office will prosecute." He took a sheaf of papers and approached Eugenia Gomez. Rinehart knew enough Spanish to follow the dialogue. "Señorita Gomez," Wilder said gently in Spanish, "this is Señor Rinehart. He's a powerful law officer here. He's on your side. I'm going to read to you some of the statement you made for us and I just want you to confirm from time to time that it's the truth. Understand?"

"Sí," the girl replied meekly.

Wilder stood up, reading from the paper, trying to put the

girl at ease. "Now, according to this testimony, you say, 'While I was employed at the Fairgrove Nursing Home in Hollywood, I was told by Mrs. Masters I could not bring my lunch to work because it might have germs the old people would catch, so I had to eat lunch at the rest home. I was charged three dollars a meal, about ninety dollars a month, for this. It was so high because I worked seven days a week at the rest home, without overtime pay. And each payday I had to sign my check and give it to Mrs. Masters, who would take out what I owed her and give me the rest.' Is that basically what you told us, Señorita Gomez?"

The girl's eyes were on the floor. "Sí," she said meekly.

"I'll read more: 'The other workers there also had to work seven days a week, and also had to eat there. We were told if we made trouble we would be fired and sent back to Mexico.' Is that also true, Señorita Gomez?"

The girl still looked down. "Sí."

Deputy D.A. Rinehart grunted and held up his hands to interrupt. "Fred. Fred . . . stop. It's no good. I couldn't go into court with this. Much as we want the old girl."

"Why not? We've *got* her this time. Involuntary inservitude, illegal withholding, possible blackmail . . ."

"Okay, I'll show you why not." Rinehart approached the girl, who still looked frightened. "All right, Señorita Gomez," he said in somewhat broken Spanish. "¿Qué dice aquí, toda es la verdad?" What you say here is all true?

"Sí. Es la verdad."

Rinehart paced slowly, continuing in his labored Spanish, taking the part of the unknown defense attorney he would have to face if this matter went to trial. "Now, Señorita Gomez, do you like living in the United States?"

"Of course."

"And even though you have allegedly been . . . taken advantage of by Mrs. Masters, you make much more money here than if you lived in Mexico. Right?"

"Sí."

"Tell me, Señorita Gomez: What has happened to the other alien employees arrested along with you at the rest home?"

"I think they were sent back to Mexico."

Rinehart stopped, showing mock surprise. "Oh? And why weren't you sent back to Mexico?"

"They said I could stay longer if I agreed to say these things about Mrs. Masters."

Wilder and Ellison grimaced. Rinehart went on, "Oh? Very interesting. And how long will they let you stay?"

"They said they'd help me apply for permanent papers if I said these things."

Wilder slumped down behind his desk until his head rested on the back of his chair and Ellison looked down, shaking his head. Eugenia Gomez leaned forward, her eyes going from face to face, sensing she hadn't said the right thing and eager to rectify it. "I'll say anything you want me to if I can stay," she said. "Did I say something wrong? What do you want me to say? It's all true."

Rinehart strode to the door and stopped. He turned to Wilder, waiting. Wilder got up and opened it for him with an apologetic gesture.

"Now imagine how that will sound to a jury," Rinehart said.

"I know. I know." Wilder extended his hand. "Thanks a million for coming by."

Rinehart nodded. "Ellison. Fred. See you around. I'm sorry."

Neither man said anything as Wilder returned to his desk and punched a button. "Jenny, would you come and get Señorita Gomez, please. Have someone take her down to the processing room," he said dejectedly. He turned to the girl. "I'm sorry," he said in Spanish. "We've done all we can for you." Eugenia Gomez stared at him accusingly and he looked away. Jenny entered. She gently guided Eugenia Gomez out of the office.

"Jesus Ochoa and a friend are here to see you," Jenny said as she left.

At the mention of the name, Wilder put his palm to his forehead and whispered, "What have I done . . . ?" Ellison rolled his eyes skyward.

"Send them in," Wilder said.

Jesus Ochoa was a Chicano attorney less than a decade out of law school and he looked the part. His hair was blue-black and the white shirt showing beneath his business suit was starched. He was clean-shaven and smelled of expensive men's cologne. The woman he was with was equally professional in her attire, her hair was equally black, and both gave the impression of a controlled hostility they were trained to handle. Each carried a leather briefcase with Mexican hand-tooling on the sides.

Wilder motioned them to seats, looking questioningly at Ochoa.

"Mr. Wilder, Mr. Ellison, this is Victoria Casimiro. She's president of the Chicano Equality Movement, which I'm sure you've heard of."

"Delighted, Miss Casimiro," Wilder said politely. "And what specific bad tidings do you two bring to my office?"

"I'll get right to the point," Ochoa said, taking papers from his briefcase. "I'm letting you have a preview of the release I'm giving to the press today. Basically, it says that the Chicano Equality Movement—I'm their lawyer—is bringing a class-action suit naming you, as an assistant director of the U.S. Immigration and Naturalization Service, and the director and the service, jointly responsible for conducting a reign of terror against persons of Latin ancestry in the Los Angeles area."

He handed the paper to Wilder.

Wilder put it down on his desk, deliberately not looking at it. "At the risk of sounding flippant or sarcastic, counselor, Miss Casimiro, so what's new?"

Ochoa fidgeted in his chair, obviously withholding stronger emotions. "That's pretty much the reaction we expected from you, Mr. Wilder." He forced a smile. "The suit goes on to say the aforementioned parties have entered into a conspiracy to harass, vex, intimidate, and terrorize persons of Latin ancestry, and have and are conspiring to deprive them of their constitutional rights with wanton raids on private businesses and homes wherein illegal search and seizure, trespassing and unlawful detention are the rule rather than the exception. . . ."

"All right, counselor, I think you've made your point. . . ."

"And we're going to ask you to show cause why you should not cease and desist from such illegal action, perpetrated against a people on a racial basis . . ." This last phrase triggered something in Wilder and he suddenly stood up, raising his voice a little. "Ochoa, we've known each other a long time and faced each other in the immigration hearing rooms many times. Excuse my language, Miss Casimiro, but

I've heard all this shit before. You know how it works and so do I. I'm tired of you people looking for a political power base and using the immigration service for a launching pad . . ."

Victoria Casimiro cut in, cool and crisp with her language, her attitude calculating. "Mr. Wilder." From her satchel she took out a pamphlet. "I want to inform you of something. A federally funded joint study by a research group from several leading universities has found that, at a conservative estimate, at least five million, *five million*, Canadians have come into the United States illegally within the past few decades. These people have merged into the flow of American society and are at present leading unmolested lives, although illegal aliens, holding down jobs American citizens need, receiving welfare benefits paid for by American taxpayers, including Americans of Mexican descent, and there is no evidence your immigration service is doing one *fucking* thing about it." She looked triumphant and Wilder thought it was because she had used the word so boldly. He cleared his throat.

"That figure of five million may be correct. But what can we do? Canadians are not as visible . . ." Too late, he realized he'd stumbled into a trap.

"That's right," Victoria Casimiro said quickly. "They're among the IAs you officially classify as O.T.M.'s—Other Than Mexican. They look like you, don't they? And they talk like you. So what the hell. If they're like you, leave them alone. But that's not all of it. No. Do you know what would happen if you sent your goddamn stooges into St. Paul, Chicago, or Niagara to chase the Anglo sons of senators and the daughters of college professors down alleys to prove where they were born? You'd probably be reassigned to Alaska, where you could hassle the Eskimos . . ."

Wilder assumed a businesslike impatience. "All right, Miss Casimiro. Counselor, I see no point whatsoever in sitting here allowing the atmosphere to become emotional. You've delivered your message. I'll see that the director is informed."

Ochoa rose to go, and Victoria Casimiro went to the door.

"We mean business, Wilder," Ochoa said. "We're going to make sure the public knows what you're doing in East L.A. And we're going to put a stop to it one way or another."

As the door closed behind them Wilder and Ellison chuckled in good-natured, exasperated defeat.

"Christ," Wilder said, "days like this come without warning."

Through the glass window to the reception room they saw a middle-aged man enter and talk to Jenny. He had the heavy, beefy appearance of a former athlete, close-cropped hair, and his nondescript suit clearly showed a telltale bulge at the beltline above his right hip pocket. Even though they could not hear what he said to the secretary, he gave the impression of professional politeness.

"Why is it you can spot a cop a mile away?" Ellison asked.

Wilder nodded in agreement. "I don't know. I think they want it that way."

Jenny stepped in. "Captain Glade, L.A.P.D.," she said quietly.

Wilder nodded. Jenny returned to her desk and sent the policeman in. He took a seat as they introduced themselves.

"You called earlier," Wilder said.

"Yes. Thought I'd stop by. We're right across the street, you know."

"What can I do for you, Captain?"

Glade had the air of a self-righteous man who knows he may be unpopular but has to press on with a tough job. "We got a warrant for an IA. Murder one. The name's Margarito Corrales."

"Have you placed a hold on her? I really wouldn't know a thing . . ."

"It's not a her. It's a him. Margarit*o*. Ends with an 'o,' not an 'a.' That's a man's name. Yeah, we got a hold notice with you."

"Well, then," Wilder said gropingly, "if you have a hold, and he's using that name, if we pick him up you'll be the first to know." His tone suggested that perhaps that was all they had to discuss.

Captain Glade hesitated before responding. "Well, uh, you see, this Corrales guy, he's evidently pretty dangerous. Big bruiser. Used to be a professional fighter. Has a record of beating up people in Mexico. Mean and vicious. I would advise extreme caution in approaching him."

"We appreciate the warning, Captain. Our agents are armed and can take care of themselves."

"I'm sure they can. But . . . this Corrales has a girl he's sweet on. She's also a wetback. I think she could turn him for us. She's probably been in contact with him and knows his whereabouts."

"Oh?" Wilder said. "Well, why don't you ask her?"

Glade smiled. "I'd like to. I think she's in your custody now. I'd like to question her . . ."

"Unless she was picked up within the past twenty-four hours, she's probably been shipped back to Mexico. You know, we have very scant facilities for holding women . . ."

"I know," Glade cut in, "but I got a tip that you picked her up just yesterday."

Ellison and Wilder sat forward. "Somebody tipped you . . . already? And we just picked her up?"

Glade saw their surprise, and a slight smile flickered briefly on his face.

"Right. And we wondered if you'd let us interrogate her . . ."

"Captain Glade, you know the law as well as I do. Illegal aliens, by treaty with Mexico, have the same rights as U.S. citizens. If she doesn't want to talk to you, that's her business."

"I know, I know." Glade was somewhat deflated. "I just wondered if you'd ask her if she'd talk to us. Her friend is a very dangerous man."

"What did he do?"

"He was hired by an elderly farmer to work the fields. He bashed his head in and took his money. We got the story from an eyewitness."

"Who told you we picked the girl up?"

Captain Glade's face was inscrutable. "I'm not at liberty to disclose that information," he said blandly.

"Well, all we can do is ask her if she'll see you. We have to protect her rights of privacy. What's her name?"

"Her name's Anastacia Herrera."

Wilder made a conscious effort not to react to the name.

He got up, indicating the discussion was about to end. "All right, Captain Glade. I was going to see her anyway on an unrelated matter. I'll see if she feels like being interrogated."

"'Preciate it very much," Glade said, heaving himself to his feet. With a curt nod, he left.

Ellison watched Glade's retreating back through the reception room window, then turned to Wilder. "You know," he said, "I get the feeling he resents not being able to put handcuffs on everybody, especially illegal aliens. But, that name . . . Anastacia Herrera . . . where do I know it . . .?"

"Remember we got a tip on her. Must have been a year or so ago. You and I went out on it. We went over to pick her up at that mansion in San Marino. Now that I think of it, the tip came from the same guy who just phoned in another tip on her. Huerta. . . ."

"Oh, yeah, yeah," Ellison laughed. "I'll never forget her. A real looker. And when she pulls a Houdini, she pulls it in *style* with a capital *S!* She was head maid for that rich old French broad."

"That's the one. But here's a good one for you. I got a call about her this morning from none other than our illustrious representative, Senator Brand."

"Brand? What'd he want?"

"Just wanted us to show her every courtesy. I'll bet he's a friend of that French woman the Herrera girl worked for. She probably contributed to his campaign and now she's putting pressure on him to pull strings." Wilder started to get up, then sat down and buzzed his secretary.

"Jenny, I'm going down to see a girl in the holding room."

"You haven't returned T. C. Segal's call yet," Jenny reminded.

"Right. I forgot. Get him on the line, will you?"

Ellison looked impressed. "T. C. Segal? The big trial lawyer? What's he want with us?"

Wilder shrugged.

In a moment Jenny informed him Segal was on the line. Wilder pushed the button that allowed Segal's voice to come in on the desk speaker, a courtesy to Ellison's curiosity.

"Mr. Segal? This is Frederick Wilder of the U.S. Immigration and Naturalization Service returning your call."

"Oh, yes. Thanks so much, Mr. Wilder. I'm calling in regard to an illegal alien you have in custody."

Something occurred to Wilder. "Tell me, sir, are you by any chance calling concerning a woman by the name of Anastacia Herrera?"

Segal paused before answering. "Why . . . yes. It concerns her. How did you know?"

Wilder smiled. "Just a lucky guess. What can I do for you?"

"I want to inform you that Miss Herrera as of now has any

funds necessary to post whatever bail is needed," Segal said seriously.

"You know, Mr. Segal, I've always been a sort of fan of yours. When did you decide to go into immigration law?"

Segal laughed good-naturedly. "I haven't, Mr. Wilder. And to put your mind at ease, I don't personally intend to get involved on a technical level."

"Well, Mr. Segal, we haven't even processed her yet. If she chooses voluntary deportation, no charges are filed and there's no need for any attorney or bail."

"I understand that," Segal replied, "but I'm informing you that my client will post any necessary bail and provide any kind of technical legal help she needs."

"I see," Wilder said, puzzled. "May I ask who your client is?"

Segal hesitated. "I don't know if my client wants to be identified at this time."

"May I take a wild guess?"

"Of course. If you know, there's no use playing games."

"Is your client by any chance a wealthy San Marino French woman?"

Segal's laugh was genuine. "No. No, not at all. You missed it by a mile, Mr. Wilder."

"Well, have you been in touch with the Herrera girl?"

"No, not yet. I'm retained to get the wheels in motion to help her. We'll be sending an immigration expert to confer with her as soon as possible."

"All right, Mr. Segal. She will receive treatment in accordance with the information you've given me."

Wilder hung up and sat for a moment looking at the desk.

"Christ, what's with this Herrera babe, anyway?" Ellison asked.

"I don't know. Huerta wants her deported, someone else wants her implicated in a murder, and a senator and T. C. Segal's well-funded client want to help her. Let's go have a talk with her."

Wilder and Ellison stepped out of the elevator on the basement floor and entered the huge cluttered room where illegal aliens were interrogated, processed, and detained only until there were enough deportees to make up a full busload.

The original low priority the INS had been assigned by the

government put any space available to the agency at a premium, and the basement of the Federal Building had never been adequate. The ceiling was a mass of wandering, twisting pipes and huge ducts leading to all parts of the structure above. Bulky, undisguised support columns preempted strategic work areas, and the overall effect contributed to the claustrophobic atmosphere. Another large area of the basement was being renovated to allow room for the ever-expanding operation of the INS, but even that would be obsolete before completion because of the increasing workload.

Even as they entered, they had to step aside while two pairs of uniformed INS agents herded a dozen and a half suspected illegal aliens in from the rear where carloads, vanloads, and busloads arrived almost around the clock. Two agents walked ahead of the arriving group and two brought up the rear.

As the procession turned from the hall into the processing room one of the agents remained at the door, a seemingly unnecessary precaution, to make sure no alien so inclined would wander down the corridor and become lost in the maze of hallways, eventually finding his way back to freedom on the streets of the city above. It had happened, Wilder recalled, as he and Ellison waited for the hall to clear.

The aliens in custody did not seem particularly despairing, although all had an attitude of resignation. One couple had several children, including an infant in arms. As this couple was passing the agent at the door, the woman stopped. "My two youngest," she said in Spanish, "they were born here. They are American citizens. What will you do about them?"

The agent motioned her on. "Go in and take a seat at a desk, please, señora. Everything will be taken care of."

The procession moved on into the room. More than two dozen desks were arranged so that INS officials could interrogate and prepare a file on each alien brought in. Wooden benches along the wall provided extra seating capacity when there were more aliens than interrogators. Perhaps twenty employees were at work, going through files, seeing to the needs of the aliens.

At the far end of the processing room were the holding facilities. These were simply large enclosures with seating facilities, drinking fountains, and lavatories. Men were in one enclosure, women and children in the other. The plastered walls were painted yellow, and graffiti from countless hapless aliens told of cities and villages across the border. The surnames inscribed—Avila, Coronado, Valencia, Palomares—traced a long-forgotten genealogy of Spain, and the hometowns and states of the deportees—Guanajuato, Vera Cruz, Mazatlan, Cuernavaca, Jalisco, Chiapas—bespoke the romance of Mexico. Some of the messages left for succeeding wayfarers were written with a mascara pencil, others were scratched into the plaster with perhaps a nail file or safety pin. This objectionable practice would be stopped with the installation of the new and larger holding facilities in another part of the basement, Wilder knew; stainless-steel walls now being installed would see to that.

The most jarring features of the holding tanks were the large glass windows which permitted observation of all occupants as they stood with dark and defeated faces, holding children and perhaps a few personal belongings, behind the glass, with nothing to do but wait and stare out at the people working behind desks or being brought in. The holding tanks always reminded Wilder of a showcase in a butcher shop: Mexico's chief export item—poor people—were on display here, waiting to be brought out, packed into giant wheeled crates seventy-three at a time, and returned to their place of origin like so much unusable or damaged merchandise.

Wilder and Ellison walked to the women's tank, and, like shoppers, stopped to view the contents. They saw Anastacia Herrera standing, talking to a woman with a small baby in her arms. They could hear nothing from behind the glass pane, but they watched. She was dressed in an off-white knit skirt and blouse with a light tan leather jacket. Her hair was shiny black, well combed, her skin was an even brown, and her face was classically beautiful.

"She's a looker, all right," Ellison said.

"A beautiful woman," Wilder added. Anastacia turned and saw them observing her. After a moment, recognition showed on her face and she nodded at them without hostility. Wilder asked a clerk nearby for the folder on her. When it came they examined the report only briefly.

Wilder stepped to a uniformed woman at a desk nearby.

"The young lady in the beige jacket," he pointed, "would you bring her out, please."

"Certainly, Mr. Wilder." The woman went to the door of the unit and unlocked it with a large key.

"You, please," she addressed Anastacia, beckoning. Anastacia walked past her through the door. "Those two men there would like to talk to you," she said to Anastacia in Spanish.

Anastacia walked toward Wilder and Ellison and she sat in the swivel chair Wilder indicated. Wilder remained standing while Ellison sat on the edge of the desk, the folder open in front of him.

"We meet again, Miss Herrera. Do you remember? You made us look like jackasses."

She looked at them a moment. "Yes, I remember. Very well."

She gave a small smile "But this time you win," she said lightly.

Ellison spoke up. "You didn't give much information in this folder."

She shrugged. "I didn't have much to say."

"You have been informed of your rights. If you choose voluntary repatriation and return to Mexico, there will be no record filed which otherwise may prevent you from ever legally entering the United States."

"Yes, I know all that."

"Do you know, Miss Herrera," Wilder said, "that you are entitled to have an attorney present when questioned . . ."

"Yes, I know that too. I choose to go back voluntarily. I have no legal status here."

"Did you know . . . a very important lawyer has been retained to represent you? If you choose to have a hearing?"

She looked at him quizzically. "Why should I have a hearing? If I lose, I can never return here legally."

Ellison spoke. "Sometimes there are loopholes . . ."

"I was born in Mexico. I lived there all my life, until almost two years ago. It is no use."

"You speak English very well."

She shrugged. "And French. Will that allow me to stay?"

Both men were momentarily at a loss for words. Then Wilder spoke. "There's a policeman wanting to talk to you." Her eyes went wide for an instant, and Wilder hastily added, "If you talk to him, you can have a lawyer present . . ."

"Why do the police want to talk to me?"

"They think you might know where a man named Margarito Corrales is."

Fear showed in her eyes. "What do they want him for?"

"For murder."

She showed no surprise at the answer. "I know nothing of Margarito Corrales."

"But you do know him."

She looked at them with defiance. "Where's my lawyer?"

Wilder checked that line of questioning, realizing it was inappropriate. That was police business. "Tell me, Miss Herrera, and you don't have to answer—we're just curious. You had a good job at the French woman's house. You're multilingual, beautiful, you have expensive clothes, and you're evidently well educated. I'm curious as to how a person like you turned up in our net." He indicated the glassed-in holding tank.

Anastacia Herrera looked around the room at the dozens of Mexicans being processed, at the scores waiting behind the glass window. She sensed the huge building above the ceiling, the streets of the stifling city outside, the countless miles of paved streets with countless cars and pedestrians. Life going on as usual everywhere, except here in the basement of this giant bureaucratic fortress which held her prisoner.

As Wilder pulled out a pack of cigarettes, she reached for one. Ellison held a lighter in front of her and she drew deeply. "Thanks," she said, exhaling. "I come from a different world. So different you would never understand. I was born in an old Buick, on a dirt road, a hundred miles from the nearest doctor, where the desert meets the ocean and men kill sharks for a living . . ."

CHAPTER 2

The city of La Paz lay sweltering in the August thundershowers and intermittent sunlight as the huge ferryboat crept toward the docks. The swaying date palms belied the oppressive heat and humidity that tyrannized man and animal alike on shore. Only the ten million frogs inhabiting the reed-shrouded lowlands around the city shrieked in delight at the water heat being delivered randomly and with abandon, to the accompaniment of flickering lightning and tenacious thunder.

The ship with its cargo of vehicles and passengers shuddered as the engine applied reverse thrust, and it seemed only to linger toward the unloading pier.

Leonceo Herrera sat in his old Buick, the fifth in the line waiting to debark. His wife, Pilar, sat beside him, and he occasionally put a hand on her distended belly and asked how she felt. Her replies were consistently stoical, neither complaining nor cheerful. Their five-year-old son Miguel, drugged from the twenty-hour sea journey from Mazatlan he'd spent jammed in the back seat with the family possessions, watched the docking procedures with fascination.

The ship rolled as it eased up to the pylons, which protested audibly at the great weight being shoved against them, and then the sensation of motion ceased. The unloading ramp clanked into place and the vehicles and passengers on foot began leaving the ferry.

Leonceo's 1941 Buick was now fifteen years old, and he was aware of its increasing senility as he drove through the streets of La Paz. The cobblestones caused the tires to hum vigorously, and the wheels transmitted the vibration to the steering wheel; Leonceo liked the tingling sensation he felt in his hands.

Miguel still thrilled whenever he entered a new city, and he stood in the rear, looking ahead.

"Papa, you said we would get some ice cream here."

"Sure, sure," Leonceo said with deceptive vitality and good nature, "just as soon as we find an ice-cream store."

Soon at an intersection they spotted an ice-cream stand next to a filling station and Leonceo pulled up to the gasoline pumps. This was a fairly nice station with a restroom, and he knew Pilar enjoyed using mechanical facilities whenever possible. She alighted and walked toward the rear of the station. An attendant, shirtless, wearing a sweatband and with sandals on his feet, approached.

"Full, please," Leonceo said. Then to his son, "Miguelito, get us each an ice cream." He gave the boy some money.

"Just get off the boat from Mazatlan?" the attendant asked.

Leonceo stretched hugely. "Yes. What a crossing. Veinte horas, no menos."

"Where you headed?"

"I got a job in Guerrero Negro."

The attendant, still filling the tank, glanced at him sharply and gave a little whistle through his teeth.

"Muy lejos." Very far.

"I know," Leonceo replied. "How's the road these days? Have you heard?"

"As good as ever. By the way, if you want to make a little money, some car parts just came in that need to be delivered to a ranch near San Javier."

Leonceo was eager. "Sure. What are they?"

"I'll show you in a minute." The attendant finished filling the tank, wiped the windshield, at Leonceo's request put a quart of the thickest oil in the engine, and led Leonceo to the workshop. He went to the bench and opened a cardboard box. "Here," he said, "a truck driver came in two weeks ago who had passed by the rancho. They had given him the money for new rings and valves. I was waiting for someone going that far to take them back."

Leonceo was a fair mechanic. He looked at the shiny parts and touched them. To him, factory-new auto parts were like treasure. One rarely saw them in rural Mexico and one protected them from moisture and dust constantly. "I'll give you directions if you'll drop them off," the attendant continued. "I don't know how much they'll pay you for the delivery."

"I'll deliver them," Leonceo said.

Miguel came back with the ice cream and Leonceo joined his son and wife at the car. They sat inside while they ate the cones. Pilar saw the worried look on his face as Leonceo studied the odometer, calculating. Then he took out his wallet and counted the few crumpled bills he still had.

Leonceo pressed the starter and the ancient Buick groaned mightily, threatened to start, wheezed, and then grudgingly began puffing regularly. Leonceo's life of perennial poverty had long since taught him to take small adversities as sort of divine little jokes, and he winked at Pilar as he put the car in gear, as though he had once more outsmarted Fate.

"Come on, car," he said, "I'm not quite through taking your life's strength."

As he left the cobblestone streets of La Paz he accelerated onto the pavement. He knew the smooth asphalt continued only a few miles beyond the city, and he used this relatively noiseless part of the journey to listen to the knock in the engine, a knock which constantly worried and gnawed at him. Sure enough, when he hit a certain speed, the loose connecting rod set up a piercing chatter that caused him to grit his teeth. He slowed down. The dirt and gravel road ahead would be a blessing in some ways, he knew. He would be forced to drive slowly, thus prolonging what little life was left in the engine, and also, he knew, bald tires lasted almost indefinitely on dirt road. It was pavement that chewed up tires, not rough terrain. The family had traveled many hundreds of miles on the Mexican mainland, some of it rough going, but almost always on paved roads. Now he was about to traverse half the Baja peninsula, three hundred miles north and a hundred miles west from the gulf to the Pacific.

He had taken many journeys in Mexico that were arduous, but he could think of nothing as forbidding as crossing the Baja desert for four hundred miles with a five-year-old, a wife due to give birth within weeks, no more than a few pesos in his pocket, and the vague promise of a steady job at Guerrero Negro. The only thing he had going for him was that he had lived in Baja until five years ago, when, at the age of twenty, he had left to find work and ties on the mainland. He knew Baja fairly well; the peninsula was a thousand miles long, as long as the state of California in the United States. And he knew the people. A subculture unto their own, they believed, with a different code of relationships and survival. They had an understanding of stark life, the Baja people did, more profound than that of any other Mexicans, a different understanding of poverty, and they understood a land that was unique in the hemisphere.

Leonceo knew Baja, knew the utter destruction that could come in seconds on the leading edge of a hurricane swooping in from the Pacific, and he knew the devil winds, hot, dry, that started as gentle zephyrs and kept building until cars abandoned in the open were rolled across the desert like empty shoe boxes, to be left crumpled and paintless, the bare metal glinting in the sunlight.

La Paz was behind them, out of sight, when Leonceo saw the end of the pavement and the beginning of the dirt trail. He braked to a crawl, easing the car into the ruts. Even so, Pilar suddenly had to grab the door grip and brace her other hand against the dashboard, and Miguel, still standing in the rear, gripped the back of the seat behind his parents as the car lurched and swayed. Leonceo had removed the rear seats to make room for the family possessions, which consisted of clothing, bedrolls, cooking utensils, and the like. Also, at night when all was removed, the rear of the car was a relatively comfortable bed for Pilar, who in her late stages of pregnancy seemed to require a great deal of room in which to thrash about.

The car rolled on, jostling, pitching, heaving, as Leonceo maintained the fastest speed permissible. He kept the wheels on the left side of the car on the hump in the middle of the road, the wheels on the right rode the shoulder. To make as much time as possible under these conditions required the utmost in concentration. Now and then a large boulder, perhaps jarred loose by the previous vehicle, had to be dodged. And if the shoulder on the right was too rough to chance, Leonceo would quickly switch to the other side, letting the right wheels ride the center hump and the left wheels ride the shoulder on the driver's side.

Loose sand and earth sometimes scraped the bottom of the car, and Leonceo's greatest fear was that one of those soft mounds might hide a large rock that would rip at the vulnerable underside of the car. Frequently he would have to plow through rocks of fist size and larger. There would be a roar as the tires hurled these stones against the underside of the fenders and chassis, and Leonceo's eyes, after each such encounter, would immediately go to the oil pressure gauge. A sudden loss of oil pressure would mean a hole had been knocked in the bottom of the engine, or the drain plug ripped out, and this old car would have only a few seconds to find a safe place off the road to roll to a stop. From there, they would have to await further developments.

The land on both sides of the road was dotted with crude farms. Occasionally they saw men plowing with horses or fixing irrigation ditches in which children played. The farmhouses were mostly made of mud, and sometimes a windmill nearby whirred in the breeze. This was the populated area of the lower peninsula, Leonceo knew, and he hurried along, anxious for the desert.

It was perhaps four o'clock in the afternoon when they left the farm country and the rugged, dry gullies and rolling hills covered with cactus swallowed them.

The radio in the Buick still worked, and Pilar kept trying to pick up a station, but all were nearly out of range. Soon, a complete sweep of the dial brought only a continuous buzzing, and she gave up.

An hour later Pilar told him he would have to stop, and Miguel seconded the suggestion. Leonceo stopped the car in the road. Pilar got out, taking with her a toilet seat with legs attached to give it the proper elevation, and tissue. She walked off through the brush and disappeared. Miguel disappeared in the other direction. Leonceo opened the door, stood in the dust, and stretched and relieved his bladder. Looking ahead, he could see the road disappearing into the rolling desert a dozen miles ahead. Twisting, he could see what looked like the identical road stretching out behind him. Nothing, other than the double dirt trail made by passing four-wheel vehicles, gave any sign that human beings inhabited this section of the planet. This was the Baja he had missed this past five years. Nowhere was there a telephone pole, nowhere an electrical tower, a house, or a billboard. Nowhere was there a sign of a building or a ship. Off to the right was the ocean.

Pilar and Miguel returned to the car, refreshed. Leonceo stood a few moments longer looking around at the deep blue cloudless sky that met the horizon two dozen miles away in every direction. He felt the hot dry air moving across the terrain toward the Sea of Cortez. In Baja when the wind came from the gulf, it was just as hot but moist. He liked that too, but somewhat less.

"Ready?" he asked them as he got behind the wheel. They nodded.

"When will we stop for the night?" Miguel asked.

Leonceo looked at the sun now to his left. "Won't be long," he said lightly.

Dusk was not far off when he came over a rise and saw a farmhouse beside the road far ahead. It was still miles away, and the road disappeared several times in gullies and draws before he could reach it. But that was the target.

He came to a little gully where a recent squall had washed the road out. He got out and saw that several other vehicles had come upon the same obstacle, and had veered off the road to find crossing points. One or all of them could have had success, so he walked down the dry bed a few hundred feet, saw where a car had tried to cross at a relatively smooth point, but had gotten stuck. He returned and then went upstream. A minute's walk and he saw the spot where the other cars had crossed, and he returned to the old Buick and crossed the streambed there.

Back on the dirt road again, he kept a steady speed, eyes ever on the road for rocks and holes, and the sun was setting when he pulled into the yard of the farmhouse.

The house was of mud, with glass windows. A lean-to housed the kitchen and eating area. Near an open cooking stove was a gas-operated refrigerator. A woman was cooking. A man seated at a rough table under the lean-to watched as the car approached. Several goats in a pen also watched, and the family mongrel got up and came toward the car, tail wagging.

Leonceo pulled up to the lean-to and cut the engine.

He got out of the car and stretched hugely. The man at the table eyed him.

"Buenas tardes," Leonceo said.

The man gestured. "Buenas tardes," he said. "Come and sit down."

The woman cooking, in her middle thirties, wearing a cotton dress and her hair in a bun, was stirring a pot with a large wooden spoon. She was about to holler a greeting to Pilar, who was just getting out of the car, when she noticed her condition. Concern showed on her face, and she set the spoon down and hurried to Pilar.

"You poor thing," she said, taking Pilar by the arm and leading her to the table. She sat her down and began firing questions at her concerning her pregnancy. "How are you feeling? Any nausea? Back pains? When are you due? What kind of a man brings a wife in this condition to this area?!"

Leonceo sat with the man, who offered him a bottle of cold beer, and learned his name was Angel Naranjo, and his family had been in the area for three generations.

Señora Naranjo took a pitcher of cold goat's milk from the refrigerator and poured Pilar and Miguel each a glassful.

"You will eat with us?" she asked.

"Sí" Leonceo said, "if your prices aren't too high."

"Don't worry about the price," Naranjo said, and Leonceo understood he was expected to pay but it would be very little.

As Angel's wife cooked, the men talked. Leonceo learned they had teenage boys who had driven livestock inland and were preparing them for slaughter. He watched as Señora Naranjo took small pieces of wood from a pile and stirred them into the coals of her cooking fire. The smell of burning dried driftwood and dead scrub pine caused memories of his past to well up, and he knew the food he was about to be served, the toasted bread or tortillas, the beans, the stewed meat, would all have this flavor peculiar only to Baja, according to his experience.

Sure enough, the steaming food did not disappoint him. Even the coffee had the flavor of the peninsula.

The long evening August twilight was still settling in as they finished the meal. The talk turned to how they would sleep.

"She will sleep in a bed in the house," Señora Naranjo said, indicating Pilar. "She shouldn't even be traveling like this. It could happen any time." She gave Leonceo an accusing look.

"We can sleep here in cots under the roof," Angel said, meaning himself, Leonceo, and Miguel. "But first," he turned to his wife, "I think I'll take Leonceo over to the town to introduce him around."

Señora Naranjo rolled her eyes skyward with a look of long-tried patience. "Have a good time," she said.

Naranjo led Leonceo around the rear of the house. There he pointed with pride to an old Ford one-ton flatbed truck, hood off, engine exposed, tires cracked.

"It's a great truck," Leonceo commented, walking around it. "Run good?"

"Very good," Angel replied, getting in behind the wheel. "If you'll just choke it by hand, we'll be on our way."

Leonceo placed his hand over the carburetor as Angel hit the starter. The engine came to life, running remarkably well, Leonceo thought. He climbed in beside Angel and they started off on a trail leading toward the ocean.

Angel was filling Leonceo in on the local history and citizenry. Angel stopped once to climb out and throw a rock at the family mongrel, which had cautiously followed. The dog slunk homeward, defeated, and Angel got back in and began guiding the truck through a narrow gully.

"We could have taken my car," Leonceo offered.

Angel shook his head. "Not on this road. This truck can barely make it over the rough spots. Besides, I heard the rod going out in your engine. You're going to try to make it to Guerrero Negro like that?"

Leonceo shrugged, hanging on as the truck inched its way over huge groups of boulders and small banks. "I have no choice. Work was too scarce on the mainland. Besides, I was raised on the peninsula, and I got tired of Mexico. You know about the big American company mining salt at Guerrero Negro?"

"Sí. A lot of our youngsters from around here went there. Some found jobs."

"Well, I have a friend there. Said there's always work for a good man."

"What do you do?"

"You name it. I'm a good mechanic. I drive any kind of machine. Some carpenter work."

They rounded a curve in the gully and Leonceo saw the town. On one side was a large building, lights in the windows, a tavern-general store-gas station. Farther down the dirt road was what was evidently the schoolhouse. Another kind of shop was on the other side of the dirt road and there were perhaps a dozen homes built mostly of adobe bricks and various materials such as plywood and corrugated galvanized metal.

ANOTHER LAND

The buildings had lighted windows. Leonceo could glance at any window and tell which kind of lighting was used inside—kerosene lanterns, candles, gas light, or electricity. All but the last were in use in this town.

Angel pulled up the truck beside the large tavern.

"Here we are," he said to Leonceo, climbing out and leading the way inside.

The tavern was barnlike inside. There was a smooth finished bar to one side and wooden tables and chairs in the center. To one side was a jukebox, now inoperative, two pinball machines, likewise not lit up, a gas furnace, and a wood stove. A grizzled old man sat behind the bar, and perhaps a half dozen other men were inside. All greeted Angel heartily, and Angel introduced Leonceo.

Two tables were pushed together so that everyone could sit together, and the barkeeper brought a fresh jug of wine for the newcomers. All joined in the conversation.

It was an hour and a couple of jugs later that the electric lights went on and the pinball machine and jukebox lit up. The lights flickered and when a coin was put in, the jukebox groaned with distortion.

Leonceo glanced quizzically at the flickering bulbs.

"Our generator," one man explained, "for months it's been acting up. We run it only from nine to eleven each night, because gasoline is so expensive."

"Mind if I take a look?" Leonceo asked.

Some of the men were staggering, but all accompanied Leonceo outside and down the street to the village generator.

One man explained, "We got this generator from a construction company that did some work near here five years ago. Everybody in town who uses electricity chips in to buy gasoline when the truck comes down the peninsula every two weeks. But something's wrong with it."

Leonceo examined the machine. It was built on wheels, like a trailer, with a hitch so it could be towed. He pushed a rod, and the generator roared louder and the lights in the town went brighter, but soon the generator coughed and slowed down. Leonceo cut the ignition switch and the machine died and the electric lights went out. Two men held lanterns.

"A screwdriver?" Leonceo asked. One was quickly produced. Leonceo expertly removed the top of the carburetor.

"Float valve sticking," he explained. He took out some

parts, wiped them clean, scraped some surfaces on them, and then reassembled the carburetor. He stepped back, a little proud and a little drunk. "Now try it," he said with authority.

A villager hit the starter and the machine began running much faster than before. All the lights in the town burned brightly. The crowd looked up and down the street, and then laughingly gave applause to Leonceo. "That calls for another drink," more than one said as they headed back toward the saloon.

The tavern was considerably brighter, the pinball machine now functioned properly, and the jukebox roared as it hadn't for months.

Some of the villagers came to the tavern, the center of activity for many miles around, to inquire why the generator was now doing its job, and when Leonceo was named as their benefactor, all offered to buy him a drink. It was a very successful evening, and when Leonceo and Angel awoke the next morning under the lean-to roof, they had trouble remembering in which gully they had bogged down the truck in the sand.

Three days later the old Buick was loyally plowing along over the rocky desert. Pilar said nothing hour after hour, silently enduring the incessant jostling. Miguel napped or looked off at mountains three dozen miles away, absorbed in private fantasy.

Leonceo kept an eye on the speedometer and an ear on the loose rod in the engine. The fatigue from dodging rough spots and boulders in the road while trying to make time was telling on him. Glancing at the surroundings, he knew just about exactly where they were. The cactus trees, cardons, towered overhead. Their trunks were sometimes ten feet thick and they rose ninety feet straight up. As he gained a rise, he idly wondered how many of these giants were in the valley around him. A hundred million? Ten billion? Then he was winding down the trail, unable to see anything but the cactus forest all around. His eyes searched for something. Soon he saw a boulder as big as a washtub, painted yellow. He braked.

Pilar glanced at him questioningly.

"The turnoff," he explained. "The attendant in La Paz said the road was beside a yellow boulder."

The ground was rocky and hard, and although the turnoff

ANOTHER LAND

was relatively well used, unless one was looking for it the dim tire marks leaving the road could easily be overlooked.

"If you didn't happen to see it, we'd never have found it," Pilar commented.

"No," Leonceo explained, "he also said when we came to a blue boulder, we would have gone four kilometros too far. It's well marked."

He eased into the less traveled road that would take them to the ranchhouse that was waiting for the parts he was to deliver. The road dropped into a dry streambed and took advantage of its relatively smooth sandy surface, then climbed out at an angle and wound toward the gulf. After a few miles he came to the farmyard. The occupants had heard the car approaching in the eerie desert silence and were waiting under the inevitable lean-to with tables, chairs, cooking accommodations, refrigerator, and water barrel.

Leonceo pulled up near the family and cut the engine.

The two families regarded each other a few moments, and then Leonceo shouted, "Anybody here need some new valves and rings?"

The man of the family leaped up, smiling. "Great! I need them desperately. My name is Lupe Zamorano." He approached, extending his hand. Leonceo got out, as did Pilar and Miguel. Lupe Zamorano's wife saw Pilar and immediately went to her, leading her back to a comfortable chair under the lean-to, and offering her food and water.

Zamorano was fiftyish, wore a cotton shirt and khaki trousers cut off at the knees, heavy work shoes, and an old felt hat.

Introductions were made and dinner was started. Later, Zamorano took Leonceo on a tour of the ranch.

Close by, a spring appeared magically out of the Baja desert, ran a few hundred yards, and then disappeared back into the rocky terrain. Zamorano had labored long and hard to delay the stream's return to the bowels of the desert, and had made several small lakes and a dam. Two windmills pumped water into a large tank on a rise. He had fowl, sheep, cattle, horses, dogs, and swine.

The meal Mrs. Zamorano served consisted of roasted mutton, beans, tortillas, vegetables from the garden, and coffee.

The sun was edging toward the horizon when Zamorano's neighbors began arriving. The first was a man and his teenage son driving a pair of horses pulling the chassis of a car with wheels and tires intact. Mounted in the center of the frame was a large galvanized metal water tank with a several-hundred-gallon capacity. While his horses grazed, the man had wine with Leonceo and Zamorano. Next to come was a farmer in an ancient Ford which had the rear cut away to form a pickup truck. He had three large barrels lashed together to carry water back to his farm. He explained to Leonceo his place was near a small spring, but the water was suitable only for irrigation and animals. He joined the others for wine. More water gatherers arrived and soon the entire population of ranchers in the area, perhaps ten altogether, was watching a fierce sunset.

A radio played. Leonceo saw it was a car radio, powered by an auto battery, which was charged by an auto generator driven by a small windmill atop the Zamorano house. Zamorano had erected an extensive antenna and could receive several mainland stations.

The long evening dragged into night, and the people of Baja who had gathered at the Zamorano ranch drank and talked, reminisced and fantasized. The few wives who had accompanied their husbands gathered around Pilar, telling of their experiences at childbirth. The men talked of everything they could think of, knowing it might be days before they saw persons other than their own families. A half-dozen children played in the small lakes with Miguel. The moon rode high, a giant, hypnotic cyclops bathing all in an unreal milky light.

"Tell me," Leonceo said to Zamorano, broaching a subject both had anticipated since early afternoon, "are you going to install the rings and valves yourself?"

"Sí," Zamorano replied, "I had planned to. I'm not much of a mechanic, but then no one else around here is either."

"I can do it for you," Leonceo said.

"You are a mechanic?"

"Sí. I have all the tools."

"How long would it take you?"

Leonceo thought a moment. "I can have it done by tomorrow afternoon if I start early."

Now Zamorano thought a moment. "That would save me

days. And I desperately need the tractor for plowing. But I have no money to pay you."

"You have other things to pay me with," Leonceo suggested. Both men had known it would come to this. "It's a deal," Zamorano said.

At midday the next day Leonceo climbed out from beneath the little tractor and washed his greasy hands.

"Give it a try," he said to Zamorano. The rancher pressed the starter and the little tractor came to life. Leonceo made a few minor adjustments on the engine and Zamorano was pleased. He cut the engine and they went to the house.

Leonceo's pay was a full tank of gasoline plus a five-gallon reserve can, cold roast meat and cured meat, boxes of vegetables, earthen jugs of wine, and loaves of bread. They said good-bye to the Zamoranos, and Leonceo headed the tired old Buick down the road. They bounced and jostled along, leaving a cloud of dust behind, and soon they came to the yellow boulder. Leonceo turned north and settled back to try to make time. He took out his wallet as he drove and glanced at the bills there, then looked at the odometer, calculating. He put the wallet back and smiled at Pilar sitting beside him. He raced the engine a little to listen to the knock, and winced.

"I have only one worry," he said, indicating the knocking engine. Then he looked at her swollen stomach and added, "Two worries, I mean." Pilar tried unsuccessfully to get a station on the radio, so Leonceo sang. Miguel sat in the back gazing out at the rocky mountain rising in the distance. He pictured their car as a baby ant making its way across the floor of a bullfighting arena. Leonceo calculated they could be in Santa Rosalia in three or four days, with luck, and then they would leave the Sea of Cortez coast and head across the peninsula and with luck make San Ignacio in a day, and then cross the rest of the peninsula in another day and be in Guerrero Negro, with luck, where there might be a job waiting for him.

He saw a huge rattlesnake in the center of the road. It saw the car approaching and coiled defensively, ready to strike. Leonceo aimed the car so it straddled the creature and continued with his singing.

The little city of Mulege. A murderous three days of being

tossed and jostled made the cobblestone streets feel like glass. At the town's only filling station Leonceo filled up the tank and the depleted five-gallon reserve can. Pilar saw the lines in his face deepen as he paid for the precious fluid with some more of the crumpled bills in his wallet. He then parked in the town plaza.

"Let's rest a while," he told Pilar and Miguel.

But Pilar knew he would circulate quickly around the town to see if he could get in a day's work somewhere.

A pushcart vendor was selling snow cones. Miguel looked intensely, pleadingly at his father for a moment, then looked in another direction. Leonceo looked at Pilar, who looked back at him without expression. Leonceo felt a coin in his pocket and pulled it out. He handed it to his son. "Here, get yourself something cold. I'll be back soon. Fill up the water cans."

Two hours later he was back, and nothing betrayed the happy-go-lucky air about him. He saw that Miguel had filled the family water cans from the public spigot in the town plaza. Pilar had found a restroom and was refreshed.

When all were seated comfortably in the car, Leonceo paused and pondered a moment before starting the engine. Then he looked around cheerfully. "¿Estamos listos?" Are we ready? They nodded. He fired the engine and circled the plaza, turned out on the road leading north, and when he came to the rocky, lumpy dirt road and the car began jerking and bouncing, the aches and sore places screamed at him that they had not yet rested enough from the grueling punishment. The one thing that made him resolve to endure his discomfort with as much stoicism as possible was the knowledge that his wife and son were hurting more than he. He grimaced and gripped the wheel harder, determined somehow to steer a smoother path through the labyrinth of chuckholes and ridges.

Two days later they were leaving Santa Rosalia. They had come a pitifully short way since Mulege, but the road had consumed time. Santa Rosalia, with mines and piers, shops and canning factories, would be the last they would see of the gulf waters. From there, Leonceo found the trail leading north and west, across the peninsula. A full day's drive, with luck, would get them to San Ignacio.

From Santa Rosalia the road ascended, winding through

ANOTHER LAND 35

canyons of giant boulders and cactus, climbing to the desert floor. They reached the plateau, and Leonceo stopped to look for a few minutes. Behind them, below, was the town on the edge of the Sea of Cortez, the sea itself a dazzling blue-green, the sky almost turquoise. Far at sea a ship headed toward the town, and another headed toward the Mexican mainland. A simple turn of the head and one was in another world of dramatic desert, as endless as the sea to the east seemed.

Leonceo turned the key, waited until he saw that the thermometer indicated the engine had cooled somewhat since climbing from sea level, and plunged the car ahead into the ankle-deep dust and jutting rocks that led to San Ignacio.

A green dot appeared on the horizon, visible only when the car climbed one of the desert's natural swells.

"What's that, Papa?" Miguel asked through dust-caked lips from the rear.

"San Ignacio," Leonceo replied, eyes on the road.

After another hour of plunging and spinning up inclines the city seemed no closer. But later the dot was a broad spot of green. And the sun had become a hideous, hateful thing when they began to make out groves of date palms, orchards of fruit trees. Now and then shacks appeared near the roadside, and occasionally a donkey or horse pulled a cart beside the road going either to or from the city.

Now there were small farms, but the city was a huge blotch of green growth beside a river.

They drove into the center of the city and parked in the shade of a giant tree at the plaza. The three sat soaking up the motionlessness their bodies cried for.

Across from the plaza towered the stone cathedral Spaniards had built more than a century before. Most shops surrounding the plaza were closed down in the blasting heat of the desert midday sun. Old men sat in the shade, mongrels lolled in the shade, occasionally a farm animal walked through the plaza. A chicken cackled and emerged from some bushes, and some naked children ran to see if they could locate the egg it had announced. Flies buzzed. The delicious smell of meat and cornmeal cooking on a charcoal fire wafted to them.

Leonceo got out of the car and stretched. His hair, his face, his clothes were a solid gray color from the dust. He began brushing it away. Then he went around and helped Pilar from the car. He led her to a comfortable wooden bench under the tree. She sat and was in obvious discomfort.

"Tomorrow, Guerrero Negro," he said in a tone of promise.

She smiled. "I'll be fine."

Miguel was on the grass, looking around. "Little one," Leonceo called to him, "bring the food from the car." He turned to Pilar. "What can I fix you?"

She tried to sound interested. "I'd like some coffee. Some hot stew. Bread warmed."

"Bring the stove too," Leonceo said to Miguel. "I'll be back in a moment."

He walked across the street, looking at the closed shops. Some were only unofficially closed, the proprietors eating or dozing inside. He found a small grocery store and bought an onion, a few ounces of sugar, and tobacco.

Returning to the plaza, he found Miguel had built a fire in the small portable stove they used for cooking. Water was coming to a boil. Leonceo cut up vegetables and some of the cured meat they had left and made a stew. As the stew and coffee simmered, he told Pilar and Miguel of growing up in Baja, but inside he was asking, Leonceo, is this the Baja you missed so much you left the mainland? Hijo!

An hour later Leonceo pulled away from the plaza, circled once to get on the right road, and pulled into the town filling station. An attendant came out of the dry-goods store and asked how much he wanted. Leonceo opened his wallet. Pilar saw a single bill there. Her husband switched on the key to study the fuel gauge. He then took out the twenty-peso bill and held it between thumb and forefinger.

"That's it," he said to Pilar with a little desperate humor. "If we don't use it all for gasoline, we won't get to Guerrero Negro. Simple as that."

She didn't hesitate a moment. "Then use it all for gasoline."

With an extremely cavalier gesture, without turning his head, Leonceo swiveled his wrist around so that the bill was offered to the attendant beside the car. The man took it and began filling the tank. Pilar and Leonceo remained looking at one another for a few moments, mirth in both their eyes. He still held his wrist bent backward out the window. She laughed. "You look like a movie star," she said.

ANOTHER LAND

He became serious as he studied the instrument panel.

"I should have been," he said.

The road ahead disappeared in a blurry haze of heat waves. The hot wind occasionally whipped a mountain of dust from the desert floor and then let it settle back. Leonceo noticed the wind shifted and he kept his eye on the heat gauge.

Soon he pulled off the road and stopped. Pilar looked at him.

"Wind from the rear," he explained. She nodded.

"What do you mean, Papa?" Miguel asked. He knew that his role in life required that he understand these things. Leonceo explained. "When the wind shifts and comes from the rear, when you're on a dirt road and can't go fast, then the air doesn't flow through the radiator. A hot pocket of air forms under the hood around the engine, and if you don't stop soon, the car will stop for you. Perhaps for good."

The hot brisk wind moved around the car, the only sound audible.

"But what can we do about it?" Miguel asked.

"Two things," Leonceo said patiently. "We can wait until nightfall, when the air is cooler, or hope the wind shifts."

The minutes dragged by and the Herrera family sat in the car, the doors wide open to act as air scoops, for although the wind was hot, the air accumulating under the metal roof of the car was much hotter when the car stood still. Presently Leonceo saw a tiny speck of dust on the horizon.

"Car coming," he said.

Thirty minutes later a battered old car stopped on the road beside them. A family with several children were inside.

"Tail wind?" the driver asked Leonceo.

"Sí," he replied. "I can wait it out."

The man started inching his car forward. "Everything else all right?" he asked.

"Everything's fine. Many thanks," Leonceo replied. The family drove on.

The Herrera family sat and waited. Leonceo's eyes swept the desert. All that was visible were the mountains in the distance, always mountains ringed the desert, the giant cirios and cardons, the rocky, sandy desert and scrub brush. Then he saw a small whirlwind out on the desert floor.

"Ah!" he exclaimed. "Here comes our knight in shining armor."

"What do you mean, Papa?" Miguel dutifully asked.

"Well, you see," Leonceo explained, "there are huge invisible rivers of air all around us. We can't see them. But when they collide, and one takes over a section of the desert, it makes a little whirlwind like that one. It could mean the wind will change soon."

They watched as the whirlwind danced around, a spiral column of dust and desert debris. It came toward them, then moved along parallel to the road and disappeared in the distance.

Leonceo reached down and took a rock from the road. He hurled it into some loose dirt. The puff of dust showed a brisk wind was now blowing in another direction. Singing, he started the engine and they moved on west and northward.

It had taken two days and two nights to reach Guerrero Negro from San Ignacio. Many transients had come to the area after learning a big American company was mining the salt beds, building processing facilities, and loading piers. Leonceo had parked the car in the shade of a tree and gone out early the next morning to catch a ride to the job site. It was a road only heavy trucks could negotiate, he had been told.

While he was gone, Miguel tried vainly to find something to do. Pilar had sat in the car, trying unsuccessfully to keep the flies away. A woman who lived nearby told her the ocean, which was only a few miles away, caused huge mounds of seaweed to pile up, and as it rotted it set up an unbearable stench and was the breeding place for billions of insects.

Toward afternoon she saw Leonceo walking toward her. She knew by his gait what news he bore.

And he saw that knowledge in her face. He shook his head, determined not to feel desperate.

"You saw Jaime?" she asked.

"Yes," he said as he climbed in behind the wheel. "He was working. His boss let him talk to me for only a few minutes. No jobs. Long waiting list."

They both sat saying nothing. Nearby Miguel was playing with insects.

"Okay, what now?" Pilar asked brightly. Whenever she saw him coming to grips with defeat, she looked admiringly, brazenly, at his wide shoulders, his shirt unbuttoned at the

ANOTHER LAND

neck, his thick arms, and then back at his handsome face. Her admiration was a tonic he always drew strength from.

"Now," he said, and framed her face with his hands, "we go to a little fishing village Jaime told me about, a hundred kilometros north. Miller's Landing."

"Miller's Landing?" His English pronunciation was fair, hers near perfect.

"Miller's Landing. He says I can help with the fishing and if I pull my own weight, I share in the profit. Don't worry about me, love, I *always* come out on top."

He turned on the switch and they both looked at the fuel gauge. It was on empty.

He looked at her and winked. "Lucky we got the five gallons extra. We'll be at our new home tonight."

She smiled. "I have a feeling we will. I felt pains while you were gone."

Leonceo lost no time in putting the five gallons of reserve gasoline into the tank, and they were on their way north, up the Baja peninsula, but this time the Pacific Ocean was on the left, and the breeze was relatively cool.

CHAPTER 3

Jaime had described a small village of fishermen near an abandoned site called Miller's Landing. Leonceo knew the area, but recalled no such specific village, but then there were many such places that sprang up and died down in Baja.

The border separating northern Baja from Baja Sur was near Guerrero Negro. Miller's Landing was roughly eighty kilometros north.

He had gone fifty kilometros when he heard the loose rod in the engine worsening. He slowed, gritting his teeth when he was forced to step on the accelerator to keep the car moving over soft spots in the road. Once the car bogged down in fresh sand washed onto the road by a small flash flood a day or two previously. He patiently took a shovel from the trunk and dug around the car until it was once more sitting above the sand. Then he climbed in and gunned the engine and somehow got across the bad spot.

A half hour later the loose rod was roaring, but he was near his destination. He began looking for something that would signal the way to the fishing village. Then he saw it, just as Jaime had described. A small shrine three feet or so high built like a cathedral beside the road. The turnoff should be right here. And then he heard the rod break loose. In his auto mechanic's mind, he could picture the piston firing, being driven down in the engine, but now the connecting rod was loose and it kept going down into the crankcase until the crankshaft came around to jam it against the side of the engine block. Although the motor had turned its last revolution, Leonceo disengaged the clutch and the car had enough momentum to allow him to steer it off the road.

He looked at Pilar. Her discomfort was such that she cared little about the engine.

ANOTHER LAND

"Is the car dead, Papa?" Miguel asked, not really impressed.

"It's dead," Leonceo said, and somehow he felt a little relief. Now, come whatever may, he would not be nursing a semi-invalid car across the world's ruggedest terrain.

"But we are here," he said to Pilar, as though they had somehow actually accomplished their mission. Then he noticed her great pain. "Does it hurt bad?"

She nodded and grasped his hand. Perspiration covered her face and neck. Leonceo looked around. Ahead a hundred feet or so was a house, built of corrugated sheet metal and mud bricks. A couple and their small son had come to the door, hearing the car. Leonceo got out as they approached.

"Buenas tardes," Leonceo said, shaking hands with the man.

"Sounds like the car has just called it quits," the man said. He introduced himself as Corrales, and his wife asked, "Is your wife sick?"

Leonceo shook his head. "No. Very pregnant." Immediately Señora Corrales went around the car to look after Pilar.

Leonceo took a deep breath and looked around, then looked at Corrales.

"Well, here I am," he said with a fatalistic edge to his voice. "I came from Mexico, thinking I could get a job at Guerrero Negro. Nothing. The man I knew there said I might find something to do here at the fishing village. I'm broke. We have enough food for a day or so."

Corrales took this news in stride. "Sí, they have lots of work to do. Killing sharks, mainly. If you pull your weight with the work, they'll give you a share. But it's rough."

Leonceo smiled, self-confidence returning. "I'm pretty rough myself," he said, taking out a pack of cigarettes and offering one to Corrales. Corrales accepted.

"You can live in your car. A water truck comes by every few days, and there's a well a few kilometros from here."

At that moment Señora Corrales shouted at them from the passenger side of the car where Pilar still sat.

"Rodolfo! It's coming! Now! Hurry, you know what to do. You, señor. Hurry to the village and get Maria. She's the expert. Take the horse behind the house. Hurry!"

Corrales hurried to the house as his wife began trying to prepare Pilar in the rear of the car. Leonceo ran around the house and saw a horse with a bridle standing in the shade of a tree. Corrales shouted to him, "Down the road near the shrine. It's only two kilometros." Then Corrales shouted to his son, "Margarito! Take the other boy to play. His mother doesn't need him now!"

Leonceo was pleasantly surprised that the horse responded well to commands. He kept the animal at a medium gallop he knew would enable it to go the required distance and return as fast as possible. The road led toward the shore, down into gullies, up over ridges, and the horse kept its pace.

Presently he saw a cluster of houses of stone, mud bricks, and sheet metal. A group of women were washing at a communal laundry area. He steered to them.

"Maria, which is Maria?" he said as the horse braked to a stop. One woman, thirty or so, in cotton blouse and skirt, barefoot, raised a hand.

"I am."

"My wife is giving birth back on the road. La Señora Corrales sent me for you."

As the horse wheeled for the return trip, Maria was swinging up behind Leonceo. She shouted to the others to bring what might be needed, and the horse sprinted back toward the road.

The horse thundered up to the old Buick and hadn't stopped yet when Maria was off and beside the car. The door was open, Pilar in the rear. Corrales had brought hot water and towels and Maria was scrubbing her hands. "Go wait in the house until we call you," she snapped at Leonceo, in the manner midwives use when talking to the useless husband.

Corrales sat Leonceo down at the wide wooden table and poured wine. Leonceo was nervous. He looked around trying to find something to make conversation. He saw a wood cookstove beside a gas range, which ran on butane, he knew. A water spigot came from a wall over a copper sink, the windows had glass.

"Tell me more about the work at the fishing village," he asked.

"It's a shark village," Corrales answered. "You know how to kill sharks?"

"I've never done it, but I've been around that work."

"It's not hard. Go out every morning. Kill as many as possible. Skin them. The meat is salted and cured. Once a month a truck comes through, sometimes a boat stops to pick it up. It goes mostly to the mainland. Sometimes Chinese want the skin and fins, but they're harder to cure. You can make a few extra dollars if you extract the shark's oil, but it's not as good paying as selling the meat. I'm sure if you're willing to work like hell from dawn to sunset, do your share, they'll give you your fair wage when they sell it."

"Fine. Anything. I'm also a good mechanic."

"That's good. We don't have one around here. Frequently, trucks and travelers break down. Now the Americans are starting to come down here in strange vehicles. Just for sport. You can pick up business on the side from them, perhaps."

"Fine. Is there a house available?"

"No. Live in your car. Several families near here do that. You can start building a house just about wherever you want."

"The owner won't object?"

"I own the land around here. All the way to the beach. My father left it to me."

"I don't like living in a car. I'll start making a house as soon as possible."

"If you spend your money on materials, you can have a house in a few months. Peralta, down the road, has lived in his car beside the road three years. He kills sharks. Every cent he gets he buys liquor. His kids are barefoot and naked. He doesn't care."

Leonceo realized he was only half interested in what was being said. His mind was on Pilar. What if something went wrong? What if that woman, Maria, didn't know what she was doing? He kept up the patter, then he heard Maria calling his name. He leaped up.

"Come on," Corrales said, leading the way out to the old Buick.

Leonceo could see Pilar through the windshield. She was pale, drawn, perspiring, trying to smile at him. Maria was beside the car holding the new baby in a blanket. She held the infant up for him to see.

"He's . . . he's beautiful . . ." Leonceo said.

"A girl," Maria corrected.

Leonceo reached out to take the baby.

"Not yet," Maria said. She handed the child to Pilar in the rear of the car and picked up something wrapped in heavy brown paper. "Here. Go bury this. Then you can be with your baby."

Leonceo was puzzled only for a moment. He took the wrapped afterbirth. It was warm and felt like . . . like what? Like meat or something. It *was*, wasn't it? He picked up the shovel from beside the car and crossed the street. The others were all gathered around Pilar. He climbed the small bank beside the road and walked a dozen feet or so. From here he could see in every direction. Now that the birth was over, he again felt great relief. All was fine. Things were working out. He looked around. To the east an extinct volcano rose between desert hills. A little farther north were the great mountains, barely visible, possibly fifty miles away. To the west he could see the ocean. He saw that the Corrales boy, Margarito, had followed and was watching. Suddenly the warm breeze stiffened to a dull roar, as though the forces of weather were flexing their muscles, then the air stilled. A few feet from him a giant old cardon stood, poised like the victim of a highwayman, hands reaching for the sky. The cardon was a monster cactus, sixty feet high, ten feet thick at the trunk, thorns covering it like the stubble of an unshaven giant. He set the package down and dug a small hole with the shovel. He placed the wrapped afterbirth in the hole and shoveled dirt over it. Suddenly he paused. A step or two away was a tiny cardon tree, struggling mightily against the overwhelming odds of desert survival. *The giant's tiny son,* Leonceo thought. What had happened in the car was happening in the desert also. Species were struggling to survive. He put the blade of the shovel near the tiny cactus and pressed with the sole of his shoe until the shovel penetrated beneath the roots. Then he gently picked up the plant and deposited it at the top of the hole he was covering up. He placed more dirt around it, patted the soil until it was firm and, shouldering the shovel, returned to the car. He had done something significant, he knew, but he was too elated to analyze it. He had helped something survive and it would be nourished by something of his, of his own doing, or was it Pilar's? It didn't matter. A tremendous load was off his back. Pilar was no longer pregnant, and he was through with an old sick Buick, and a new life was starting. As he reached the car, he suddenly felt a deep emotion for it. It had done well for him. And it was the birthplace of his daughter. Then a thought occurred to him and he frowned a little. It was also now his home.

That night there was a festive mood at the place where the two roads crossed in front of the Corrales home. The residents of the fishing village came to get acquainted with the new arrivals. Pilar remained in the back seat of the old Buick nursing her new baby, and the midwife, Maria, proudly took the others to see the result of her handiwork. Leonceo fondly held the infant, and Pilar said they should give her a name. He thought deeply, looking around at the surroundings in the bright moonlight. He looked at the giant cardon, and then thought of the little tiny one next to it. It should have a better start in life than the others had, and it should turn out to be the king of them all, barring some unforeseen mishap. And if it turns out to be the king, somehow the little girl is related to it, and is therefore royal kin.

There was a princess named Anastacia, wasn't there, in Europe? Yes.

"We'll call her Anastacia," he said to Pilar.

Pilar smiled and looked at the baby. "That's a good name. Our little *Tacha,*" she said, using the nickname for Anastacia. She looked at her husband. "And, like you promised, as soon as we have a house we'll send for my mother. She'll love her new granddaughter."

Leonceo's expression was one of mock resignation. "If that's what I promised, that's what we'll do," he said affectionately.

The Herrera family of four lived in the old car while Leonceo worked in the fishing village. The car served as a bedroom mainly for Pilar and the baby. After a few months Señor Corrales made a deal with Leonceo. The Corrales home was the gassing-up spot for vehicles in the vicinity. He had several fifty-five-gallon drums, and fairly regularly a huge gasoline truck would make its way down the peninsula, taking a month and a half to go from where the paved highway ended south of Ensenada to the lower end of Baja Sur. Along the way it refilled the drums of several dozen gassing-up spots such as the Corrales place, and Corrales, who was considerably older than Leonceo, said he would deed him property nearby to build a home on if Leonceo would build up a service-station trade with his knowledge of automobile engines.

So Leonceo had three jobs: He worked with the men of the fishing village; he tended the station at La Tijera, where the Corrales place was; and in whatever spare time he had he worked building his home.

By the time Anastacia was four years old she knew how to avoid scorpions and rattlesnakes, both abundant around La Tijera. The house had long since been built and her father finally had acquired another old car. This increased his range of work availability, and he might help pour a concrete foundation forty miles north, and help round up cattle the next day fifty miles south. He still worked at the fishing village, and among all his jobs he earned enough to make ends meet and feed his family. Pillar's mother came over from the mainland and helped with the family chores.

When Anastacia was six there was a severe epidemic among the children of central Baja, a throat infection, and while the girl survived it, her older brother, Miguel, did not. And it was after that that the Corrales boy, Margarito, four years older than Anastacia, began following her father around whenever he could, and she saw that at least in part he filled Miguel's place in her father's heart.

The family moved about, Leonceo sometimes finding work across the peninsula, sometimes up or down, and always she found herself attending school in little adobe schoolhouses with the children of other families that also moved around.

She was eight years old when old man Corrales said he had made arrangements to open a filling station in Ensenada, and offered Leonceo the chance to work there during the busy summer months. So the family began moving back and forth between Ensenada and La Tijera. They found a house to rent a few miles outside Ensenada. The tourist season was booming, and Pilar got a job making beds in a motel where Americans came. Pilar's mother had decided to remain in La Tijera. At the end of the summer each year, Leonceo and his family would go back to La Tijera, taking the little dirt road south of Ensenada, traveling at a snail's pace for days, and then reopening the little station.

Anastacia helped her mother at the motel, making beds and cleaning rooms. At the age of ten, when Margarito was fourteen, her father caught him and Anastacia as they were about to explore each other. Leonceo took Margarito behind the house and told him if he ever learned of such a thing happening again, Margarito's rear end would look like raw hamburger. By the time she was thirteen Anastacia was filling out in more ways than one. In the various schools she attended she did well, particularly in English, as her mother spoke it almost fluently.

Frequently during her childhood Anastacia had heard talk of how her mother had learned English. Pilar's parents had been migrant workers off and on in the United States, her father taking his family to various states in different seasons, following the crops. Anastacia was fascinated by the stories of her mother's early life in the United States.

When Anastacia could read fairly well she discovered the wealth of interesting material in the vacation reading left behind by the tourists at the motel. She began collecting magazines and other useful items abandoned by the visiting Americans. Her life since the age of eight had consisted of going to school and coming home early to help her mother. Saturdays and Sundays she had little time to herself. What little time she did have she often spent reading an American book or magazine.

Leonceo worked seemingly night and day, but the family had a television set and a radio, which placed them materially among the "haves" in their Mexican peer group.

Occasionally Tacha became acquainted with American children more or less her own age, and she gradually came to realize that there were many people who did not work, work, work from dawn to dusk, on weekends, for the sake of a few luxuries such as television.

Some American children, at least, she knew, came home from school and no work was required of them. Frequently the mother in the family did nothing in the way of supporting the family, and the father spent a relatively small number of hours away from home each day, came home nights, and never worked weekends.

Anastacia received no pay for working at the motel during this time. Her mother was only too glad to have her job for a flat fee. Such an arrangement was common in Mexico, and if a working parent had children who were able to help, it made the work that much easier and less time-consuming. It was not thought of as a child being exploited by the employer, but rather as two people doing a certain job together for a certain amount. A certain amount of money was available for a certain job, and how the worker chose to accomplish the task was of little concern to the employer.

On one occasion as they were talking, Pilar reminisced about her childhood. "My earliest memories," she said, "were of helping your grandfather in the fields. He picked crops, getting paid by the crate. If I helped, more was picked quicker. Sometimes I went to school. When I did, Papa made less money. I didn't mind working."

"How old were you?" Anastacia asked.

"That went on until I was about sixteen, then I worked in a hotel until I married your father."

"Where?"

"That was in Texas. And many times our family worked in the United States. When the crop seasons were over, they took us by train back to Mexico, and we picked crops there. But that paid much less."

Anastacia was looking at a children's geography book. The family renting the room was out on the beach. She turned to a map of the United States. "Mama, show me where you traveled. Do you know where you were born?"

"Not exactly," Pilar said, looking at the map, "Your grandparents went north from the border in Texas. Always, they took families. Many women were pregnant. I was born on one of those trips, just as we were being returned to Mexico."

Anastacia was thinking. "Then . . . you were born an American?"

Pilar laughed. "No, heavens no, child. We were Mexicans. In those days we had no papers. All of us were Mexicans. Sometimes children were born on the train, like me, sometimes on one side of the border, sometimes on the other. It didn't matter."

"How come you learned English and your mother and father didn't?"

"I learned it because I must have spent almost half my childhood going from camp to camp in the United States, attending schools, sometimes with all English-speaking children." She laughed, remembering. "As soon as I was old enough, Mama made me go to the store, or to pay a bill, because I was the only one who could speak English. The other kids didn't think my English sounded so good, but Mama thought it was great. She never learned."

When the family renting the room checked out, the geography work book was among the items left behind, and Anastacia added it to her growing collection of abandoned American paraphernalia.

When she was sixteen, the motel in Ensenada had expanded and so had the tourist business, so that Anastacia and her mother were able to work there full-time year-round; since there was more than enough business to keep Leonceo busy at the Corrales station, they no longer returned to La Tijera for the winter. One day when Margarito was twenty, and working alongside Leonceo in his father's station, a new, powerful sports car came in with a brake problem. The dapper man who got out to talk to Margarito about repairs regarded him with something more than casual interest. The man watched Margarito, who was working naked to the waist, as he put the car up on the hoist, took off the lug bolts, and lowered the huge wheel and tire with ease.

When the brakes were repaired, the man said, "My name's de Baca. I'd like to talk to you if you have time. You'll find it interesting."

Margarito agreed and de Baca took him to a fairly nice restaurant nearby. "Have anything you like," he told him. Margarito ordered lobster. "I'm a fight promoter and manager," de Baca said after he had heard a little about Margarito. "You're a natural heavyweight. You know how rare Mexican heavyweights are? I've managed two out of a couple hundred fighters. I'm willing to invest a few bucks in you if you want to give it a try. I run a stable of fighters in Tijuana."

De Baca made a show of being a spender, and before he left Margarito to return to Tijuana he gave him money to cover bus fare and make up for missing a day or two of work should he decide to come to see de Baca.

That night after work Margarito felt good, simply because he had another option. It wasn't easy to make a decent living in Baja, and he took pride in being able to do a number of things well. As he walked down Avenida Juarez he saw a group of mariachis carrying their instruments. They were on their way to play at various restaurants in town where the tourists would be.

He called to them and they crossed the street to talk to him.

"Fernando is sick," the leader said. "Want to take his place on the guitarrón tonight?"

He considered. He'd planned to stay in his little room and watch television and perhaps go out later to see if a loose gringa was among the town's tourists.

"Okay. Soon as I get the grease off me and change. I'll find you."

He'd learned to play the mariachi instruments as a boy, in the little villages down the peninsula where there was little else to do nights but play and sing. He was a fairly accomplished musician on several instruments, and his singing voice was more than adequate.

That night after the group had played all the spots where the tourists went, they found it was still early and went to a tavern where tourists never came—except perhaps a daring few who would sit quietly, almost fearfully, as the natives of the land indulged in their own music for their own sake. It was there he saw Chata, the sexy little pug-nosed waitress, and as she sang, danced, and served drinks, he remembered how she would squeeze him with her legs, how in bed she was all sex organ, thighs, breast, and mouth, and he said, "Can you come home with me after work?"

At ten o'clock the next morning he was absolutely drained. Chata was up, fixing breakfast, in his tiny kitchen, singing nonsensical popular songs. He put on his trousers and at that moment there was a knock on the door.

He went to answer it. Chata didn't have a stitch of clothes on, but that didn't bother her. He opened the door and Anastacia stood there.

He saw her eyes go past him to Chata in the kitchen a dozen feet away, and he saw her react. He stepped out into the corridor and pulled the door closed behind him.

"Tacha. How are you, baby? Why aren't you working at the motel?"

Now her attitude was one of aloof control. "I had to come into town. Papa wondered why you didn't show up this morning."

"Well," he said casually, with some measure of defiance,

"now you know. Anything else?" He was trying to analyze his emotions, reason out why he suddenly felt so hostile toward her. She stood looking at him, standing a little farther from him than she should have, one hand near her throat, defensively. He thought her attitude was saying, *You rotten thing, you touch me and I'll scream.* And he looked at her in her simple clothes, the body he knew so well, but really didn't know at all. She was sixteen now, and for years he had yearned in vain for her, she always pushing him away, saying *Papa's near, he suspects us,* something always interfering. Well, goddamn it, it was her fault he was shacked up with a sexpot, and none of her damned business.

"Besides," he went on after they had been at a loss for further words for some moments, "I'm quitting. I'm going to Tijuana today. I probably will work there for a while."

"All right," Anastacia said calmly, turning to go, "I'll give him the message." In her eyes he thought he saw jealousy, envy, anger, and hurt.

He watched her as she walked away. He leaned over the second-story rail and watched as she went down the stairs to the street. He saw her look up at him, and he knew, and knew she did too, that he wouldn't be in Tijuana long.

CHAPTER 4

Anastacia Herrera walked down the dirt road toward the highway in the gathering dusk. She greeted, waved, or nodded at the inhabitants of the shacks alongside the road. Occasionally a carload of American vacationers went by traveling one way or the other. More often than not, going in her direction. This was Saturday night. The vacationers for the most part had arrived at Velasco Beach Thursday or Friday, would leave Sunday, and tonight most had left their children in bed either in the tents in the camping area or in the motel rooms on the beach at the end of the dirt road.

The houses she was walking by were no better than her own, for the most part. They were made of discarded building materials or clay bricks. Most had but one or two rooms to house the families living inside, but Anastacia did not dwell on the poverty of these people who had been her neighbors for a decade off and on.

Her timing was right. Just as she reached the highway she saw the bus approaching. "ENSENADA," the sign above the driver read. The vehicle rumbled to a stop and she boarded, handing the driver the fare for the three-mile trip into town. She didn't look directly at him, but was aware the driver looked at her the way men in their thirties or forties look at a nice-looking girl in her late teens. She didn't mind.

There was no empty seat. She stood, holding the overhead bar. She saw only a few familiar faces among the passengers; no one she knew by name. The bus groaned into Ensenada.

She alighted, walked to the main street, and turned south. The street was a seething mass of tourists and shops, street vendors and taxicabs. Anastacia picked her way through the milling crowd, ignoring the suggestive glances and whistles from young men and middle-aged, Mexican and American.

She heard her name and glanced up to see a street vendor selling tacos that dripped chili sauce. She stopped. "Hola, Señor Saenz," she smiled. The vendor prepared a taco for her and refused payment. She ate it, chatted with the gaunt man, thanked him, and then resumed her search for her father.

She had a good idea where to find him. On Saturday nights he got off work at six. And once or twice a month he would visit a tavern where he would spend a few hours talking with other men, singing to the music of mariachis, and drinking beer. Then he would catch the late bus back to the dirt road that led to Velasco Beach. Only a few times within her memory had he stayed late and drunk too much and spent all his money. But this night she had a message for him and had to make sure he was home early; hence the journey into town and the search. She came to a dirt cross street and turned toward the bay. Halfway down the block she entered a doorway. Steps took her down to a basement tavern. She stood a moment at the bottom of the stairway, surveying the interior.

The place was crowded, smoke filled the air, the strong smell of liquor predominated. To one side a group of musicians played while the men crowding around the bar sang. On a bench to the side sat several girls dressed in flashy clothes. It was Saturday night in July in Ensenada. Soon the demands of the thousands of tourists within the small town would have to be met, and the musicians and the girls would go out on the streets. But before—and after—in the small hours of the morning, they would be here.

She saw her father standing at the bar, a beer bottle in his hand as he sang lustily. She was always pleased to see him enjoying himself. She waited for the end of the song.

One of the girls seated on the bench called her name. Anastacia looked at her. "Cora! How are you?"

"Muy bien," the girl answered. "How's the family?"

"Fine," Anastacia said. The prostitute laughed self-consciously and turned back to her companions.

Anastacia watched her father. He sang and gestured as though he were singing grand opera instead of Mexican folk songs. He wore gray cotton trousers and a matching shirt, the uniform of the gas station. He was mostly bald, but what little hair he had was still black, as was his small moustache. He was not tall, not short, squarely built with a slight paunch, a handsome man for his forty-odd years, she thought. As she watched, the bartender noticed her and poked her father's arm with a finger, then ever so faintly jerked his head in her direction with the typically Mexican economy of communication, no surreptitiousness intended. Her father looked at her, his face breaking into a fond grin as he made his way to her, staggering only slightly. The music stopped momentarily while the next possible song was discussed.

"Mi hija, mi hija," he said loudly, embracing her.

Some of his friends at the bar turned. "Ho, Leonceo," one man called, "your daughter has to come to drag your drunken carcass home now, eh?" They all laughed.

"Is something wrong, Tacha?" Leonceo asked.

"No, Papa," Anastacia answered. "A tourist at the motel needs work on his car first thing in the morning. If you came home too . . . too late, you might miss the job."

Leonceo was pleased. "Oh? What's wrong with the car?"

She shrugged. "It just won't start. They're at the Valdez motel. Valdez told them a very good mechanic would fix it in the morning." She smiled. "That's you, Papa."

Leonceo looked serious. "Good, good," he said. "I can make a few dollars maybe. What kind of car?"

"Volkswagen camper."

He gestured with an arm. "Nothing to it. All right. We'll catch the next bus back." He glanced at the clock on the wall. "But we have an hour to kill." He led her to a small table that was unoccupied. "Have a beer while we sing a little more, okay, pretty one?"

"Fine, Papa. I'll wait here and listen. Get them to sing the one about the bay horse."

"Ay! 'El Caballo Bayo.'" He rose to rejoin the singers and musicians. "¡Muchachos! Para mi hija, por favor, 'El Caballo Bayo.' ¡Andale!"

A waitress brought her a small bottle of beer. She sat watching. The prostitutes were a dozen feet or so to her side. They also listened attentively as the masculine voices reached for the high notes beginning the song, and then marched down the scale in harmony. Anastacia suddenly felt the girls grow tense, and sensed someone had come down the stairs into the tavern. Casually, she looked in that direction and saw a man in his thirties, well dressed, with straight black hair.

ANOTHER LAND

The man's eyes searched the room until he saw the girls seated along the wall. He approached them.

Anastacia could not make out the words, but got the impression the girls were afraid of him. One of them asked a question, and the man raised his voice angrily, stiffening as though he were about to strike her. Two of the girls got up and left, evidently at his instruction. The man talked rapidly to the others for a moment. She heard him say sternly, "You understand? Got it?"

The remaining prostitutes nodded and also left.

Anastacia's eyes were on the men singing near the bar, but she felt the man looking at her. Suddenly he was standing beside the table. She looked up.

"Mind if I sit with you?" he asked, trying a good-natured smile that didn't work. She shrugged and he sat down. She still looked at the singers but could feel his appraisal. A bolt of anger shot through her, but was gone a minute later.

The man lit a cigarette and offered her one. She refused without looking at him. She was dressed in an inexpensive cotton blouse and skirt, but she knew they were neat, clean, and fit well.

"My name is Huerta," he said, still looking at her.

She looked at him evenly. "My name is Anastacia. That man dressed in gray at the bar is my father."

Huerta looked at Leonceo a few moments, then turned back to her. "Came to drag the old man back home before he spends his paycheck, eh?" He said it neither mockingly nor viciously. She looked at him coolly a few moments and didn't answer.

"I didn't mean to be offensive, but . . ."

She cut him off. "But you are."

He laughed a little. "I'm sorry. But I've been around a lot and seen it all. Your father works in a gas station?"

"Yes."

"And you work too, don't you? You're a clerk in a store? Or a dishwasher?"

She looked at him with slight annoyance. "I make beds and clean motel rooms."

"I see," he said with a little sigh, "and so does your mother. And any sisters you may have. You make maybe a hundred pesos a day. Five dollars, perhaps. Right?"

Her attitude remained casual. "I suppose." She finished her beer and Huerta snapped his fingers at the waitress and signaled for two more bottles. The waitress brought them and Anastacia noted he paid in American money, giving her a dollar tip. It was an old story, so far. Even though only eighteen years old, this wasn't the first time, nor the hundredth, that a man had sat by her and wanted to buy her drinks.

Huerta set his expensive cigarette lighter on the table and toyed with it as he spoke. "Look, Anastacia, you're a good-looking girl. There's a way out of all this." He waved his head, indicating the surroundings. How old was she when she'd first heard this from a man. Fifteen? Sixteen?

She regarded him. "I saw you talking to the girls."

"Of course you did," he went on. "But listen to this. Those girls make fifty, a hundred, a hundred and fifty dollars a night with me. Dólares, not pesos. And all of them were like you once. Making beds, cleaning rooms for a few dollars a day. You know what one girl did? After six months with me she went back to her shitty little town in Sonora and bought new instruments and uniforms for a group of musicians who played for free every night in the town plaza. She paid their way to Mexicali and now they're one of the most successful mariachis in Baja. That's what money can do."

The anecdote had aroused her interest somewhat. She seemed pensive as her eyes wandered to those singing at the bar. Her father, head tilted back as he bellowed, a bottle of Mexican beer in his hand, his greasy clothes, dirty hands, always seemed ready to laugh.

She turned back to Huerta. "You know, I've heard all this before. Many times."

He gestured impatiently. "I don't doubt that. But when I see a girl like you wearing mercado clothes, combing her hair like an Indian, not knowing how to make a beautiful face out of a pretty face . . . believe me, I know women. They are my commodity. You could be the top doll in any city."

"Except Ensenada."

"Yes. Do you speak English?"

"Perfectamente."

His eyebrows went up. "Good. You don't know what a clean young babe can do. It's not just lying on your back in a whorehouse as the gringos pass through one after another all night. The type you could be, in the right clothes with the right hair style, spends half her time on private jets going to places like Puerta Vallarta and Cabo San Lucas."

He offered her a cigarette again and this time she accepted. He lit it. He drew heavily on his cigarette, watching her face. "Tempted?"

She smiled a little, tilted her head, and looked at the table surface. "Men whistle at me like I am."

"What men?" he said contemptuously. "The American college boys who come here to buy firecrackers? The men with their wives and kids in a tent on the beach?"

She sat looking at the table. He went on. "I can pick you up at nine in the morning. I have to be in Tijuana before noon . . ." She said nothing. "Tomorrow night you can be in a hotel room with air conditioning. With a dressmaker outfitting you."

She looked at him, and her feelings were impossible to read. "My folks need the money I make."

"Jesús Cristo! You'll make a hundred times more . . ."

"They need it . . . this week. Every week."

"Look. You live here in town?" She nodded. "I'll give you a hundred dollars advance and pick you up at nine tomorrow morning."

She sat looking at him. He persisted. "You've got to cut the umbilical cord sometime. Are you waiting for some cabrón who makes huaraches? Or drives a fishing boat?"

His hand was on the table, fingers folded. Now he opened it to show a hundred-dollar bill. With his other hand he took one of hers and placed it over the bill, then drew his empty hand from beneath hers. His face showed excitement, and hers seemed more alive as with one smooth motion she tucked the bill in the halter under her blouse.

"Where do you live?" he said tensely, and his words were barely audible over the music.

"Up Valencia Avenue, third house on the right past Insurgentes."

He got up to go. "I know where it is. I'll pick you up at nine on the corner." Her eyes were on the table surface as she nodded.

It was noon as Anastacia approached the motel suite occupied by the Liggett family. She pushed a linen cart ahead of her as she enjoyed the cactus garden and shade trees abundant within the horseshoe-shaped Valdez Motel. The trees and vegetation were placed to give each unit maximum privacy and a view of the beach at the mouth of the semicircle. The number of units including the outer perimeter and those within totaled more than a hundred, and at this time of year all were full. At noon on Sunday nearly all guests were either on the beach or at the motel's restaurant and recreation center. Only the stiff breeze from the sea kept the Baja sun from mercilessly punishing the coast as it did the state's interior.

As she pushed her master key into the lock of the Liggett suite, she paused and looked between cacti and trees and saw her father's feet protruding from beneath a Volkswagen camper a hundred feet away. She smiled, imagining she could hear him curse as he always did when he worked on a car. He had been working on the car for hours. She pushed the door open and entered.

The rooms were as she expected. The Liggetts were very neat people, as tourists and vacationers go. Trash had been put in the proper receptacles, the bathroom was well used but not a mess. Clothes were in closets. The beds were unmade, naturally. The reading material, which all Americans brought in quantities on vacations, was stacked neatly on a writing desk. She looked through the magazines and paperback books, knowing they would be left for her as usual. She had been making up rooms and cleaning in this motel for so long now, she felt she had grown up with it. Ten years, had it been? At that time Valdez had just completed a dozen units and she and her mother had done all his work. During the following years she had come to know many families very well. Those who were friendly with Pilar and Anastacia would give them the food left over at the end of their vacation, and frequently liquor, too, as there were severe penalties for taking more than one's quota of liquor from Mexico into the United States. Anything else the visitors didn't feel like lugging home might find its way into the Herrera household.

As a result, Anastacia's library of books and periodicals grew to proportions which were fantastic for a girl of her age and background. Her appetite for reading had become prodigious, and that along with the many long conversations she had in English with her mother was responsible for her excellent command of English.

As she looked over the magazines before plunging into her work, she thought a shadow momentarily darkened the window. She glanced out at the cactus garden screening the adjacent motel unit, but saw nothing moving.

Quickly, deftly, crisp clean sheets were stretched over the bed. Fresh pillowcases. Next she scoured the porcelain and tile in the bathroom. New soap, clean towels and washcloths, fresh water glasses. The carpet was clean. One trip with the wastebaskets to the plastic sack on the linen cart at the doorway, and the Liggett suite was done.

She closed the door, making sure it locked, and started for the unit across the garden of cactus trees. It was good to see Alvin, the Liggett boy, who was about her own age. In ten years he'd grown up. And Monica, the little girl, now thirteen, had been a toddler when the Liggetts first came, that summer ten years ago. She had baby-sat for Monica many times when the Liggetts and Alvin had gone into Ensenada to shop or eat dinner.

As she pushed the cart almost leisurely toward the next unit, the breeze caught her hair, at the same time wafting gently to her nostrils the scent of ocean water and hot clean sand. Let's see, the family in the next unit was . . . a strong hand closed cruelly on her arm. She let go of the cart as she whirled. Huerta stood there, eyes glaring, the muscles of his jaw protruding. She gasped.

"Now listen, little whore," he rasped, "I'm going to give you a beating, but it'll only be half as bad if you give me my hundred dollars back." He tightened his grip and drew back his other hand. She tried to twist loose.

"Go to hell, puto!" she hissed.

His face twisted with rage and his poised hand trembled.

"You made me spend two hours waiting at that phony address, where they never heard of you. Nobody does that to me."

His heavy open palm crashed across her nose and mouth, and her consciousness reeled as she fell to the gravel walk. She sat up, trying to see him. He was upon her, grasping her hair with one hand, tilting her face up, drawing back again to strike her.

"Papa! Papa!" she screamed, and then felt again the sickening, paralyzing blow to the mouth. Again he seized her hair, lifting her head from the ground. "Your father can't help you now, whore." He continued talking as he struck her. She tried to cry out, tried to focus on him, tried to protect herself from his blows. Then her eyes picked out a blurry form, moving fast, dressed in gray, hurtling toward them, and the air was jarred as her father's form crashed into Huerta. Leonceo was bellowing like a bull as he ripped into Huerta with feet and fists. Anastacia picked herself up, trying to assess the action. Concern for her own wounds diminished as she witnessed the horror of what her father was doing to Huerta as he screamed, "Strike my little girl, will you, hijo de la chingada . . ."

She was suddenly aware that guests were responding to the noise. Two men arrived at the scene and hesitantly pulled Leonceo from the supine Huerta. "Easy, Leo, easy, Leo," one said. Leonceo allowed himself to be pulled away. He was puffing heavily, glaring at Huerta, who stirred, trying to sit up. More vacationers appeared, uncertainly looking from Anastacia to Leonceo to Huerta. Then Edmond and Patricia Liggett pushed through the gathering. Mrs. Liggett gasped when she saw Anastacia holding her bloody face, and hurried to her.

"My God, child, what happened? My God!" Tenderly she held the girl's head to her neck. Anastacia was sobbing uncontrollably. Mrs. Liggett began leading her to the motel suite.

At that moment the motel owner, Valdez, shouldered his way through the gathering crowd. "What the hell's happening?" he demanded. He looked at Huerta, now sitting up, blood spewing from his face. Then he looked at Leonceo and Anastacia. "What happened, Leo?"

Leonceo was still trying to catch his breath. "He was beating up my little girl."

Valdez looked back at Huerta. "I know that pimp," he said with loud contempt. He called to an employee, "Lalo! Call Captain Ramos. You men," he said to those holding Leonceo, "let him go. But hold that snake on the ground for Captain Ramos. Whatever he did, his big mistake was coming on my property."

Edmond Liggett and Leonceo followed as Mrs. Liggett helped Anastacia into the suite. Inside, the girl turned to embrace her father as Pat Liggett brought damp washcloths.

"How awful, how utterly awful," Mrs. Liggett said as she cleaned away the blood. Anastacia winced with pain but was able to stop her sobbing. Soon she looked much better, but her lips and face were beginning to swell. The Liggetts looked at each other, something unspoken and affirmative passing between them.

Anastacia faced her father. "How do I look, Papa?" she asked in a small voice. Leonceo carefully examined her face, beginning to smile.

"You look terrible. Just terrible," he said with some humor. "Tell me, what started this?"

Anastacia stepped back, hands on hips. "That bastard. It was last night. In the tavern where you were singing. Some of his girls were there."

"Yes, I noticed them."

"I bet you did. Anyway, he approached me and wanted me to work for him. He offered me a hundred dollars in advance if I would go with him. I told him yes, he could pick me up at nine in the morning. I gave him a false address. You know the rest."

Leonceo's brow wrinkled for a moment, then he threw back his head and roared with laughter. She started to laugh too, but winced with pain when her bruised lips curled.

"That's great, bebita! Tell me, did you keep the money?"

She became a little indignant. "Of course!" She put her hand into a pocket of her apron and drew out the bill, handing it to him. He laughed louder as he took it.

"Good. We can use it. But tell me, why didn't you hold out for two hundred?"

She shrugged, smiling a little coyly. "I don't know . . . you think I'm worth that much?"

They both laughed and embraced. Mrs. Liggett motioned her husband to the next room and he followed.

"Ed," she said when they were alone, "do you still want to do it? As far as I'm concerned, this clinches it."

They could hear Leonceo and Anastacia joking and laughing in the next room. "Yes," Ed Liggett said. "But as I said, she'll have to make her own arrangements for getting to L.A.

If she can get herself there, she can have the job. She can live in the guest room. I agree. I don't want her to have to grow up in this."

Pat Liggett studied her husband. "She *is* grown up, Ed. She'll hate to leave her family. God, if we could only do something for *all* of them. But . . . we can only do what we're able to." They returned to the other room.

"Well, we've got to go," Leonceo said, walking Anastacia to the door.

"Leo," Mrs. Liggett said earnestly, "we'd like to meet with you and Mrs. Herrera tonight. We have something to discuss."

Leonceo looked puzzled. "Sure, Mrs. Liggett," he said.

She went on. "About an opportunity for Tacha. Could we come to your house? About eight?"

A troubled look passed quickly over his face. "We'd be glad to have you," he said, with the utmost courtesy. "Hasta luego, señora, señor. Y muchas gracias."

They walked through the cactus garden to the gravel drive that ran in a circle around the motel, then stopped as they saw Police Captain Ramos talking with Huerta, in handcuffs, beside a police car. Captain Ramos was a large man who kept his hair neat and always smelled of cologne. He wore an immaculate uniform and liked displaying his gun, club, and badge. He opened the rear door for Huerta. A few of the guests were watching from nearby.

"Get in," Ramos said with authority and impatience as he turned and got in behind the wheel. Huerta did not get in.

"But Capitán, you must let me say this . . ."

The captain said in a controlled voice, "Get in the back seat, pendejo, and close the door!"

"Please, Capitán, allow me just to say . . ."

"¡Puta madre!" the captain said, twisting out of the car. He grabbed his heavy club and raised it high, as though to strike the mightiest of blows. Huerta dived headlong into the rear seat.

Captain Ramos drove slowly toward the highway. Huerta, in the rear of the car, was soaking up blood from his face with a handkerchief.

"Capitán, what are you going to do with me?" he asked.

The captain was in no hurry to answer.

After a few moments Huerta repeated, "What are you going to do with me?"

"I have to put you in jail."

"What for?"

Ramos looked back at him with annoyance. "Don't get smart, Huerta. You've pushed your luck in this town a long time."

Huerta was more solicitous. "What I'd like to know, Señor Capitán, is how long I'll be locked up and how much I'll have to pay."

"Well, Huerta, I think if I let you out of jail right away, you'll be begging me to lock you up in about a week."

Huerta was puzzled. "Why? Don't play games with me."

"I'm not the one who's going to play games with you. Do you know Margarito Corrales?"

Huerta mulled over the name. "You mean Rito Corrales? The fighter?"

"That's the one. He used to be a fighter."

"Yes. I tried to buy a piece of him when he was a popular boxer in Tijuana a year or two ago. What's he got to do with this?"

"Well, Rito Corrales and Anastacia Herrera kind of grew up together. He says he feels like a brother to her, but he only says that when her father's around. He really wants to screw her so bad he can taste her."

"You're trying to tell me he's going to come after me."

Captain Ramos chuckled. "That's putting it mildly."

Huerta was silent as they reached the highway and Captain Ramos turned north toward Ensenada. "Where is Margarito now?"

Ramos divided his attention between the road ahead and speaking to Huerta in the mirror. "I sent him away on a job."

"You sent him away?"

"Yes. A couple of months ago he got into a fight with two American Marines. They were drunk, causing trouble, and they happened to pick on the wrong guy. Rito sent them both to the hospital—one with a broken jaw, the other with a dozen broken ribs."

"Why'd you send him away?"

"When the Marines went back to Camp Pendleton they got a whole platoon and came back looking for Corrales. I locked him up but they were waiting. So I found a job for him fishing over in San Felipe. I drove him there to work until it all blew over."

Huerta waited but Ramos showed no inclination to continue.

"Okay, when is he coming back?"

"I got word he'll be back at the end of the week."

Again, Huerta waited futilely. "Okay, what should I do? You think I'm scared of him?"

Captain Ramos chuckled again. "You do whatever you think you ought to do."

Huerta sat thinking for the rest of the trip.

The Ensenada jail was not new to Huerta, and he made no move that would antagonize Captain Ramos as he was locked up in a tank with a dozen and a half other men.

Through the bars, as Ramos was leaving, he said, "Capitán, what are you charging me with? How long will you hold me?"

As he walked away, Ramos said over his shoulder, "We'll see, we'll see."

Several of the prisoners knew Huerta, and he knew there was no use trying to conceal what had led to his arrest.

"So Ramos tells me Margarito Corrales is a man to be feared above others."

"He's right," one prisoner said simply, helping himself to Huerta's cigarettes and passing them around. Each said thanks to the helpless Huerta and then they returned the empty package to him, ignoring his glare. "I don't know if Rito is in love with that girl, he's got lots of girlfriends, but if he is, you'd better get away from here while you can."

They discussed Huerta's plight at length, mainly because there wasn't much else to do, and when they saw his fear they perhaps exaggerated Margarito's ferocity. After a few hours Huerta went to the barred gate. The turnkey on the other side was reading a magazine.

"Hombre," Huerta said to him, "I'd like to talk to Capitán Ramos."

The turnkey regarded him blandly a moment. "He's busy," he said, and returned to the magazine. Huerta fumed a little and paced back and forth in the tank. One prisoner approached him. "Señor Huerta, I have a boat. If you want to get away, I'll be out tomorrow and can land you anywhere on the coast."

Huerta asked the man's name and recognized it as that of a man he'd heard would take people and land them on the other side for a fee, going out to sea to detour the Coast Guard and border patrols. The problem was, some of the people he took were never heard from again and there was considerable controversy concerning what actually happened to them after they set foot on the boat.

Huerta huddled with the man. "How much will you charge me to take me somewhere up the coast, past the border?"

"Actually," the man said, "I'm a water taxi. I have a standard rate of about five dollars a mile."

"*Five dollars a mile?*"

"Yes. Dollars, not pesos. Roughly a hundred and fifty to go to San Diego. Six hundred to Los Angeles."

"That's a lot of money."

"Not really. It's safe. We go when it's dark. Travel all night without lights. I land you at the place of your choice, right up on the beach."

Huerta was thinking. This was an idea he'd had a long time.

"You'd charge the same rate if I took other people with me?"

The man looked puzzled only for a moment. "Oh. You mean your whores. No, no listen. I'm not greedy, but I'd have to charge more for more people. How many would go?"

Huerta pondered a moment. "Say, six girls."

The man tilted his head. "I'd have to get triple price for that."

"I'll pay you double."

The man considered. "You make a hard bargain, Señor Huerta."

"I think I can be ready to leave night after tomorrow. Is that okay?"

"Yes. I can leave any evening. Dusk is the best time. Oh, by the way, have the money with you."

"That's one of the things I have to take care of. I'll have half the money with me. The other half I'll have waiting for us when we get to the place I choose."

The man looked a little hurt. "You're a very cynical man, Huerta. You should be more trusting."

Huerta walked back to the jail door. The turnkey was still on the other side of the bars, reading.

"Hey, hombre," Huerta called to him, "I want to see Capitán Ramos."

The guard set the magazine down and looked at Huerta solemnly. "He's still busy," he replied simply.

Huerta ground his teeth a little. "How do you know he's busy?"

The guard shrugged. "I just know, somehow," he said, resuming his reading. "I have a feeling about those things."

It was after midnight when the turnkey informed Huerta that Captain Ramos wanted to see him in his office. Huerta found him behind a desk, expansively smoking a cigar.

"You're in big trouble, Huerta," Ramos said, leaving his desk to stand before him. "You got money for a lawyer to beat this?"

"Of course. If I have to."

"No, you don't have to. I figure you'll pay a lawyer a thousand dollars or so to defend you, and then maybe he won't get you off. And that'll take time. And if you hang around this town until the end of this week, I think you'll be very sorry."

"You mean Margarito Corrales will get me. I can hire some one to take care of him."

Ramos laughed heartily. "Who you going to hire to fight him? In Ensenada? You'll need a platoon of Marines. You better save yourself half that thousand by paying your way out of here and getting your ass out of town."

Huerta ground his teeth, the jaw muscles twitching. "I'll pay," he said at length.

"Okay, Huerta. I'm letting you go now. I'll have someone drive you to get the money to bring back here. And this should be a lesson to you. All this you brought on yourself just because you couldn't stand to have that little girl beat you out of a hundred dollars. Now get your cheap, chiseling ass out of my office and you'd better be a long way from here when Margarito comes back. I don't want to have to take you to the hospital and lock him up again."

Huerta took the envelope with his personal belongings and at the risk of jeopardizing his freedom, he said, "Capitán, this isn't over. I've never yet let anyone beat me out of a hundred dollars. You don't know me very well."

Captain Ramos came out of his chair with his club held high and Huerta scurried out the door.

It was a week after the incident with Huerta that Anastacia stepped out the back door of the kitchen and started to call to her father and Margarito, but she stopped, watching. The two men had rigged a rope over a tree branch in the Corrales back yard and were lowering an engine block into a car. They grunted, groaned, and wheezed as Leonceo gave instructions: "Easy, man, a little to the left. Okay, down another inch. A little more. Forward now a fraction. Watch your fingers, now, you'll lose one . . ."

She smiled. They were as close as father and son. Now with the possibility of her leaving soon she was suddenly aware of her tremendous love for both of them, these two who had endured desert, sea, and poverty all their lives.

Suddenly with a loud thunk the engine block dropped an inch or so and the two men let go and straightened up, sighing loudly.

"Jesus! What a heavy cabrón that was," Leonceo said, wiping his forehead with a blue bandana.

Margarito smiled as he stepped to a workbench and began cleaning his greasy hands with a gasoline-soaked rag.

"You see, we didn't need a chain hoist. Saved you ten dollars."

Leonceo began cleaning his hands also. "Yes, but that's the hard way. I almost got a hernia. Lucky I don't plan to make babies anymore."

Anastacia called, "Hey! Dinner's ready. That job can wait."

The men filed past her into the tiny kitchen. She followed and when they had washed their hands and doused their heads, she handed each a towel. In the living room Leonceo and Pilar sat at either end of the small chrome breakfast table. Margarito settled himself next to where Anastacia would sit after she served the meal.

Three trips to the kitchen and she had the heated, heaping plates and other things necessary for the meal on the table. Then she sat down beside Margarito. Leonceo served himself a generous quantity of stewed meat, mashed beans, and rice, poured chili sauce over all, and began eating. The others did the same.

"Okay," Margarito said, finally breaking an almost strained silence, "you've decided to accept the job offer from the gringos from L.A."

Her voice was quiet and firm. "Yes. I have. I hate to leave all of you. You're my life. But I can't pass up this chance."

Margarito chewed and swallowed. "You'll have to go illegally."

"I know. Thousands of others do it every day. I can too. I just can't pass this up. No telling what it may lead to . . ."

For a few minutes no one said anything. Then Margarito said nonchalantly, "I'll take you. I'm going too."

She stopped eating and looked wide-eyed at him.

"No. I don't want you to. I don't want you to become a fugitive. It's different as a housemaid . . ."

He faced her, stern but not angry. "How is it different for you? I work, work, work like hell for five or ten bucks a day here. I hear a good mechanic can make that much an hour in the States. Or a musician or ranch foreman. I've thought about it many times, but . . . you kept me here." He said it looking at her, but then looked quickly at each in turn to include them all. He plunged ahead. "I'm tired of having to buy hundred-dollar cars that you have to work on a week to get running. Tired of being so goddamn poor that all I can look forward ever to owning is a shack like this. You know, the only halfway decent clothes I own are my mariachi costumes. No. I'll take you across—my father knows the best authority on crossing the border in Tijuana—and I'll go too. Don't worry, I won't bother you at the rich gringos' home. But Tacha, baby, I want to be near in case you need me."

They had all dropped their eyes to their plates and continued eating in silence for some time. "All right," Anastacia said at length. "You can take me across. But . . . you know, when I was growing up we used to spend most of the year in La Tijera. That's more my home than here. I want to go back to visit. See Grandma, all the people I grew up with, the places I love, the little village near the roadside shrine." She stopped and they were looking at her. "Will you take me back for one last visit, Rito?"

He smiled and put his hand on hers, looking into her eyes before replying.

"Sure, baby. When do you want to go?"

"I'll tell Mrs. Liggett tonight that I'll take the job. Can we leave for La Tijera tomorrow?"

She looked at her father and saw a small measure of hurt in his expression; she supposed it was because she had not consulted him about any of her decisions. *He's got to get used to the idea that times are changing,* she thought.

Margarito rose, looking down on her. "You bet we can. But I gotta get the old heap running and ready. I better start on it now."

CHAPTER 5

The roosters across the dirt road were beginning to crow when she heard the Volkswagen come to a stop in front of her house. She picked up her traveling bag and went to her parents' door. She tapped. "Mama? Papa?"

"Sí." She heard her father's sleepy voice.

"Margarito is here. You don't need to get up. I'm leaving now."

Her father's voice was a grunt as he answered, getting up, "I want to see you off. Besides, I want to talk to him."

She went out to the car. She put her bag in the rear seat, looking at the rack on top of the car piled high with camping equipment. Anastacia's eyes went to him only momentarily and he returned the look. Her father came out, buckling his belt, wearing only trousers.

"Rito, good morning."

Margarito nodded good-naturedly as always. "Buenos dias, Leonceo."

Anastacia watched a large camper coming down the road. It slowed and as it passed she saw a bleary-eyed American family staring at them. They must have traveled all night to get to this place, to start a vacation. God, how they gape at us, she thought, as the children in the rear of the camper rubbernecked.

"So you're taking my little girl away for a couple of weeks, eh?" Leonceo was saying. He had walked around to the driver's side to talk to Margarito.

"Only for ten days," Margarito replied, lighting a cigarette with a little flourish, "and besides, she's not a little girl anymore."

Leonceo doubled a fist and gently put it next to Margarito's jaw. "Don't you get ideas, boy." He tried to sound as though it were a warning.

"And I'm not a boy," Margarito said. Leonceo threw back his head and laughed, but it wasn't the most carefree of laughs. He went around to Anastacia. She put her arms around him and kissed him.

"Don't worry, Papa," she said, "I'll say hi to everybody at La Tijera. Tell Mama I'll make sure Grandmother is okay. Now go back to sleep some more."

Margarito put the car in gear and pulled away, leaving Leonceo waving in the dirt road.

At the highway, they turned south and in minutes were going through Maneadero on the stretch toward Santo Tomas. She adjusted the window so that she was comfortable and was pleased to find a mirror on the other side of the visor on her side. She made final touches on her hair and what little makeup she wore.

She said with detachment, still looking in the mirror and aware he observed her, "The mirror comes in handy . . . for whoever sits on this side."

He mulled this over a moment and then nodded in agreement.

She went on: "I guess . . . the girls who ride in your car . . . they have occasion to get . . . pretty mussed up."

He shook his head slightly, blinked, and made a little whistling noise through his teeth. "Wow! Do they!" and continued driving in silence. Her anger, she found, was not entirely feigned.

She suddenly faced him. "You want to tell me about them?"

"No. Not particularly. Well, okay, if you want . . ."

"Please. Never mind."

They drove in silence for a time. The countryside went by, the road winding through low mountains, into small valleys where farmers and their children were already working in the fields and pastures.

Soon she looked at him again. "The car is loaded down with camping equipment."

"Yes," he said, "for camping."

"Are you going to camp?"

He shrugged for an answer.

"Tell me something, Rito," she said, but before she could finish he cut in.

"No, Tacha, you tell me something. Do you love me?"

"Rito! How do I know if I love you? You've never had a serious thought in your life . . ."

"You know better than that."

She reconsidered a moment. "Yes . . . I know better. But you act like you haven't. How would I know?"

"Easy," he said in his laughing way. "You just ask yourself how you feel. Do you feel love for me?"

"I don't know, Rito. You're the only boy I've ever really known. We grew up together. You say you saw me being born. I've found out that's a lie."

He laughed. "How'd you find out?"

"My father. He said when I was born at La Tijera you were in the house. Besides, you were only four years old. How *could* you remember?"

"Oh, you never forget a sight like that. Believe me. And besides, you *have* gone out with other guys."

"That's right. And boy, is that a big blast, to go to a third-rate movie in Ensenada, or to the bullfights in Tijuana. God, how great it would have been if we never had to grow up. If we could always stay little kids living by the ocean in the desert . . ."

"But we did grow up, Anastacia. And also, you dated some of the gringo guys who come down on vacation . . ."

"And man, is *that* a trip . . ."

"What do you mean?"

"Well, I guess it's not fair to judge gringos by the guys I've gone out with. People, Americans especially, act different when they get out of their own country. They really don't know how to act. The Europeans who come here are different. Probably because they've traveled more. But the young Americans who come here, they think we're primitives, they think they should educate us. And the biggest deal for them is to run into someone they know from the other side. Especially when they're with a Mexican girl. This seems to prove something or other."

"Did you screw any of them?" There was a little tightness in his voice, and then he continued casually, "and if not, why not?"

She recoiled inwardly and physically, and the hurt she felt

made her voice almost inaudible. "I don't have to tell you things like that."

They rode in silence a while, listening to the road noise and the air rushing by. Then he said, "No, you don't have to tell me things like that."

She contemplated the sentence, mulled over its duplicity, then mused that there were *three* ways it could be interpreted. That made her smile and when she glanced at him she saw the trace of a smile on his face also.

They rode in silence, commenting occasionally on the surroundings. After a while he said, "Santo Tomas coming up. Ready for a stop?"

"No. Keep going. I'm good for hours yet."

Hours later Margarito turned toward the ocean, and they traveled rapidly along the packed wet sand next to the surf, keeping off the treacherous dry sand. In a few hours they traversed 150 miles of uninhabited beach, refueling once from a gasoline drum at a small fishing village.

The sun was still relatively high in the sky, yet poised for its quick plunge behind the sea, when Margarito pulled the little car up near the high-water mark and cut the engine. They sat listening to the wind and ocean a few minutes. Pelicans patrolling the surf landed and waited to see what the newcomers were going to do, past experience reminding them there might well be some unearned reward. The white sand of the beach stretched interminably before and behind them. The rocks and stones and plant life of the desert stretched away to the east, ending in rugged low mountains a dozen miles to inland, which evidenced no sign of life of any kind from this distance.

Margarito got out of the car, gazing at the ocean. He walked toward it a few feet and then stopped to pull off his shoes. Again proceeding, he whipped off his shirt. Fifty feet farther he unbuckled his belt and took his trousers off. She watched him. He always amused her somehow. He was still trying to walk forward to the water as he took his pants off his legs, started to fall, took them off and threw them over his shoulder. A wave was just receding as he reached the water. He followed it as it retreated and then dived into the next breaker. She watched as he wallowed in the water, swimming farther out with easy, powerful strokes. He was brawny; in fact, he almost looked like a fat man with ridiculously small hips and waist. She watched him play, trying to entice a slow-flying pelican. He disappeared beneath the surface and was out of sight a long time, then came up with a large white object in his hand. He turned toward her and shouted, "Clam bed! Big white ones!" She could see it was six inches in diameter. He hurled it in the manner of a discus thrower up onto the beach, and again disappeared beneath the water, returning in a half minute with another big clam. "We'll save the veal for tomorrow and have clams tonight," she heard him shout above the sound of the crashing surf.

She got out and sat on the fender of the car. After Margarito had thrown more than a dozen clams up on the beach, he came out, breathing deeply. At the water's edge he donned his trousers only and approached her, carrying the clams in his shirt.

He stood there, dripping, looking at her, and his intensity was obvious. She wore cut-off jeans, frayed at the knees, a loose blouse, and thongs of leather on her feet. She returned his gaze evenly, an almost awkward smile playing on her lips. She looked around.

"Is this our . . . campsite?" she asked.

"This is it," he said without taking his eyes from her. "While you take your swim, I'll set up camp."

"How long will we be here?"

He considered a moment. "That depends . . . on a lot of things."

She laughed. "That means . . . if things . . . if I'm . . . if things aren't as good . . . as they could be, we'll be getting along to La Tijera soon."

He threw the clams down and stepped to the car, reaching for the cords that tied the equipment on the rack. "If I'm any judge of . . . woman flesh, we'll be here a while."

She started to turn toward the ocean, then faced him again. "So this is how . . . casually . . . you would strip a girl of her virtue."

He took her face in his hands. "Believe me, Anastacia Herrera, I don't feel casual. Do you know how long I've . . . loved you?"

"I know how long you've wanted me."

"And we almost made it once or twice."

ANOTHER LAND

"Good God, Rito, I was only fourteen or fifteen that time you were taking me to school on the horse."

"You were old enough. But you didn't want me."

"Ha! How wrong you are. But you wanted to stop right on the road. And Papa already suspected you were trying to get me."

"He guarded you a long time, like a possessive old billy goat."

"That's right. You don't know how many times since I was twelve years old that he checked on us when you and I went someplace together."

"Oh, yes, I know. But he gave in this time, didn't he?"

She mused. "I don't think he gave in. We're supposed to be visiting relatives in La Tijera."

"He knows. Go take your swim." Margarito turned to the task of unpacking.

Anastacia walked toward the beach. She stopped just above where the waves retreated and took off her clothes. As she folded them neatly, she was looking out to sea, where the sky and water met, but she felt his eyes on her back. As she waded in she felt the cool-warm sensation of the ocean in summer. Then she plunged in, feeling the clear salt water everywhere on her. She held her breath underwater as she scrubbed herself everywhere, then she floated a few moments, then dived under again. She came up facing the beach, and burst out laughing as she saw that Margarito had walked halfway to the water and was standing with one hand shading his eyes, Indian scout style, staring at her. They both laughed and he returned to the campsite to put up the tent and prepare the evening meal while she swam and dived with luxurious abandon.

Wearing only her jeans and blouse, carrying her other garments and thongs in her hands, she approached the driftwood fire he tended. The fire was on the lee side of the tent he had erected, and a frame metal device held a kettle above the low flames. The clams steamed within the kettle. Two folding aluminum chairs were beside the fire and they both sat down. She watched the kettle as it began to boil. The bubbles came from a single spot at the bottom of the kettle, then suddenly began coming from another spot. The smoke was momentarily caught in an eddy of the breeze and drifted around her, then returned to its path away from the tent and the chairs.

He had set up a small folding table with a chopping block and she watched as he opened a can of prepared chili sauce and then chopped fresh onions, garlic, tomatoes, and coriander into the sauce.

"You're a marvelous camper, Rito," she said.

"It's not camping. It's Baja living. The gringos come down here and try to live like this for ten days. But they don't know how. Because they never really had to."

"Have you ever been afraid when you've had to live like this?"

"Not really. You remember about five years ago, when my father and I went to Bahia de San Rafael?"

"Yes."

"That was an adventure. We drove in a stripped Chevy pickup. Thirty-five miles from the road. The hurricane hit two days later. We knew it was coming, but we had supplies to wait it out, we thought. We were there to build a place to dry fish and work on fishnets and boats. We planned to return the next year with a launch and fish the area. Well, four days of the hurricane, and it was plain no one was going to get in or out of Bahia de San Rafael by auto for at least a month. Steady drizzles kept the terrain muddy. We had found a clay basin and we dammed it to keep us in fresh water, but we forgot about the high tide and two weeks later we had no water. My father's old, but on dry ground he could have made the thirty-five miles and then somebody would have come along."

He stopped talking to add water to the steaming clams and sample the sauce. She found she was listening for every word.

"Well anyway, that's the only time I was scared. Myself, I could have walked out, even in the mud, but my father, he got weaker on just fish, that's all we had to eat for three weeks when our food ran out."

"How'd you get out?"

"Gathered lots of firewood. Climbed a hill and waited till we saw a boat at sea. Built a giant fire. Finally a fishing boat came to investigate."

He handed her a bowl of clams. Tortillas and sauce were on the table. She savored the delicious combination of flavors, feeling his eyes on her. She looked down the beach. It stretched away into the distance, curving westward to a point near the horizon. Fish were leaping high out of the water every few seconds. In the brush she got a glimpse of a dog-sized animal prowling, watching them. Then her eyes went to him and he watched her as he ate. Soon he put his bowl down and stood up, approaching her. He took the bowl from her hands and put it on the table. The canvas walls of the tent flapped in the warm breeze. One wall of the tent was folded back and he led her inside. She only felt his fingers briefly at her blouse and at the waist of her jeans and then she was naked. He knelt and pulled her down onto the bedroll. He threw his pants into a corner.

"Will you bleed?" he asked.

"No, I won't bleed, I don't think. But take it easy."

He lay on his back, eyes closed, arms folded across his chest. She was beside him, watching his face, trying to guess his thoughts.

At length he said, "It hurt you, didn't it." It was not a question.

She thought a moment before answering. "It was . . . bittersweet. More sweet."

"You mean it felt good."

She put a hand on his stomach and rubbed it. "God!"

He sat up. "See what you been missing all these years?"

"I'm not going to apologize."

He lay down again. "It hurt me too."

"Very much?"

"Not too much. I screwed a gringa with a bad sunburn once in San Felipe. It was hurting her so bad on her tits and stomach she'd scream. But she wouldn't stop."

Anastacia laughed. "I don't believe half of what you say."

"You should. Half of everything I say is the absolute truth. But you won't be too tight very long."

She was running her fingertips along his chest.

"It depends on a lot of things."

"That means you don't know. I'm the first virgin you've . . . had."

He sat up again, assuming a professional, clinical attitude. "Luckily, you oiled up quickly."

She forced herself to seem unembarrassed. "Quickly? I could feel myself starting to get slippery inside when you took my pants off."

"And you claim to be a virgin?"

"You think that's something a girl learns from practice?"

He looked at her and he looked serious but she knew that meant nothing.

"Talking like this is getting me all ready again."

"So I see."

"How about you?"

"Yes. I'm still sore."

"I know a joke about that. You see, once Thor, the god of thunder, met this virgin . . ."

She laughed. "I've heard it."

"Well, I'm Thor."

"Maybe they make a salve of some kind."

He got up, pulling her to her feet. "The best salve is seawater. Come on."

She reached for her pants and blouse.

"Why are you getting dressed?"

She paused, thinking, then dropped them, shrugging. "Force of habit."

They walked toward the beach. He went on, "Too bad we're not a couple of Indians in the year 1546."

"Why?"

He took her hand as they walked. "That's when the Spaniards discovered all this."

"You sure of the year?"

"Okay. One of the nice things about other girls is they're dumb. You read too much. Anyway, we could be a couple of Indians here back then, nobody owns any part of the peninsula, and we see this Spanish ship out there and they drop anchor and send a boat here and Señor Cabrillo steps off and greets us and says, 'I claim all this land in the name of the King of Spain. Get some clothes on.' And I say, 'You can't claim all this land. I'm an Aztec prince. . . .'"

"There were no Aztecs around here."

"Shut up. Don't spoil my story. And I explain to him that this peninsula is my kingdom and we don't wear clothes here and if he can give me one good reason why we should, we'll get dressed. Then Cabrillo looks at you and says, 'I see what you mean. I got to carry the word about this back to Spain. Who's this broad you're with?' And I say, 'This is my wife, Princess Thundertits . . .' Why are you laughing?"

They had reached the water and she let his hands go and plunged in. She came up still laughing, allowing the seawater to enter her. He was in the water too.

"Man, that feels good, doesn't it?" he said, swimming toward her.

She faced the setting sun, again feeling the gripping remoteness she'd felt all her life when she was far from bustling villages and towns. A huge fish leaped twenty yards away. A pelican seemed suspended a dozen feet above, looking at them with what she considered a stupid, curious expression. The water was breast deep and the same temperature as her body. She turned as Margarito swam around her, she looked at the surroundings, the desert sloping up from the beach, the beach turning into cliffs ten miles away, the water meeting the sky to the west.

He surfaced inches from her. "Margarito, can we have a big fire tonight?"

"Big as you like. Help me gather driftwood?"

"Sure. Did you bring some wine?"

"And tequila. I feel like drinking."

"Not too much, though. I don't want it to affect you."

"See? The seawater has soothed you. You're wanting to screw again."

She stood in the water, arms hugging her breast, feeling the faintest chill. "Yes. Because I love you."

"Well, don't worry about me drinking. Mexican tequila is the one drink in the world that makes you screw more. They feed it to rabbits, you know."

She started toward the shore. "Well, I'll be in the tent. Swim as long as you like."

He followed her. "You know I'm behind you. A pair of tits can pull harder than a pair of mules."

"That's an old saying."

"It's one of the few that's as good in English as Spanish. Come on, let's run."

She started to, but then resumed walking. "I can't run," she laughed.

"That's right," he said. "You're not built for running without a bra."

"Yes. I flop too much."

"A woman is supposed to flop too much. You weren't meant to be an Olympic track star."

They disappeared into the tiny tent on the beach that separated the desert from the ocean as the sun was setting.

CHAPTER 6

Mark Summers, south-of-the-border sports figure and full-time riveter at Lockheed Aircraft Corporation in Burbank, California, kept his eyes on the dirt road ahead as he depressed the clutch pedal and revved the motor. The powerful Porsche engine in the dune buggy responded by blatting profanely in the still Baja air. Night was coming and Mark wore a worried look as he kept the vehicle at a pace that allowed him to maneuver the hogbacks and swales along the road. He put his hand on the knee of the girl beside him and smiled at her between quick glances at the road.

"How you holding up, Honey?" he said above the sound of the rushing air and road noise.

She took her eyes off the road to smile into his face. She hung onto the dash grip with one hand while her other arm was locked behind the seat. "Great," she said, smiling, "just great."

He skillfully rounded a bend in the road, a look of deep concentration on his face, and saw the lights of the small village ahead.

"Here's the goddamned town now," he said. The approach to the town was a relatively straight and even stretch of several hundred yards, and he floored the accelerator to cover it. The rear wheels spun, the engine roared, and the car shot the short distance across the stretch at phenomenal speed. Then he was braking to a stop in front of a little restaurant with an electric sign in the window.

Cutting the engine and leaning back on the seat, he closed his eyes and rubbed the bridge of his nose with thumb and forefinger. Then he gave a tired smile and looked at Honey.

"You okay, Honey?"

She nodded eagerly. "Fine," she said.

He jerked his head, indicating that they were going inside. They unbuckled their harnesses and stepped out of the doorless vehicle. As they walked toward the door a parked vehicle caught their eye. It was an old Volks, rear fenders cut away to allow oversize tires, a rack piled high with traveling equipment tied to the roof. On the bumper was a Baja California license plate.

Mark nudged Honey along with a hand on her hip. "Mexican dune buggy," he quipped. Her laughter rippled briefly.

She followed Mark to the door. He swung it open and stood aside, allowing her to enter ahead of him. He scanned the room as they entered. Near the door was a young couple. The girl was very good-looking, and her companion was powerful and muscular, but he had no time at this moment to make critical assessments. A man in an apron stood behind the counter, and three or four men sat on stools, bottled beer in front of them. All eyes were on the newcomers. Mark strode aggressively across the floor, one hand barely touching Honey's back. He stood well over six feet tall, wore tight jeans and a cotton shirt unbuttoned at the front, covered by a fur-lined windbreaker. His hair was close-cropped and he wore expensive new heavy shoes which laced halfway up his calves.

Honey was in skin-tight, rust-colored jeans with shirt to match. She also wore heavy shoes, but they were carefully designed to accent her femininity. Her orange-red hair was matched by her heavy lipstick. She took a seat beside Mark and looked to him for leadership.

"Señor," Mark said to the man behind the counter in an adequate voice, "do you speak English?"

The waiter approached, wiping his hands on a clean dishcloth.

"Sí, señor."

"Thank God for that," Mark said, looking to Honey for approval; she did not disappoint him. "Have there been any other Americans come through here? I mean, in the past hour or so?"

"No, señor, you are the first Americans to come by in a long time."

Mark and Honey looked at each other. "Jim and Tess and

ANOTHER LAND

Ken and Marge must be right behind us," Mark said. Honey nodded.

"Would you like something to eat?" the waiter asked.

Mark looked around the room. The couple by the door were eating a meat dish in a red sauce. "Give us some of what they're eating over there," he said.

Honey was straightening her windblown hair. "Ask if they have a mirror," she said to him.

"Do you have a mirror?" Mark asked the man. The man shook his head no. "They don't have a mirror," Mark said to her.

The waiter, who was also the cook, turned to a stove behind the counter to prepare their food.

"God, it's good to see electric lights, isn't it, Honey?" Mark asked. She nodded in assent. "Let's see," he went on, "it's been, well, we were in El Rosario night before last. That was the last time we saw electric lights. Seems like ages ago, doesn't it?"

She nodded. Then she leaned toward him and said something under her breath. Mark looked to the waiter, who was dishing out chili and meat onto the plates. "Rest room?" he inquired. The man indicated the door to the rear.

He turned to her. "It's out in back," he said in a confidential tone. "Don't expect too much." She nodded and left. In a few minutes she returned and took her seat beside him.

"Flush," she said, "what a pleasant surprise. But there was only one. And no lock on the door."

He digested this information. "That figures," he commented.

The waiter brought two plates of red chili and meat. "Do you want tortillas or bread?" he asked.

Mark and Honey regarded one another a moment.

"Oh, what the hell. Give us tortillas," he said. Over by the door, the powerfully built youth seated at a table with the good-looking girl said something and her laughter rippled briefly. Mark and Honey jerked their heads in that direction.

Honey's voice had a threatening quality to it. "I'd sure as hell like to know what they think is so funny," she said.

Mark was about to comment when something caught his attention. "Listen!" he said, holding up a hand. They both froze. A high-pitched whine could be heard, the sound of a high-powered engine bringing a vehicle to a stop under compression.

Mark grinned broadly at her. "Jim and Tess!" he said. They hurried to the door and Mark flung it open. The roar of the engine filled the little restaurant. A street light illuminated the area in front of the restaurant and now the vehicle appeared in the lighted area. It was like Mark's—custom-built, doorless, giant tires on the rear, painted bright colors with an elaborate air-filtration system atop a chrome pipe at the rear.

Jim parked beside Mark's vehicle and cut the engine.

"How'd it go, Jim?" Mark bellowed. "When we left you like you were standing still this morning I figured I'd seen the last of you two!"

"Not a chance," Jim replied, climbing from the dune buggy, pulling off his driving gloves, and wiping dust from his shoulders. "Generator light came on for a while couple hours ago. Had me pretty worried. But everything's okay now."

Although Jim and Tess had approached the doorway, Mark continued in a loud voice, "Where's Ken and Marge? See any sign of 'em?"

"Climbing outa that last valley, I could see their headlights ten, fifteen minutes behind. But I was really pushin' it tryin' to catch you."

Tess embraced Honey briefly and then all four approached the counter.

"Is there anything edible in this godforsaken hole?" Tess asked, laughing.

"We don't know yet," Mark answered, sitting down, "We were about to plow into that red stuff there." He turned to the waiter. "Señor," he pointed to his food. "Más, por favor." He held up two fingers.

"Sí, señor," the waiter replied.

The conversation among the Americans centered on details of the trip, and they seemed oblivious to the others in the room. Mark placed a map on the counter and used a pencil as a pointer.

"We're right here, at this minute," he said seriously. "This here is where we were this morning."

"God!" Tess exclaimed. "They don't even show the dry gullies we had to cross to get here. What happens to people who try to get down here in passenger cars?"

ANOTHER LAND

Mark smiled grimly. "They don't make it. We've got the proper machines or we wouldn't be here right now."

Honey looked serious. "Mark, you still determined to try to make La Tijera tonight?"

Mark was silent a moment. "It's sixty miles down the road. Twenty of that we can cover in half an hour. The other forty, you go ten miles an hour or it'll pound your machine to pieces." He glanced at his watch. "We can be there by midnight. There's accommodations there, such as they are."

Tess shrieked, "I've heard! Dirt floors. And you have to build a fire under the hot-water heater to take a shower!"

She and Honey shook their heads, smiling.

Jim returned to eating his chili, but stopped suddenly, listening. He and Mark looked at one another, then all dashed to the doorway and stood on the step. They waved as Ken and Marge came into view, motor roaring in a vehicle similar to the others. Ken saw them, but continued through the town at a high speed, gunning the engine, spinning the rear wheels. At the far edge of the town, a hundred yards farther, he made an abrupt U turn and the dune buggy spurted back toward the restaurant. He went past and again turned around, gunning the engine, spinning the wheels, and making a cloud of dust in the still night air.

As he went past them again, Mark cupped his hands to his mouth and hollered, "What's wrong, Ken? Got problems?"

Ken coasted by, motor disengaged but revving up thunderously. "She's not breathin' right!" he shouted above the noise. "Hear it? She's missin'." He spun the tires to the far edge of town, wheeled about, and after a burst of speed he cut the engine and coasted to a spot beside Mark's vehicle.

The men, women, and children of the town were coming out to see what was happening. Ken and Marge alighted and the six Americans were ostensibly oblivious to any other human beings.

"Coming up the last big grade," Ken was saying, "I heard her cuttin' out. Thought it might be dust gotten into the distributor. But I checked and it was still sealed tight with plastic tape. Did you hear it?"

The group moved to the engine at the rear of Ken's dune buggy. Mark took over.

"Ken, you and Marge go inside and get some chili inside

you. It's not bad. Jim, start the engine. I think it's the jets. I want to be on our way to La Tijera in ten minutes."

All looked at their watches and Ken and Marge went inside to eat. Jim roared the engine time after time as Mark made adjustments on the carburetor.

Tess and Honey stood mute, watching, as Mark worked. Presently he announced, "That ought to do it. Sound better?" looking at the women. They nodded.

Mark strode back into the restaurant, followed by Jim, Honey, and Tess. Marge and Ken were just finishing their meal.

"Let's get going," Mark said matter-of-factly. "Check your gas and supplies. We'll be there by midnight. Waiter! ¿Cuánto?"

"A dollar each, señor."

Mark carelessly tossed a ten-dollar bill on the counter and led his five companions outside.

Anastacia was looking across the table at Margarito as Mark and the other Americans left the restaurant.

"I know what you're going to say, Tacha. 'They're not all like that.' Right?"

She smiled faintly, nodding as she sipped her hot chocolate.

"But that's unimportant right now, isn't it."

They seemed to share a morose mood as Margarito paid the bill and they went outside to the little car piled high with equipment. He drove out of the village and abruptly left the well-traveled dirt road and headed toward the beach. Within minutes they were gliding almost noiselessly along the damp sand, Margarito occasionally veering away from the sea to avoid the breaking waves.

They said little. Their ten days were ending. La Tijera had been almost exactly as it was when they were growing up. The people there still fought the same battles and talked of the same things. They had spent their nights there playing cards and singing by kerosene or gaslight. On the walls of the grocery store and tavern where the villagers gathered evenings were newspaper clippings telling of Margarito's boxing matches in Tijuana.

Doña Carmela still tended the lush grapes hanging from the vine that covered the hand-hewn wooden arbor behind the gas station Anastacia's father had managed for so many years. The old woman had looked askance at her granddaughter traveling with Margarito, but had eventually acquiesced with a mischievous smile. They were no longer children, she realized, and the world, even down in the land where the desert meets the sea, was changing.

Now night was coming on and Margarito drove along the beach as long as he could without headlights, then continued with the lights on for an hour or so. The Americans coming down the peninsula in their dune buggies didn't know you could travel several times faster than the ten-mile-an-hour rate the torturous dirt road sometimes allowed. But you had to have spent a good deal of your life in Baja to know how and where to travel on the damp sand, skirting the surf.

They stopped to camp for the night, but their mood was not what it had been a week and a half earlier, when they were traveling south. They walked along the beach for hours, looking at the black ocean and the dazzling universe above.

In the tent, ready to go to sleep, with only the sound of the ocean and the flapping of canvas in the warm evening breeze, she turned to him.

"I'm afraid about tomorrow," she said. "Aren't you?"

He rolled over and looked at her in the dim light of the kerosene lantern. "I'm nervous about it, I guess. But we'll get across the border somehow."

"I know, but . . . it's scary. Sneaking across the border into that big giant country. I feel like maybe it will . . . swallow us up or something. Anything can happen to us . . . once we're separated."

"It's got to be, Tacha. It's our only chance. We've both worked since we were seven or eight years old. And we've managed to save two hundred and twenty dollars between us. We stay here and in another ten or fifteen years we'll have four hundred dollars between us. I can't take this work, work, work for next to nothing forever . . ."

She stilled his lips with a forefinger. "I know, I know. It's the only way out of a dead end. But I'm still scared."

He squeezed her hand. "Sleep, querida. Tomorrow in Tijuana we'll work it all out."

CHAPTER 7

Anastacia and Margarito got off the bus in Tijuana and made their way toward the bullring.

"This Samaniego we have to see," Margarito explained, "my father told me a lot about him. He's the leading authority on how to get across the border, and how to survive once you make it. He lives down here, and runs a little shop of some kind by the stadium."

It was a cobbler shop the old man ran. "So you're Corrales' boy, eh?" he said after Margarito had introduced himself and Anastacia. "Come to get advice on how to get across, eh?"

He locked up the shop and invited them to stroll with him. "It's not like it used to be," he said, leading the way toward the Colonia Libertad. "Now another big danger is from the polleros."

"Polleros?" Margarito asked, taking in the utter squalor of the slum through which they walked.

"Yes. The polleros are those that prey upon the pollos. Pollos are the people who scamper through the holes in the border fence after dark. That's why they call them pollos. Like chickens, they scoot through any hole in the fence, and in the twelve miles between here and the ocean there are dozens of bands of thugs waiting for them on the other side."

"Where are they from? The polleros."

"They're just bands of guys who wait there in the brush. Some are Mexicans. Some are Mexican Americans from the barrios in the United States. Some are Anglos. They have camps on the U.S. side and they wait to find some poor Mexicans trying to sneak across. They rob them. Screw the women, if there are any, take whatever they have, because they know no one can go to the police."

They were walking through the colony, ironically called

Liberty. Only a narrow road separated the Colonia Libertad of Tijuana from the chain link fence that was the international border. Margarito could see dozens of places where the fence had been cut and later patched, literally within a stone's throw of the houses and shacks of the colony. Entire families lived under pieces of tin, or in stacked wooden crates. There was an overpowering odor of decaying matter, half-naked children wandered about, men limped by on bare feet, and cheaply dressed young girls headed for the bars and cheap hotels of downtown Tijuana. Starving dogs nosed through piles of debris in vacant lots, their naked skin covered with flies. "Come to this house, I'll show you something," Samaniego said, leading them to a shack. The old man banged on the door and a woman answered. She invited them in.

Once inside, Anastacia wanted to bolt. Several mattresses were on the floor. Two sick children stared at them through feverish eyes. But the most hideous thing was a man, literally beaten to a pulp, who was lying facing them. He breathed heavily through his mouth, his smashed nose useless. His blackened eyes were swollen shut. He was naked and a blanket covered him from the hips down.

"This man," Samaniego said, "crossed over the border two nights ago with his wife. He came from Mexico City with his life savings. Fifty dollars. He didn't ask advice about crossing the frontera. The polleros caught him. They left him for dead. You can see he almost is. He will be soon."

Samaniego led the way out to the street. "He's one of hundreds."

"And his wife?" Anastacia asked.

Samaniego shrugged. "Who knows? He can't even talk yet. He crawled back here by himself."

They were again strolling parallel to the border fence. Samaniego went on. "They come, by the thousands. Along the twelve miles of border around Tijuana there are only a couple of hundred U.S. border guards. They try to patrol, but all they can do is discourage the swarms of people. And then there's a hundred miles or more of border from here to Mexicali. And more than a thousand miles of border to El Paso."

"But why do they come here? Wouldn't it be easier to cross fifty miles inland?" Margarito asked.

"Sure. Some do. If you can walk the fifty miles, and then

walk maybe another fifty across desert in the United States. But then you're out in the country, easy to spot. No, they come here because in great numbers chances are better, and once you cross around here, there are the big cities of San Diego and then Los Angeles. You make it there, and if you're smart you're pretty safe. Now, look at this."

They had stopped near a Mexican border official station. Several large buses were there, and men and women were debarking.

"Mojados," the old man explained, "wetbacks, the Americans call them. Those are the ones the United States is returning to Mexico today. Count them. Hundreds. And tomorrow there will be hundreds more being returned. And tonight hundreds will slip back across, through the holes in the fence, like chickens. Lots will get caught. The thugs in the brush will get some. But many will make it."

"What happens when the Americans catch you?"

"They treat you well, for the most part. With such a big Mexican-American population, the U.S. Immigration service is watched carefully for mistreatment. Rarely do they do anything other than send you back. If you get caught, don't resist. Accept voluntary repatriation. They'll send you back here and you can sneak back the same night."

"Okay. We're determined to go," Margarito said. "What more should we know?"

They resumed strolling through the city as the old man lectured. "Walk a couple miles out of town when night comes. Be careful. The thugs will leave you like that man back in that shack. And *you*, pretty one!" He whistled. "You both have money? How much?"

"A couple hundred dollars."

"Ay! How those thugs will like you! But good. Take nothing extra. Just the clothes you're wearing. Be careful. Take nothing that makes you look more like a wetback than you do naturally. Get to a big city close by. San Diego or maybe Oceanside. Establish yourself. Take a job as a night clerk for just a place to stay, if you have to. Then get a California driver's license. I'll tell you how. It won't do you any good if the Immigration finds you, but with a driver's license you can start a checking account. Then you can function in the American society. If you have to travel, to Los Angeles or San Francisco, you can rent a car. Nobody will think a wetback is traveling by rented car. It doesn't cost much. You turn the car in wherever you go. If you're questioned, say you're a Chicano from someplace like Pasadena, Texas, and then start to explain it's not the Pasadena where the Rose Bowl is. *That* rings true. Learn to say it like a Chicano . . ."

The lights of Tijuana were lighting up the sky when Margarito and Anastacia returned to the chain link fence separating the United States from Mexico. They followed it out of the city for a few miles. In the dark many shadowy figures waited to scurry across when no one was in sight. On the other side of the fence only brush country could be seen—sandy dunes covered with mesquite and scrub oak, sage, and cottonwood. There was an occasional border patrol outpost, and U.S. government vehicles cruised by. But watching every point where someone could sneak across would require an army, they saw.

He held her hand as they walked along. It was dark here, as the city and the streetlights were farther behind them, but the moon gave some light. Now they walked beside the chain link fence, and the next time he saw a place where it had been cut, he bent low and scooted through, and then pulled her after him.

Looking about, he saw only brush country. He took her hand and led her at a dog trot, glad of his physical prowess, which would enable him to cover several miles in an hour or so; he hoped she could keep up the pace. They crossed the road used by the vehicles of the border patrol and kept running. The ground underfoot was fairly firm and the light from the moon was adequate. They topped a rise and could see in the distance the lights from a residential section. That would be the housing developments of San Ysidro, in the United States. Once there, they would at least be out of the wilderness.

She was soon breathing hard.

He glanced off to the side and movement behind him caught his eye. Looking around, he saw two figures hurtling at them. In a flash he pushed her into a thicket and turned to confront the danger. Border patrol? Or thugs? He had but an instant and his decision was made for him. The closest man was rushing at him headlong, an object raised high over his head. Margarito's sudden stop disrupted the assailant's coordination. The raised club would go far over his head. Margarito grabbed the man and using the attacker's own momentum, heaved him high into the air. He came down head first a dozen feet away. The second assailant was now upon him, trying to brake his speed. Margarito hit him hard in the face with his fist and felt the unmistakable crunch of bones as the man fell. A third man was coming up fast. Margarito had just time to pick up the club dropped by the first man and face the new threat. The man stopped, plainly discouraged by the fate of his accomplices, and in the instant of indecision, Margarito became the aggressor. He lunged toward the man, flailing with the club. The man jumped backward, and Margarito felt his club strike the man's ankle. The attacker went down and screamed as he tried to crawl away. Margarito was about to pursue him when he heard the sound of feet approaching, and three more men came into view. They were momentarily at a loss in the near darkness as they assessed the situation; three of their accomplices out of action in almost as few seconds. Margarito chose that moment to act again as the aggressor. Quickly he charged the closest thug, swinging the club in great swift arcs. He felt it strike bone and flesh and suddenly the other two no longer had the stomach for the situation. They ran.

Margarito didn't even pause to catch his breath. He ran back to the thicket and found Anastacia trembling, whimpering, transfixed in terror. He shook her by the shoulders.

"Come on, snap out of it," he said gently, and then pushed her ahead of him in the direction of the lights.

No telling how many more thugs were nearby, or whether the six he'd chased were regrouping. As they tried to avoid the patches of brush that would make noise he headed for a small rise a half mile away, and when they got there he stopped, holding her by the arm, looking in all directions, breathing deeply.

To the south were the lights of Tijuana. In the other direction was the residential section of San Ysidro. In between was this no-man's-land of border patrol agents, gangs of thugs, and the objective of both: the economic refugees.

As he looked about, listening to the sounds in the night, the insanity of it all struck him. There was Baja, with two thousand miles of virgin beach, thousands of square miles of land undeveloped and unpeopled, and here this, a savage

ANOTHER LAND

strip of nothing next to a chain link fence that ran for fifteen hundred miles, tens of thousands of people wanting, plotting, risking life, limb, and liberty to get across. A giant nation spending tens of millions of dollars in a futile attempt to stem an irresistible tide of poor people. He thought about how terrified Anastacia must be. From where he was right now, at this moment, everything seemed remote, their possible life together in the future, their past life, all of it was remote, like a story in a book, and right now they had to survive. His musings were cut short by the sounds of a woman screaming. He strained his eyes in the direction of her voice, but could see nothing among the gullies. He felt Anastacia's fingernails digging into his arm. Suddenly the voice was muffled, as though somebody had clamped a hand on the woman's mouth, and then a man was yelling in terror. His voice rose in a crescendo of profanity and then was cut off in midsyllable. Margarito listened moments longer, and then, club still in hand, cautiously began walking fast, pulling Anastacia along.

Dawn was breaking as they walked into the city of Chula Vista. He had hoped somehow to get to San Diego by morning, but they were still some miles from it. He saw a gas station attendant who looked as though he spoke Spanish and they walked toward him. "Is there a bus that runs into San Diego?" Margarito asked.

The attendant glanced at them. "Got papers?"

Margarito hesitated only a moment. "No."

"Pretty risky moving away from the border around here." He eyed Anastacia a moment. "I get off in half an hour. I'll give you both a lift in."

During the ride into San Diego the attendant spoke freely and sympathetically. "You kids speak English pretty good, man. That's in your favor. But you gotta learn more slang. Say 'man' a lot when you talk to someone. Like a Chicano. This your first time here, you gotta learn the ropes. See this underpass we're going under?"

They both nodded, looking up at the bridge. Stenciled on a girder were the words, *Clearance: 13' 7"*. "Well, you know these big hay trucks go by all day long? Stacked with bales of hay? They're stacked to clear the bridges by less than a foot. Three, four days ago a bunch of wetbacks climbed on for a free ride north. Driver didn't know it. He hit that underpass doing about sixty. The wetbacks were sitting back to the wind. They didn't see it coming. They were cleaning up pieces of wetbacks all day long. Parts of 'em stuck to the girder. What I mean, there's lots to know about getting along up here." The frontera certainly takes its toll, Margarito mused.

In the course of the conversation they volunteered the information that Anastacia had a job waiting for her in Los Angeles—if she could get there. The attendant was immediately full of helpful advice.

"Look, pretty one, have this family come and get you. Don't try to make it yourself. La migra has a checkpoint at San Clemente. And they watch the airports. Call the people you'll work for to pick you up here in San Diego. I can tell you the best bet to dodge the spot checks of la migra between here and L.A."

They checked into a cheap hotel in the sleazier area of San Diego. As the desk clerk handed Margarito the key, Anastacia said, "Please. Go on up to the room. I'll phone Mrs. Liggett from the pay phone here. I'll be right up."

When he let her in a few minutes later she clung to him. "I'm still afraid. The Liggetts will pick me up here at noon tomorrow. We have twenty-four hours together. That's all."

He took her arms away. "Okay. It's our first day in the States, as they say. We have no change of clothes, don't know anyone in town, or anyplace. But let's go out and eat and see a movie and then come back here and have a night we won't forget."

The afternoon movie they saw failed to make them forget the uncertainty and danger of their circumstances. Afterward they found a small cafe and sat finishing their meal, looking out onto the crowded streets and sidewalks where derelict and businessman, transient and working man trod past one another unconcerned. They said little throughout the meal and then sat staring through the window.

"Have you decided what you'll do?" she asked.

Margarito signaled the waitress to bring more coffee.

"I'll stay here, find a job. You said you don't want me to call you."

"I said not for a while. I want to get into this job with the Liggetts without a lot of distraction. And it would be dangerous for you to call. It's better if the Liggetts know nothing about you." She took her purse, rummaged through it, and found a slip of paper with a name and address. She began copying it on another slip. "This is the name and address of the Fuentes, a family my folks know in East Los Angeles. If you have to get in touch with me, contact me through them."

Margarito took the slip and placed it in his wallet.

"Okay. I won't get in touch with you unless there's very bad news or very good news."

They sat, looking out the window in silence. He was watching her dreamy expression.

"What are you thinking of?"

She looked at him, coming out of her reverie. "I was just thinking of the giant old cactus at La Tijera. I'm glad we visited it when we were there. It's always been special."

"I guess cactuses represent Mexico," he said absently.

She went on. "My father says that cardon poked its head into the world at almost the very same moment I did."

He smiled, looking at her. "I know. I remember. I was there."

She continued, "When I was little, Papa would take me when he carried a bucket of water to it. He'd pour the water on and step back and say, 'See? It's bigger and stronger than all the others. Because I give it special attention. It's kind of your twin.' And for years, if he was away working somewhere else, I'd take a bucket of water from the barrel you used for filling car radiators, and I'd walk up there and pour the water on it. It grew much faster and better than the others. I'd look around, seeing everything struggling to live in the withering heat, and wish I could take every cardon a bucket of water. But there must be millions within a mile of La Tijera."

Now he smiled in his own reverie. "Once, when I was about fifteen, some American tourists gave me a dollar to put on a sombrero and pretend I was sleeping under that cactus. Then they took my picture." He thought a moment. "I did it, but I wouldn't do it now." Then he smiled his usual mirthful smile. "Not for a dollar, anyway."

The waitress brought the check. They rose to go, Margarito glancing down at the littered table. "Our first American meal," he said to her as he paid the cashier.

They walked slowly in the direction of their hotel, she holding onto his arm. Wordlessly and seemingly without interest they looked at the cheap clothing stores, pawnshops, thrift stores. Men stood on corners wearing trousers that were too short, revealing dirty, scrawny ankles, no socks, and tattered shoes. A wino lay asleep on a bus bench. A group of dark young men came by, talking loudly in Spanish, wearing new but cheap clothes. At this time of day traffic in the streets was bumper to bumper.

They entered their hotel. The clerk at the desk glanced up from his newspaper, tossed them the key, and returned to his reading. They ascended the steep, narrow stairs, turning sideways to allow a pregnant woman to go by.

The dark unlit hallway contributed to their sense of despair. Inside their room they stood at the window overlooking the street below, listening to the sounds of traffic and the throngs.

Finally she said, "I don't even have a change of clothes."

"Me either," he said, trying to sound cheerful.

She made an effort to snap out of her mood. "Well, I have to have a shower. It's just down the hall, isn't it?"

He nodded. "Go ahead. I'll take my first American shower after you."

When she returned he still stood silently looking out the window. She undressed and stood beside him in the near darkness. He turned and held her close.

"I'm so scared," she said quietly.

He tilted her chin up to him. "It'll be okay, Tacha, baby. Just wait and see."

The next day Margarito watched from the cheap room on the second floor of the sleazy hotel as Anastacia got into the Liggetts' station wagon. He stood staring out the window long after the car had disappeared around the corner. Then he left the room and tossed the key on the desk as he went out and started looking for work.

He was unsuccessful at first, and spent his days wandering about the city. He bought T-shirts and khaki shirts and trousers. More than a week later he was offered the job of night clerk in the hotel. His salary was small, but he got his room free. He went about learning how to get a driver's license. He had no trouble passing the test, was given a temporary permit and within a few weeks the real thing came in the mail.

The hotel was in a neighborhood populated mostly by

blacks, Mexicans, and many Southeast Asians. Margarito soon saw the tremendous advantage of being bilingual. In his spare time he hung around bars, soon becoming bored with the Mexican hangouts because the conversation was always about getting jobs, dodging authorities, and helping relatives get across the border.

One man he met was called el sobreviviente—the survivor—and when Margarito asked why he was so called, he found the story would cost him a drink. The man related vividly how he had been approached by Americans with a scheme to get into the United States that was foolproof. He and a dozen other Mexicans gave two hundred dollars each to the Americans. They were put aboard and locked inside an enclosed truck during the night and driven across the border—they thought. But after only a few minutes of traveling, the truck stopped. Those inside heard or felt nothing more in the rear, and soon the morning sun was beating unmercifully on the top and sides. By noon the men were collapsing from heat prostration. This man, el sobreviviente, was for some reason the only one to live through the day. And the following day someone happened to stop to investigate the locked truck. The drivers had simply driven the truck, which they had rented, out into the desert and abandoned it, leaving those inside to die.

"I saw ten of my best friends, and two of their wives, sweat themselves to death, beating on the door, trying to tear metal with their bare hands, their voices too hoarse even to cry out."

Others in the bar had elaborated on the story, fantasizing such additions as that el sobreviviente had drunk the blood of the dead to survive. The survivor enjoyed his legendary status, and when somebody accused him of this atrocity he would neither confirm nor deny it, saying in a profound manner, "Believe me, when you're face to face with death, you'll do anything to live. *Anything!*" and let the story rest on that cryptic ending.

Another man he knew came into the tavern. "Hey, Rito," he called, motioning him to take an adjoining stool. "You want a good job? I'm quitting."

"Sure," Rito said, indicating two beers to the bartender. "Doing what?"

"I work at that big chemical factory. The work's not too hard, but it's messy. Filling the big tank trucks with chemicals. You have to wear rubber overclothes and it gets very hot."

"You think I could get the job?"

"Yeah. It takes somebody who is fairly good with arithmetic and can read and write English well. They'll take you if I recommend you."

Within a month Margarito was one of the fastest truck fillers the chemical company ever had. The trucks would pull in, he would take the paperwork from the driver, scramble up on top of the tank, flip open the hatch, insert the right nozzle, and flip the valve. While the tank was filling, he would be handling the paperwork, giving the driver a copy saying what he was hauling, to where, how many gallons were aboard, how much it weighed, and so on. He wore rubber overclothes, but still the company warned him that if any of the chemicals splashed on him, he was to change clothes and bathe immediately upon getting home. He left his rubber clothes in a company locker room every night.

One day as he filled trucks he suddenly realized six months had passed and he'd had no contact with Anastacia.

"I'll call tonight," he said to himself.

But when he called from the booth in his hotel lobby he got a recording saying that the number had been changed and there was no new number.

With foreboding he mulled that over in his room as he watched a program on the tiny black and white TV set he'd bought. He cursed himself for not knowing the Liggetts' phone number, or the area in which they lived. Well, he still had the Fuentes' address, and as soon as circumstances permitted he would go there and find out about her.

The telephone by his bed rang. It was an ancient model with no dial and would only take incoming calls. When he answered he heard the voice of Alicia, the waitress at a nearby cafe.

"Rito!" she said with her customary exuberance. "I'm downstairs in the lobby. Let's go to the wrestles tonight and then have some fun later, eh?"

He laughed. Alicia was a fellow illegal alien. She loved

ANOTHER LAND

practicing her poor English and had introduced him to many friends in the area. She had a terrific body and this had done a lot to get his mind off Anastacia when his nights had become unbearably lonely.

"Come on up, baby," he said, warming to the occasion, "the door's open. We'll start having fun now."

And they did have their fun. And then he took her to "the wrestles." And afterward they stopped at a tavern where they both had many friends and where mariachis sang the old songs of Mexico, and they drank so much they had a difficult time getting back to the hotel. Margarito was late for work that day, for the first time, and his boss glanced at his wristwatch when he saw Margarito come scampering up to the loading dock where a half-dozen giant tankers already waited with motors idling.

"What the hell," Margarito said to himself, "it's the first time I've been late in months. If they don't like it, tough."

More months passed, and he was feeling fairly safe. One day a huge tanker pulled in. The driver climbed out to go to the office. "A load of MEK, Rito," he hollered. "I'm going right back."

Margarito nodded. MEK was methyl ethyl ketone, he knew. A powerful substance, toxic if you breathed the fumes too much. He opened the hatch atop the tank, inserted the nozzle, went about the paperwork. He happened to glance up at the hatch as the tank was nearly full, and saw the chemical stream splashing out, as though it were hitting something inside the tank. He shut off the valve and climbed up on the tank. The hatch was a foot and a half wide, and floating on the surface of two thousand gallons of methyl ethyl ketone was the body of a man.

Quickly he jumped down and ran to the dispatch office to inform the chief dispatcher. A secretary called the police. Several employees returned with Margarito to the tank truck. The body was no longer in sight, and a rod with a hook was brought to the scene. Margarito probed down in the chemical and located what he sought. But when he raised it to the hatch, he saw it was the body of a woman.

"Could you have been wrong?" the dispatcher asked.

Margarito shook his head. "There's a man in there too."

The dispatcher sighed in disgust, climbing down. "Okay, pump it out. Take the truck out of the way and drain it. No telling how many are in it."

When they lifted out the fourth and last body, Margarito flinched. It was that of a small, gaunt man, one he had known well in Ensenada, who sold tacos from a steaming pushcart on the streets. He had been a poor man, living on the side of a hill in a hovel among other hovels. And he'd finally made it across the border.

The police, a man from the coroner's office, and an immigration agent arrived. Margarito heard the dispatcher talking. "It's what we call MEK—methyl ethyl ketone. It's a powerful solvent, used among other things as a degreaser in garages and machine shops. The truck had delivered a load to Ensenada. Obviously, at a truck stop these people climbed in. MEK doesn't seem to be noxious, but its fumes are deadly. After they closed that hatch, they were all dead within minutes. It's happened before . . ."

"That one," Margarito sullenly indicated one stretcher, "I know him. He's from Ensenada. He has family there."

The man from immigration looked at him sharply. "How do you know?" he asked curtly.

Margarito looked at the man, aware he had given away something about himself. "I just know. His name's Saenz."

The immigration man approached him. "May I talk to you further about your knowledge of this man?" the agent asked.

"Sure," Margarito said casually, "just let me go to the locker room to get out of these overclothes. I got some of that stuff on me. Be with you in a minute."

Margarito walked into the locker room, took off his rubberized overclothes, threw them in a hamper, opened the window onto the parking lot, and climbed out. He went directly to his hotel, packed his belongings, walked to a car-rental agency a few blocks away, and rented a car.

CHAPTER 8

Pat and Ed Liggett drove Anastacia from San Diego to their home in a pleasant suburban neighborhood of Los Angeles. As soon as the car rolled up the driveway, Alvin and his sister came out to greet her. They showed her the house, the kitchen, the dining room, the guest room where she would stay, which had its own private entrance, and then the whole family talked with her in the living room. She noticed no mention was made of her illegal crossing at Tijuana; in fact, they stayed away from that, until fourteen-year-old Monica blurted, "How did you get across the border?"

There was an awkward little silence, and then Pat Liggett said, "That's none of our business. And besides, it's bedtime for you."

Pat promised to take her shopping for clothes the next day, and to show her the supermarket, which was within walking distance, and while they stayed up chatting, she noticed Edmond had three drinks to Pat's one, and was a little glassy-eyed by the time she said good night and went to her room.

She liked the room. The bed was soft and snug, and a small bathroom adjoined the bedroom. The little bathroom was perfect, it smelled nice, and the scented toilet paper caused her to smile. As she made herself comfortable in bed, she realized she was tired and aching. Something else ached, too. Yes. She thoroughly enjoyed the feeling that came from that part of her that had so recently been awakened. Now an emptiness was pronounced there, while previously that emptiness had been vague and ill-defined. Somehow this, and the memory of it all, pleased her immensely, and she fell asleep with a smile on her lips.

Anastacia had long realized that many Americans talk about the supermarket the way Parisians talk about the Louvre. But she was still unprepared for the magically opening doors, the rush of refrigerated air, the seemingly endless corridors of items. All that's missing is the candlelight, she mused, as she listened to the quiet music which courted, almost seduced each person who entered. Quiet but cheerful, encouraging.

She counted twelve different types of chicken soup alone. The varieties of breakfast food were staggering. But in the produce department Anastacia stood looking at the vegetables, at first unable to define what was amiss. Then it came to her. All the vegetables were incredibly identical. She walked down one row to make sure she was right. She was. Where were the carrots that turned a right angle halfway down the shank? Where were the tomatoes with rough green spots that always seemed to add to the earthiness of the flavor? Where was the potato that doubled back on itself? She knew it was impossible to grow things as perfect as this, so that must mean . . . either the malformed specimens were thrown away, or were sold somewhere else. She pointed this out to Pat.

"I've never seen misshapen vegetables," Pat said. "Those must have been diseased."

Anastacia saw a fat woman with two equally fat teenagers arguing vehemently about buying such items as whipped cream, chocolate syrup, and pastry. "All right!" the mother finally snapped. "Get what the hell you want. See if I care what you look like." A family with real problems, Anastacia surmised.

Pat and Anastacia walked by two girls who were obviously maids, leaning on their shopping carts as they chatted in Spanish. She wanted to talk to them but thought better of it. There would be plenty of opportunities later.

She quickly caught onto the routine at the Liggett home, and at the end of the first month, things were going almost too smoothly.

The supermarket became a minor focal point in Anastacia's life. On a subsequent visit she became acquainted with the two Mexican maids she'd seen on her first visit. Within the structure was an eating area with small circular tables, and Anastacia had coffee and snacks with the two girls, and then she met others. She found that this was a place where criadas mejicanas met one another to talk of their jobs, their experiences, and of news from down home. She was astounded to realize that in this West Los Angeles area alone the number of Mexican maids must number in the tens of thousands. At each meeting the talk eventually came around to their illegal status in the country and the resulting problems.

A few months passed and on one shopping trip three regulars at the supermarket did not appear.

"They were picked up," one knowledgeable domestic reported. "Their boyfriends took them to a movie in downtown L.A. The migra raided the place."

Anastacia got the standard advice: If picked up, don't tell where you're working. That way the job will be safe to return to. Also, always say you're from Tijuana, Ensenada, or Mexicali. Then when you accept voluntary deportation, as the alternative to criminal charges of illegal entry filed by the immigration officers, they take you there and it's much easier to find your way back.

As she sat talking with her new friends at the supermarket one day, one girl kept looking at her. "Tacha Herrera, your name is?"

"Sí."

"Where did I hear it mentioned? Oh, yes. I was shipped back to Ensenada a few weeks ago. There was a man, recruiting girls, if you know what I mean, and he was asking if anyone knew the whereabouts of a girl by that name. Was he looking for you?"

Anastacia felt a chill. "What was his name?"

"Uh . . . let's see. Huerta, I believe. Did he get hold of you?"

After that conversation, Anastacia went about the housework unable to concentrate the rest of the day. It was a small world. It had to be the same man. Huerta was looking for her, and would exploit the grapevine among illegal aliens to whatever ends he could. A gnawing fear began to set in. By this time, many housemaids either knew her by name or knew of her. It was only a matter of time before one would cross paths with Huerta, wherever he might be. The last she'd heard he had set up shop somewhere near the two big U.S. military bases at Camp Pendleton and San Diego. She had no idea what he would do if he found her. Would he seek revenge for the trouble and humiliation she had caused? Or would he just inform the immigration people?

Well, at this point, there was nothing she could do. She decided to put it out of her mind as best she could and be a good housemaid.

That afternoon as she folded the laundry in the washroom she heard Pat Liggett call to her: "Tacha! Telephone for you."

Her pulse quickened as she hurried to the phone. Margarito hadn't called and it was six months now since they'd parted. But disappointment showed on her face when she recognized the voice of the Fuentes woman in East Los Angeles.

"Tacha?"

"Sí, señora."

"I just want to let you know, we had some trouble with a caller bothering our daughter, so we had our phone number changed. Got a lápiz?"

Anastacia took a pencil from her apron pocket and jotted the number on a pad.

"Thank you so much, señora. How long have you had this new number?"

"Just a few days."

"And . . . no one's called to ask about me?"

"No, Tacha. Nobody called."

Anastacia thought a moment. "Okay. I got it. Thanks again."

As she returned to her work she was more anxious than ever. What if Margarito called now? He had no way of getting in touch. Then with more dismay she realized she did not know the name of the tiny hotel they had stayed in for one night. Even if she could remember, he probably wouldn't be there now.

That night as she cleaned and polished some crystal after Pat and the children had gone to bed, she heard Edmond Liggett's car drive in. Soon she heard his key in the back door and then he walked into the living room, staggering slightly.

He looked surprised to see her. "Oh, hi, Tacha. Say," he

stopped in front of the wet bar she was working behind, "how about having a tiny drink with me."

She smiled. "I'm going to bed as soon as these are done."

"Oh, come on. One little one for kicks."

She thought a moment. "Okay. I'll have just a sip of sherry."

He came around the bar and she suddenly sensed his intent. As he walked behind her he stopped and she felt herself holding her breath. Then she felt a hand on each hip. She stood still a moment. Then she set down the crystal she had been polishing and whirled, pushing him away firmly. She walked around to the other side of the bar and stood looking at him.

He let his eyes droop, assuming an attitude of superciliousness.

"Well, excuse me all to hell," he said. "I didn't realize you were made of gold."

She returned his gaze coolly, then moved toward the door. "Good night, Edmond." She went to her room and heard him go into the master bedroom a few minutes later.

For a day or two he was remorseful, though she attributed that as much to a bad hangover as to his guilt at making a pass. Within a week he was trying to be cheerful and jolly with her, as though to reassure her, and she decided that she should forgive and forget the whole episode. But one night a few days after her resolution she was lying awake in bed and heard his car drive in. She heard him fumble with his key at the back door and guessed his condition. She could hear his footsteps as he walked across the kitchen linoleum. Then nothing as he trod on the plush living-room carpeting. Soon she heard the clink of glass against glass and knew where he was. Silence for some minutes and then again the clinking. Five minutes passed and she heard his quiet footsteps coming down the hall to her room. With mounting panic she tried to remember if she'd pushed the little locking button on the handle of her bedroom door. She heard the handle rattle, ever so faintly. Then it rattled again a little louder. Finally it rattled vigorously and she guessed he was angry. Soon his footsteps faded away in the direction of the master bedroom. She wondered if Pat or Alvin or Monica had overheard.

Suddenly she was sobbing quietly as she found her thoughts

racing from her life at the Liggetts to Margarito and his whereabouts; Huerta; her parents; and then to La Tijera—the sloping desert disappearing into the turquoise sea, and the giant, proud cardon cactus standing tall at this moment in the incredibly bright desert moonlight. She fell asleep crying.

Anastacia had been writing to and receiving letters from her parents in Ensenada, but now that she knew that Huerta was looking for her she doubted the wisdom of any correspondence from home. After she mulled it over, however, influenced by her need to maintain close family ties, she decided no harm would come of it.

She had visited the Fuentes family occasionally and now at their invitation began spending weekends there. This allowed her to become acquainted with the barrio, and she enjoyed starting to build a circle of friends in the area. She became almost a regular at the Fuentes home from Saturday mornings until Sunday nights.

Another three months dragged by and still no word from Margarito. Then four months.

One afternoon she had just returned from the supermarket and was putting things away in the kitchen when Pat Liggett came in.

"Oh, Tacha, dear. There was a phone call for you. He left a number."

"Who was it?"

"He wouldn't give a name. He said he would be at this number at ten tomorrow morning."

Anastacia took the slip of paper with the number on it. She felt a coldness in her stomach. A man who wouldn't give his name. Margarito? Huerta? An immigration agent? When she was alone that evening she decided to call the number. The anxiety of not knowing had become too great. The number rang, and at length a male voice answered.

"Hello," gruffly.

"Ah . . . hello . . . who is this?"

"Who'd you want?"

"I was told to call this number. What's your name?"

"Oh, I'm just passing by. This is a phone booth on the corner. I heard it ringing and answered."

"Well . . . is there someone else around there?"

"Ain't no one around here but a bunch of winos, lady. Can I help you?"

"No. No. Thank you."

She finished the dinner dishes but as the evening wore on she became more unnerved. She was in her room, lying down, having one of the two cigarettes she smoked during a day, when Pat rapped at her door.

"Tacha? May I come in?"

"Sure."

Pat came in and sat on the bed. "I know you're terribly upset, Tacha. Want to talk to me about it?"

And in a monotone, Anastacia told her more or less what life had become for her, watching the other girls at the supermarket vanish, fearing any moment there would be a knock at the door, a raid when she went anywhere in East Los Angeles. She did not mention her fear of Huerta, nor the fact that Edmond Liggett had been making advances, or a few other things that were bothering her.

Pat Liggett was sincerely moved even by the abbreviated account Anastacia gave her. "I had no idea life here would become so complicated for you. You've been here nearly a year. It's time you had a vacation. I want you to take it. Soon. You've got to. We've all got to get away from the workaday world now and then, or we don't function right."

Anastacia nodded without much enthusiasm.

At ten the next morning she looked at the phone a long time before finally dialing the number. She was alone in the house, and found her hands were trembling. When she heard Margarito's voice answer, her pent-up anxiety exploded in great sobs. Pat was due back momentarily, so they made plans quickly. She would take her vacation at the end of the week and meet him. For convenience, she would tell the Liggetts she was going to the Fuentes home. Margarito was unfamiliar with the locale, and she gave exact instructions where she would be at what time. No, his position was precarious also, much more so than hers, and there was no way she could contact him in the interim.

"I got your phone number from the Fuentes," Margarito explained. "I finally went there after they had their number changed. They wanted me to stay but I look too suspicious, so they couldn't have me hanging around their house. Also, I had to memorize your phone number and I almost forgot it."

"Why did you have to memorize it?" Anastacia asked.

"Maybe you haven't found out what it's like yet, out on the streets. If the immigration agents pick me up and find this phone number on me, they'll go there and get you next."

"Listen, Rito, we don't have much time to talk. I have vacation time coming. Write this down. I'll meet you Saturday . . ."

Pat Liggett came in just as she finished talking. Anastacia looked at her. No, this woman could never in a million years understand what it's like to have the man you love afraid to carry your phone number, to have no place to call him.

It will work out eventually, she told herself. She attempted a smile at Pat and the tears she squeezed back were as much from anger as anything else.

"You're sure you don't want a ride to the Fuentes house, Tacha?" Pat Liggett asked. She was wearing slacks and a loose blouse, thongs, and her hair was in a bun, her usual Saturday morning attire. Anastacia was dressed in traveling clothes. They were talking on the front porch while Alvin went to Anastacia's room to get her suitcase.

"Positive, Pat," Anastacia replied, "just drop me at the bus stop and forget me for two weeks. Everything's taken care of."

"Well, we're certainly going to miss you. But it won't hurt Alvin and Monica and Edmond one bit to do a few things for themselves. After this vacation maybe they'll appreciate you."

The front door opened and Edmond emerged, wearing slippers, light blue denim trousers, a square-tail shirt and dark glasses. He looked slightly hung over.

"Pat, I'll be glad to drop Tacha off. In fact, we ought to take her over to the Fuentes'."

"Edmond, she doesn't want us to take her to the Fuentes'."

"Well, why not?"

Pat's voice betrayed annoyance. "That's *her* business. It's her vacation and she asked us to take her to the bus stop."

Edmond walked toward the car. "Okay. I'll take her."

Pat put her hands on her hips, and her voice had an edge. "Edmond, she asked me to take her. Now forget it."

Edmond stopped and faced them. He looked down and shrugged.

ANOTHER LAND

Anastacia suddenly moved toward the car. "Really, please," she laughed lightly, "it's not worth a fuss. Thank you, Alvin."

Alvin placed the suitcase in the back seat and returned to the house. Pat got in the driver's seat and Anastacia got in beside her. Edmond stood looking at them from the porch, hands in his pockets. He called out to the car, "Tacha, is there a number where we can reach you?"

Anastacia smiled at Pat.

"Edmond, why would we want to reach her? She's going on vacation."

"Well, just in case. Maybe her folks will want to get hold of her."

"Well, they'll just have to wait."

"I'll keep in touch," Anastacia called. "'Bye now."

Edmond Liggett waved without enthusiasm and turned toward the door.

Within minutes Pat pulled the car up to the bus stop on Santa Monica Boulevard. "Here you are, Tacha. Have a lovely time. Don't worry about us."

"Thanks, Pat," Anastacia said, taking her suitcase from the back. "I'll call you if I need you."

"Good. The bus ought to be here in a few minutes. If it doesn't come, please call me."

Anastacia laughed, but said with some conviction, "If it doesn't come I'll hitchhike."

Pat eased into the traffic and left Anastacia waiting beside the bus stop. At home she sensed Edmond's remorseful mood. She went about her household duties. Alvin was watching television in the den. Monica was on and off the telephone. Toward evening Pat went to the bar in the living room to mix a drink. Edmond was there, nursing an Old Fashioned glass of Bourbon on the rocks.

"Hitting it kind of heavy, aren't you?" she asked carefully, as she poured and mixed.

"Got a lot of business problems. Need to unwind."

The next day Pat attributed the morose mood that permeated the house to Anastacia's unusual absence and the fact that it was Sunday. At midafternoon Edmond and Alvin were watching a football game in the den. Edmond held a dark drink.

Suddenly he said to his son, "When you took Tacha

to the Fuentes house that time, did you remember the address?"

Alvin looked at him blankly. "What?"

Angrily, "I said when you took her to the Fuentes house, did you notice the address?"

Alvin gathered his thoughts. "No. On Barnhart Street near First in East L.A."

When his father didn't respond he turned his attention back to the game.

"What house?" Edmond asked after a few moments.

Alvin again looked at him. "What house? Why?"

"Never mind why! We might have to get in touch with her. Which house did you take her to?"

Alvin concentrated. "I went out First to Barnhart. Then turned left. It was about the third or fourth house down."

"On which side?"

"On the right."

Pat came into the room with a sandwich and a soft drink. She took a chair between them and fastened her eyes on the screen. "Who's winning?" she asked.

"Rams can't get untracked. Ten to nothing Atlanta."

"I'm tired," Edmond said, draining his glass and rising. "I'm going to take a nap."

Pat Liggett stepped out of the dressing booth, buttoning her blouse. She faced the doctor.

"I'll give it to you straight, Pat," he said.

"Please do."

"Ten to one you should have that breast removed. I'd do it as soon as possible, if I were you."

She paused a long moment. "And if I don't?"

He shrugged. "I don't think there's much choice. Even with the mastectomy, we won't know the full story for a while."

"How long do I have to decide?"

"I'll have it nailed down by the end of the week, but there is little chance I'm wrong. How soon can you have it done?"

Pat retained a remarkable amount of composure, but the doctor wasn't surprised. "Oh, God," she said as though her tolerance for inconveniences was at an end. "Our maid just took off on vacation. I *can't* have it done for a couple of weeks. It'll just be too complicated."

"All right, then. Let me set it up for two weeks. I'll arrange for a bed for the week of the twentieth. We'll let you know when to check in."

It was early evening when she arrived home. She entered the house by the rear door and could tell Monica had heard her drive in and had rushed into the kitchen to make it appear as though she had been preparing the evening meal for some time. Pat smiled and kissed her.

"God, Mom! Tacha's only been gone two days and already this house is a shambles."

"It won't hurt any of us to do a few things for ourselves. Believe it or not, Monica, there are millions of people in this world who don't have housekeepers."

She walked through the dining area and looked into the den off the hall. *Monday Night Football,* she realized, as she saw Edmond and Alvin in front of the television. *I'll tell them after the game.* She greeted them more or less successfully, she guessed, as they seemed to notice nothing, and then she refreshed herself in the bathroom. Emerging, she went to check on Monica in the kitchen.

"God, Mom," Monica said, trying to set up TV trays, "what a hassle trying to fix dinner trays for those two boob-tube boobs in the den. You'd think they'd have had enough watching football all day yesterday."

"I guess we'll get to appreciate Tacha while she's gone. Here, I'll fix my own plate and take it in the bedroom."

She took the plate into the bedroom and set it on her desk. She snapped on the reading light and went to the bookshelf, where she found a small book titled, *Hints for the Convalescing Housewife.* She was about to begin reading and eating when the phone rang.

"Hello?" she answered.

A voice with a pronounced Spanish accent replied, "Hello, is that Mrs. Liggett?"

"Yes it is."

"This is Ramon Fuentes."

"Yes, Mr. Fuentes. How are you?"

"Fine. We are wondering if you've located Tacha yet."

". . . What?"

"Did you find Tacha? Is something wrong she should know?"

"No, not that I know of. Why?"

"Just because, when Mr. Liggett came today there was only our youngest daughter home, and she couldn't help him."

"Couldn't help him?"

"Yes, but if it's important you locate her, we can maybe reach her mother and father in Ensenada by phone. They might know. Is there trouble or something?"

Pat Liggett took a few moments to reply. "No. There's no trouble. Tacha left Saturday on her vacation. Mr. Liggett wanted to know where she'd be if anything urgent came up."

"No, we don't know where she is. But if we hear, we'll tell her to call you right away."

"No, don't do that, Mr. Fuentes. It's not necessary. If you hear from her tell her to enjoy herself."

When she replaced the receiver she sat thinking and listening. From the kitchen she heard Monica saying, "God!" amid clanks and clatters. She heard Alvin and Edmond suddenly laugh with glee at something that happened in the football game. The small reading light on the desk could not overcome the gloom and darkness in the room. From the den she heard the sports announcer saying, ". . . and they're calling that one back, and the home crowd doesn't like that *one bit!*" And the great swelling boos that came from the crowd covered the sobs she finally allowed herself.

The bus that was to deliver Anastacia to Margarito rolled to a stop, air brakes spitting as the automatic doors at the front and rear opened simultaneously. Anastacia found her heart was pounding as she stood in the aisle, waiting for the other passengers to file out with what seemed agonizing sluggishness. Then as she stepped down onto the sidewalk, suitcase in hand, she saw him coming toward her. The bus stop was crowded, and for a moment she got lost in the mob of passengers waiting to board, then he was lifting her nearly a foot off the ground so their lips would meet. After the better part of a minute she tried to wriggle free, turning her face.

"Put me down! I want to look at you."

Reluctantly, he lowered her. "And I want to feel you," he said with his customary good nature.

She laughed. "Rito. You'll never change, will you?"

"You wouldn't want me to."

ANOTHER LAND

She stood back, taking him in from head to foot. "You look marvelous, Rito," she said.

"You too, baby. Come on." He picked up her suitcase. "I got a place rented. We can walk there."

He was wearing a blue polo shirt and denim trousers. His shoes were brown loafers. She wore a cotton print dress and high-heeled white open-toed shoes. Her purse was almost an overnight bag.

They walked slowly, almost strolling, in the manner they had traversed countless miles of empty beaches together when they were growing up. But here, along Ocean Boulevard in Santa Monica, the traffic was jammed, bumper to bumper, as were the cars parked along the curb. The walkway was next to the sand, and a few hundred feet beyond was the ocean. Thousands of people jammed the beach, running, playing, lying on blankets and promenading. Sun bathers argued over a few square feet of space, as did car owners on the street trying to squeeze their vehicles into absurdly small spaces. Teenagers raced by on foot or bicycle or skateboard.

They walked.

"How far is our . . . love nest?" she asked.

He glanced at her and then his gaze returned to the unending throng about them. "Couple of miles. These gringos are crazy. You know that by now. They run five miles every morning, but they won't walk a half-mile when they need to. Remember at La Tijera? How many times did we walk to the store? It was six miles."

She nodded. "Sometimes we walked three or four times a day. I remember one time some gringos threw away four or five beer bottles worth two cents each. We found them and took them back and got a dime's worth of candy."

They walked in silence for a while. Rito was looking out toward the sea. "Remember walking to Punta del Diablo?"

She smiled, looking down at the sidewalk. "Many times. How far was that?"

"That was about fifteen miles. We were kids and we thought nothing of it."

They again walked in silence. Soon he led her down a side street, away from the ocean, for a block, and then they turned into an alley lined with garages at the rear of houses. To the side of one garage was a wooden gate. Passing through, he led her up a rickety outside wooden staircase into a tiny one-room apartment above a garage. He set down the suitcase, closed the door and gave her an embrace that lasted nearly five minutes. When he released her she stepped back, looking serious, shaken by feelings she had never really felt before.

She shook her head slightly, as though to clear it.

"Rito, let me get my bearings." She looked around. "This reminds me of that little apartment you had on Avenida Vegas for a while."

He laughed and walked toward the area used as a kitchen. "Oh, yeah. Where you caught me with that little waitress, Chata. Remember that?"

"I remember. I was only sixteen. She wasn't much to look at." Then she added, "In the face."

He was opening the small refrigerator. "Oh? I never noticed her face. What'd it look like?"

Anastacia laughed and felt herself entering into the spirit of the occasion. She watched as he removed most of what was in the refrigerator and placed all of the items on the little breakfast table for her inspection.

"Good grief, Rito!" she exclaimed, sitting at the table. The food consisted of trays and cartons of Mexican food prepared by a delicatessen. "That must have cost a fortune."

"It did. So did this apartment, by the way. Can you believe, I had to pay five hundred dollars for this for two weeks?"

"Five hundred!"

"That's right. Because it's two blocks from the ocean. Rents are high here. Mostly only vacationers rent in this area. And I bought food already made so we won't waste time cooking." He gave her a ridiculously significant glance and she laughed again.

"Funny," he went on. "All day yesterday I wasn't hungry. This morning I had butterflies in my stomach. Then when I met you at the bus stop, and walking here, I was starving. And now suddenly I'm not hungry again." He took her hands and pulled her to her feet.

She also became serious. "Okay," she said, "show me the shower. I have to get out of these clothes."

He crossed the room and threw open a door, revealing a small bathroom. She looked about, puzzled. "Where's the bed?"

ANOTHER LAND

He went to a flimsy tapestry and pulled it back, revealing a bed standing against the wall.

"They call it a Murphy bed. I don't know why. I guess some guy named Murphy who had a small room invented it."

She stepped out of the shower and saw him lying on the bed, undressed. She lay down beside him and put her hand on his hair, but suddenly he was rolling over on top of her. Only for a moment did she feel discomfort at the penetration, and then she felt as though her womb was being filled. An intense longing to receive, receive, coursed through her body. She wanted him. All of him. All the time. Now. Later tonight. Tomorrow and every day thereafter.

Finally, when they lay still together, still engaged, she spoke, "Eres mi vida, querido."

He sat up, looking down on her, and started to say something, but she pressed a finger to his lips; "I know, you're starving."

He nodded. "I'll fix it."

"Oh no you won't," she said, rising. From her suitcase she took a linen half-length bathrobe and put it on. She spent a few minutes in the bathroom and then busied herself at the stove while he sat at the table watching her. Soon she had a pair of pots simmering on the small two-burner stove and a minute later she was heaping his plate full. Suddenly she stood still, staring at nothing, surprise on her face.

He paused with the spoon halfway to his mouth.

"What's the matter?"

She put down a dishcloth and started toward the bathroom door, glancing around at the floor behind her.

"I've got to get to the bathroom quick," she said. Margarito roared with laughter. She paused at the bathroom door, fist on hip, looking at him. "I *am* fairly new at all this, you know," she said with humor.

"Stick with me, Tacha baby, and you'll get a whole new education."

She turned away, pulling the door closed as she said, "I intend to stick with you."

That night on the beach they walked quietly. There were couples on the sand in the shadows. Two joggers came by. A woman passed leading a large dog on a leash. The ocean roared and in the opposite direction the city lights reflecting from the overcast sky gave more illumination than a full moon would have. He studied her face in the vague light.

"You look angry."

She shook her head. "Not particularly. A little, I guess, when I think of you. You've worked hard since you were a boy. I saw the ditches you dug, the bricks you carried, the clay pipes you laid, the cars you fixed, and not much has changed since then except now you work hard *and* you run and hide."

"You have to hide too."

"Yes."

"Do the Liggetts treat you all right?"

She thought a moment before answering. "Yes. I'm getting along fine there. They think I'm visiting the Fuentes."

"But you miss Mexico, don't you?"

"Terribly. I miss the lower Baja country. Not Ensenada so much. I try not to think of Mama and Papa. I miss them so."

He was looking out at the ocean, which appeared black. "Then why are we here? What are we doing here?"

She stopped and looked at him. "You know why we're here. We have a chance to earn money that will get us out of working from dawn to dusk the rest of our lives. Maybe when we return to La Tijera you can make a fine addition to your father's little gas station and roadside café. Someday it'll be yours, and if you have money you won't have to make a new building by buying one sack of cement every other week and ten bricks at a time. Maybe I can set my father up in his own little business." They resumed strolling and she continued, "All we have to do, Rito darling, is stick it out. If we can last a few years up here we'll be able to do what we want. Mama and Papa can have a place of their own. And we can be together. But we have to wait. I won't go back and give up hope. I won't return to work, work, work for someone else forever." She looked at him. "And neither will you."

"You're right, Tacha. This two weeks will be over before we know it, but remembering this will be enough to keep me going. I know you think I'm strong, but sometimes I want to give up and go back where there's no migra to hassle everybody."

"You are strong, Rito. In every way. Let's just remember what we're working for, how it will be someday. And we'll make it."

ANOTHER LAND

He was looking at the ocean again. "Yes, we can do it."

They walked silently for a while. Then, "Tacha, there's something you should know. Remember today when I was telling you about finding the bodies in the tank truck?"

"How could I forget."

"Well, what I didn't tell you was, one of the bodies was Señor Saenz. The skinny old taco merchant."

She stopped, looking at him, and he knew there were tears in her eyes. "Saenz? The one who pushes his cart around Ensenada?"

"The same."

She had trouble talking. ". . . Rito . . . he's been giving me free tacos since I was eight years old. He has a daughter my age I went to school with. Rito . . . not him!"

"Yes. Harmless old guy who tried to support his family and never quite could. His wife, Doña Alma, works in a restaurant making tortillas in a glass window so the tourists can stare at her."

"Does she know?"

Margarito shrugged. "I told the migra man who he was. They usually try to notify family."

For a few minutes neither said anything. Then she said with quiet determination, "We'll make it, Rito. We will because Baja made us strong."

She put her hand to the back of his neck and pulled his face to her level. Their mouths touched for a long time, and he drew her tightly to him. Then he turned her around and they retraced their steps back to the little apartment, but this time they walked much faster.

Then it was over. They stood at the bus stop where a local bus would take her the few miles back to West Los Angeles. Her suitcase was on the sidewalk beside her. For a few minutes as they waited they said nothing.

"Well, Rito, what will you do now?"

He answered unenthusiastically. "Go back to the little apartment. Pack my things. I sent for my mariachi outfit while I was in San Diego. I'll go to Oxnard. Try to get on as a mariachi."

"When will I hear from you?"

"Not until I have something good to tell you."

She digested this a moment, then nodded. "I figured that."

The bus pulled to the curb and they moved to the door. "Let's make it quick, Tacha. It's not the end of the world."

She smiled. "No. It's the beginning." He stooped to kiss her and they didn't part until the bus driver started making threatening noises with the air system.

Anastacia had finished getting the kitchen in order and was readying the family laundry when the phone rang. She sat at the breakfast table and answered.

"Liggett residence."

"Ana. How are you?" She recognized Pat's voice.

"Fine, Pat. How are you feeling?"

"So great that I'm coming home today. They insist on sending me by ambulance for some reason or another. I'll be home about one this afternoon."

"Wonderful. It's not home without you."

"I'll be in bed for a week or so. How's everything been?"

"Good as can be without you," Anastacia replied sincerely. "We don't see much of Alvin. He comes in when he's hungry. Monica is a great helper."

"Ana, don't you fix Alvin's meals at ungodly hours. If he's not there at dinnertime, that's tough."

"Right."

"All rightie, dear. Would you call Edmond at his office and tell him I'll be there about one? He's got to be warned, you know."

Anastacia chuckled. "Sure, Pat. Everything will be ready for you."

She hung up and dialed Edmond's office. A voice she recognized answered.

"Hi, Kitty. The boss man in?"

"Hi, Ana. Yeah, just a minute."

Edmond came on the line, a trace of apprehension in his inflection. "Hello, Tacha. What's up?"

"Pat called. They're bringing her home about one today."

"Oh . . . that's good. All right. I'll see you in a little while."

There was a slight awkward pause, then Anastacia hung up.

An hour later she was putting slips on pillows for a backrest for Pat's bed when Edmond entered the bedroom. She looked at him and went about her work. The pillows done, she walked past him, out of the room. He followed her and in the living room he called to her.

"Tacha." She stopped and faced him. "Tacha, I'm sorry." Briefly her eyes flickered to the bar and she saw he had had a drink.

"Yes, I'm sorry too," she said mildly.

"I'm sorry for what I did. But I had to let you know how I felt."

"Then what are you sorry for?"

"I'm sorry because . . . now you're troubled . . . ?"

"Yes, I'm very troubled. I'll be leaving soon."

He was a little angry. "Well, I hope you won't leave the minute Pat comes home. It'll be so obvious . . ."

Anastacia smiled. "You don't know women very well, do you, Edmond? Pat's an extremely perceptive woman."

He sat on the sofa and hung his head slightly. "Yes, I suppose so. I'm sorry about the whole goddam thing. How long have you been here, about a year?"

"Almost."

"But I didn't feel that way at first. At first you were just . . ."

"Please, I don't want to hear it. I should have known better than to stay so long."

There was a silence. She went to the bar to tidy up, putting away the bottle and cleaning the glass.

"I do love Pat, honest to God I do. But . . . I've become unable to have sex with her knowing you're alone in a bed a hundred feet away . . ."

"You told me all that the other night."

"Well, it's true! Goddamnit."

She stood behind the bar, looking at the glass she was polishing. He sat watching her. Soon he rose.

"I have some work to do in the den," he said, then he looked at his watch. "Pat'll be here in an hour or so." He left the room.

In the den, he went through papers, arranged some files, then heard her rap softly on the door.

"Come in," he said. Anastacia came in with a tray of rolls and coffee. She set it on his desk and poured him a cup, smiling as she handed it to him.

"No hard feelings, Edmond," she said. He tried to make it

seem the most platonic of gestures as he put an arm about her waist and hugged her, but they were both aware that she involuntarily tensed until he let go.

It was four days later that Anastacia rapped on Pat Liggett's bedroom door.

"Come in, dear," Pat called. Anastacia approached the bed.

"How are we today?" she said with a wry smile. Pat laughed.

"We're fine," she said. The bed table before her was piled high with books, stationery, address books, and the like. "Everybody should be bedridden occasionally, if only to catch up on letter writing and reading." She patted the bed beside her. "Sit down, Tacha. What's on your mind?" She took a cigarette from her bedside and offered one to Anastacia. "Have your daily cigarette with me."

Anastacia sat and took the cigarette. Pat lighted both from a table lighter. Anastacia blew the smoke upward, and then smoothed her hair during the little silence that developed.

"I want to leave here soon," she said quietly.

Only the almost imperceptible twitching of a facial muscle belied the equanimity Pat tried to project. She too blew smoke toward the ceiling. And her voice came out a little flat behind her forced smile.

"He made advances to you while I was away, didn't he." It was not a question.

Anastacia looked at her evenly. "I want to leave."

Pat drew heavily on her cigarette. "Tell me, did he need a lot of liquor in him to do it?"

Again there was a silence, and Pat reached out and touched her hair. "I'm sorry, dear. That really was bitchy of me. No man would require booze to make a play for you. You do know how beautiful you are, don't you." Again, it was not a question.

Anastacia was thinking, *Now is the time for me to hang my head and apologize for being the beautiful home-wrecker, but that is not me.* "Pat, we've been very good friends for a long time. And I don't want to talk about why it happened or anything like that. I want to go, and to remain your friend."

Pat was silent a longer while. "When I saw it happening, I really didn't know what to do. I'd like to know what a marriage counselor would say. At what point would he have said, 'Get that girl out of your house!' Would it have been after the first six months, when Edmond had his eyes on the door every time he knew you were about to enter the room? Or when he'd tell me at bedtime he'd be right in and then sit out there at the bar drinking? You know, Tacha, we've got to give him credit. He did behave like a gentleman for a while after he felt that way about you," and then, bitterly, "didn't he?" It was a question.

Now I do feel like hanging my head and crying, she thought, but she said, "Pat, believe me, the best thing for me to do is pack and get out of here. Now."

Pat was still trying to smile. "Tell me, did you have to fight off Alvin too?"

Anastacia's mind raced with emotion as she thought of a half dozen replies to the question. Then she pictured the tall, straight giant cardon at La Tijera.

"Yes, I did," she replied simply, "but he was easy to handle—he's a baby. And maybe I should be given a little credit too, because I knew after I first came here that someday you would come to hate me. I had to live with that." She paused, then added, "I *had* to. I had no choice!"

"Alvin's not a baby, Tacha. He's your age," Pat said.

Anastacia looked at her for a moment, then said softly, "No. He's not my age. He's a baby."

Pat closed her eyes, squeezing out tears that hadn't really formed yet. She extended her hand and Anastacia took it with both her own. "Yes, Tacha," she said, her voice a little hoarse, "you had no options here, did you. Isn't that funny? The very reason we brought you here from Baja was because down there you didn't have options and here you would. Now I'm learning what it's like to have no options. I have to go through the rest of my life with one breast. Would you like to know what goes through the mind of a woman who's had a breast removed?"

Anastacia contemplated various answers, then said suddenly, from the heart, "Yes, I would."

"It's only been four days, so I haven't had to face it yet, but, when he does want me again, what do I do? Do I lie there with a bra on, one cup collapsed? Or do I stuff that one and say, 'Let's pretend I have two of them'? Or do I lie naked and let the incision and sutures stare back at him . . . ?"

Anastacia rolled back the bed table and came closer to her. "Pat, please . . . it's not . . ."

"It's not what, Tacha? What are you going to say to me? 'Sex isn't everything'? You, looking like you do, are you going to tell me that? After what's happened?"

"I'm not going to tell you anything. Except maybe that I'm sorry for what happened but don't think that any of it is my fault. I'm not responsible for the way I am, and you can't help . . . being the way you are."

Again, Pat Liggett regarded her. "What do you mean, 'the way I am'?"

Anastacia let go of her hand and sat back a little.

"It's just . . . just how you are. Your people, I mean. Your belief. If you're going to believe everything that's worthwhile is over because of your operation, and because of what's happened, well, there's just nothing I can do about it. I'm sorry for you. But we can both see I can't stay here anymore."

"What do you mean, 'how my people are'?"

"I just meant, about your values. I can't do anything about that."

"What about our values?"

Anastacia was deep in thought, framing her words. "Well, let me tell you a little story about a woman in Baja. It was a little town, on the dirt road . . ."

Pat had regained a good measure of composure. "Tacha," she offered her hand again, "before I get another philosophical pearl from your past, do me a favor. Mix us a drink."

Anastacia smiled warmly. "Sure. Kind of early."

"Maybe it wouldn't be too bad if we became the stereotyped suburban female daytime drinkers. But I need one."

Anastacia left the room and returned shortly with two of Pat's favorite drink. She sat on the edge of the bed and they toasted.

"Now," Pat said, "let's have your story."

"Well, you've heard of the flying doctors?"

"Yes. Wealthy American doctors who have a club, they own their own airplanes and fly all over Baja treating the people in the back country."

"Yes. Well, there was this woman, she's still there, I guess, and she owned a tavern. The only tavern on a hundred-mile stretch. A real shrew. She had no trouble attracting men, owning the successful tavern. She went through two or three husbands, and countless boyfriends. They all figured running a bar was better than harpooning sharks or working in the quarries. Well, one day the flying doctor showed up, giving free breast cancer tests. The tavern owner had it. He talked her into going to La Paz to have a breast removed. And do you know, when she came back, twice as many guys were hanging around, trying to make her."

Pat was serious. "Why?" They both sipped their drinks.

"Think about it."

Pat Liggett pondered a few minutes, then laughed.

"I see. She became a *cause célèbre*. But would a man want to have a wife like that?"

"They fought over her. One night I heard two men, drinking. One of them said, 'Once you've had a woman with one, you'll never go back to two.'"

"But they were drunk."

"But it didn't matter to them."

Pat continued to smile. "Can you see, Tacha? Can you see? To your people, life is fun."

"Yes. It's the thing I noticed first when I was a little girl. To your people, only parts of life are fun, and as you grow older, it's harder and harder for your people to decide what parts are fun."

They sat looking at one another for several minutes. Then Pat closed her eyes. "I'm tired, Tacha. I just want one last favor from you."

"Sure."

"Let me find you another job. And stay long enough to break in a new girl."

Anastacia rose. "Sure, of course. Now you sleep, and call me if you need anything." She went to the door, but Pat called to her. "Yes, Pat?"

"I think you do know that Meme de Beauclair, that obscenely rich French woman, who was here the last two times we entertained Edmond's boss, has been dying to steal you away from me. You knew that, didn't you?"

Anastacia smiled absently for a moment, pleased at the prospect. "No, not really."

CHAPTER 9

Anastacia was standing by the front-room window of the Liggetts' house looking out with a little sadness when she saw the sleek black limousine pull slowly into the driveway and stop. A graying man in a tasteful chauffeur's jacket and cap got out and came to the door. She opened it just as he was about to ring. He looked at her face and she noticed that he didn't allow his eyes to take in the rest of her.

"Hello. I'm Madame de Beauclair's chauffeur. Ruel's the name. R-u-e-l. I've been sent to pick up Anastacia Herrera."

Anastacia smiled at his stumbling pronunciation of her name. She stepped aside. "Oh. Fine, Ruel. I'm Anastacia. They call me Tacha for short. Here are my bags. Can you manage?"

"No problem, no problem," he said quietly, stepping past her. He expertly hoisted one bag under an arm, picked up the remaining two in either hand, and went out to the car.

Pat Liggett appeared from somewhere inside the house. The two women stood facing one another at the door, Anastacia ready to turn and go. They looked at each other in silence for a long moment and then Pat took both of Anastacia's hands in her own.

"Tacha, dear," she said only a little hoarsely, "it's been marvelous having you here. I only wish your stay with us could have been one big pleasant memory for you."

"It will be, mostly," Anastacia said, nodding in sincerity. "I'll remember you always. You've been a real friend. I'll never forget."

Then the tears welled and each clutched the other. They stood apart, blinking.

Forcing a smile, Pat said, "And I'm so glad you told me all about. . . ."

"My 'young man,' as you put it?" Anastacia said with mirth.

"Yes. Is that how I put it? Oh dear, is that expression terribly dated? If he calls here, should I . . ."

Anastacia shook her head. "He won't call here. On vacation last month I told him I'd probably be leaving. He can find me through the Fuentes. But he won't call unless he's got very bad news or very good news."

"Where is he now?"

"He was going to Oxnard. We found out about a restaurant up there that hires wetbacks on the run. He was hoping to get on there. He's got that macho streak and I won't hear from him until he's able to show me he's made good."

They were quiet a moment, then abruptly Pat kissed her on the cheek and said quickly, "Look. Let's not drag it out. There's too much to say. Take good care of yourself and please, please, if there's anything I can ever do . . ."

"Don't worry, Pat. Good-bye. We'll keep in touch."

Anastacia closed the door and walked lightly to the waiting car. Ruel stood holding the back door open, his face even and expressionless.

"Thank you, Ruel," she said as she got in. He nodded and climbed in behind the wheel.

The de Beauclair mansion hugged the side of a hill among terraced gardens and oak trees. The ambience bespoke tasteful and quiet wealth and the comfortably aged colonial exterior belied the contemporary convenience of the house plan. The broad concrete driveway wound to the front entrance between molded curbs, and life-size statues stood arrested in oak-shaded alcoves.

Ruel parked the limousine at the front entrance and alighted. Anastacia made no move to get out. Ruel moved almost casually around to the other side of the car, the while eyeing the driveway for oil spots. He opened the door for her, then closed it and went to the trunk to get her luggage.

She walked beside him across the wide veranda to the door and he rang.

"Yep, ten years, almost, I been driving for the de Beauclairs. Meme has only been divorced two or three years. I keep the cars running, keep oil spots off the driveway, and stuff like that. You met Amelia yet?"

They were still waiting at the door. "No. I've never been here before."

"You'll like it. Amelia's the chambermaid, I guess you'd call her. Dumb. Doesn't speak English and refuses to try. She could have had your job if she'd only tried, but if you try to get her to speak English, she grins and goes away."

Amelia had opened the door while he was talking, but Ruel made no attempt to speak confidentially.

"Anastacia?" Amelia appeared delighted.

"Sí."

"Thank God for you. I'm having an awful time because I can't speak a word of English." She looked at Ruel, then back to Anastacia. "Tell him to take your things to your room. See? I'm helpless."

Anastacia relayed the message, then Ruel said, "Ask her if lunch is ready. I'm starving."

Anastacia complied. "Tell him in half an hour. In the breakfast room," Amelia said. "Come, we can talk while I fix lunch."

They went to the kitchen, where Amelia had food cooking on the stove. Anastacia saw that she was shy, lacking in self-confidence like so many of the people from the Mexican mainland back country. She was also very plain, almost homely, rather squat with Indian features, short, with straight black hair and dark skin. Her grammar told Anastacia she came from uneducated people.

Anastacia sat at a kitchen table while Amelia worked at the stove, testing, adding ingredients to the stew she was cooking, the while talking.

"I just can't learn to pronounce the names of the dishes la señora likes prepared. Since the last chief maid quit, I've had a terrible time."

"Why?" Anastacia asked. "The señora speaks very good Spanish."

"Yes, but she likes things done, food and work, in a French manner, and she gets so angry at me because I don't understand. I thought she would fire me, and I was so glad when she said she hired you. I'm happier doing just the housework."

"You were doing everything yourself?"

"No. I couldn't. But Señora de Beauclair tried to teach me

complicated things, like how you serve and what you put on the table."

"Does she have trouble keeping or hiring help?"

"She has trouble trying to get the kind of help that can understand what she wants. I don't like that kind of work."

Ruel came in and took a seat in the breakfast room that opened onto the kitchen. "Tacha, would you tell her I'd like a hamburger patty done well? Jesus, it's been murder around here lately."

Anastacia translated for him.

Amelia went on. "La señora gets very angry because Ruel has to tell her to tell me things. It's been going on a long time. Señora de Beauclair finally got a French maid from Europe who knew how to do everything the way she wanted. But she couldn't speak Spanish. La señora is the only one who can speak all three languages."

An hour later Amelia and Anastacia were finishing putting things away after the lunchtime snack when Meme de Beauclair entered.

"Tacha, Tacha, Tacha," she said with fondness, briefly embracing her and planting a quick kiss on each cheek. "How good to have you here! Tell me," she said, as though it mattered a great deal, "Do you like my house?" She even held her breath waiting for an answer.

Anastacia looked around. "It's a little bit . . . overwhelming. I haven't seen much of it yet . . ."

But Meme was turning to the others. In Spanish she rattled off a string of instructions to Amelia concerning the housework, then gave Ruel an itinerary of errands. When they were gone, she pulled Anastacia into the living room.

"Come. We'll take a quick tour. And then I've got to show you how to prepare for the dinner. . . . Good grief . . . it's only two nights away. We'll never make it. . . ."

Meme de Beauclair was a heavy woman who had maintained a surprising amount of youthful glamor. She dressed casually but expensively, even in her own home, and she talked in a rapid-fire French-accented English.

The tour ended in the dining area.

"I brought you here last for a reason," Meme said. She pulled back some drapes to reveal an anteroom lined with glass-enclosed shelves containing the de Beauclair tableware.

She was silent as she allowed Anastacia to walk around the room, viewing the hundreds of plates, silver pieces, shakers, and bowls as well as items Anastacia had never seen. When Anastacia had made her way entirely around the room, Meme said, "What do you think?"

Anastacia turned to her. "Why, I've never seen anything like it. It's incredible."

"Well," Meme said, walking to a shelf and taking down a large old leather-bound volume, "I want you to look at this." She leafed through it, found the page she wanted, and handed it open-faced to Anastacia. It showed a very formal elegant table setting for eight, with several forks for each place, tiny individual salt and pepper shakers, and a variety of strategically placed little spoons and bowls. Anastacia studied it a few moments and then looked at Meme.

"The night after tomorrow we're having twelve for dinner. It must be set just like this. Exactly. There will be people from Europe who know. Turn the page."

Anastacia did so and saw the next photo and illustrations showing what should be cleared for the serving of the second course, in what order, and what should be left or moved around. On the facing page were the instructions for the serving of the dessert.

Anastacia looked up helplessly. "But . . . the instructions are all in French. I can't make out a word . . ."

Undaunted, Meme snatched an English-French dictionary from the same shelf and handed it to her. "With this you'll be able to make it out."

Anastacia was still unsure. "But . . . I . . . Amelia and I can't serve a dinner like this . . ."

"Oh, nonsense, dear," Meme said kindly but firmly, "we'll have a chef who knows about this type of thing. You don't have to worry about the food. We'll have extra help. I just have to have someone in charge who will make sure everything goes like clockwork." She snapped her fingers several times. "I know it's unfair to ask you to do this so soon, but . . . you can be prepared for it in two days . . . can't you?" Her voice pleaded.

Anastacia turned away, looking at the leather volume for almost a minute. Then she turned back with a bright smile. "If I start now, I think I can."

ANOTHER LAND

Meme waved a hand in the air. "Start now. Retire to the drawing room with those books." She turned to leave, talking over her shoulder. "Everything and everybody in this household is at your disposal. Even me, if you can help me pull this off successfully . . ."

When the last guests had left, Madame de Beauclair joined Anastacia in the kitchen.

"You were magnificent, Tacha. Everything was perfect."

"I really enjoyed it, Meme. It was hard, remembering everything, but I'm glad you're pleased."

They worked side by side, storing the silverware and crystal. Anastacia saw how she examined each piece by allowing the light to reflect from the surfaces.

"Now let's not be coy, Tacha. You saw Paul Foster ogling you, didn't you."

Anastacia paused, her hands in the water, a little smile on her lips. "No more than the others, I didn't think."

"No more, perhaps," Meme said in her confident way, "but differently. Donna allowed her lack of sophistication to become obvious by not concealing her annoyance."

"She was annoyed?" Anastacia asked, still smiling.

"Plain jealous. Shows absolutely no *savoir vivre*."

Anastacia looked at her. "No savwah . . ."

"*Savoir vivre*. Good breeding, polished manners."

"Who is she?" Anastacia asked.

"God knows," Meme said, returning a wine glass to the suds. "Paul's been divorced a couple of years. He owns a very successful public-relations firm on Wilshire Boulevard. She's his head typist or something or other."

"Well," Anastacia said, musing, "he's a very attractive man. I hope I see him again."

They worked quietly together for a while. Then Meme asked, "Tell me, Anastacia—oh, how I love that name—is there a man in your life?"

Anastacia looked at her, thinking. "I suppose. His name is Margarito. I grew up with him in Baja, more or less."

"Where is he now?"

"He's here, somewhere in the United States. We try to keep in touch but it's difficult. As you know, if one of us is caught we're sent back to Mexico."

"What does he do?"

Anastacia smiled, reminiscing. "Everything. He's a mariachi, among other things. Do you know what that is?"

"Certainly. It comes from the French word *mariage*."

Anastacia tried to pronounce it. "Mah-ryahzh? I didn't know that."

"You have the makings of a good French accent," Meme said. "The Mexicans learned the custom of having strolling musicians at marriage celebrations from the Europeans. Anyway, Ana, tonight's occasion was a *succès fou*."

Anastacia did a fair job of repeating the phrase, with an interrogative intonation.

"*Succès fou*. A smashing success, the British would say. And I'm very pleased."

They were putting the final touches on the kitchen. "I'll show you how to prepare my breakfast in the morning," Meme said, "and then we'll go grocery shopping. To me, that is the most important thing in my household. It's a European art, and I'm sure you'll love learning it. Next week at the local college there's a six-week course in conversational French starting. We'll get you enrolled in that. Then across town in the fall there's a course in European antiques. You'll get time off for those. I'll pay any tuition. Ruel will take you and bring you back. And don't thank me. I'm the lucky one to have found someone like you equipped enough to handle my home."

CHAPTER 10

The endless commercial developments, apartments, and housing tracts drifted past the window of the bus as it labored up the northbound Ventura Freeway leaving the San Fernando Valley.

Margarito stared out the window with no interest. He was reliving the past two weeks with Anastacia during her vacation. With regret, he forced himself to realize the futility of that, and his mind snapped back to the present.

When boarding the bus, he had narrowly avoided an encounter with an immigration agent at the terminal, as they randomly checked the papers of those appearing to be illegal aliens. That had shaken him somewhat, but now on the bus, within a few minutes of Oxnard, his destination, he felt safe.

When the bus reached Oxnard, he got off, carrying only a small traveling satchel. He had to find del Rio's Restaurant. Old man Samaniego in Tijuana had told him about del Rio's, and he was hungry right now. He had noticed a hamburger stand a half block away, and he went there and ordered a hamburger with everything. It was one native American dish he liked. As he stood near the serving window eating, a black-and-white police car cruised slowly down the street. Two uniformed officers looked at him with perhaps a little more than idle curiosity, but he was prepared; he gazed back at them without apprehension or malice and turned his attention to his hamburger. He knew that local police in the United States were not as a rule preoccupied with immigration problems. They continued on down the street.

The first person he asked directed him to del Rio's Restaurant and he walked the few blocks to its location. He saw a sign saying "Closed," but went to the door. There was a porch a few steps from the sidewalk with tables for dining.

Inside he saw some activity. He peered through a window and rapped on the glass. A smallish, dark, dapper man came to the door and opened it, standing as though to block passage.

"Yes?" he said in English.

"Del Rio?" Margarito asked.

"Sí."

"My name's Rito Corrales. I was told you might be able to help me."

"Oh, come in," del Rio said. He locked the door behind Margarito and turned to him. "You're a musician?"

"Yes."

"What do you play?"

"You name it. Mariachi."

"¿Vihuela?"

"Fairly well."

"¿Guitarrón?"

"My specialty."

Del Rio motioned him to a table and asked a waiter to bring coffee, after making sure Margarito was not hungry. Margarito saw that there was a cocktail area on one side, a large dining room on the other, and between them a passageway to a well-planted courtyard with yet more dining tables.

"Tell you how it is," del Rio said, when coffee had arrived. He spoke English and seemed perfectly at home doing so. "This Mexican food business is competitive. I have to cut corners everywhere. So I don't pay my musicians anything. You can eat when the kitchen's open, and you got a room to sleep in. The group splits what they make in tips."

Margarito nodded. "I understood all that when I came here."

"Well, that's the way it is. I've operated this restaurant without live music, and it does just about as well. In fact, I'd be better off without music. But if it'll help guys like you as you're passing through, okay. The migra hassles us from time to time. They're liable to come busting in here any hour and haul all your asses back to Mexico. But then you're no worse off than before."

"I've been dodging them for more than a year now," Margarito answered as he looked around at the relatively plush decor and furnishings. There were the portraits of matadors, the decorative arches built into the walls, with tiny bits of red-tiled roof protruding a foot or so into the room, a big replica of the Aztec calendar on one wall. "How long do your mariachis usually stay?" he asked.

"Turnover's terrific. This whole area is kind of a jumping-off place for wetbacks. Musical scouts from the big night spots in L.A. come up here to look for good musicians for their restaurants. If a guy's really good, they'll give him a job in L.A. and sometimes get a lawyer to try to get him status papers. They even married one guy to a chamaca who was a citizen so he could stay."

"Okay," Margarito said, "I'd like a shot at it. They said you'd maybe have an instrument."

"Our guitarrón player got picked up last week. Not in here. You can use his till he finds his way back."

Margarito rose, picking up his travel satchel. "Okay, where do I flop?"

Del Rio showed him to a small room off the courtyard. Inside were two bunks, a chest of drawers, and a mirror. Another musician was lying on a bunk reading. Del Rio left them. They introduced themselves, and the other man offered to show Margarito a dry-cleaning shop where he could get his mariachi uniform pressed. Margarito got the flavor of the town, set in a rich coastal valley, as they walked the few blocks to the cleaner. It was a town that tried hard to retain some of the original Mexican flavor in its architecture and landscaping. They attracted no attention as they went and returned.

Back at the restaurant the other three musicians appeared and all decided it would be a good idea to rehearse for the coming evening dinner hour, to coordinate styles and decide on solo and harmony parts. Margarito was pleased that all the musicians took one another's musical expertise for granted.

The first night they each earned eight dollars. Not bad for a weeknight, they told him. Their uniforms did not match, other than that they each wore tight trousers that flared at the bottom, and each had an embroidered satin shirt. Two wore sombreros and one wore a chrome-plated replica of a .45 revolver.

On Friday night a couple dining summoned the group to their table. "How much would you charge to provide music for a reception in our home tomorrow afternoon?" the woman asked. One musician who was a self-appointed bandmaster quickly replied, "We have a flat charge of $250 for an afternoon."

And on Saturday night when the group had returned to the restaurant and were playing for the dinner crowd well after midnight, Margarito found they had each made seventy dollars. Not bad, he thought as he hung up his mariachi uniform and climbed into the bunk to the snores of his roommate. He had worked many a ten-hour day in Baja for less than one tenth of that amount.

As his head touched the pillow and he drew the blanket around his shoulders his thoughts went to Anastacia. He closed his eyes and concentrated mightily to relive the times he was with her. He remembered the scent of her hair, the sound of her voice. In his mind he created a vision of her walking in her knee-length dress, and he stopped the action at just the right moment, one leg ahead of the other, showing strong, round, brown calves, the dress clinging to an ample hip as she was caught in midstride by his mental camera, a strand of her hair flung out in front of her face. Was this the reaction of a love-struck boy? No. No, Tacha was surely the most beautiful of women, but she was more, she was the most desirable, the softest, most scented, firmest piece of wet female flesh ever to wear a pair of handmade sandals.

"Good God," he thought, as he found himself more wide awake than when he'd lain down, "I've got to do *something*."

A few weeks later the group was rehearsing in the early afternoon. It was a warm day and the front door of the restaurant was open. An attractive woman in her midtwenties came hesitantly to the door, then entered and took a table near the musicians. She was blond, dressed as though she liked to look nice when she shopped, and was absorbed in the music.

Del Rio, bustling about, saw her and approached her table. He mustered his best and thickest Mexican accent.

"I am sorry, señorita," he said, "but we are closed. We won't be open until the evening."

"Oh," she said, "I'm terribly sorry. But couldn't I just sit here and listen? I won't be any bother."

Del Rio glanced at the lead musician, who shrugged ever so imperceptibly. They did not break their rhythm.

"I suppose it would be all right," del Rio said at length.

Thereafter she reappeared frequently during the early afternoon and just sat while the group rehearsed. When they were through, she would leave a generous tip, thank them, and walk to her car at the curb.

Margarito was becoming thoroughly bored and impatient with his latest relocation. He had expected some kind of break before this. But nothing had come. He had learned little of the environment, from the point of view of an illegal alien. He occasionally heard of great farms and ranches in the area, of labor movements working to shut down production at the farms, but he could make no connections to the outside world that were solid enough to warrant leaving the relative safety of del Rio's Restaurant.

Anastacia entered his thoughts no less frequently. He realized he had subconsciously anticipated he would somehow own a boat, perhaps, and fish or take fishermen out to sea, or maybe somehow wind up owning an auto repair shop, and she could then join him. He wondered what she was doing. Maybe the migra had picked her up and she was back in Ensenada. He thought about calling her. No. She'd said not to. The last time he'd called the Fuentes' he'd gotten the name and address of the new people she worked for. He wondered if she was being sexually harassed by the man of the house. If the woman of the house shouted at her.

It didn't matter, Anastacia was a woman who could take care of herself better than any woman he had known. Thinking of her in that manner gave him comfort. And he knew she felt that way about him.

Soon afterward, on a warm afternoon as the group rehearsed, the blond woman came in and sat alone, listening, as she had often done before. One of the musicians suddenly stopped playing, staring out the window. The others looked at him curiously, then quit playing to follow his gaze. The man set his instrument down and strode quickly to the window. He beckoned the others.

"See?" he said, pointing with some apprehension. "That car with the man sitting in it down the block? That's Immigration Agent Rafferty!"

The others tensed. "Are you sure?"

"Positive. See? He's now talking on his radio."

Margarito could see the man, sitting with one arm casually

on the car doorsill. Yes, the man was speaking into something in his other hand.

"What's he doing?" Margarito asked.

"He's coordinating a raid. He's got us spotted. Let's get out of here!"

The group set aside their instruments and prepared to leave through the courtyard. One of del Rio's maintenance men came hurrying in. "Looks like la migra agents behind the restaurant," he said, hurrying toward the front door.

"Out there too!" one of the musicians shouted.

"Quick," another said, "tell the kitchen help. Let's make a break from the side door and run for it. They can't chase us all!"

Margarito realized this was probably true. There was a chef in the kitchen, several helpers, three or four dishwashers, and various other employees of del Rio. A worthy catch for any immigration agent. Among the bits of advice illegal aliens passed around was always keep your most important possessions on your person. No time to go to your room for your wallet if the migra shows up.

But Margarito now saw that the chances of eluding the agents, if indeed they had the place surrounded as it appeared, were slight. As the others bustled about and ran here and there, he calmly approached the blond woman seated alone. Not understanding Spanish, she was confused about what was going on. She looked up at him, trying to remain composed.

"Please, lady," Margarito said quietly in English, "we are about to be raided by the American immigration people, because some of us here don't have papers. Would you please just walk out the door with me to your car?"

She tried to hide her disconcertion. "I . . . you mean, they're going to raid . . ."

"Yes. In a moment. I don't think they'd bother me if I were to walk out the door with you." He was thankful the rehearsals were held in street clothes.

The blond woman was tense, but rose to the occasion, and Margarito saw the faintest trace of a daring smile at the corners of her mouth.

"All right," she said evenly, taking her handbag.

As they walked through the front door, Margarito reached back and pulled it closed. She started to walk hurriedly.

ANOTHER LAND

"No! Don't hurry," he said quietly. He paused and put a cigarette in his mouth, then fumbled for a match. "Don't look up the street," he told her. She waited and then casually walked with him toward her car at the curb. He held the door open.

"Want me to drive?"

She considered a moment, and he saw her fear. "No," she said, scooting across the front seat. He got in behind her. In a moment she had the key in the ignition switch, and he put his hand on hers, stopping her.

"No! Slowly. Like we have all day." She was staring at him intensely in her excitement. Margarito looked in the rear-view mirror and saw that the agent was still in his car some fifty yards to the rear. Then the agent got out of the car, still talking into the microphone.

Margarito released her hand. "Now," he said. "Not too fast."

She started the engine and pulled away. The agent made no move to follow them. They had gone less than two blocks, and Margarito told her to stop. Together they watched as a carful of agents joined the one near del Rio's, and they all began running toward the restaurant entrance. Margarito nodded. She put the car in gear and slowly pulled away. He puffed thoughtfully on his cigarette. She was obviously nervous.

Finally she said, "Where can I drop you?"

He shrugged, blowing smoke. "Anywhere. I am very grateful for your doing that."

Now she shrugged. He saw her looking at his massive physique, hands, and arms, and he saw more fear than admiration in her.

"Can I take you to a friend's, or something?"

"I don't know anybody or anyplace around here," he replied.

She looked at him. "You have . . . no place to go?"

"No," he said, relaxing for the first time since the agents had been spotted. "I'm new here. Thanks again for what you did. Just anyplace will be fine."

They had left the town and she turned south on the highway. "Well, I can't just leave you here. They'll . . . capture you . . ."

He laughed and then so did she.

"I guess you can take me down the road a ways and let me out."

She glanced at her wristwatch. "I do have to be getting home. I'm married to a policeman and I never dreamed I'd be helping a fugitive escape from federal authorities. There's a roadside café a few miles down the road. I can take you that far."

They rode in silence. Soon she pulled into the gravel parking lot of a restaurant and bar. This was an open stretch of highway with no other business in sight.

He got out and said through the window, "Thank you again, and I wish I knew your name."

She smiled genuinely for the first time. "Gretchen." He looked surprised, and she said, "It's unusual. What's your name?"

"Margarito," and she was surprised. "Spelled with an 'o' at the end. It's not a girl's name. It was a pleasure being rescued by you."

"And if you ever get straightened out, I'd like to know about it."

"How would I tell you?"

She shrugged, thinking. "I'll be stopping at del Rio's now and then. Leave word. I'll ask."

"All right, Gretchen. Good-bye."

"Good-bye, Margarito."

He stood watching as she turned and headed back to town. He saw her wave to him and then she was gone. He looked about. He didn't feel like getting out on the highway and hitching a ride so soon after his narrow escape. He turned and walked into the restaurant bar.

Inside he found the place divided into a short-order food counter and a bar, joined by a swinging door. He chose the bar, sat on a stool, and ordered a bottle of beer.

It had been a close call. Perhaps his escape had been luck, but he preferred to think that he might be a little better equipped for survival than his ill-fated fellow musicians. He thought about calling Anastacia and relating the incident, but realized it might make her panic and there was certainly nothing she could do. He had some money on him but he had no plans. He knew he had to make some soon.

The wall was lined with booths, some taken by couples or

groups drinking and talking. A wiry man in his sixties, unkempt and bearded, sat at the bar talking in a relatively loud voice to the bartender. Margarito half listened, eyes on the bottle in front of him as he mulled over his predicament. The old man seemed to be talking of the past, when he was evidently some kind of a grand figure in this area. He and the bartender laughed frequently, more often than not at some catastrophe or other that had contributed to the financial downfall of the old man. Suddenly Margarito realized the old man was calling to him.

"Hey! ¡Amigo! Wake up, there."

Margarito looked at him with a good-natured smile. "Me? What can I do for you?"

The old man seemed friendly. "Well, for starters you can come over here and let me buy you a drink. Looks like you need a little cheering up."

Margarito considered. What the hell, he thought, maybe the old guy has connections around here. He moved down the bar and sat on the stool next to him. The bartender opened another bottle of beer and set it before Margarito.

"You work around here?" the old man asked.

Margarito gave a characteristic little chuckle-snort.

"I was recently gainfully employed, but was forced to terminate without notice," he answered in good humor.

The old man laughed and slapped his knee. "The migra busted in and you went out the rear window, zat about it?"

"Good guess," Margarito answered, hoisting his glass. "Salud."

"Salud, amigo," the old man answered. "My name's Sloane." He drank deeply. "What you going to do now? Got a job lined up?"

Margarito reflected on his beer. "No. I don't know what I'll do. You got anything for me?"

"What do you do?"

"Name it. Mechanic. Farmhand. Leatherwork. Cook a little."

"You speak English pretty good for a wetback."

Margarito was not offended. "I was raised in Baja. Learned pretty young. You know anywhere they need help?"

Sloane ordered another drink. "Yeah. I need help. Lots of it."

Margarito waited, but there was no immediate explanation forthcoming. "You look like a grower down on his luck. You got a place around here?" He had picked up this much from overhearing the conversation.

Sloan drank again and wiped his mouth with the back of his hand. "Yep. I got two hundred forty-seven of the best acreage in Ventura County."

Margarito shook his head slightly. "Let's go to work, man."

Sloane laughed, and the bartender laughed with him. "Okay. You come to work for me. And a bunch of your compadres to boot. If they'll work free, that is. I got no money."

Margarito thought a moment. "You have crops coming ripe?"

"I got fruit rotting on the trees. Not very good fruit. I was in jail six months. Place went to hell."

The bartender, wiping the counter, broke in, "Come on, Sloane. That place was going to hell long before you went to jail. Wouldn't a' made no difference."

Sloane cackled and showed he had few teeth left on one side of his mouth. "That's right, I guess."

Margarito persisted. "You have crops you can salvage?"

Sloane turned to face him, swiveling on the stool. "I got citrus about ready, only it'll yield maybe ten percent of what it should. Nobody pruned last year. Got sugar beets in the ground. Lots. Hundred acres, maybe. But if I don't thin 'em, I'm outa luck there. Couple other crops failing."

He laughed and the bartender again laughed with him.

"Why don't you hire some help and get it going?" Margarito asked.

"I'll tell you why," the bartender volunteered, sitting on a stool behind the bar and putting a foot on the beer bin, "'cause he owes everybody and his brother money. They shut off his water, so he can't irrigate. He ain't got electricity 'cause he didn't pay his electric bill. He uses kerosene lanterns. He chops wood for the fireplace for the same reason."

Both the bartender and Sloane were laughing, Sloane so hard he could only make a gesture indicating all should have another drink on him.

ANOTHER LAND

Margarito accepted the drink. "You're messed up," he commented. "But you got enough money to drink on."

Sloane stopped laughing and eyed him. "Oh, I always got enough for that. Keep a little hidden away."

They talked and drank for an hour or so more, Margarito learning more and more of the old man's holdings and problems.

"Tell you what," Sloane said at last, "you want to come out and see my place, you're welcome. Maybe you can come up with some ideas. Can't do no harm, and you can spend the night and at least be safe from the migra."

As they turned off the pavement onto the long dirt drive that led up the hill to Sloane's house, Margarito saw the farm's almost unbelievable state of disrepair and neglect. Trees whose juices should have been going into fruit were instead sagging from lack of pruning and trimming. Irrigation ditches flattened out to nothing.

They walked past a rusted tractor. "Ain't had it running in a year," Sloan explained. The house stood on the top of the hill. The dirt drive was really a road that went from the paved road on one side to the highway in the opposite direction. There were dwellings for migrant workers, but in such poor condition as to be uninhabitable. A spigot was behind the house, and Sloane turned on the water. He stooped and drank of the gushing water.

"I thought they shut off your water," Margarito said.

"They did," he said, straightening, "but the only thing that works on the place is my windmill. It pumps water up here. They can't shut off the goddamn wind," he cackled.

The sun was setting when Sloane took him into the house. Inside, it was much as Margarito expected. Sloane had hooked up a potbelly stove. To one side was a large, squarely cut tree stump that served as a table for a huge washbasin. Sloane lit a kerosene lantern and put some wood in the stove, and in a few moments the chill was out of the room. He went into the kitchen and returned with a gallon jug of wine. He found two tin cups on a shelf, shook the dust out, and poured them full. Margarito took a seat on a wicker couch, and Sloane sat on a wooden rocker.

"Well, what do you think?" Sloane asked, then went on

without waiting for an answer. "I figure twenty men, who'd be willing to wait maybe four months for their pay, might be able to pull it off."

Margarito was thoughtful. "No," he replied. "Ten, maybe twelve. We could work on the citrus, push our luck, pick a little early, and maybe have ten men's wages in a couple of months. Then they'd wait longer next time."

Sloane sat thinking. At length he shook his head, refilling his tin cup. "Nope, too many ifs. *If* you can find some men who'd wait. *If* you can get the tractor running. *If* we can get the gasoline pump working. Goddamn, I got a beauty of a 'lectric pump. Lotta goddamn good it does with no electricity. Those mangy bastards."

"Who?"

"The whole goddamn bunch. Gas company. Electric company. Telephone company. You know, Margarito, I don't got one single person in this country who'll give me credit. Goddamn 'em all, anyway."

Margarito thought a while. "I'm willing to try. If I can get the equipment running, I think I can find some help. We'll have to fix up the bunkhouses at least a little. And we'll have to pay them something. For cigarettes and wine, anyway."

Sloane was a little evasive. "Don't worry about that. I can keep 'em in tobacco and booze, at least. But what you gonna want outta this?"

Margarito didn't hesitate. "I want half of what you make. After we pay off the crew at the end of the season. And room and board and pocket money in the meantime."

"And what if we don't make nothin'?"

Margarito shrugged. "At least I've had a place to stay where the migra probably won't find me."

Sloane cackled. "That's right. They're out there raidin' the big boys, who got big crews and bumper crops every year. They don't look sideways at me. That's one plus in our favor. When you find a crew, tell 'em we can promise the migra won't bother 'em here."

They talked until midnight, and then Margarito blew out the kerosene lanterns and went to lie down on the cot in the next room, leaving Sloane asleep in the wooden rocker.

CHAPTER 11

Margarito labored mightily on the tractor, improvising with odd-size bolts and washers when he had to, and sending Sloane into town only for the essential new parts. In a few days he had it running. "This is why I said we could bring about a harvest with only ten men," he said to Sloane. "I'm not satisfied with the way it runs. It was too rusty inside. But if we baby it, it'll probably see us through."

Next he tackled the gasoline pump that would lift water from the well into the irrigation ditches, which either didn't exist or needed repairing. He'd need a crew to fix the ditches. But he couldn't have a crew until he fixed up the workers' quarters at least a little. So he and Sloane started on the bunkhouses as soon as the pump was running.

It was nearly two weeks after his arrival on the farm that he went into town to make discreet inquiries. Three men were living under a railroad bridge, once a hobo jungle, north of town. He found them, stealing vegetables by night, staying off the roads, and walking across the fields by day to look for work. One refused to go to Sloane's ranch when he found he might have to wait months for his pay. The others were desperate enough to grab anything.

He called del Rio and learned that two of his employees had eluded the immigration officers that day and were living in a shed nearby.

"By the way," del Rio said, "where'd you go with that babe who got you out of here?"

"Why?" Margarito asked.

"I just wondered. She was in the other day and asked if we'd heard from you. She's married to a cop, so I wouldn't trust her."

In the rear room of a crowded Mexican-American household Margarito found a man and his six-months-pregnant wife who were desperate enough to wait for a payday, as long as they had a place to stay, and back at the farm he fixed an outside kitchen where the wife could cook for everybody when the weather permitted, which Margarito figured would be just about every day for the rest of the season.

He found more desperate men, and the following Sunday he counted eleven faces around the outside fire in front of the workers' quarters at the Sloane ranch. Some had miraculously managed to keep guitars intact, and when they had eaten Sloane brought out several jugs of wine and poured for all.

"To the resurrection of the Sloane ranch," Sloane said, proposing a toast. "Amigos . . . and señora," he said to the wisp of a woman with the huge belly, "I am once again el patrón. I'm a very poor patrón, but I'm patrón again." He drank with a pleased expression, and then added, "Goddamn it," for no particular reason. Margarito translated all but his last words for those who couldn't understand.

Some of the men were in no condition to do a day's work. They had spent weeks, even months in cramped quarters, daring to venture out only when it was safe to do so, and their diet had been poor. Margarito assigned the work accordingly at first, and within a few days he could see them responding to regular food and hours. He tried to keep them occupied during the evenings before bedtime, but by the end of the week, in spite of the terms of their verbal contract, some were badgering him for spending money to go into town. Sloane, appearing to have a good knowledge of human nature, had anticipated this, and doled out a few dollars, warning Margarito that he had precious little left and they had to put by enough for gasoline, groceries, and the like. Sloane, when he had to, would go into the house and shortly return with what cash he needed.

By the end of the second week the man with the pregnant wife was complaining loudly of the drafty, unheated bunkhouse, and Sloane allowed them to move into a room of the main house. She still came outside to cook in the open-air kitchen.

The work was proceeding more or less on schedule. With

ANOTHER LAND

luck, some of the citrus crop could be harvested within a few weeks. It would be a fraction of what it would have brought if the ranch had been under the continuous care of experienced workers, but Margarito and Sloane agreed they might squeeze by until the fast-growing crops, the radishes, carrots, etc., could start bringing in money, and meanwhile they were tending the largest crop, the sugar beets, and if they could hold out until that harvest, there was a possibility the ranch could get back on its feet.

In his nearly twenty-four years, Margarito had done some farm work in Baja. He didn't know a lot, but now he carefully gleaned all he could from each man about farm work. His Baja experience had taught him how to get things done with a minimum of mechanical equipment. He knew how to get the men working in rhythm so that by the end of the day all were surprised at what had been accomplished without machinery other than the tractor.

The pregnant woman washed clothes for the men, at a trough, beating the items on a large boulder, the way her mother had, and her grandmother, and her great-grandmother.

Sloane made himself as useful as possible. Having the only vehicle, he was frequently going into town for items such as gloves, fuel, groceries, wine, and tobacco. He joined in the work when he could, and the men near him always commented on how good he smelled, meaning he smelled of liquor. Once when Margarito started to translate for him, Sloane stopped him. "I may not speak it, but I savvy most of what's said."

Once again a weekend came, and the men were not content to strum guitars and sing. "I feel like we're on one continuous stag party," one complained, and the others agreed and the talk began about what they could do about it.

Again Sloane went into the house and when he came out, he doled out spending money. He loaded them into the rear of his truck, took them to town, and dumped them in a dark back alley, saying they'd have to find their own way back. Margarito stayed at the ranch, drinking wine. He went to his bunkhouse and lay down. He heard Sloane return and go into the house where the pregnant woman and her husband always were. Sloane kept them in batteries for their portable radio. Margarito fell asleep.

It was well after midnight when he awakened, hearing activity about the quarters. He heard subdued talking and laughing. Going to investigate, he found a half dozen of the workers had returned with women and they were trying to drink and have a good time without waking the others.

"Ho, Margarito! You caught us, eh?" one shirtless man said, sitting on the edge of his bunk, one arm around a shapely woman, the other around a jug of wine. When Margarito discovered the extent of the debauchery, he heaved a sigh and built a fire in the outside kitchen fireplace and sat down at a table. Soon the others joined him. The girls were not bashful, to say the least.

"Where did you find them?" Margarito asked, a little irate.

"Where else do you find such beautiful women?" said one worker, his girlfriend on his lap. "In the whorehouse in town."

Sloane was awakened by the noise and came out. When he saw what was going on, he went back and brought out more wine and a bottle of whiskey for himself.

A half hour later, as some of the couples danced and some men sang and played their guitars and some negotiated with the women, Sloane, whom Margarito noticed had taken a liking to one girl, said, "Now, this is what I call a party."

Margarito looked at the house and saw the pregnant woman watching the goings-on with hearty disapproval. Her husband also watched from the house, but not with disapproval.

The party was breaking up as the eastern sky showed light. One of the conditions of the girls' visit was that they be back at their place of employment before daybreak. They, too, were illegal aliens, and severe punishment awaited her who risked her boss's investment by taking a chance on being spotted by la migra. And their boss had invested a great deal of money and effort in getting them set up in the rural agricultural areas to service the tens of thousands of workers who swept up and down California's vast farm belts.

The work went on. The faces that were a yellow-tan two months before were now a handsome copper. Sinews stood out on arms, and hands pridefully grasped the shovel handle without need of gloves. Margarito and Sloane conferred frequently as to just when to harvest the first of the citrus. The longer they waited, the sweeter and larger the fruit would be, but the men could not go much longer without a real payday.

One day when Sloane had left the ranch on an errand, Margarito was servicing the tractor when he saw his workers had stopped their labor and were talking to a small group of men in the field. He strode toward them to investigate. The newcomers were obviously not Anglos, and from their dress were not officials. As he approached, they quit talking and faced him, and he assumed they knew who he was.

Margarito introduced himself and faced the leader of the new arrivals. He was a small man, but commanded great respect from the others. He began telling Margarito of the struggle for better working conditions for all farm workers, of the terrible injustices the men faced, how the Mexicans from Mexico and the Mexican Americans alike were being exploited by the growers in order to put cheap food on the dining tables of America, and the man talked of what had happened in the automobile factories in Detroit, and the packing houses in Chicago, and the aircraft plants in California after the workers banded together to form a union and make their demands felt.

And when he got through, Margarito beckoned him to walk alongside, away from the others, and Margarito talked. "I fully appreciate what you're doing, Mr. Chavez," he said politely, "but please, understand what I have here. These men have told you we are paying them next to nothing, but I will see they share in the harvest. I have the dregs here. I got them from under bridges, from cots in broom closets. That thin man there has a wife at the house who will shortly give birth to a U. S. citizen. You know what that means to them. We have here a gringo patrón who is giving them his life savings, and they in turn are saving a ranch. You talk these ten men into demanding better conditions and more money now and next year instead of me having two dozen field workers, all these will be dodging the migra in back alleys again."

The testing of the citrus showed the fruit had ripened beyond expectations. The yield would still be a fraction of what it should, but it would bring several thousand dollars and possibly see the ranch through until the sugar beets were ready. Testing and sampling of the sugar beets showed

Margarito and the crew had done everything just right. The watering had been timed perfectly, the thinning had been timely and not overdone, and the weather had cooperated. That yield was months away, but Margarito was already making plans.

On a Thursday the citrus was boxed and stacked, and the next morning the trucks from the packing plant came to load up. The field workers were jubilant. Within a few hours the trucks were loaded and pulling out of the ranch road, Sloane following in his pickup. He shouted to them he would be back as soon as he cashed the check. They waited.

Within a few hours he came roaring up to the workers' quarters. He jumped out of the truck carrying a bag. Margarito helped total each man's earnings, which he had kept track of in a notebook he carried.

Then Margarito spoke to them. "Listen, muchachos. You all agreed not to go into town at once and attract attention. I'll take one or two of you in to buy drinks and to call the girls. I don't want any of you picked up by the migra now. This is our first real payday, but better ones are coming."

The pregnant woman and her husband sat in the front of the truck as Margarito drove into town with two of the workers in the back. He stopped in front of a bar and let them out. The man and his wife would shop and then return to the ranch later.

Margarito parked and went into a thrift shop and bought a fairly respectable jacket and shirt. As he walked out he happened to look toward del Rio's and saw the blond woman, Gretchen, entering the restaurant alone. He went into a different bar. He was truly tired of this jumping at shadows that illegal aliens lived with. He reflected on what *had* happened to him and speculated on what *would* happen to him. He ordered strong drinks, which he usually didn't do, and soon he saw one of the workers at the door, beckoning him.

Outside, he saw the men had engaged the same girls who had visited the ranch previously. "They wanted to return," one worker told him. "The other girls wouldn't come because the whoremaster wasn't there, but these girls went without his permission, because they'd been there before."

Returning to the ranch, Margarito sat at one of the outside eating tables and watched as the revelry began. It was pretty much as before. Sloane was a little more aggressive with the girls. The men outnumbered the whores about two to one, but solutions to this were being worked out.

The evening wore on and Margarito sat off to one side, almost in the shadows. Somehow, the merriment and fun were making him sad, and he knew why. He thought about Anastacia a while longer but knew that soon he would cast her out of his mind and join in the fun. But he wasn't quite ready yet, and he poured another tin cup full of wine.

They scarcely noticed the car that pulled up quietly just outside the circle of light thrown by the fire. The driver sat, his features indistinct, watching, and soon the girls nudged one another and stood looking at the car. "Our boss," one of them said fearfully. The man got out of the car and approached. Margarito's eyes were on him. Something about him was familiar.

"Who told you you could come out here?" the newcomer hissed at the whores. One girl retreated, near terror on her face. "What kind of deal did you make with these cabrónes?" he said coldly, advancing toward them. One of the workers stepped forward to protest, but a girl stopped him. "No," she said, "it'll be worse if you interfere."

As one girl began a halting explanation of their actions, Margarito recognized Huerta, the Ensenada pimp, and it all came back to him: the battered face of Anastacia; trying to find Huerta after Captain Ramos had released him; his vowing to all that Huerta would never operate in Ensenada again. But Huerta had eluded him. Now he was here, still plying his trade. Margarito downed the full glass of wine before him and strode to Huerta. He stood facing him. All eyes were on the pair. Huerta didn't recognize Margarito.

"Don't give me any crap," Huerta said. "I came to get my girls. It cost me a fortune to bring them into the country, and by God they don't make a move unless I tell them."

The two men were a step or two apart, and Margarito was aware he was swaying a little. "You don't remember me, pimp?" he asked.

Huerta squinted at him. "Do I know you?"

"Yes, pimp. You beat up a little girl in Baja because she wouldn't screw for you. Remember?"

Huerta looked puzzled. "I don't remember . . ."

"I guess you beat up girls so frequently you can't remember

all of them. But this one was Leonceo Herrera's daughter, in Ensenada. And Leonceo and I ran you out of Baja, son-of-a-fucking whore!"

Margarito's open palm smashed suddenly across Huerta's face, and the nose spurted blood as he stumbled backward. Margarito was staggering only a little as he lunged after him, but the other workmen and Sloane grabbed him.

"Take it easy! Take it easy! You're drunk, Margarito."

Huerta had fallen back against his car, and now stood holding a handkerchief to his nose.

"Don't ruin our night, just because you got a grudge against him," Sloane said. Margarito stood, breathing heavily, eyes fastened on Huerta. The others all pulled Margarito away from Huerta, and Margarito suddenly allowed himself to be pulled, knowing the ultimate futility of revenge.

"Okay, pimp," Margarito said to Huerta, "how much do you want for the girls? For tonight?"

Huerta was still fearful. The girls stood back, uncertain what would happen. "How much would the girls bring in for you tonight, pimp? You'd better tell me quick and be glad you're getting out of here in one piece."

Huerta still held the blood-soaked handkerchief to his smashed nose. "They better each bring me twenty dollars," he said with some difficulty.

The men started going through their pockets.

"Sloane!" Margarito barked without taking his eyes from Huerta. "Go get a hundred dollars!"

Margarito spoke in such a manner that Sloane didn't question the command. The old man hurried into the house and in a few moments came hurrying back, carrying the bag of money. He held it so that the firelight reached inside and managed to pick out two fifty-dollar bills. Margarito, his eyes still on Huerta, grabbed them and threw them at the whoremaster.

"There are six girls . . ." Huerta said, picking up the money. He left the sentence unfinished, looking around. Somehow, he had lost ground. The whores now stood with the workers, and they no longer seemed to fear him. He got into his car and drove off.

Slowly, the frivolous spirit that had so abruptly departed began to return. Inquisitive glances were cast toward Margarito, who again sat alone at a table, drinking wine. But no one bothered him.

When he finished the jug of wine and went to get another, no one noticed. He poured another tin cup full and drank it. And he sat and remembered. It wasn't often that he gave into this self-torture. He remembered vividly. Huerta had brought it all back clearly. In his mind he saw her at the helm of the fishing boat. How had that come about? Oh yes, he had plunged his harpoon into a giant of a shark, so big that two other men had to hold him by the waist as he twisted and jerked until he killed the shark all by himself. How old had she been then? Not more than thirteen. And when the shark was dead he had looked first at her to see if she had seen it all. And the slight smile on her lips as her eyes traveled over his body, naked to the waist, had said, "I knew you could do it. You didn't surprise me." And later, walking back to the village when they'd beached the boat, she had said, "Rito, you're already stronger than any man around here, and you're only seventeen," and she had seen how he looked at her and she liked it, and knew that only his fear of her father's wrath kept him from exploring her.

He was jarred from his thoughts by the tin cup falling from his fingers, and he realized how groggy he was. The workers and Sloane were in various states of drunkenness and Margarito stood up, suddenly realizing what he wanted. He needed to get away from here.

"Sloane," he called to the old man, "I'm going to use your truck a while." Without waiting for an answer he drove off.

It was not late when Gretchen Heath came out of del Rio's Restaurant and went to her car. As she inserted the key in the lock she was startled to see Margarito stepping out of the shadows.

"Hello, Gretchen," he said.

She stood looking at him a moment, then smiled.

"Hi. I wondered what happened to you." She appraised him. "You're looking better than when I left you at the roadhouse."

He stepped to her. "Yep, I'm doing all right. You on your way home?"

"I was," she said uncertainly.

"How come your policeman husband doesn't ever go to del Rio's with you?"

She hesitated. "He . . . doesn't care for . . . that kind of music."

Margarito picked up on an unspoken message. "Oh. And you do."

She smiled broadly. "I love it."

"And he lets you out alone?"

"He's married to his wörk. And besides, this week he's attending a peace officers' symposium. In San Diego."

They stood facing each other a little awkwardly. Then he said, "Well, I could get picked up standing here, you know."

She finished unlocking the car and held the door open for him. "I guess we could go somewhere . . . somewhere a little safer."

Dawn was breaking when she pulled up to Sloane's truck near the center of town and stopped. He got out and came around to the driver's side, looking at her. She returned his gaze. "I don't know how it happened," she said quietly, "and please don't ask the question I know you're going to, because I can't answer it."

"All right. Good-bye, Gretchen."

"Good-bye, Rito. I know it will happen again."

He stood in the empty street looking after the disappearing taillights. Then he got into the truck and returned to the ranch.

The sun was high and all was quiet when he awoke in the bunkhouse. He got up, still fully dressed, and went out to the scene of the previous night's activity. Nearby was a hand-operated pump, and he tugged on the iron handle and splashed water on his face, drinking deeply. He ran his pocket comb through his hair. Still there was no sound except that of a few chickens as they scratched and pecked with unconcern. Looking about he saw half-emptied wine jugs, cigarette butts strewn about, a pair of women's panties. He walked toward the bunkhouse and hollered, but there was no answer. The door of the ranch house was ajar. A dreadful premonition settled on him as he mounted the steps and entered the living room. His eyes quickly focused on the body of Sloane on the floor, head smashed in, neck at an awkward angle, rheumy eyes open. Then Margarito saw that the huge stump used as a table for the washbasin was overturned and he could see it was hollowed out. Sloane's hiding place for the money. He turned and looked back at the outdoor kitchen as he reconstructed in his mind what must have happened: Huerta had seen the bag of money, knew Sloane kept it hidden in the house. Huerta had assessed the situation and knew that all would sleep the sleep of the drunk before morning. He had returned, killed the old man, perhaps forced him to reveal the hiding place first, and left. The workers had discovered the body when they arose, and had fled, quite understandably.

It was nearly noon. No way of knowing when exactly all this had transpired, or what was going on now. Quickly he hurried to the bunkhouse and put on a clean shirt and street shoes. Not wanting to appear to be traveling, he took nothing he couldn't carry in his pockets. Sloane's old truck was nearby, but it would be foolhardy to be caught in that now.

From the house on the hill he looked off to the highway and thought he saw a black-and-white car approaching rapidly. He waited until he saw the car turn onto the dirt road to the ranch, and then he broke into a trot in the opposite direction.

He left the ranch property and chose a little-used road that would lead to town. He kept to the ditch when a car came by and at length saw an old produce truck coming. He waved to the driver.

"How about a lift toward town?" he asked.

The driver nodded and he climbed aboard. In town he started for del Rio's, but then thought better of it. He went to a phone booth and called. Del Rio answered.

"Margarito!" he said with some excitement. "What's happened at the Sloane ranch?"

"Somebody killed the old man. How did you know about it?"

"That babe that got you out of here the day the migra came, she came in a half hour ago, very upset. Said she'd heard there was a killing, on her husband's police radio, and the cops had your name and description."

Margarito cursed under his breath. Del Rio went on, "Where are you now?" Margarito told him. "Stay right there. I'll pick you up in five minutes. Don't move."

Margarito reflected a moment. "Where can you take me?"

"I can leave you in the barrio in Los Angeles within two hours. At least you'll have a chance there."

Margarito hung up and waited. In less than five minutes del Rio drove up to the booth. Margarito got in and sat low in the front seat as del Rio headed the car south.

CHAPTER 12

Rogelio Huerta had no trouble getting past the Mexican border crossing going into Tijuana. He had all the proper papers allowing him to enter and transact business in the United States and return to Mexico at will.

A few hours in Tijuana convinced him it was not the best place to locate new girls for his whorehouses in California. Too many whoremasters and pimps, too many prosperous prostitutes, who could make good money with little effort from the tens of thousands of tourists who came there weekly.

He got in his car and drove on the toll road south to Ensenada. He'd been away a long time; ever since that cabrón Captain Ramos had driven him out of business. After the incident with the Anastacia girl.

Huerta spent a lot of time brooding, and whenever he did he ground his teeth. He had been raised a street waif in Mexicali, never having known his parents. He knew several trades by which he had always earned a living. He was an expert at burglarizing tourists' cars and motel rooms, at rolling drunk U.S. servicemen, and at several other things, but running a crew of whores had been his forte for years.

He'd settled in Ensenada and had never had any trouble until the Anastacia incident. That had happened more than a year and a half ago, but he still ground his teeth when he recalled his subsequent incarceration at the hands of Captain Ramos. Ramos hadn't been too hard to pay off, but when he had gotten out of jail he'd had to leave town because of Margarito Corrales. Margarito's reputation was legend. Aside from his nearly killing two U.S. Marines in the fight Ramos had told him about, Huerta had heard that many times Corrales had cleaned out a local tavern in brawls.

Huerta had been unable even to hire bodyguards when it was learned Margarito Corrales was after him, so fierce was the man's reputation. Huerta, with his contacts, had gotten papers to do business in the United States, and by posing as a legitimate businessman, eventually had had the opportunity to spend considerable time setting up a prostitution operation above Los Angeles. Again, all had gone well until the incredible coincidence of running into Margarito at the Sloane ranch. But it had been worth it. Remembering, he fingered his broken nose gingerly. He'd only recently been able to remove the bandages. He looked into the rear-view mirror and saw the nose was only slightly discolored, hardly noticeable. Yes, it had been worth it. Not only getting the money from the old man after he killed him, but also framing Margarito for the murder. It had been simple: The next day, hearing nothing about a murder at the Sloane ranch, he had made one single call to the police, faking a heavy Mexican accent, saying, "Señores, I saw a killing last night. I saw a man name Margarito Corrales, he ees beeg and strong, he keel his boss at the Sloane ranch and steal all his money. Maybe he ees steel there and you can catch him if you hurry." Yes, it had been well worth it. He knew Margarito was a long way from Ensenada now.

Arriving at the town, Huerta drove to a motel near the waterfront and checked in. Then he set out on foot through the town. "I'm looking for girls who want to work in the States," he told all the cab drivers and other likely persons. He gave the name of his motel and the room number. Then he returned to read the newspaper.

It was a half hour later that there was a knock on the door. Huerta glanced at his watch, a little surprised. Girls coming so soon? He paused in front of the mirror and combed his straight black hair, tucked in his shirt, then went to the door.

The man who stood there was familiar, but Huerta couldn't quite place him. He was tall, lean but muscular, light-haired but unmistakably Mexican. He was dressed almost casually; his light sport suit looked new and expensive. He eyed Huerta calculatingly.

"Can I help you?" Huerta asked, uncertain as to what his attitude should be.

"Señor Huerta?" the man asked.

"Sí."

"May I come in?" the man asked politely. "I think we have some things to talk about."

Huerta hesitated only a moment. "Certainly. Pase usted," he said.

The man took the only upholstered chair in the room and Huerta sat on the bed.

"My name is Nachez," he said, and Huerta remembered him then. He had been a police official in La Paz. "I've been observing this town and its inhabitants for some time," Nachez went on. "And I think I have an interesting proposition for you."

"I wish I could offer you a drink or something," Huerta said apologetically.

Nachez waved him silent with a clearly authoritative gesture. "I'll get right to the point, Señor Huerta. I believe you are familiar with a certain Captain Ramos?"

"Yes, I know him well," Huerta said.

"Well, his job, in the upcoming reshuffling of political positions, is up for sale."

"Understandable," Huerta said. He was familiar with the political structure.

"The person who will be, shall we say, put in his present position, as you must know, must have qualifications other than just the money that goes to the right place. I want that job, Señor Huerta. I am an experienced policeman, I know the right people. And I want it."

Huerta shrugged. "I hope you get it." Monetary contributions to the politicians in power to ensure getting a certain job, Huerta knew, was a universal practice, carried on with varying degrees of openness depending on what country you were in.

Nachez went on: "I need a fairly large amount of money to get this job."

Huerta nodded. "There are people to go to in this town, if you're prepared to make certain . . . concessions."

"But I'm not," Nachez said simply. "I don't want to be beholden to a group of taco merchants, or firecracker dealers. What I'm saying, Rogelio Huerta, is that the man who puts up the twenty thousand I need can have things pretty much his own way in this town."

Huerta was excited by these words, but not yet optimistic. "I see. Everything is . . . worked out? For the transition of power?"

Nachez pulled out a cigarette case and took out a cigarette. He said nothing until it was lit and he had inhaled deeply. "Everything is worked out. The newspapers will announce Ramos has been offered a position with the party that will necessitate his resignation. He will bow out gracefully. There will be a search for a qualified successor, one who has had experience dealing with the problems peculiar to this area. It's all worked out. I need but to put the money in the right palm and I have it."

Huerta got up and paced. "And you want twenty thousand from me," he said casually.

Nachez regarded him solemnly. *"Only* from you. I've checked you out. You're ambitious. I know what you're into. I could put a stop to your activities in the United States with a single phone call to the U. S. Immigration and Naturalization Service. Instead I'm giving you a chance to build an empire."

Huerta saw the not-so-veiled threat. And the promise. He realized that once Nachez had singled him out to finance his venture, there was no backing away. Nachez would, if he had to, go to a group of taco merchants, and then when he was in command, Huerta would be sent packing in short order.

"I don't have twenty thousand dollars," he said.

Nachez was unconcerned. "I'll accept your pledge that it will be delivered within sixty days."

Huerta's mind raced into the future. He had already made the decision. There wasn't much choice if he wanted this town as a base of operations. He didn't have the twenty thousand. But, if he pushed, hired extra girls, cut their percentage, borrowed from everyone he could, he could have the money in two months. It would leave him broke. He envisioned a classy operation, with girls picking men who carried credit cards, hotel rooms rigged to enable someone to go through pockets of trousers hanging on the wall, and he pictured a future of running things his own way in a town where at present the police didn't respect him. This was his chance at the big time.

He wheeled and faced Nachez squarely. "Where do you want the money delivered?"

Nachez smiled. "In sixty days, I will call on you." He got

up and went to the door. "Have the money then. Don't worry, I'll call on you wherever you are two months from today." He walked out.

Huerta was exalted. Plans began forming in his mind. This was too good to be true. He'd have the town in the palm of his hand. Then he remembered. He'd spread the word about girls. They were the key to the whole thing. He looked at the clock. Some should be arriving soon.

It wasn't long before there was a knock on the door. Huerta answered it and he saw a young girl, cheaply dressed, shapely.

"Are you Señor Huerta?"

"Yes," he replied. "Come in."

She entered and he motioned her to the chair. "My name is Maria Colima," she said uncertainly, when she was seated. "I understand you're looking for girls? To go to the United States?"

"Yes. You understand what for?"

"Yes. You have a way of getting there?"

"I have a safe way. But tell me, do you have ties here in Mexico?"

The girl shook her head. "I have no one."

"Good. How old are you?" He guessed she looked perhaps fifteen.

"That doesn't matter," she said evenly. He raised his brows slightly. She either knew her way around or had learned the answers.

"Yes. I can take you there. If you want to work."

"I want to work."

"You've worked before?"

Her smile was decades beyond her years. "I'm not a beginner."

He looked her over. "Are these the best clothes you have?"

"Won't they do?"

"They're not too bad. I hate to start out having to buy clothes for a girl before she proves she can bring in money."

"I can bring in money. Where will I be?"

He looked at her sharply, and she lowered her eyes.

"Don't worry. I'll take you to a place up the California coast. We'll go by boat. Tonight or tomorrow. And you leave the questioning to me, understand? Now tell me, in bed with a customer, are there any things you have qualms about doing?"

Her face was expressionless as she shook her head. "I know my business."

Now Huerta sat back in a chair. "Take your clothes off," he said curtly. She rose and in a moment stood naked before him. He stood up, his eyes traveling over her. Then he went to the bed and lay down on his back. "Come here." She obeyed. He clasped his hands behind his head. "Now, let's see you work."

A practiced smile came on her face as she sat on the bed and reached for his belt buckle.

A few minutes later she rose and went into the bathroom. When she returned Huerta was tucking in his shirt in front of the mirror.

"Will I do?" she asked.

"You'll do," he said curtly, motioning her out the door. "Come back tomorrow at noon."

She hesitated, looking at him. He turned and glared at her. "Señor Huerta," she said in a small voice, "would you be kind enough to advance me a little money? I'm hungry . . ."

He took a few crumpled bills from his pocket and tossed them at her.

Maria Colima left the motel and walked down the street. Tourists and peasants crossed the broken dirt sidewalks. In a small store she bought a freshly baked bolillo and some cheese and a soft drink. Hungrily she ate and drank as she walked toward the post office. She had finished her meal by the time she got there. "How much in stamps to send a letter to La Ciudad de Mexico?" she asked.

Next she went to a small drugstore and was able to get a large envelope. Then she bought a newspaper.

She walked out of the business district and turned up a hill on a dirt road. High on the hill were scattered the uncountable hovels, with uncountable small dirty children, and women cooking over open fires or on gasoline or kerosene stoves.

She picked her way through, passing men who sat watching her lithe form climbing the hill. Occasionally she greeted someone she knew. Near the top she entered a house built of mud bricks with two rooms made of cardboard boxes that had

ANOTHER LAND

been added. Inside an older woman looked at her. Maria handed her the remaining money.

"Good," the woman said. "Now we have enough to buy ingredients for stew. Watch the little ones. I'll go to the store."

When the woman was gone, Maria made sure the children were occupied and then began writing a letter on paper that had been a grocery bag.

"Dear Mama and Papa," she wrote. "Forgive me for not writing sooner, I know you must be worried frantic, but I did not want to write until I had good news. I am near the border and I met a man who is taking me to the United States to work. It is good work, don't worry. The best news is that which you can see in this newspaper I'm sending along. The U.S. President, Señor Carter, will soon pass a law allowing all Mexicans in the United States to stay permanently as citizens. Thousands are arriving around here every day to take advantage of this. I wish you would come too. You can see by the headlines I am telling the truth. I'm staying with a family that is waiting to go north as soon as they save money. I am lucky. This man I met is providing me a way to get there. As soon as I am a citizen, I will send for the whole family, if you cannot come sooner. I knew I would have good luck sooner or later. I may leave today or tomorrow and I might not get another chance to write, but I wanted to put your minds at ease. I am fine. I miss you so much I cry at night, but things are working out slowly but surely. I'll write again."

By the next afternoon, Huerta was ready. The boat would be at the private pier by dusk. The girls, he had gotten seven, would be there. Seven was just the right number because he had plans for six. He had engaged the boat owner whom he had met in jail after his fight with Leonceo Herrera.

A few phone calls to some people up the California coast and all was ready.

He had some time to kill so he went to a tavern. He was remembered in Ensenada, but no one was concerned about him.

He was drinking alone when he happened to overhear a mail carrier mention Velasco Beach. That was where Anastacia Herrera had lived. He befriended the mail carrier and asked if a family by the name of Herrera still lived there.

"Leonceo Herrera? Sure. He's on my route."

"Tell me, does he get mail from the United States often?"

"Only from his daughter. She's working for a rich family near Los Angeles."

"You don't happen to remember her address, do you?"

"The daughter in Los Angeles? No. But I think I got a letter from her in my bag out in the car."

Huerta pulled out a bill. "I'll give you this if you tell me the return address on that letter."

The man looked at the bill. "Make it twice that and I'll get it for you right now."

The man left and returned in a minute or so and handed Huerta a slip of paper. Huerta studied it. He read, "Tacha Herrera, in care of Meme de Beauclair," and the address in a town named San Marino. "Thank you, my friend. Have another drink." And Huerta pocketed the paper.

At dusk Huerta and seven prostitutes stood on the pier waiting to board the boat. The boat owner arrived. Huerta gave him five hundred dollars. The man took it to his wife waiting in the car and handed it to her. Then he got on board.

Huerta followed, snapping orders to the women as they climbed on board and took seats. "Now you all had better have enough food. We'll be traveling all night. Don't attract any attention and stay seated. Is that clear?"

He sensed their resentment and their contempt, but he warmed inwardly at the thought of how he would correct that attitude.

The boat started out slicing smoothly through the calm waters of the bay. Then when it hit the ocean it began pitching and heaving, bouncing and rolling. The pilot knew his business and made good time, but as Huerta knew, it was five or six hours to Los Angeles, and they were going many miles above that port.

Within a half hour, the girls began showing signs of regret. As it got darker, their fear of the rough sea became more intense. Huerta looked at each one in turn. He had been through this more than once. Which one of the girls would it be? Which one would become the catalyst that would weld the others into a disciplined group that understood what the name Huerta was to mean to them?

His eyes settled on Maria Colima, the youngest, the most hysterical. She would do. Too bad she owed him ten pesos.

Dawn was breaking when the small boat edged up to a makeshift pier and the prostitutes, sick, weak, and tired from the ordeal, filed ashore, the remaining six of them hypnotized by the utter terror Huerta had inspired during the night.

A gentle breeze lifted the gauze curtains of the drawing room and Anastacia felt its warmth as she sat on a cane and velvet couch. She felt tired. It was early afternoon, Meme was off with Ruel somewhere, Amelia had caught up on most of her work and was in her room watching a Spanish-language soap opera, a luxury Anastacia allowed her only when time permitted. She heard the muted gong of the great grandfather clock in the front entry. It was a sound she'd come to love in the eight months she'd been with Meme, a sound she'd even missed during the month she and Meme had spent in Europe.

The breeze coming through the window warmed suddenly, and it brought back memories of the hot winds blowing through the giant cactus at La Tijera. Then her thoughts raced to Margarito, and a worried look came over her face. No word since he'd left for Oxnard. Amelia had told her a man called several times during her visit to France, but would leave no name or number.

Meme had taken her partly as an apprentice to the European manner of doing things, partly as a traveling companion, and the trip had been a whirlwind of dinner parties, museums, antique and dress shops, and social engagements. The French lessons Meme had paid for during the preceding half year had served her well, and in the month since they'd been back she found herself lapsing unconsciously into an occasional French phrase, much to Amelia's chagrin. Now when she looked back on it, their time in Europe seemed an extended, hazy dream.

She decided to get busy doing something to get her mind off Margarito. She started to rise but at that moment the phone beside the couch rang.

She picked it up and gasped when she heard his voice.

"*Rito!* Where *are* you? I've been worried to death . . ."

"Listen, Tacha, baby. Are you alone?"

"Yes."

"Is there any chance someone is listening on another phone?"

"No. No chance. Why? What's the matter, Rito?"

"I'm in trouble. I called you a month ago a couple of times. The Fuentes told me where to find you. Some dumb criada kept answering. She seemed to think I might be la migra and I thought she might be planted there by them. Who is she?"

"She's just a housemaid. Don't worry, she's all right. I've been away in Europe. We got back nearly a month ago. Rito," her voice became pleading, "what kind of trouble are you in? Can we meet?"

"No, we can't meet. Tell me, do you think there's any chance someone may be following you?"

She thought, but her growing apprehension dominated her thinking. "No. I'm sure. Tell me, what happened?"

He paused, and she could tell he was gathering his thoughts.

"Well, after I left you I went to Oxnard, and I found del Rio's Restaurant. Del Rio was a great guy. Gave me a job, working for tips, room, and board until I found something better. That lasted a month or so and la migra raided the place. I got away. I met an old down-and-out rancher, Sloane's his name, and formed sort of a partnership with him, working his land. Then one night about a month or so ago, Huerta showed up." He paused in his narrative.

She was shocked. "Huerta? Rogelio Huerta from Ensenada?"

"The same."

"What was he doing there? How'd he find you?"

"He's still in the same business. Had a string of girls. Some of them showed up at the ranch with the workers. He came looking for them."

"What happened?" She was feeling more and more apprehensive.

"I beat the shit out of him and kicked him off the place. Then I went into town and met . . . this babe I'd come to know. You know how it is, baby. I just knew her casually . . ."

She was angry with the inane diversion. "That's not important. Go on. You shacked up and then what?"

"Well, while I was gone, Huerta, it had to be him, none of

my men would have done it, Huerta came back and killed Sloane. Stole his money."

"Killed him! *Rito!* But what's that . . ."

"Let me finish. I got back to the ranch early and went to sleep. When I woke up about noon everything was quiet. I went into the ranch house and found the old guy dead. He'd been robbed. All the help—they were all wetbacks—had split, naturally. I looked down the road and saw the cops coming. I split too. I went to see del Rio and he said he'd heard the cops were on the way and I was the main suspect. He took me to Los Angeles. I'm here now."

There was a prolonged silence, and then she said, exhaling, *"Rito!"*

"That's it, Tacha, baby."

"Rito! What are we going to *do?* What are you doing now?"

"Well, when I got here, the only place I could find was an empty boxcar in the freight yards with a half dozen other wetbacks. I finally got a job as night janitor in a building downtown. One night I didn't go to work and it happened the office building was raided. I was just lucky. Then I tried out for this real good mariachi group, and I made it. That's what I'm doing now."

She was still in a state of shock. "Rito! When can I see you?"

"You can't, baby. I'm afraid Huerta may have told them about us and you might be staked out, by a migra, in the hopes you'd lead them to me. I'm wanted for murder."

"Where are you staying?"

"I can't tell you that, Tacha. I won't put that burden on you."

She sensed his utter desperation, and some of it transmitted itself to her. She said fiercely, "Rito, I want to see you. If only for a minute. I've got to see with my own eyes that you're all right. I *have* to . . ."

"Take it easy, Tacha. It would only put you in danger . . ."

"I don't care! I've got to see you."

There was a long silence and she knew he was thinking. Finally he said, "Okay. This mariachi group I'm with, we're having a mano-à-mano at the Million Dollar Theater this Saturday night. Can you get someone to take you? So you look like you're just on a date, in case you're being followed?"

"Yes, I'll find someone to take me. But . . . couldn't I just see you for a minute? Before the show, maybe?"

Again he was thinking. "No. But . . . we'll see how it is after. Maybe you could come up on the stage after the show and we could look like we're just casually talking or something."

"All right, Margarito, I'll be there." She cradled the phone in her hands and closed her eyes. "Please, *please* be careful. Oh, how I love you!"

"Adios, querida."

She hung up and sat thinking a long while. Of course, she'd known immediately whom she'd use to take her Saturday night. Paul Foster, who had ogled her since the night of her first dinner at Meme's, had asked her out several times. And Paul might be a good person to be in good with if there was trouble on the horizon. He hinted frequently, if not boasted, that he had important connections. He knew famous lawyers on first-name terms. He knew powerful politicians and government officials, and wealthy and influential people such as Meme. Anastacia felt only fleeting guilt at using him. The stakes were high. From the drawer of a nearby reading table she took Meme's address book and dialed a number.

A professional female voice answered, "Foster Advertising."

"Hello. I want to talk to Mr. Foster."

"I'll give you his office."

In a moment another female voice came on. "This is Paul Foster's office."

"I'd like to speak to Mr. Foster."

A pause. "Was he expecting your call?"

"No, but I'm sure he'll want to talk to me."

"He is *very* busy right now. May I ask what this is regarding?"

With what she knew might be slightly irritating self-confidence she said, "Tell him Anastacia Herrera is on the line." She gave her name the full Mexican treatment: the broad *a*'s in her first name and the rolled *r*'s in the last, knowing the girl would never be able to pronounce it but Paul would instantly be able to interpret whatever she came up with.

Foster came on the line almost immediately. "Tacha, what a surprise! To what do I owe this pleasure?"

She chuckled over the phone. "Hi, Paul. How are you?"

"Fine. How's yourself?"

"I'm all right, Paul. You know, you've asked me out a couple of times. Right?"

"Six times, to be exact. But this is too much. Where do you want me to take you and when?"

"Well . . . do you have plans for Saturday night?"

"I just canceled them."

CHAPTER 13

Paul Foster slowed his expensive foreign car and eased into the de Beauclair driveway, looking at the house. He had been a guest in the de Beauclair mansion many times, but had never seen it in the daytime. The crescent drive sloped up from the street and leveled off near the front entrance. He saw Anastacia in one of the gardens, pointing to flowers as she told the gardener which she wanted to decorate the house. She saw Foster and waved, squinting a little in the bright sunlight, and turned her attention back to the gardener. Foster cut the engine a dozen feet from where they stood and listened. He could hear their conversation, Anastacia telling the gardener she wanted the Iceland poppies for the following weekend and the Shasta daisies for tonight. She started to turn toward Foster as he sat in his car, but at that moment the housemaid, Amelia, came out carrying a pair of vases. Anastacia spoke to her in Spanish, but Foster could tell by a slightly exasperated expression that the maid had not brought the right vases. The maid looked momentarily crushed by Anastacia's gentle scolding, and hurried back into the house to bring the proper receptacles.

Foster regarded the house; it was lordly, he decided. White columns supported the high overhang protruding from above the second floor. Deep red bricks somehow suggested a quiet superiority. Olive trees were grouped at either end of the portico. The azaleas were trimmed as perfect little trees across the front of the mansion, the snowy white blossoms contrasting vividly with the dark green leaves. Lobelias and deep blue pansies, backed by brilliant patches of yellow and orange tulips and poppies, lined a brick walk that ran around the house. It seemed that if the powerfully built live oaks hadn't been right where they were, Meme would have had them put there. Perhaps she did, he mused.

"Hi," Anastacia said. Her elbows were on the door of his car, her face less than a foot from his. She took a step back as he opened the door and climbed out.

"Tacha!" he said, taking her hand in both his warmly. Before he could say more, she nodded her head, indicating he should watch what was about to take place in the nearby garden. Amelia had returned with the proper vases and was holding them for the gardener to judge the cutting lengths of the flower stems. He asked her to put the vases down, but she did not understand his English. He raised his voice and said something rapidly in Japanese. Amelia became indignant and cursed him in Spanish. They ended up each talking his natural language yet working together. Then they smiled at one another, Amelia returning to the house, the gardener turning to his soil.

"Amelia believes speaking one language is enough," Anastacia said. "She refuses to try to speak English."

They strolled toward the wide veranda. "Why is that?" Foster asked. "I mean, it seems so many people from Mexico have that trait. They refuse to learn another language."

Anastacia looked at him. "That's odd, isn't it. I always thought that was an American characteristic."

He said nothing as they stopped on the porch.

"You said you'd like to see the house before we go."

"Right. If we have time. You know, Meme's husband has been a major client of my firm for many years, and Meme and I have remained close friends since their divorce, but I've never seen this place in the daytime, or any more of it than the living and dining rooms."

She took his arm and guided him through the high carved oak doors. The entry-hall floor was of polished marble with subtle traces of soft rose. To the right stood a grandfather clock, towering a foot over Foster's head. He stopped before it.

"Now, this is something," he said. "An original piece."

She didn't try to hide her suppressed giggle. "Not a copy," she said. "If Meme heard you suggest such a thing she'd have a tantrum. No. It's Louis XV."

He examined the instrument, lightly touching the gold leaf

and bronze and green-tinted horn. He looked at her almost skeptically. "How do you know it's Louis XV? And why isn't it Louis XVI?"

"I am Meme's confidante, and I'll tell you some very confidential gossip. In many homes like this you'd find Louis XVI. It's more classical. But Meme prefers the Quinze. Partly because she likes the less developed style—in that era Parisian masters were still motivated by rococo designs. But mainly because when she was a flaming debutante in Paris many years ago, she had an affair with a Louis XV collector and gallery owner that colored her whole life. And she likes to be reminded of that every hour. The French are different."

Paul was amused. "Is that really true?"

She held up a hand. "So help me God," she laughed. "When she took me to the family chateau in Briançon . . ."

"Briançon?"

"Yes, that's a town in Dauphiné. I went there with her last month. She met the dealer again."

"That must have been romantic."

"Yes. He'd been having a tough time, and Meme fixed him up financially with lots of orders when she came back."

To the left of the entry an arch opened onto a drawing room. They strolled in.

"Tacha," he said, and he was careful in choosing his words as well as his sentences, "you know an incredible amount . . . I mean, how did you pick up so much knowledge so quickly . . . ?"

She stopped and faced him, not belligerently. "You mean, with my background, how do I know about such things?"

He retained his composure. "I suppose that's what I mean. How long have you been with Meme? Six months?"

"A little more. First, she has a magnificent library. Not full of novels, but about such things as period furniture and continental architecture. I spend much of my spare time reading. The house happens to run very smoothly with me in command, and I have free time."

"Now, what about this room? It looks modern." They had gone beyond the drawing room to the family room, which adjoined the kitchen.

As she turned from him she smiled with a sidelong glance. "This is . . ."

He interrupted, "Why did you laugh at me?"

"Paul, please don't be offended. I suppose you could call this 'modern,' in the sense that the furniture designer is of this century. Hans Wegner, opus two or three."

He stopped, looking at her with pleasant humility. "Now you're showing off at my expense."

Her reply was not completely good-natured. "Well, you come in here with the attitude, 'Now let's see what the peasant girl has learned,' and then you holler 'foul' when you can't keep up."

He resumed walking through the room. "I'm terribly sorry if I offended you."

She took his arm again, walking with him. "You didn't . . . quite."

As they entered the salon past the kitchen, he asked, "Now, why is this room different from the last?"

"Meme does most of her informal entertaining in here. This is Antti Nurmesnievi. He was Finnish. Wegner was a Danish wood sculptor, and that room is Michelle's favorite, except that it's pretty close to the ever-observant parental eye," she smiled.

"And you learned all this by reading Meme's books."

"Not really. Meme sends me to a contemporary furniture importer when he gets a shipment in. She wants first choice. I took two classes this fall. And I'm *very* flattered because Meme's adding a kind of playroom out by the pool for Michelle to entertain in when she's home from school, and I'm assigned the task of furnishing it. I'm thinking of Mexican murals, with free-form wood and leather furniture. There's a fellow in East L.A. who does really exciting things."

"Which reminds me," he looked at his watch. "What time is this . . . concert thing we're going to?"

"We'd better be going soon. Meme's at the racetrack," she said as they returned to the entry.

"That kind of surprises me. I didn't think she was the gambling type."

"She's not. She took me with her once. You know what she does at the track? She meets with three or four other ladies at the clubhouse. They have drinks and talk, always about decorating, landscaping, their children, and domestic help. They are Europeans too. I said before that the French are different." She tilted her head thoughtfully. "No, it's not the French. The Europeans are different."

"Don't they bet?"

"When they think about it, they pick a horse and place a bet with the waiter. Mostly they drink, eat, and talk." They stood near the front doors. "It'll just take me a second to get Amelia squared away and change. Be right back and we'll go."

"This thing we're going to . . . you call it a . . . mano-à-mano?" Foster asked as they hurtled over the freeway toward downtown Los Angeles.

"Yes," Anastacia replied. "It means 'hand-to-hand.' Let's see: In English you'd call it an eyeball-to-eyeball meeting."

"And it's two mariachi groups playing at one another?"

"Not quite. There's a band called Mariachi de Los Angeles. They're the best group in the area, supposedly. Well, the Mariachi Nacionales from Mexico challenged them to what's called a mano-à-mano. One plays, the audience reacts with applause, then the other tries to top them. It's fun."

"You've been to these playoffs before?"

"Uh-huh. At celebrations in Baja. One band claiming to be the best would challenge the champions. The audience decided who was the best."

"You said you know one of the musicians, right?"

"Yes. I know one."

"From Baja?"

"I grew up with him."

"Childhood sweetheart?"

She looked at him evenly before replying. "Something like that."

"What's his name?"

"His name is Margarito."

"Margarita?"

"No, Margarito. We call him Rito."

"Have you been seeing him regularly since you've been here?"

She turned her attention to the road ahead, ignoring the question, and he felt helpless anger for a fleeting moment.

He turned east on the Santa Ana and then took the Temple Street off ramp to North Broadway. He realized he had never been in the Million Dollar Theater. North Broadway for several years had been almost exclusively the territory of

Spanish-speaking people. It was "downtown" for the people of East Los Angeles.

As they crossed First Street he became more aware of the almost complete lack of Anglo faces among the throngs on the sidewalks. A sign on a parking lot near Fourth Street promised a two-dollar maximum fee and he pulled in. He took the parking ticket from a man whom he could swear looked fleetingly about in fear of immigration authorities, and they joined the crowds on the street.

Loud Mexican music blared from amplified speakers in the doorways of record and radio shops. The aroma of cooking corn and chili came from the many snack shops fronting the sidewalks. A black man on a corner shouted to all that doom was impending and one and all should fall to their knees to accept the Savior here and now.

"They don't pay much attention to him," Foster remarked, aware that somehow he was an alien here in downtown Los Angeles.

"Most can't understand him," Anastacia smiled.

A sideshow attraction caught his attention. It was a trailer, enclosed but evidently open at the top. A tape was playing nearby where a ticket taker stood. The tape and the sign on the trailer told of what was being offered.

"Now, for the first time in the United States, on exhibit for ten cents, see genuine giant rats from the sewers of Paris!"

"Want to take a look?" Foster asked her.

She was a little amused. "Sure," she said.

Foster handed the ticket taker some coins and he unhooked a rope blocking the railed passageway to the trailer. They walked up and looked down. The huge rats, big as alley cats, scurried about in the trailer searching for scraps.

Foster and Anastacia looked at each other and laughed, realizing this experience was rather thin.

"Well, we can tell our grandchildren we've seen the giant rats from the Parisian sewers," he said as they walked down the street toward the theater.

Foster saw that North Broadway was the outlet for hundreds of shops and stores selling cheap items. A leather-goods shop sold the cheapest and gaudiest of handbags. Another shop sold imitation jeans and T-shirts with either football stars' names or dirty words across the chest. Hand-painted large red letters advertised children's tennis shoes for three dollars. Little if any of the merchandise related to Mexico, but the throngs of patrons were dark, black-haired, and spoke Spanish.

Inside the Million Dollar Theater Foster felt less an alien than he thought he would. His mind was on Anastacia and what her reaction would be at the sight of the man she'd come to see. The musicians filed onto the stage and took their places on one side. No reaction showed on her face. Then the opposing group took the stage, and Foster saw it was the sixth man, with a giant guitarlike instrument, who brought her reaction. When the second group was introduced she applauded as long and hollered as loud as anyone else in the audience.

Foster understood less than a few words of the songs on the program, but learned Rito was a member of the group opposing the Mexican nationals. The participation of the audience, the audience reaction, the pitting of one group against another with robust good nature were new to him, but he found himself responding to the verve projected by the musicians. Then it was over.

Foster followed her between the seats to the aisle. There she turned. "I'm going to see him. I won't be long," she said.

"Fine. I'll meet you out on the street."

She turned and walked down the aisle to the stage. The curtains had not been drawn, and the stage was crowded with people shouting and greeting the musicians. He saw Rito with his huge guitar shaking hands with people, his eyes searching. Foster saw them as they saw each other. Rito handed his instrument to a bystander and she was in his arms, and they clenched one another fervently. Then he held her back to look at her. They talked, and Foster knew if he could overhear he wouldn't understand. Rito introduced her to several of the musicians. Foster took a good look at him. He was tall, as tall as himself, but heavy in the shoulders and neck. Thin-waisted, accentuated by the tight trousers and form-fitting mariachi shirt. The chromium-plated pistol at his side was ridiculous, of course, but the large white sombrero that dangled on his back from a thong about his neck somehow wasn't.

Rito's face showed a reckless good humor as though he

were ready to laugh at everything. As he talked to Anastacia she took a kerchief from her purse and dabbed at the perspiration beading his face. He was talking and she was laughing at what he was saying.

Then suddenly they were both listening seriously to a man who had hurried to them. Foster saw Anastacia and Rito look at one another, and there was no humor there now.

Quickly, Rito conferred with another musician, who reacted with excitement. Anastacia took a pencil and pad from her purse and wrote something, and then they were saying good-bye hurriedly, reluctant to part. Foster turned and walked to the front of the theater so that he would be there when she came out.

They were almost to the de Beauclair mansion and she'd scarcely spoken.

"I was watching when you went up on the stage," he finally said.

She looked at him without much reaction.

He went on. "He seems like quite a guy."

"He is quite a guy."

"I couldn't help but be curious about the excitement when that other man ran up to you."

She lowered her eyes and he felt she was about to cry.

"Look, Ana, if I can help in any way . . ."

"How can you help? That man simply said the apartment where Rito and some of the other mariachis stay is staked out."

Foster was astounded. *"Staked out?* What do you mean? Is he a fugitive?"

"Staked out by the immigration."

Foster looked at her, beginning to understand. "Immigration? You mean he's . . . an illegal alien?"

"A wetback. Don't you read the papers? They have one of their drives on. Two thousand last week alone, in just the L.A. area. That's what Rito was laughing about before that man came up. He said wherever he's been, an immigration officer comes in, shouts 'Immigration! Everybody freeze! Show your papers!' And then they catch them in nets when they start dropping out the windows." In spite of herself she was laughing at retelling the story. Foster laughed too.

"Yes, I've heard of the raids. All over. Hurts me too. Last

week a big client called and canceled an advertising campaign. He can't fill his orders because the immigration people raided his factory and took half his work force."

She looked at him fiercely. "That really hurt you, didn't it!" And he regretted what he'd said.

He pulled into the drive and parked in front of the house.

"Meme will be home soon," she said. "I'd better go in."

"What's your friend going to do?"

"I don't know. He gave me the number of a place he worked. The owner will relay messages so we can keep in contact until he can go somewhere where they aren't raiding."

"What will he do, do you think?"

She shrugged. "Pick grapes, maybe. Work in a filling station. He always manages."

"And then he'll call you."

"That's right. I'm sorry if you don't like it."

"But God, Tacha, you can't blame the authorities. Why doesn't he come here legally?"

She got out of the car, the door on her side still open. "You *are* stupid, aren't you, Paul."

He leaned across the seat and took her arm, gently pulling her back into the car.

"Listen, Tacha. Maybe I'm not as stupid about you people as you think I am."

She raised her eyebrows. "'Us people'?"

"Yes. In college my best buddy was a Chicano."

She threw back her head and laughed. "You really are a trip."

"Why is that so funny?" he asked defensively, a little angered.

She shook her head. "Paul. Please. 'Chicano' is a word we never use. In fact, in some places in Mexico you'd get a black eye for calling us that."

"Why? There's nothing wrong with it. This guy's name is Ben Garza. I roomed with him for two semesters."

"Good God, Paul," she said sarcastically. "How goddamn liberal can you get? Next you'll be telling me you screwed a Chicana."

He had started to plunge ahead with his next sentence but suddenly remained comically frozen with his mouth open. He tried to stem the rising frustration he felt. Regrouping his thoughts, he managed to salvage his dignity and went on, "My point is, I had a chance during those two semesters really to be exposed to your culture . . ."

"Paul! You can't be *serious*."

"Yes I am. I admit, I had really been culturally isolated. When I moved in with Ben I didn't even know what a burrito was."

She was suppressing laughter and it irritated him.

"What's so funny?"

"I'll tell you what's so funny. Growing up in Baja my family went South at the end of the tourist season and we ran a little café-gas station in a tiny town on the dirt road far down the peninsula. I still remember the time some gringos came bursting in, telling my mother they wanted burritos. My mother looked at them blankly—little *donkeys?* They were amused and a little mad because we'd never heard of *their* kind of burrito. My mother was raised off and on in the United States because her father was a migrant farm worker, and she spoke English very well, so she understood when the gringos laughed because they thought they'd come to such a backwoods place that we didn't even know the national dishes of Mexico. The fact is, Paul, burritos are an American thing. Like chili beans or chop suey. Now please continue about how much of our culture you learned from your Chicano roommate . . ." And then she added, "We're worlds apart, Paul."

"It doesn't have to stay that way, Ana . . . does it?" Without realizing it he tightened his hand on her arm.

She carefully pulled her arm back and looked at him in a new way. "I don't know, Paul. I truly don't," she said slowly.

He was silent for a while, at a loss for words. "Well, getting back to your friend here illegally, if he can't get immigration papers, why can't he get a passport? Or a visa or something . . ." His voice trailed off when he realized she was shaking her head, looking at him with sympathy.

He felt frustration, and realized it was because they *were* worlds apart, and he really knew nothing about immigration. "But what are we supposed to do? We can't let every wetback stay here who sneaks across the border, can we? We've got to try to catch them and send them back."

She got out and closed the door. He still sat behind the wheel.

She bent down, talking to him through the open window. "Paul," she said quietly, "I am a wetback too." And she turned and walked toward the vast de Beauclair mansion that was her domain.

CHAPTER 14

Acting Assistant District Director and Agent Fred Wilder, of the United States Immigration and Naturalization Service, walked to the window of his office and looked down on central Los Angeles, eight stories below. His desk was cluttered with papers, outside in the hall was a constant bustle, the day was hot, and his fatigue was as much from dealing with so many different tasks as from the effort he put forth. He went to the water cooler and filled a small paper cup with ice-cold water, drank it, and returned to his desk. "Send in Rogelio Huerta," he said into the intercom.

Huerta came in and shook hands, smiling.

"Good to see you, Mr. Huerta," Wilder said, motioning his visitor to a seat. "Before I take the information you're passing on to us, I want to say how much we appreciate the cooperation you've given us."

"Don't mention it," Huerta said in his broken English. "The least I can do is abide by the regulations you people set down for us."

"I know it's inconvenient for you to check with us and keep us posted, but if we don't keep track of Mexican businessmen with permits we find they will take jobs that U.S. citizens might take. That's the reason for all the reports about your business transactions."

"Understandable," Huerta said. "I'm still just negotiating business here. In fact, with the services and goods we order from your country, I'm putting more Americans to work."

"Good. The immigration service has a policy of encouraging commerce between the two nations. Now. You said you have information about a specific illegal alien . . ."

"Yes. I'm not a . . . what do you call it, a telltale, understand. I just want it understood I intend to abide by every rule and regulation of the service. I know there are untold thousands of my people illegally here, but I have specific information about only one. If I knew of others . . ."

"Of course, of course," Wilder said, not impatiently. "Now, do you have the name of the person? And where we can find him?"

"Her," Huerta corrected, taking a small notebook from his coat pocket. "She is Anastacia Herrera. Currently residing, at least until a few months ago, as a housemaid, I believe, at 2301 Oakhurst Street, the city of San Marino. You know where that is?"

"Yes. It's a suburb a few miles from here. Now, there could possibly be many Anastacia Herreras. Where is she from?"

"She is from Ensenada, Baja California."

"I see. That's where you're from, isn't it. Do you know her from there?"

Huerta shifted in his chair. "No. I know of this girl only because an American woman who lives near her said she had supplied her children with narcotics. I told this American woman I have no influence, but I am in legitimate contact with the immigration authorities and I would see that they knew of this girl's presence."

"You did the right thing, Mr. Huerta," Wilder said, showing him to the door. "We'll take care of it." Huerta left.

Another man was waiting outside Wilder's office, and Wilder beckoned him in. "Come in, Ellison."

Ellison entered and sat down.

"That guy who just left. He's on an unlimited entry visa, isn't he?"

"Yeah. He's a legit businessman. Our consulate in Tijuana checked him out."

"Giving us trouble?"

"No. Came in to renew. And give us the name and location of a suspected illegal alien."

"Just *one?* Jesus."

"Yeah. But coming from him, we'd better check it out as soon as we can get around to it." He stood up and took his coat from the back of his chair. "Ready for the Green Elms job?"

Ellison, also rising, clapped a palm to his forehead. "Christ. I'd forgotten. We just hit them last year. Where'd we get that lead?"

"An anonymous call. But you can be goddamn sure it came from their competition. And we'll hear about it if we don't go out on it soon."

Wilder was driving on the Pasadena Freeway.

"Maybe if we wind up Green Elms quick we can catch the San Marino address on the way in."

"Fine. Everything's all set in Pasadena?"

"Yeah. The crew will be in place"—he glanced at his wristwatch—"about right now."

"Has anyone checked it out? Maybe we're on a wild goose chase."

Wilder snorted. "How we going to check it out? Those wetbacks can spot an immigration man a mile away. If we checked them out, when we got there the place would be empty."

Wilder drove slowly up to the sanitarium. He saw the three other cars of agents parked randomly on the street in front. He nodded at each as he went by, then pulled up directly in front of the main entrance. He and Ellison got out and went to the front door. Before entering they turned and saw the other agents approaching, two stopping to question a gardener.

Inside the lobby all was quiet, as befitted an old folks' rest home. They approached the reception desk. A girl in her twenties looked up, speaking in a quiet voice.

"Can I help you?"

Wilder and Ellison produced their identification.

"We're from the immigration service, miss," Wilder said. "We have to question some of your employees here."

The girl looked shocked. She pressed a button and spoke into an intercom. "Mrs. Linden, I think you'd better come to the front desk . . ."

Wilder and Ellison waited patiently, and in a few moments Mrs. Linden appeared. She was in her late fifties, slender and stern, and her eyes narrowed when she recognized Wilder and Ellison. "What's the meaning of this?" she hissed, trying to keep her voice down.

"I'm sorry, Mrs. Linden. We have to question some of your employees. We have a man at each exit. We can do it with your cooperation or without."

Mrs. Linden stood rooted, her fury poorly concealed.

"Who told you to come here? It was the Fairgrove Nursing Home, wasn't it?"

"That doesn't matter, Mrs. Linden," Wilder said. "We have to check . . ."

At that moment a janitor came down the hall with a large pushbroom. The man was small, dark, unmistakably of Latin descent. Wilder and Ellison stepped to him. Mrs. Linden followed and stood, seething. "I'm sorry, señor," Wilder said to the janitor in Spanish, flashing his identification. "We're with immigration. Papers, please?"

The janitor's jaw dropped open. "I have my papers at my home."

"Well, we'll have to ask you to come with us . . ."

A door opened and a youth of perhaps eighteen came out of a room, wearing a white uniform and carrying a bedpan. Ellison stepped to him, accosting him in the same manner.

At the end of the hall another door opened and several white-uniformed persons appeared, followed by agents who had been in the parked cars. "Got five here, Wilder," one agent called.

A skirmish almost developed when one employee refused to answer a question, shouting loudly he was a Chicano and they'd better not violate his civil rights. Within minutes eighteen sanitarium employees were filing out the door in custody, to be taken to the Federal Building in vans.

It was then that Mrs. Linden turned her wrath on Wilder and Ellison. "You have no right to do this. How am I supposed to run a sanitarium with no help. What am I supposed to do?"

"The same as other rest homes do, Mrs. Linden."

"There are dozens, hundreds of other rest homes that hire these people. Why pick on me? *Twice in a year?*"

"Give us the names of those you suspect of employing illegal aliens and we'll look into it."

They started to leave, but Mrs. Linden stayed with them.

"I'm going to start proceedings against you. Illegal trespass, illegal search, discrimination . . ."

Wilder stopped and cut her off. "Look, Mrs. Linden. You're damn lucky you're not being charged with harboring illegal aliens . . ."

"How was I to know any of them were here illegally? Law forbids my discriminating on the basis of . . ."

"Mrs. Linden, I'll tell you something and you'd better shut up and listen. You get a thousand bucks a month for each of these old folks you keep here. Then you hire these poor wetbacks for next to nothing to empty the bedpans and bathe them."

She was screaming. "Well, how am I supposed to bathe them *now?*"

"The same way other rest homes do. Hire American citizens to work for you."

"They want three, four, five dollars an hour, and then they sit on their butts, hoping to get fired so they can go on welfare. I'm telling you I'm having you charged with illegal entry . . ."

"You're not having anybody charged with anything. And I'll tell you why. All those poor wetbacks you pay a dollar and a half an hour, I happen to know you take out Social Security, federal taxes, unemployment insurance, only you don't send it in. You keep it. Because you know these people are illegal and will never claim what's theirs. So you keep it. And *that,* Mrs. Linden, is a serious offense that can send you to prison, and the next time I have to waste the taxpayers' money to come out here and pick them up, I'll see to it your books are looked into. Now, if you don't want the health authorities to close you down, you'd better call the state unemployment office and get some help out here to bathe these senior citizens and empty their bedpans. Agent Ellison and I will drop around next week to see how you're doing."

The last Wilder and Ellison saw of her she was standing in the doorway, her face white, her bony knuckles trembling with rage.

On the drive back to downtown Los Angeles, Wilder and Ellison were pensive. "Oh, by the way, are we going to go by San Marino and see that . . . what's her name? The girl Huerta reported?" Ellison asked.

Wilder glanced at his watch. "Oh, Christ. We don't have time today. Might as well give her another day or two of washing diapers and cleaning toilets. Probably some poor little Indian broad from Yucatán, happy as hell she can earn her keep and thirty bucks a week and watch the Mexican television station every night. We'll check her out first chance. Right now we got a lot of wetbacks to process."

Anastacia finished arranging the fresh-cut flowers in the entryway and then went into the kitchen, where Amelia was working.

"We'll be using the Persian china for eight tonight," she told her in Spanish, "and the Damascus crystal."

"Sí, yo entiendo," Amelia replied obediently.

Anastacia took her knee-length trenchcoat from a chair where she'd left it. She was buckling the belt when Meme came in.

"Tacha, did you say you're taking Paul to do your shopping with you?"

"Yes. If that's all right. He said he had something to talk to me about. And when I said I had to shop for tonight, he asked to go along."

Meme seemed to digest this a moment. Then she said, "Do you know what he wants to talk to you about?"

"No."

"Tell me the truth. Don't you have an idea?"

"Well . . . I guess he thinks I was offended the other night. He said some things about wetbacks and he was shocked when I said I was one too. Guess he wants to apologize, but there's no need to."

"No, I don't think that's it. He wants to hire you away from me."

Anastacia smiled, bewildered. "Hire me . . . ? What could *I* do for him?"

"Lots, don't you know that? But you must promise me this. If he does offer you a job, please consider it carefully."

Anastacia shook her head unbelievingly. "You . . . you can't mean that, Meme. Leave you? After all I've . . ."

"Tacha dear, listen to me. This is a dead-end job, and you know it. God knows, I could never replace you. But whatever Paul has to say to you, consider it."

"What makes you so sure he's going to offer me a job?"

"I just know. From the questions he's asked me about you. You're very young but in a way you're far beyond your years. I don't know just what you'd be getting into with Paul, but I'm sure you'd handle it well."

Anastacia thought a moment. "Well, I don't think I'd be interested in being a secretary for Paul Foster and his advertising firm. I'm very happy here."

"Yes, but you won't be for long. I know you've enjoyed taking classes evenings, learning the way things are in this house, but I know your type. It'll be old to you soon, and eventually I'll lose you one way or another."

At that moment the horn of the limousine sounded, a liberty Ruel took only when he was driving other members of the household staff.

"All right, Tacha," Meme said, dismissing her. "Go have your talk with Paul. I'll be expecting the worst of news when you get back."

Anastacia pressed her arm around Meme's shoulder as she went past her toward the front entrance. "Don't be silly, Meme," she said.

Still a little taken aback by the possibility of an offer from Paul, Anastacia made herself aware of the utter grandeur and grace of the de Beauclair home. The polished oak doors were magnificent, and she asked herself as she walked through and reached out to close them if she felt they were hers. No, she didn't.

At the foot of the half-dozen brick steps leading down to the driveway, Ruel waited with the rear door of the limousine open. She regarded him as she went by. She'd never really paid much attention to him. She knew that in her beige trenchcoat, which wasn't needed now but would come in handy later in the day, she was a woman who caused men to stare. But Ruel didn't stare. Neither did he avert his eyes guiltily, the way many men did when they felt it improper to absorb her with their eyes.

"Can we pick up Paul Foster at his office on Wilshire? He's expecting us," she said.

"Sure thing, Tacha," he replied.

She wondered how Ruel felt about working for Meme. Ruel was late fortyish, scrawny-limbed, with thin gray hair, and he seemed content living in the room above the garage. The glass partition separating the driver's area was down, as was usual when he was driving house staff.

"Ruel, what do you do in your spare time?" she asked on impulse. She realized she knew very little about him, that perhaps he wanted it that way.

He reacted with some surprise, and she saw him looking at her in the mirror.

"Me? I don't have much spare time, what with cleaning the driveway and keeping the bucket of bolts polished."

"Yes you do. Sometimes days go by when we hardly need you, and most evenings you're free, except when I have a class."

He laughed a little. "Oh, I hang out at a bar down on San Gabriel Boulevard. Why?"

"I just wondered. Don't you get tired of your job?"

"Why should I get tired of it? I watch television. Go to the bar."

"What do you do at the bar?"

"Meet with guys I know. Drink. Look for babes to pick up."

She started to laugh but thought better of it. "Do you find any?"

"I'm always trying."

There was a silence and he drove in his rather majestic manner that befitted a car such as they were riding in. He was watching her in the mirror. "You seem surprised."

"I don't know why I should be. It's just that . . . you've never shown such tendencies toward me. Or anyone in the house."

"As I said, I like my job."

She mulled this over a few moments. "If you saw me in your bar, and didn't know me, would you try to pick me up?"

He paused before answering. "No."

"No? Why not?"

"Don't play games with me, Tacha. You know I'm not in your league by a long shot."

"What do you mean?"

"I mean, the babes I pick up are usually over the hill. My age a few years one way or the other. Usually the other. They're divorced, because their old man found a younger broad. They got two, three teenage kids who're giving them all kinds of trouble, they work their asses off at a bank-teller job all day, and when they get tired of daydreaming about Burt Reynolds they go to a bar where they can find a guy like me."

She waited, then said, "A guy like you."

"Yeah, you know. I'm white. I don't have muscular

dystrophy, I got a job, I can buy her a steak and maybe a ten-dollar bottle of hooch, I'm not a bum, you know what I mean?"

She tried to imagine the bar he frequented, the people in it. "Is there a billiard table in the bar?" she asked.

He showed surprise. "Yeah. Fact is, I'm on the championship team. You know the place?"

"No. And you wouldn't even . . . approach me if you saw me in there?"

"Like I say, Tacha, you're way outa my league. Water seeks its own level."

But she was thinking of another tavern, on a dirt road that ran through a little town, where wiry men came to drink beer and wine after they'd fought all day trying to raise crops or animals in the desert or killed sharks and set lobster traps, where they came to play billiards by kerosene lantern or gaslight, and women came there too, and no one thought about water seeking its own level. Or perhaps they did.

Paul Foster was waiting on the sidewalk in front of his office building as the limousine pulled up to the curb. Ruel started to get out but Foster stayed him with a hand on the arm.

"I'll get it," he said, opening the rear door and getting in beside Anastacia. "Hey, you look good."

"You look good too, Paul," she said. She appraised him, his immaculate clothes, of material that always looked as though it had just been pressed, the carefully chosen colors of his slacks and coat, the tie that blended, and the off-white shirt, making it all seem as though it were one piece.

"Ruel, please go to Grand Central first."

Ruel nodded. She explained to Foster, "I'm getting some things for Amelia and me first. Now, you said you had something to talk to me about."

He took her hand in his and was surprised at how firm and full it felt. "You have strong hands," he remarked.

"I earned them."

"You told Ruel to drive to Grand Central Market. The one on Broadway, downtown?"

"Uh-huh."

"Don't you and Amelia shop at the same market you go to for Meme?"

"No. We . . . at least she, prefers other kinds of food."

The limousine circled the block and headed toward downtown Los Angeles. Foster looked with obvious pleasure at the surroundings. Complexes of high-rise office buildings mixed with carefully landscaped plazas to create a luxurious atmosphere.

"You like it over here? On Wilshire Boulevard?"

"Yes, I like it fine."

"It's another world over here, Tacha."

"I can imagine."

"Do you think you'd like to work here?"

"You're offering me a job?"

"Right."

"Why?"

"Well, I could give you lots of reasons. Such as, you deserve a chance at something with a future. And I'd really be giving you a chance. And reasons like, you shouldn't have to be involved with housework all your life. But actually, I think my corporation needs you."

"What would I be doing?"

"I'm starting some new projects. I have to bring in some new talent. I want a woman. One who looks like you."

"You mean has sex appeal."

"Yes, that's part of it. In the public-relations business looks mean a lot. Followed by charm and personality. Followed by brains. Fortunately, you've got them all."

"Your priorities are weird, Paul."

"Well, I'm sorry. That's the way it is, if you're in this game."

"What makes you think I'd quit Meme?"

He took out a pack of cigarettes and offered her one. She took one and then he took it back, lit it for her himself, and placed it between her kips. Her expression gave no indication as to whether she approved or disapproved of this impetuous act. "Thank you," she said evenly.

"I think," he said, lighting his own cigarette, "that you'd love having an apartment of your own. Your own car. Your own telephone, television. Maybe even your own maid."

His last sentence made her stop and contemplate, a little amused. "It sounds nice. But, you know, I don't have it too bad right now."

"I know. But that's the easy way. Making all your own decisions is what's tough."

"Suppose I did. What about you and me?"

He inhaled, and then stared at the burning end of his cigarette. "I'm a single man. Of course, I hope something could develop between us. I need you. And I think my company needs you. Either one—or both—I can't lose."

The people who happened to be at the parking-lot entrance on North Broadway stopped and stared as the sleek limousine with its uniformed driver glided noiselessly in and Ruel opened the door for Anastacia and Foster.

The conversation about the job offer was held in abeyance by tacit agreement while they went to Grand Central Market. The street was not new to Foster, but the store was.

"Everybody's heard of the place, but I've never been inside," he remarked as they pushed their way through the throngs of shoppers milling about. "It's really fantastic."

She went to a produce bin and spoke to the man behind the counter in Spanish. Foster watched through the glass as the man shoveled a bag full of black objects and handed it to Anastacia.

"What in the world are those?" he asked.

She took a handful and held them out. "Black beans. Frijol negro. You've never seen them?"

"No. They look just like regular beans, except they're pitch black. What do they taste like?"

Anastacia was moving on, he following. "Pretty much like the pink or pinto. But they're prepared differently."

"And you prefer these?"

"Not particularly. But Amelia thinks she can't live without them."

She stopped in front of the butcher counter and watched Paul's face as the meat cutter filled her order of raw octopus and tongue of beef.

"How is the octopus cooked?" he asked as they made their way toward the street.

"Fried."

"I've had it raw, in sushi bars, but I've never heard of frying it."

"It's practically a national dish in Mexico. At least in some parts. Amelia loves that too. And I don't mind it."

"I thought you'd eat what Meme eats in her house."

"In Meme's house everybody eats just exactly what they

want to eat. Amelia loves the dishes of the interior of Mexico. I like most of them too."

"But you also like the gourmet dishes Meme has prepared."

She smiled. "Oh, yes. I like those too."

Back in the car Ruel needed no directions to the next stop, and Foster was surprised when the car stopped in front of a large warehouse with no sign on it. He saw other cars like the limousine in the parking lot.

Paul followed Ana through the swinging doors and saw it was a storehouse for fresh produce. The temperature was kept in the low forties, and he was chilled.

"I see why you wore the trenchcoat now."

A man approached carrying a ledger.

"Ah . . ." he fumbled only a moment for the name, "Miss Herrera. Good to see you again. How's Madame de Beauclair?"

"She sends her best, Garth. Here's the list."

Garth took the list and went off down the endless rows of produce in crates, in small boxes of earth, and on spray counters.

A woman in her fifties, slender and with the unmistakable elegance of great wealth was walking by, but suddenly saw Anastacia.

"Tacha, dear!' she said, coming toward them. "How's Meme?"

"She's fine, Mrs. Leonetti. This is my friend Paul Foster."

"Good to meet you," Mrs. Leonetti gushed. "Please give Meme my best. Tell her I'll call her."

Foster was still looking after the woman as he said, "Do you know who that is, Tacha?"

"Yes, I know."

"That's Giovanni Leonetti's wife! The savings and loan man."

"I know, Paul!" She smiled as she mimicked his excitement and he smiled back, a little embarrassed.

At that moment Garth came back with a tray of produce. He held it before Anastacia. "Take a look at the strawberries, Miss Herrera. They're perfect. And the truffles are exceptional."

Anastacia picked up a fist-sized strawberry and squeezed it

gently. "Yes. Give me an extra two pounds of these. But those sprouts are a little pale."

"Yes, I know. But you can bring out the color . . ."

"I know, Garth. The spinach is superb too. A pound or so extra on that, please."

"All rightie," Garth said agreeably. "Will you want to see the fresh crab and ricotta?"

"No, I don't need to."

Garth turned and disappeared along the rows of chilled produce and soon reappeared with a ledger. "Sign here, Miss Herrera. It's all in the trunk of your car."

As they got into the limousine Foster said, "Wow, so that's how the super rich live. They have a whole different world."

"Yes. Different from Wilshire Boulevard. Meme's house is a different world. Ruel, can we go back to Paul's office now?"

With the glass partition sealing off their conversation, Paul continued trying to persuade Anastacia to take his job offer. A few times she seemed to entertain the idea, but wound up by saying, "Please, Paul. I don't want to say no right now." He looked a little hurt, and he lit a cigarette and placed it between her lips, leaning toward her.

"And I'll never come to work for you if you're going to do that with my cigarette during office hours."

His hurt was more pronounced. "Why? Don't you like it?"

The car was in front of his office building and Ruel was holding the door open for him. He got out but stood facing her, waiting for her to answer. She puffed on the cigarette and held it between her fingers. "That turns me on, Paul," she said, shaking her head as she looked at him evenly. "It makes me feel closer to you than I want to."

His face broke into a broad grin. "Anastacia Herrera, you've made my day. I'll look forward to hearing from you."

"Good-bye, Paul."

Ruel drove to the service entrance at the rear and Anastacia went into the house, leaving the groceries to him. Meme de Beauclair was in the breakfast nook, having coffee.

"Sit down, sit down, Tacha, and tell me what Paul had to say."

Anastacia sat, and Amelia set a cup of coffee before her, then busied herself at the sink. When Meme would just as soon Amelia not understand, they spoke English. Anastacia related the gist of the afternoon's exchange, and added, "Actually, he was rather vague, and I made no promises."

"Well, I think you should seriously consider it. I mean, who could blame you for looking for something with a possible future . . ."

At that moment the chimes sounded, announcing someone at the front entry. "I'll get it," Anastacia said, rising.

When she opened the door, it was with foreboding that she assessed the situation. Two men stood there, dressed in business suits. Their countenance conveyed a measure of official authority and they looked as though they regretted their job required they do something unpleasant.

"Is this the de Beauclair residence?" one asked, stumbling somewhat over the pronunciation of the name.

"Yes, it is. Can I help you?"

Simultaneously, they opened their wallets to show identification. "We're with the immigration service. Are you the head of the house?"

Anastacia fumbled for words, trying to collect her thoughts.

"No . . . no, I'm not. Who . . . what did you . . ."

It was with great relief that she felt Meme beside her.

"I'm Mrs. de Beauclair. May I help you gentlemen?" And Meme had risen to the occasion; a lioness ready to defend her cub.

One of the men addressed her, "I'm Agent Wilder and this is Agent Ellison. We're with the immigration service . . ."

"And what do you want here?" Meme demanded. Anastacia knew she was trying some kind of delaying action. She stepped back to let Meme handle it, feeling the color drain from her face, her knees turn weak and shaky.

Wilder, the spokesman for the pair, knew he was dealing with a tough customer, but he'd been through all this many times. "We have reliable information that you may be, knowingly or otherwise, harboring an illegal alien," and his face looked as though he were waiting for a firecracker to go off.

"I beg your pardon," Meme said deliberately, taking off her glasses the better to view this . . . this working man.

"I said, Mrs. Day . . . Daybow . . . clar," he glanced at a pad, "that we have reliable information you may be harboring an illegal alien. You may be unaware of that person's status, we're not accusing you, understand. But we have to check these things out . . ."

Meme still stood in the doorway, twirling her glasses by the stem in one hand, one hip thrown out in an attitude of belligerence. She spoke English with an exaggerated accent, also very rapidly. "And just where, may I ask, did you get this so-called reliable information?"

"I can't tell you that, ma'am. Or madam, I guess . . ."

"And *don't* call me 'madam.' The way you pronounce that word it definitely has another meaning."

Wilder knew he must appear crude, but he also knew he represented the United States government. "Well, I'm sorry, Mrs. de Beauclair, but we must insist on interviewing any possible illegal aliens here."

"Do you have a warrant?"

"It's complicated, ma . . . lady, but I don't believe we need one if we have probable cause for suspicion . . ."

Meme was relenting but arrogant. "I know all about your probable cause. All right, give me the name of the person you're looking for and if that person is here I'll summon him or her."

Anastacia realized that Meme was not sure if they were after herself or Amelia, and whichever one they wanted, did not want to jeopardize the other.

Wilder referred to his pad again. "We're looking for one Anastacia Herrera of Ensenada, Baja California. Is she here, and if so, would you please take us to her."

Meme was momentarily at a loss for words, and Anastacia saw that prolonging the confrontation would only place Amelia in jeopardy. They evidently were looking for just one wetback.

She put a hand on Meme's arm and stepped forward. "I am Anastacia Herrera," she said.

The agents looked surprised. "You're Miss Herrera?"

"Yes, she is," Meme was at them again. "You're surprised, aren't you? You wouldn't suspect her because she looks elegant and doesn't cringe like the others you chase through back alleys every day. Oh, I read the papers, and . . ."

"Please, Meme," Anastacia said, then to the agents, "I'm Anastacia Herrera."

"Are you from Ensenada?"

She nodded, defeated, afraid. "Ensenada, Baja California."

"I'm sorry, miss. We'll have to ask you to come with us."

She looked at them, then at Meme, then back at the immigration men. "Where will you take me? What will happen to me?"

"We'll have to take you downtown. To the Federal Building. You'll have the right to legal representation and you can have a fair and impartial hearing if you think your rights are being violated, or you can choose to have no hearing and choose voluntary deportation with no criminal charges filed."

Meme addressed Anastacia in Spanish. "Tacha, let me handle this and do as . . ."

Wilder cut her off politely. "It's only fair to warn you, Mrs. de Beauclair, that my fellow agent and I are bilingual."

"True," the other agent said in Spanish, as though to verify this. "We both speak and understand Spanish fluently."

Meme held her glasses by the stem between her teeth, standing with her hands on her hips. "All right," she conceded, "but can't this girl go change and get a few things?"

Anastacia had regained some composure. "Yes, may I? There are . . . a few things I'll need."

The agents understood the implications of her request. "Yes, but one of us should go with you . . ."

Meme exploded. "One of you should go with her to her room to watch her dress? Listen, she's going with you willingly, and if you two are going to act like two-bit TV cops in my home . . ."

Anastacia cut her off gently. "Please. I'll only be a moment. My room's just upstairs."

The agents looked at one another and acquiesced. "All right. But you'll have to return within two or three minutes or we'll have to . . ."

Meme turned to Anastacia, and to the surprise of the agents, spoke to her at length in French. This upset and unnerved them considerably, but before they could say anything Anastacia turned and ran lightly up the stairs.

Meme kept the agents occupied at the door, badgering them, then listening with some compassion to their explanations and justifications of the actions their profession demanded.

When after a minute or so they saw the long, sleek

limousine come around from the rear of the house and pass a few feet from them, the darkened windows revealing nothing in the rear, Meme said, "My chauffeur is going to get my husband. Please wait. He'll want to hear what you have to say."

And when another several minutes had passed and there was no sign of anyone else in the house, the agents looked at each other and demanded to look upstairs.

"Go ahead," Meme said lightly. "When you've searched the house, I'll be in the kitchen. If the girl is gone, I'm sorry. I can't keep her here by force."

CHAPTER 15

The transition from the de Beauclair mansion to the Fuentes' screened-in rear porch was less traumatic than Anastacia had expected. She had long wanted to get better acquainted with the giant barrio of Los Angeles; now she was having her chance—though the circumstances were not what she would have chosen.

She had brought Amelia with her, but Amelia had taken a factory job in the downtown garment district almost immediately, and she soon found her own place to live, while Anastacia stayed on, doing housework for the Fuentes family in return for her room and board.

She enjoyed having little or nothing to do during most of the day, when the younger children were at school and the Fuentes were at work. In the evening she went out with them, sometimes to a nice restaurant, frequently to a tavern, where they danced and listened to a mariachi that switched from Mexican folk songs to Latin rock on an instant's notice.

The house was a block from Brooklyn Avenue, which ran for miles from near downtown Los Angeles through the Spanish-speaking barrio within and contiguous to the city limits.

Two weeks passed, and she still didn't know what to do. She wondered how the immigration people had learned of her presence at Meme's. She didn't like the idea of calling there. She had little contact outside her immediate surroundings, as there might be risk involved in contacting those who had helped her. She was reluctant to correspond with her parents until she better understood the practices of the immigration service.

Well, there was no rush to make decisions. When the opportunity came, she would establish herself someplace, and when it was safe, she would re-establish her acquaintances and somehow be in touch with Margarito. And Paul . . .

On a warm midafternoon Anastacia left the house on Barnhart Street and walked to the corner. She turned east on First, strolling leisurely. A woman in her forties was herding three small children ahead of her, threatening one who was evidently the troublemaker. "Raúl, I'll twist your ear good for you if you do that again to your sister." The boy paid her scant attention, being safely out of reach and obviously more agile.

Anastacia entered the supermarket, did her shopping carefully, recalling the days she shopped at another kind of store. She waited in line while a woman who spoke no English paid with food stamps. The checker painstakingly explained to the woman that some of the items had to be paid for in cash. The monolingual shopper considered this information at length, then said, "All right, I won't take those things." Patiently, the checker called a box boy to return the items to the shelves.

"They never understand," the checker said to Anastacia as she rang up her purchases.

As Anastacia was returning with the groceries, she looked down a side street and saw considerable commotion a half block away. She stopped, studying the scene. The unmistakable, nondescript sedans used by nonuniformed law-enforcement officials were parked at the curb. Then she saw the vans of the U.S. immigration service arriving. It was evidently a raid on an old duplex apartment and a dozen agents in plain clothes were about, escorting men into the apartment, bringing others out with their possessions.

Hesitantly, Anastacia approached the activity. A small crowd had gathered but was getting bigger by the minute. She fought an impulse to get away from the scene as fast as possible. *No. I haven't yet been reduced to scurrying through back alleys.*

The agents were shouting to one another, keeping an eye on the crowd of dark faces watching. "Okay, Ralph. Let him get his sewing machine. If it's portable. Red! How many's that make? Twelve? We got twenty-five then. Jesus! How'd they all live in two rooms?!"

No guns were drawn, but each agent was armed with a

pistol in a shoulder holster. The men being rounded up were sullen, none appeared terrified, and none offered resistance. Some were wearing ragged clothes, others had on working attire. As she watched, two low-slung cars, old but impeccably restored, idled down the street and stopped. Nearly a dozen youths in their early twenties or less got out, approaching the scene. The agents cast leary glances at the new arrivals, who joined the crowd watching the activity.

One of the youths shouldered through to be nearest the agents. "Hey man!" he shouted in the English vernacular of the bilingual barrio. "You assholes having a field day, huh?"

The agents, writing on clipboards and escorting arrestees, ignored him. "Motherfuckers, why don't you pick on us?" another shouted menacingly, thumping his chest. "Go on. Ask me for my papers. Ask all of us. We all speak Spanish too!"

The youths had moved forward so that they were all but impeding the agents' actions. "Why don't you hassle the Japs down on First Street?" another said belligerently. "Or the Jews over in Beverly Hills. We know you're scared of the niggers in Watts."

"Pinchi gabachos," another youth cursed loudly, "why don't you go back to Germany? Our people were here first. You're the invaders!"

One agent stopped to address the youths, who were inching forward, and Anastacia gasped as she recognized him as one of the men who had come for her at the de Beauclair mansion. "We have no quarrel with you," he said to the youths, doing his best to disregard the mounting hostility, "we're federal officers. We have a job to do for the federal government. If any of you interfere, we'll have to arrest you."

Anastacia saw the agent nod over their heads to someone behind the crowd. Turning, she saw another agent at a car with the radio microphone in his hand. She could make out the words, "Request local police help. We have a dangerous situation developing . . ."

The militant Chicano youths continued their heckling, becoming bolder and more offensive in their racial slurs and profanity, and at that moment Agent Wilder looked directly at her. She returned his gaze evenly, but she felt her heart pounding. Standing there, holding a bag of groceries, obviously living within walking distance, she felt . . . caught. But he looked at her for only a few seconds, and then turned his attention away, having given no indication he recognized her.

She stood rooted. He *must* have recognized her. Then she realized why he would make no move to apprehend her. Well he must know what the reaction of the militant youths would be if one agent were suddenly to single out a girl such as herself, an apparent bystander, to arrest on a public street. And she suddenly felt a deep camaraderie for these brave . . . low riders, they were called, who had delivered her by their taunting words and hostile presence, just as surely as Meme de Beauclair had by telling her in French to take the limousine and get away.

Her mind began working fast. In a moment, local police would arrive to calm the situation. And if Agent Wilder had indeed recognized her, he would then have the opportunity to pursue his interrogation of her safely.

She turned, not quickly, and began walking down the street, still carrying that bag of groceries that must have told Agent Wilder so much. She saw a black-and-white cruiser round the corner, proceeding toward the scene of the raid with deliberation, light flashing, but no siren sounding. In a moment another police car appeared. Then another. A short block away she glanced back and saw that the controlled show of force by the police had had its effect; the immigration officials were proceeding with their duties, the crowd was watching peacefully.

She turned at the first street, then turned again at the next intersection. Now was Wilder following? Would he come after her on foot? Or in an unmarked car? He was a trained detective; he could follow or have her followed without her knowing. Perhaps he would see where she went, in hopes of catching other wetbacks there. What would they do to the Fuentes family for harboring her? She didn't worry about reprisals aimed at Meme de Beauclair; she had the resources to protect herself; but would they put the Fuentes family in jail? She couldn't lead the agents there. She got to Brooklyn Avenue and turned west, somehow feeling safer among the throngs on the sidewalks. She wanted to lose herself among them. Two old men sat talking in Spanish on a bench at the corner bus stop. She approached them.

"Here," she said to one, in Spanish, hurriedly handing him the bag of groceries, "I can't use these." The old man looked at her with suspicious surprise, and she turned and walked away. She felt less encumbered without the groceries. She walked, block after block, trying to see if she was being followed by looking at the reflections in the storefront windows. She couldn't tell. Well, either she was, or she wasn't. She had to decide to do something. A pay telephone hung on a store wall. She went to it, taking a coin from her purse. She inserted it and dialed a three-digit number. "Yes, operator, the listing, please, for Foster Advertising. On Wilshire Boulevard."

Anastacia stepped out of the elevator on the fifth floor and paused to look around. She saw that Foster Advertising occupied the entire floor, and large swinging glass doors marked the main entryway. She pushed them open and approached two young women who doubled as switchboard operators and receptionists. One of them looked up at her questioningly.

"Hi. I'm Anastacia Herrera. I guess I'm going to work here . . ."

The girl nodded, smiling and extending her hand.

"We're expecting you. Welcome aboard. Just a second. I'll have someone walk you back to Mr. Foster's office."

She inserted a jack and spoke briefly. Within seconds another girl appeared from the maze of offices beyond the switchboard.

"Hi, I'm Jackie. You . . . do we call you Anastacia?"

"Tacha, for short."

"Come with me. Mr. Foster's expecting you."

The corridor down which she followed Jackie was lined with desks near office doors, and Anastacia noticed she attracted a minimum of attention. The dozen or so women were mostly under thirty, she noticed, and attire was chosen to combine the maximum in smart fashion with sex appeal. The plaques on the doors indicated these were the offices of vice presidents, associates, and account executives; Paul Foster's was the only door without a plaque title.

Foster was seated behind an enormous desk. He looked up as they entered.

"Tacha!" he said, rising and coming around the desk. He

took her hand warmly. Jackie exited without being told and Paul Foster closed the door behind her.

"How are you, Paul?" she asked.

"Fine, fine. Please sit down." He returned to his high-back chair. "Well, how do you like the looks of Foster Advertising?"

"It's unbelievable. Exciting. You must feel you've really created something."

"You're all settled in your new place?"

"Yes. I love it."

"You have your driver's license?"

She smiled. "It was easy, just as you said. No questions."

"And you're all set to go to work here."

A pensive pause. "I suppose so."

"'Suppose'?"

"I don't know exactly what's expected of me."

Paul laughed lightly. "You made it all clear. You said you're not looking for a wealthy husband. Then you said '*necessarily.*' And you won't be a working mistress. You just want to get ahead."

"And I don't want to get into any sticky situations."

"And I promised you wouldn't. You must think places like this"—he made a sweeping gesture—"are a hotbed of . . ."

She smiled quickly and finished for him, "Sexual activity. Yes, I do."

He turned in his chair. "And how did you put it the other night? You won't be thrust into a competitive situation with some little secretary who has her sights set on me."

"Is that what I said?"

"More or less. I told you, Tacha, I'm a square shooter. I'm hiring you because I believe Foster Advertising can use your talents."

They regarded one another a moment, and their mutual admiration was obvious.

"I didn't see Donna when I came in."

"She has her own office. Just as you will."

Anastacia sat thinking a moment. "Okay. I'm ready to start."

"Good." He pressed a button. "Get your office arranged to your satisfaction." He glanced at his watch. "Then let's go to lunch at noon. I'll give you your first assignment then." There was a light rap on the door. "Come in, Jackie." Jackie opened the door, "Jackie, be a dear and show Tacha her office. Then give her the tour. Supplies, and all that, and Tacha, I'll meet you at the switchboard in two hours."

The Wilshire Continental Restaurant bustled with quiet activity as they entered. The carpeting was plush, woven tapestries hung from the walls. They paused only briefly at the waiting area, and a headwaiter approached.

"Mr. Foster. Good to see you," he said.

Paul Foster presented Anastacia. "Kenneth, this is Anastacia Herrera. She's new with us, and she'll be a regular, we hope."

Kenneth bent ever so slightly at the middle. "Very pleased to meet you, Miss Herrera." He looked at Foster. "How many will there be?"

"Three, anyway. Maybe more. I'm expecting Emery."

"Right this way. I'll bring him to you when he comes in." Kenneth led them to a crescent booth. "The usual?" he asked when they were seated. Foster nodded. "And Miss Herrera?"

She shrugged, "I'll have the usual also, if it's ladylike."

A protrusion from the wall above their heads proved to contain a work light, and Foster switched it on, placing a folder on the table. She saw the entire establishment was geared to the working executive, and there were many luncheon conferences under way. Foster opened the folder.

"Here's what I want you to do first. See this letter?"

She took it and read it swiftly, then nodded at him.

"Well, that's the pitch for a new service we're offering our clients. It's self-explanatory. We send out a letter to every client, telling about this, how the demand for it has made us move in this direction, and all that. We have the typing machines that individualize the mailing list. Know what I mean?"

"So the clients think they're getting personal attention."

"Right. Only thing is, everybody's wise to that. So here's a list of all our account executives and associates," he handed her the list, "all in our office. I want the personal touch for every client. Like if Account Executive LeRoy Geotz—you'll meet him later—if he met a certain client in Las Vegas last time out, it'd be nice if we started his letter something like, 'Dear Klottzenbach: Remind me not to go to Vegas with you next time. I dropped three big ones, and I seem to remember

ANOTHER LAND

you did worse. By the way, Klottzie, we're offering a new service, because of demand . . .' and then we get right to the meat of it, and let the typing machines take it over. Jackie will show you the mechanics of it."

She had taken brief notes as he talked. A waitress in continental peasant costume arrived with the drinks.

"What I really want, Tacha, is for you to do this thing, and figure out the most efficient way of applying this to *all* our correspondence. Take your time. Maybe when an account exec or associate comes back from out of town, he should be debriefed, concerning all he talked to and about what, who he went to a nightclub with. Maybe he should just hand in some notes. Or perhaps you can come up with a form he can fill out. But I don't want each one wasting a half day or so trying to personalize his correspondence two or three weeks later when we need to make contact."

She still took notes. "Shouldn't be impossible."

"And *then,*" Foster went on, "when you have it all down to the most efficient way possible, pick one of our girls who you think can handle it on a permanent basis and make the operation part of our system."

"And that shouldn't be hard."

He put his hand to his forehead. "You don't know. You see, we pick girls for their appearance and presentability. They're all sharp, sexpots. Right?"

She nodded. "That was very apparent."

"Well, when you go for that type, and it's essential in this business, you sacrifice other qualities. They're all so vain I had to have the mirrors on the fifth floor removed."

Anger flared in her eyes. "Paul, you're really . . ." But at that moment Emery arrived, and almost simultaneously the waitress brought him his usual drink.

"Paul, Paul," Emery said, "I hope I'm not too late."

"No, no," Paul said. "Emery, this is Anastacia. Tacha for short. Emery is our chief account exec. I've briefed him on how you fit into our organization."

"Welcome aboard, Tacha," Emery said, shaking hands with her and nodding sincerely. "I'm famished. What are you two having?"

Almost magically, Kenneth was tableside with three menus. They took them and pondered the contents. Emery wrinkled his brow. "What's that third thing there? *Filet*

... *de boeuf* ... *aux* ... *sh* ... *cha* ... *champignons* ... why the Christ don't they print them in English?"

"Because then people wouldn't think they were getting their money's worth," Paul Foster said. He looked knowingly at Anastacia, and when she didn't respond he raised his eyebrows, coaxing. Obviously he wanted her to show off her knowledge of French. She looked at him evenly, giving the slightest negative shake of the head. Foster dropped his eyes and thought for a moment.

"I think that's steak and mushrooms," he said.

"Well, why the hell don't they say so? Sounds good to me." Emery handed the menu to the waitress. Foster and Anastacia ordered the same.

CHAPTER 16

Amelia Moreno sat sewing the cuffs on shirt sleeves at her machine as she had been doing for many months. At least fifty other girls sat at machines doing similar tasks in the second-floor garment factory in downtown Los Angeles.

All but a handful of the seamstresses were illegal aliens from Mexico; the others were either from other Spanish-speaking backgrounds, or were Asian. She was paid by the number of pieces she completed, and in some ways she liked it this way. There were no serious objections when she took a day or an afternoon off, as it cost the employer nothing.

Periodically, the factory was raided by U.S. Immigration and Naturalization Service agents, and more often than not, it was practically a clean sweep, leaving only a few workers who could produce proof of citizenship or show documents legalizing their presence. Then the factory bosses would place a call to someone south of the border offering to finance the smuggling of a new batch of I.A.'s.

As she worked she chatted in Spanish with the woman at the next machine.

"Do you ever hear from the girl you lived with who disappeared? What was her name? Tacha, was it?"

"Sí," Amelia replied, turning the material to a different angle. "She called. I thought she had maybe run off with a man, but on the way home from the market one day she ran into a migra raid and one of the agents recognized her, so she was afraid to come home."

"Where did she go?"

"Oh, Tacha is lucky. She speaks English perfectly. She called the other day and said she had a job with a fancy company in the rich financial district. As a head secretary or something. She always has good jobs. She was the head maid when I worked for the rich French woman."

"You were a maid for a rich woman? Did you like that job?"

Amelia finished and took another shirt to begin work on. "It was the best job I ever had. I had my own room, with my own television set. I got to eat whatever I wanted free. It was a dream job. But"—she sighed as she put yet another piece of material in place—"la migra again. They came one day and, oh, it was *so* funny." Amelia laughed, recalling. "While the French señora was arguing with the migra agents at the door, she told Tacha to take me and escape in the limousine with the chauffeur. She said it in French so the agents didn't know. They thought Tacha was packing her things to go with them, and we got away right in front of them."

A buzzer sounded announcing the lunch break, and the garment factory suddenly was emptying. Amelia liked to buy her lunch at a quick-food stand nearby. She walked down the stairs and out of the building onto the street. The lunch break in the garment-manufacturing district of downtown Los Angeles was a reassuring thing to her. Literally thousands of women such as herself, ranging in age from teenagers to elderly, suddenly took to the sidewalks. At least nine of every ten persons looked Latin American. The men and boys working the lunch counters, the parking-lot attendants, the janitors, the clerks, the shop owners, all spoke in Spanish and all went about their business with a slightly fearful and expectant air. Undoubtedly, Amelia knew, there must be a sizable proportion who had legal status here, but who? It seemed those who did have legal status deliberately did nothing to make the fact apparent, in this way tacitly protecting the tens of thousands who had no documents. She enjoyed the safety of numbers. An immigration raid in this district meant only that the garment factory would stop production a few days, and then word would get out they were hiring, and one way or another a flood of available workers would appear.

She started walking down the crowded sidewalk toward a hotdog stand and was suddenly aware a man had fallen in step beside her. She stopped, facing him, fearful, looking about for reassurance of the passersby. The man faced her.

"Amelia Moreno?" he asked.

She was still afraid. "What do you want?"

"I am a friend of Anastacia Herrera. I must find her."

"I don't know where she is. What do you want with her?"

The man looked sincere. "I have a message for her. I know she is dodging the migra." He paused, looking around warily. "We all are. But I have an important message. About a job."

Amelia still didn't trust him. "Who are you?"

"I'm a friend of her family."

"Tacha has a good job already."

The man was a little exasperated. "Look, I'm doing her a favor. This person told me to be sure and give her a message. Do you know where she can be reached?"

Amelia thought a moment. This man was also afraid of the immigration people. It was true she didn't know where Anastacia was, but she had called and left the phone number of the company she worked for, with strict instructions that only in an emergency was it to be given out.

The man was persistent. "I must reach her soon. Or a great opportunity will be lost."

Well, Amelia thought, if he had only her work number, it couldn't do much harm. Anastacia could choose whether to tell him her whereabouts when he called.

"To the merger," Paul Foster said, raising his wine glass. Anastacia smiled from the end of the table and raised hers also. Two of her guests, Carol and Frank Getlin, did likewise.

"Really," Getlin said, "I've never been so sure of a move in my life."

Emery and his date, Gail, also made the toast.

When they had put their glasses down, Gail said, "I don't know what you've got coming for dessert, Ana, but whatever it is, it couldn't top the dinner."

Anastacia laughed, enjoying the compliment. She rose to go to the kitchen. "It's only flan," she said, and at that moment the telephone rang. She stepped to the oak table in the adjoining living-room area and answered it.

Only Paul was watching her face when she heard the voice on the other end. He sat forward.

Anastacia looked stunned, even fearful, and had trouble finding her voice as she turned to her guests.

"I . . . I'm sorry . . . I'll have to take this in the other room. Please excuse me . . ."

The conversation at the dinner table continued lightly, the guests commenting on the apartment and the good taste with which it was furnished.

In a few minutes she returned and Foster could see it was all she could do to maintain her composure.

She attempted to listen to the conversation as they finished dessert and moved into the living-room area, but her distraction was obvious, and when the Getlins suggested it was getting late she said, "Yes, tomorrow is a working day."

Soon Paul Foster was the only remaining guest.

"Tacha, something happened . . ." he said.

She opened the door for him, shaking her head. "Please, Paul. Not now. I . . . I need to be alone."

With exasperation, he attempted to embrace her, but she turned her head. "I'll see you in the morning," she said absently. He stalked out.

She shut the door to the hallway and went into the bedroom. She had jotted a number on a pad on the nightstand and now she dialed it hurriedly.

"Margarito?"

"Sí. Are you alone now?"

"Yes, yes. God, how good it is to hear you."

"It was only luck I happened to call del Rio and got this phone number . . ."

"It was the only thing I could think of. Come over now." She gave the address. "It's a security building. Ring 204 and I'll have to buzz you in. Can you catch a cab?"

"Yes. I'll be there in an hour."

She hung up and tried to analyze her agitation. A lot of reasons, she thought. Now to kill an hour. She could tend to the dinner dishes and then shower. No. That way she might not hear him ring. Shower first.

She was almost through with the dishes when the downstairs door buzzer announced him. She pressed the talk button on the wall.

"Rito?"

"Sí."

She admitted him.

At the door she only momentarily took in his gauntness and loss of weight. He held her close, his mouth on her lips, then her eyes, then her cheeks and ears.

Finally, she pushed him away to see him again.

ANOTHER LAND

"You look tired."

"I should. I've been through a lot."

"You've lost weight."

"You look so beautiful, Tacha," he said, pressing her close to him again. She was quiet a moment, feeling his arms and chest. He started to say something but she pressed a finger to his lips.

"First things first," she said, turning away and pulling him along by the hand. "The bedroom's this way."

An hour later he was lying on his stomach beside her, propped on his elbows, looking down at her. Neither had said a word for some minutes.

"You know what?" he asked, a measure of his boyish casualness returning.

She smiled. "What?" she said, moving suggestively.

"No. No more of that. I have my limits even if you don't. I'm starving to death."

She ran her fingers through his hair.

"Funny that you just thought of it."

He thought a moment. "Yes, it is," he agreed.

She rose and put on a quilted blue bathrobe.

"Come into the kitchen. You're not going to want for anything tonight."

He pulled on only his trousers and followed. He sat at the breakfast table and watched her.

"Pretty nice place you have here," he said, looking around.

"I haven't been here long."

"You must have a pretty good job."

"I do. But let's not talk about that now. God, I've been worried out of my mind. Where have you been? Is there anything new about the Sloane killing? What have you been doing? Are they still looking for you?"

"It's a long story, Tacha. I've been out of my mind also. I . . ."

He stopped as he saw her eyes had suddenly riveted on something behind him. Sudden fear went through him as he realized she was looking at someone else in the room. He turned. She came and stood beside him, a hand on his shoulder. They faced Paul Foster.

"Rito, this is my boss, Paul Foster," she said calmly. "Paul, how did you get in here?"

Foster stood looking at them. Then he held up a set of keys.

"When I rented this apartment for you, Ana, I took the liberty of keeping a set of keys. That is customary, you know."

There was a little silence. Foster and Margarito regarded one another.

Her voice was still calm. "Well, I'm not a customary woman, Paul. Please set the keys on the table and leave."

Foster swung the key set by the chain a moment, then with a bitter smile he set them down and turned. "Okay, Ana. I'll see you around." He turned and went to the door, then paused and turned to them. "And I don't have another set, in case you're worried." He left, closing the door behind him quietly.

She looked at Margarito and he looked at her, and then they laughed. "Does this mean you lost your job?" he asked.

"I don't know. It doesn't matter." She went to the stove and finished piling food on a plate, then she set it in front of him. "There. Will that do for openers?"

"For openers," he said, his mouth already full.

When he opened his eyes sunlight was coming in the window and she was putting the finishing touches on her makeup in front of the mirror. She noticed he was awake.

"Hey," she said, and her voice announced pleasure in looking at him. "I'm going to work. I don't know what will happen, but I have to find out. We'll talk about what we'll do when I get back. Here's a set of keys. I already went through your pockets and saw you have money, so shop for some clothes and get a haircut. There aren't many suspicious police or migra in this neighborhood."

"What time will you be back?"

"I don't know. No later than five-thirty." She came over and sat on the bed. He reached up and pulled her to him. She resisted.

"Not now. You'll muss me."

His hand went beneath the covers. "I'm Thor," he said with a straight face. She remembered and chuckled, grimacing a tiny bit. "So am I," she said. "But we'll get over that."

"When?" he said seriously. She returned his serious look, but then said lightly, "We'll talk when I get back. Be careful."

ANOTHER LAND

As she got to the door, he said, "Does your boss know you're a wetback?"

She paused. "Yes, he does," she said, and left.

The advertising agency was buzzing normally when she entered. The receptionists at their PBX greeted her as usual. She walked down the hall and saw Paul Foster had not yet arrived.

A few minutes after she was seated at her desk a girl came in with a folder.

"The new individualized form letters," she explained, setting them in front of Anastacia. "Let me know if you have any changes in mind."

She looked over the letters and set them down. No, this would never work. She couldn't do this job now. Too much was happening. She forced herself to go over them.

An hour and a half later she was still at her desk trying to concentrate on her work when one of the receptionists came in uncertainly, ushering two men in business suits. Anastacia had never seen them before, but recognized them instantly for what they were.

"Tacha," the girl said hesitantly, "these men insisted . . ."

"I know, Jeannie," Anastacia said with resignation. "It's all right." She stood and approached them.

"Are you Anastacia Herrera?" one asked.

"Yes, I am."

"Are you from . . ."

"I am from Ensenada, Baja California," she said in a flat voice.

"I'm sorry, Miss Herrera, but unless you have something to prove you have legal status in the United States, you'll have to come with us."

She thought a moment. "Are you going to put me in handcuffs?"

They looked at each other. "I don't think that's necessary," one said.

"Thank you," she said, getting her coat from the hanger.

"You may call the payroll department here to make out a check for what you have coming."

"Can I ask who called you?" she asked, picking up the phone.

"I'm sorry. We can't give out informers' identities. Matter

of fact, the caller asked for a different agent, but he wasn't in so we took this one. Shall we go?"

She went with them out of the office, down the hall. The receptionists looked very upset, but said nothing as they passed. At the payroll desk her check was ready within a few minutes.

On the street level they led her to a car. As she got in, one said, "If you like, we'll stop by your home for any personal things you might want . . ."

"You've already checked to see if the company had my home address, didn't you."

"Yes, we did. The secretary said you hadn't gotten around to filling out the papers yet. We get that one all the time."

"No, I don't want to go home first."

CHAPTER 17

Paul Foster walked briskly past the receptionists, nodding a greeting, on his way to his office.

"Oh, Mr. Foster," the girl said.

He stopped. "Yes?"

She got up, putting her headphones down. "I . . . can I talk to you in your office?"

"Sure," he said, leading the way.

When she had closed the door, she began, "Mr. Foster, two men came . . . looking for Tacha. They took her away . . ."

"What?"

"Yes. They said they were from . . . the immigration service."

Foster was thunderstruck. "They came right in here? Into my company offices?"

"Yes."

"And they took her away?"

"Yes. She went with them."

Foster sat thinking. "All right, thank you." The girl left. He pondered a moment, then looked through his desk secretary for a number and punched it out on the phone.

"De Beauclair residence," a voice with a thick Spanish accent said.

"Mrs. de Beauclair, please. Paul Foster calling."

In a moment Meme came on. "Yes, Paul, what can I do for you?"

"Meme, Tacha has just been arrested by the immigration people. They took her away."

"Mon Dieu!" Meme said, genuinely distressed. "What can we do?"

"I don't know, but we'd better do it fast. I understand

when they pick them up they're on the way back to Mexico within hours."

"Well, I'll see if I can do something about that. I know Senator Brand quite well. Many thousands of dollars' worth, in fact. I'll see if he can intercede on her behalf."

"Good, Meme. And I know the biggest trial lawyer in this town. He owes me a big favor. And now's the time to pay up."

"Good, Paul. I'll check back with you later. Keep me informed."

Rogelio Huerta drove up the winding street to the top of the hill that overlooked the city, and parked in the parking lot of the restaurant. He entered and walked through the dining room to the patio and took a seat at a table with a commanding view of Ensenada Bay. He was weary from the long drive down from L.A. and was feeling contented and relaxed. Chief Nachez had not yet arrived for the luncheon date, and Huerta ordered a drink from a hovering waiter and also asked for the daily newspaper.

He had hardly started to scan the news when Nachez walked up.

"Rogelio, hombre," the chief said.

"¡Jefe! ¿Cómo estas?" Huerta said, rising. The two men embraced briefly in the manner of old friends and Nachez took a seat, indicating to the waiter he would have the same drink Huerta was nursing.

"So," Nachez said when his drink was in front of him, "you've come back for more . . . recruits?"

Huerta nodded. "Among other things. How is it going here?"

Nachez shrugged. "Pretty good. In fact, no complaints. My policemen are very busy with tourists. All appear happy. The merchants are pleased because I've eased up on selling fireworks to the Americans. And how is it with you?"

"Good. I'm expanding operations all the time. Are there plenty of girls in town?"

Nachez knew Huerta meant transient, unattached, good-looking young women looking for gainful employment. "Many. More arriving all the time. That fool Jimmy Carter keeps dangling the carrot in front of them, doesn't he? Los pobres are piling in here every day, spilling over from Tijuana and Mexicali and everyplace else. It's worse than ever."

"Good. I can probably wind up my business quickly and be on my way back to el otro lado. Do you have any suggestions . . . ?"

Nachez lit a cigar expansively. "Just try to be a little discreet in your recruiting. No use attracting attention to the fact that we have a good thing going around here. Do you still move them north by boat?"

"Yes. That's the best way. As long as you keep it safe at this end."

"Rogelio, a promise is a promise. I am indebted to you and as I said, you can have things pretty much your own way, as long as we don't get into any areas of conflict."

The waiter with an order pad arrived, seeing their drinks were gone, and they ordered expensive entrees. They talked casually until the meal arrived.

"I do have one other thing you could do for me, Jefe," Huerta said, patting his lips with the napkin.

Nachez swallowed a mouthful of food and nodded. "Anything. Within reason, of course."

"Well, no doubt you have heard there is ill feeling between myself and a family by the name of Herrera."

Nachez nodded. "I heard something to that effect, yes."

"Jefe, they did me a great injustice. Leonceo Herrera and his daughter, Anastacia. I intend to see that injustice is righted. But it would be much more to the advantage of all if they saw fit to leave the area and go back to where they came from down the peninsula somewhere."

Nachez mulled it over. This was the payback—or a good part of it. He had known when he asked Huerta to be his backer that someday he would be asked to return a favor that might rock his boat. But a debt was a debt.

"The girl is in the United States now, isn't she?"

"At present," Huerta replied. "But I have a feeling she will return very soon."

After a moment's thought Nachez said, "I know Leonceo a little. It will be no problem to make his life here . . . problematical. He frequently leaves the drinking spots a little too tipsy for his own safety. And of course he works on cars without the proper credentials. Yes, he is a frequent violator of the law, and I can quickly make the family see they would enjoy life more elsewhere. Consider it done."

Huerta smiled broadly. "And one more thing, Jefe. This is to your advantage. The Herrera family's friend Margarito Corrales is currently wanted for a brutal murder in the United States. If he were to show up here and you arrested him and notified the proper authorities—I'll give you their names and numbers—they would extradite him and it would be quite a feather in your cap."

CHAPTER 18

Anastacia sat finishing the brief details of her life story which Agents Ellison and Wilder had asked to hear. She put out the last of a half-dozen cigarettes she had smoked in the previous hour or so.

"So you see," she said, and her smile was a little bitter, "I'm not much different than the others who fall into your net." She indicated the other women being processed in the basement of the Federal Building in downtown Los Angeles. "It's nice to know I have influential friends trying to help me. But I've been dodging you people for going on two years. I know what's coming."

She looked at them frankly, unapologetically, as she accepted another cigarette from Ellison. Finally Wilder spoke.

"So you're choosing voluntary repatriation, even though you know a well-known lawyer is ready to try to help you?"

She thought a moment. "You said if I asked for a hearing before an immigration judge and it was ruled I had no legal right to be in the United States, then I would be deported anyway and could never again legally enter this country."

"Yes," Wilder said, "that's the way it is. Accept voluntary repatriation and you can then apply for a quota number at the U.S. consulate nearest your home."

"How long is the waiting list for immigrants?" she asked.

Wilder shrugged. "We allow twenty thousand a year from any Western Hemisphere nation. Get on the waiting list and you may get in legally within, say, five years."

She again pondered. Undoubtedly it was Paul Foster or Meme de Beauclair, or perhaps both, who were employing a lawyer for her. And no doubt she would be giving up any hope of ever coming back with the proper documents.

At last she shrugged. "I'm a Mexican citizen. My parents are Mexicans. I don't see how having a hearing would help me."

"I think you're right, Miss Herrera. I can't think of a single loophole you might fit into," Wilder agreed.

"There are loopholes?" she asked, mildly curious.

"In some cases. For instance, if you have a peculiar skill and are holding down a job that can't be filled by a U.S. citizen. Or if you can establish a minimum of seven years' residence here, even illegal, and are self-supporting and have equity, such as a home and business and material things."

She shook her head. "No. I have no right to be here. How soon will you send me back?"

"Immediately. We can have you on a bus back to Tijuana within hours."

She looked down. She feared desperately for Margarito's safety, and she had the feeling the quicker she herself was removed from the area, the safer he would be at her apartment, until he figured out what must have happened to her and then took some action. But what could he do?

"All right," she said, and for the first time there was a tone of defeat in her voice.

At that moment another immigration agent approached bringing with him a girl in her twenties. She was wearing tight pants and a clinging blouse, her hair was smartly styled, and her heavily made up eyes flashed angrily from one to the other of the agents.

"Mr. Wilder," the man said, "would you take a look at this case file?" He introduced the girl, gently taking hold of her elbow. "This is Rosa Montoya."

The girl jerked her arm free. "I am not Rosa Montoya," she said spiritedly, "I am Anita Misquez. And keep your goddamn hands off me." She spoke English with scarcely a trace of an accent.

Wilder took the file and looked through it, while the agent explained, "She says she's Anita Misquez, and these papers say she's Anita Misquez, and everybody in the bar where she works says she's Anita Misquez, but our files say her fingerprints are those of Rosa Montoya, whom we've picked up three times previously."

"Screw your files," the girl spat. "I can prove I'm Anita Misquez. I've been a legal resident here for ten years."

Wilder looked up from the file. "Miss Montoya, fingerprints don't lie. And at great risk of sounding like a bigot, illegal aliens frequently do. I suppose you want a hearing."

"Friggin' right I do," the girl said. "I want a lawyer and bail. My boss will make the two-grand bail for me. And I'm gonna teach you guys a lesson!"

Wilder motioned an attending matron to the scene. "Please, Lilian, take Miss Herrera, here, and . . . Miss whoever-she-is back to the holding room. We'll deal with them separately in a little while."

Inside the holding room, Anastacia appraised the girl, who stood angrily looking through the glass at the goings-on in the processing room.

Anastacia stood beside her. "Are you Rosa? Or Anita?"

The girl turned to her, still looking angry, but then her face softened and she chuckled. "I'm Rosa, for Christ's sake. These dumb bastards here really lucked out. Yes, they caught me before. More than three times, but they aren't even computerized here. It takes them forever to come up with your file, and then they usually only have half of it or can't find the rest."

"How'd they pick you up?"

"Luck. Pure luck. I work in a classy nightclub. I make thirty, forty bucks a night in tips alone. They raided the place—they were after the janitors and kitchen help. One goddamn agent saw me and happened to remember me from five years ago. Some of them have fantastic memories. Just my luck. I showed him my papers but he trusted his memory more than he trusted them."

The door opened and a long list of names was called out. Those called filed out singly, to be put aboard buses going back to Mexico.

The girl's attitude puzzled Anastacia. "Why are you fighting it?"

The girl sat on a bench now that the departing aliens had left the room. She suddenly became resigned. "I guess I won't. In a few minutes I'll say I changed my mind and want to go back voluntarily. Then once I'm in T.J. I can come back across that much sooner. I can't miss more than a night or two or they won't hold my job for me."

Through the glass they could see a cart being pushed toward them.

"Here comes lunch," Rosa said. "Christ, I'm hungry."

The processees were all given a burrito wrapped in foil, a piece of fruit, and a small carton of milk.

Rosa watched Anastacia as she unwrapped the burrito. "See this wrapper?" Rosa said, reading the print on the label. "It's made right here in East L.A., this burrito. And guess who makes it? Take a wild guess. What a gas. A factory full of wetbacks, making burritos dripping with food coloring and monosodium glutamate, for lunch for wetbacks going back to Mexico."

Anastacia saw the food was just what Rosa had described, but found it very tasty. Rosa went on, not caring if anyone listened. "And see that milk carton? It comes from a dairy, right? And who do you think you'd find shoveling up the manure and spreading the hay and loading the trucks at the dairy? Right, sweetie. And who do you think picks these apples?" She held up the apple and then bit into it. "Christ! You take all of us out of here and the whole fucking country would collapse, believe me."

After finishing the snack, Rosa asked to see an official and when she was brought back, she said, "I volunteered to go back. We'll both be leaving within an hour."

Soon their names were called, along with the others who would be on the bus, and Anastacia was taken out and boarded a bus waiting at the rear of the building.

For a long time Anastacia sat thinking next to Rosa on the trip southward. Anastacia tried to analyze just how she felt about this dead moment. Here she was, on a bus, under lock and key with more than a score of others. Beyond all help from Meme de Beauclair and her wealth, Paul Foster and his connections, and certainly from Margarito. The countryside went by. Santa Ana. San Juan Capistrano, San Clemente, where traffic in the opposite direction on four lanes of the freeway was being stopped and searched by immigration agents trying to stem the tide of illegal aliens being smuggled across in car trunks, hidden compartments in trucks, under rear seats.

"Are you coming back right away?" Rosa asked.

"I don't know. I have family to see. It's been a long time. I don't know what will happen."

"Well, if you do," Rosa said, "let me tell you how. There's this guy owns a little airplane outside Tijuana. Every day or

ANOTHER LAND

two he makes a trip, before dawn. His plane will hold five, maybe six wetbacks. All he charges is about a hundred bucks, and he lands you in a vineyard twenty-five miles from downtown L.A."

Anastacia thought. "It's that easy."

"Right. Look, honey, I'll be staying at the El Rey in T.J. until I make contact with him and he's got a load. Give me a call if you want to go back. I'll be there a couple of days, probably. It's a snap. This guy flies at treetop level and he's back in T.J. empty in a couple of hours."

The bus pulled into the west gate at the San Ysidro U.S.-Mexican border and Anastacia was aware there was no difference in feeling, going from San Ysidro, U.S.A., to T.J., Mex. A Mexican official approached the driver's side of the vehicle and spoke briefly to the bus driver, who shook his head.

"Nope. No criminals," she heard the driver say. Then the driver, who had been seated beyond the heavy wire mesh partitioning off the rear area, unlocked the door.

"Everybody out," he called, standing at the doorway. The passengers filed out. Anastacia followed Rosa. Once outside the bus she had expected some additional red tape or interrogation, but Mexican border officials watched in boredom as they debarked. A small crowd also watched, and a half-dozen persons came to meet those they were expecting.

"Well," Rosa said, "I'm off to get a drink and a meal. Nice meeting you, Tacha. And remember, if you're going back, better call me soon at the El Rey."

"Thanks so much, Rosa," Anastacia said sincerely. "Best of luck to you."

Anastacia watched Rosa walk off toward the center of Tijuana. Somehow, the girl's walk announced her independent, indefatigable nature.

Anastacia's attention was caught by a small, dirty woman with a child of three or four looking at those who had debarked. The woman approached several persons, questioning them in turn. Then she approached Anastacia.

"Perdone me, por favor, señorita," she asked, "but have you seen a man by the name of Antonio Cervantes?"

Anastacia stopped. "No. Were you expecting him on this bus?"

Poverty, defeat, desperation were all on the woman's face.

"Not particularly. He's my husband. The migra separated us in Los Angeles last week because he asked for a hearing. Somebody said they may have sent him to Mexicali. I have no way of knowing. Maybe he's here in Tijuana."

Anastacia studied the woman and child. "Don't you have a place where he'll look for you?"

"No. We're from Yucatán. But I'm telling everybody, if you see him, tell him the baby and I are staying under the first bridge west of the circle."

"You're staying under a bridge?"

"Yes. I've got to find him soon. I have no way to get to Mexicali to look. He doesn't know where I am either."

Anastacia thought a moment more. She slipped a hand inside her purse and took out five dollars. "Here," she said, "at least you'll have food for a day or two."

The woman was still thanking her as Anastacia walked away, and suddenly it struck her. How many times had the level of resentment risen in her when she saw an American finally reach into a pocket or purse and give a poor person something; any amount, even a dollar, or half dollar, would then allow the American to walk away feeling relieved of any responsibility to his fellow man. Suddenly she wanted to run, and she didn't know where or why. "Well, it's the truth," she said, half aloud. "That's all I can do for her." But she knew it wasn't.

Almost as in a dream, she walked through the crowded dirty streets of Tijuana toward the bus terminal. She realized she was now looking at the scenes about her through different eyes. Only a few years she had been away from Mexico, and the city seemed unreal.

She had seen it all many times before, but now she was overwhelmed by the realization that all this, the barefoot children, the old ladies in rags trying to sell live chickens dangling in bunches upside down, the young adults with a desperate look, that all this had been going on each and every day since she and Margarito had slipped across in the dark so long ago.

The buses were no different than before, and by the time the vehicle was braking down the steep road leading into Ensenada her life for the past few years was already becoming remote.

She remained on the bus while it discharged passengers and

ANOTHER LAND

took on travelers going south of the city. Then she asked to be let off at the little dirt road leading to Velasco Beach.

The road had been leveled and new gravel spread. As she walked along she saw that a few new houses had been built; cheap frame houses on tiny lots. Then she was turning into the walkway of her home.

Just before she knocked she realized it had the look of a house that was not lived in. The door was locked, she could find no key in any of the usual hiding places.

She turned and looked about. A few children played across the street, oblivious to her. A few cars went by, slowly, so as not to raise too much dust. She began walking to Valdez' motel at the beach, a quarter of a mile down the road.

Luís Valdez was at his desk when she walked through the open doorway. He looked up, froze for a moment, then went to her, smiling.

"Tacha! Tacha bebita! What in the world are you doing here?"

They embraced like old friends, and he motioned her to a seat and returned to his swivel chair.

"I just decided to come back, Luís."

"Tacha, you've been out of touch for so long . . ."

"Yes. I . . . couldn't take the chance. Once before I was traced because I kept in touch with Mama and Papa. Where are they?"

Valdez looked away for an instant and a pang of alarm went through her.

"Then . . . you haven't heard about the . . . changes . . . that have been going on around here," he said, groping for a beginning.

She sat up. "Changes? No. Where are Mama and Papa?"

Valdez sat back in his chair. "I guess I have to tell you. There has been a change of regime here. A new police chief named Nachez is in power now. He is a good friend of your old enemy, Rogelio Huerta."

She absorbed this, considering the possibilities.

"And what has happened to Mama and Papa?"

"I'm coming to that. Huerta backed Nachez and got him in power. Now the two of them are running things here. Nachez started harassing your father. Little things. Testing him for drunk in front of his friends. Leonceo took it and took it, and then took the bait. He fought back when the policeman harassed once too often. Nachez had him thrown in jail. He said your father started more fights there and was badly beaten."

A look of horror was coming over Anastacia as she listened. "They beat him? My father? What about Mama?"

Valdez waved her quiet. "Let me continue. Finally, Leonceo realized he could no longer stay here. And he was afraid for your mother. He sent her away . . ."

"Where? Where is she?"

"I don't know. Your father said he was going to find any kind of work in Tijuana. Your mother worked for me here, but Huerta was putting pressure on Nachez. Nachez followed two American boys here and came in the motel and arrested them for smoking marijuana, right in front of all my guests. When they objected, he threatened them all. You know how scared Americans are of being thrown in jail here. Nachez hinted that his harassment of my guests would probably stop when the Herrera family was no longer around here. Your father sent your mother to someplace safe. Then he disappeared. I don't know if he went to Tijuana, or if Nachez is holding him in that dungeon."

She slumped, putting a hand to her forehead. "Oh, God!" she murmured. "How did all this happen?"

Valdez regarded her with great sympathy for a few moments. "But there is more bad news, Tacha," he said.

She composed herself and sat straight, looking at him. "Yes?"

"Nachez has learned Margarito Corrales is wanted for a serious crime in the United States. His men are watching for him. You know what will happen if he returns here?"

She nodded, dumbly. "If they try to take him, he will fight back."

"Yes. And then they'll shoot him."

She sat still, thinking, and Valdez remained silent. She shook her head as though the fragments of life might somehow fall into order. Almost with a start, she realized that only ten hours earlier she had said good-bye to Margarito in her bedroom, going to work to see if she still had a job after . . . was it only last night? The party? With a chill she realized if Margarito found she had returned to Ensenada, he would come to her. And there were many ways he might find out. He could call the immigration service. He could call the company. If Meme de Beauclair knew, she might call her apartment. And when he knew, he would be on his way. She continued thinking for a minute or two and Valdez didn't interrupt. She made a decision.

"Luís," she asked in a low voice, "would you give me a ride into Tijuana, please?"

He rose. "Of course, Tacha," he said.

It was nearly dawn when Rosa and Anastacia got out of the taxi a dozen miles outside the city of Tijuana, paid the driver, and walked to a barn a hundred yards off the road.

Inside was Alex, the pilot and owner of the small plane that was parked inside. A couple in their twenties and a man somewhat older were also waiting to make the flight.

Alex eyed Anastacia only briefly, then said to Rosa, "Give me the money and climb aboard. I want to get back here before noon."

The five passengers boarded the plane. Anastacia and Rosa took seats together. Alex sat at the controls, started the engine, and taxied through the wide door onto a hard dirt runway scarcely twenty feet wide.

"Here we go!" he said with a grin as he gave it full throttle and the plane accelerated down the strip and was airborne in a matter of seconds.

"So you decided to go right back, eh?" Rosa asked as the plane flew over semidesert country.

Anastacia regarded Rosa in the near-dark of the plane's interior. Here was a girl who knew her way around, a girl much like herself, but wiser in the ways of survival in the illegal alien world. She twisted in her seat to face Rosa more comfortably. "Rosa," she said earnestly, "will you listen to the mess I'm in? And maybe give me some advice . . ."

"So you see," Anastacia said, near the end of her story, "I don't know what's happened. I called my apartment from Tijuana and he didn't answer. It could be he left; or maybe he's afraid to answer, if he knows I was picked up."

Rosa thought for some time, then turned to Anastacia seriously. "Look, sweetie. Want some advice? No. 1, go to the immigration and beg them, *beg,* to find your boyfriend before the cops do."

"Why?"

"On account of, honey, I'd'a hell of a lot rather see the migra after my man than the cops."

"But . . . they'll take me in again . . ."

"That's right. And what you do, get a savvy lawyer and ask for a deportation hearing. Ask to be released on your own recognizance—O.R., they call it. That means no bail. You say you got a good job, a nice apartment, furniture, they know you aren't going to split if they grant you a hearing date."

"But if I lose the hearing case . . ."

"Oh, Christ. Worry about that when the time comes. A good lawyer can find loopholes galore. Like establish you have a certain time in the States and are of good moral character. Or maybe you can marry this boss of yours. Then dump him after you're legal. Or maybe you can show special skills that can't be replaced by a citizen. A good lawyer can make a case for you, I'm telling you. But the main thing, see if you can get the immigration on your boyfriend's trail before the cops blow him away, the way they do wetbacks wanted for murder."

Anastacia looked doubtful. Rosa persisted. "Look, if the immigration catches him, at least he'll be alive and able to come up with a defense. Especially with all the good connections it sounds like you got. Then, when he gets clear of the murder rap, the cops will give him over to the immigration and you can start on his papers."

"You make it sound so easy . . ."

"Believe me, it's not."

"But you . . ."

"Right. Look, I don't have anybody. Just me. You have this Margarito. A good job, a boss who sounds like he's gone on you, parents—and an asshole like Nachez ready to make life miserable. I'm telling you, for your own good, and everybody else, do like I say."

With what seemed like miraculous good luck and directional instinct, Alex found a small airstrip and set the plane down smoothly. He taxied to the far end, away from the control tower and hangars, and stopped. He opened the door and lowered a set of steps. "Everybody out," he called. "I got to take off before anyone comes to investigate what we're doing here." A minute later he was airborne.

The other three passengers began walking north on the street adjacent to the airport.

"Over the other side," Rosa said, pointing, "is a little restaurant. We'll go wait there until time to catch the bus into L.A."

As they walked, Anastacia looked up at the departing plane. "This operation . . . it's so, so open. Doesn't the immigration suspect Alex . . . ?"

"What can they do? Send an immigration helicopter after every private plane they can't identify? And what if they did get onto him? What are they going to do, shoot him down? He comes in and leaves so fast nobody knows what to think. Private planes crossing the border don't exactly trigger the Strategic Air Command early-warning system."

It was nearly noon when Anastacia and Rosa walked out of the bus terminal onto Sixth Street in downtown Los Angeles.

At the first corner they discovered they were going in different directions. "I know I'll be seeing you, Tacha," Rosa said. They embraced briefly. "And do me a favor."

"Sure, anything."

"Whichever one you choose—the big handsome Mexican or the rich boss—give me the other one."

Anastacia laughed. "I'll see you."

"Don't forget. I'm at the Bali Hai every night from nine to two."

The moment Anastacia unlocked the door to her apartment and pushed it open she could feel the emptiness. No, he's not here. She went through the rooms. He'd left not a trace, except the keys she'd given him were on the nightstand next to the bed.

Then she went into the living-room area and sat on the plush couch. She took a cigarette from an inlaid wooden box on the coffee table and lit it, looking around. By the standards of the people she came from she was surrounded by luxury. The large gilded antiqued mirror by the entry, the telephone which was a reproduction of a half-century-old European model, an oak dining table in the dining area, an original oil of the Duomo Cathedral in Milan. Paul had been insistent in helping her set up housekeeping, and though it was certainly not decorated in the manner Meme de Beauclair would have suggested, it was luxury, nonetheless.

Well, life was pretty much a mixed-up mess right now, and

she was unable to cope with it alone. In her mind she now knew what she needed to do and in what order.

She went to a console cabinet and got a phone book. Back on the couch she looked up the number of the Los Angeles office of the U.S. Immigration and Naturalization Service and dialed the number. It was busy, but she knew there must be a switchboard with many outlets. She dialed again, hearing the rotor at the other end search all outlets and report back with a busy signal.

She dialed repeatedly for the better part of an hour and finally got through and asked for Frederick Wilder.

Eventually Wilder came on the line.

"Hello, Mr. Wilder. This is Anastacia Herrera, of Baja California. Do you remember me?"

"Of course I do, Miss Herrera. How are you?"

"I'm fine, I suppose . . ."

"At the risk of it sounding like a sick joke, how was the trip back home?"

"It was all right."

"Where are you now?"

"I'm here in Los Angeles. I need to talk to you."

"If you have something to say, please come over."

"All right. But . . . I need to talk to *you*. Not one of the ordinary agents. I need help . . ."

"Miss Herrera, I have to tell you that if you are illegally in this country, the best thing for you to do is come in as soon as possible. You may bring legal counsel with you, but I can't talk about anything or advise you on the phone."

She thought a long moment, could hear him waiting.

"All right. But I must see you this afternoon."

"I'm on the eighth floor, room 821. I'll be waiting."

She hung up and sat thinking in the soft quiet. Then she picked up the phone again and called Foster Advertising.

Paul Foster sat at his desk, the telephone to his ear. A secretary came to the door and he put his hand over the mouthpiece and raised his eyebrows. "Schumacher on the phone. Says it's important," the girl said a little fearfully.

Foster angrily shook his head and mouthed the words, "I'll call you the minute I know anything . . ." He was listening to the voice at the other end of the line.

". . . and I finally got through to the motel she used to

work at in Ensenada. And Paul, she and her family are in big trouble there. She has no place to go . . ." Meme said.

"Meme, I'm doing everything I can to locate her. We may have to wait until she surfaces . . ."

The secretary returned to the door and he looked at her angrily.

"Tacha is on the other line, Mr. Foster," she said.

"What? Thanks, Jackie. Meme, she's on the other line right now. I'll call you back." He punched a button on the phone. "Tacha, how are you? Where are you?"

"I'm back in Los Angeles, Paul," she said calmly. "I just wanted you to know I'm on my way to the immigration service to turn myself in."

He digested this a moment. "Tacha, please, if you've made up your mind, just let me talk to you first."

"I decided I have to. For many reasons. I can't go on like this."

"All right. But let me try to help: I know an expert in these matters. A guy I went to school with. He's studying immigration law now. Promise you'll come by and see me first."

"Why? I've made up my mind."

"Well, just get the advice of an expert. It can't do any harm. He'll know what's best."

She considered a long moment. "All right, Paul. I'll be by the office in an hour or so. I've got to get a little sleep first."

CHAPTER 19

Ben Garza was lying comfortably on the couch in his small apartment near Chavez Ravine in north-central Los Angeles. He stopped reading the textbook on U.S. institutions and reached for the package of cigarillos on the painted wooden coffee table beside him. Seven left, he noted. He glanced at his wristwatch. Nearly one in the afternoon. No wonder he was hungry. He set the book down, decided not to have a smoke, and went into the kitchenette. He didn't need to look into the refrigerator. He went to a cupboard and saw a half-full plastic bag of pinto beans. He took them down, thinking. The goddamn gasket on his pressure cooker was leaky, which meant he would have to boil them without pressure, which meant it would be two hours before they were ready.

From his pocket he pulled a five-dollar bill. He studied it. He'd need two bucks for parking tomorrow; that left three. Two bucks for gasoline, leaving one. One for coffee on campus left enough for a package of cigarillos. He'd better have boiled beans instead of buying a can of Rosarita at the corner Seven-Eleven.

He put the beans in a pot, added water, and set it on a burner on the stove. In the refrigerator he found two strips of bacon. Not the best bacon he'd ever seen, he had to admit, but it would do. He diced them and threw them in the pot. In a drawer for vegetables he saw a lone onion nestled in a corner. In had only one black spot, which he removed. He diced it and threw that into the pot also. Last, he put in a generous portion of salt. He had factory-made flour tortillas in the frig and in a couple of hours he would have bean burritos laden with Tabasco sauce.

He started back to the book and couch, but remembered

the daily mail was due. He walked out, leaving the door to the hall open, and went to the building entrance. In his mailbox he found several letters. None from the insurance company that owed him two days' work for investigating a disability claim. Well, goddamn them, he would just give them a call right now and offer to drive over to pick up the check. It should be over sixty bucks. Enough to see him through the week with maybe a chuck steak or roast for dinner.

Yes, he thought, as he entered the apartment and headed for the phone by the couch, he'd call those bastards right now and tell them the check hadn't come and if it's not in the mail he'd drive over and get it. He flopped on the couch and reached for the phone just as it rang.

It took him a few moments to place the voice.

"Yes, Paul, this is Ben. How's the old boy?"

"Ben, I don't have time to catch up now. You want a job?"

Ben thought a moment. "Well, not really. There's this school business. You know, studying, homework, law degree, and all that shit."

Foster had to laugh. "Really, listen, I need you. I have this girl, Anastacia, who works for me. Only, she means a lot more than that. She's an illegal alien. She got picked up and sent back, but she's here again. I've got a big-time well-known lawyer willing to help, but he says what he really needs is an expert in immigration law. She's got to turn herself in today, and I talked her into listening to an immigration expert before she does anything rash."

"I'm the expert?"

"Right. Can you get over right away? She's on her way here now. Just talk to her, Ben. And if you see a chance to save her, I'll pay you like hell to work on the case."

Ben thought it over. Pay me like hell. "Well, Paul, every individual case is different. I don't know if anything can be done . . ."

"No. And you won't until you talk to her. I know you're not a lawyer yet, but you're the best investigator I know. Will you just come over and talk to her?"

"Right now?"

"Right now. In my office."

He thought again. What the hell. He did volunteer work for a legal advising agency in Los Angeles, helping all kinds of aliens. It might be an interesting case.

"I'm on my way, Paul."

So the boy wonder of Wilshire Boulevard, Paul Foster, his former college roommate, had hot pants for a Mexican housemaid, Garza thought as he drove to the Foster Advertising Agency.

Well, you never know. I'll bet she's the sexpot of all sexpots, fiery, tight clothes, very poor English, and begging for a chance to stay in the United States. And if he were going to fight the U.S. Immigration and Naturalization Service, he knew where and how he had to begin, and she wouldn't like it a bit.

When he met her in Foster's office he went through the motions of the formal introduction, all the while assessing her, trying to place her, at least physically, in a niche. Yes, if those Madison Avenue type-casters could ever get off their Anglo-Saxon hang-ups, she would be perfect in those late-night commercials selling commodities for the female body. She had it all.

When he had heard the bare essentials of her case history—he already thought of it that way—Ben Garza took command.

He addressed Anastacia and Foster. "Miss Herrera . . ."

"Please call me Tacha."

"All right, Tacha. I am a law student, emphasis on immigration law. I am also connected with a community aid agency in East Los Angeles, which allows me to represent clients in immigration cases, acting as their counsel in the hearing rooms in front of the immigration judge. I support myself by doing investigative work for insurance companies and legwork for lawyers. I am qualified to represent you in the immigration hearing room, if you decide you want me to. However"—he looked at her and then at Foster—"I must tell you that based on what I've just heard, you are an illegal alien, perhaps with a chance to obtain legal status, and I cannot help you further unless you go immediately to the office of the U.S. Immigration and Naturalization Service and report yourself."

Foster started to stand. "Ben! You're supposed to help her, not turn her in . . ."

Garza waved him down. "Paul, I know what I'm doing. As long as there's a chance I may represent her, I have to tell you that any attempt on my part to keep her presence a secret from the immigration people may seriously jeopardize her chances later."

Paul was angry. "They'll just send her right back. And Ben, there are a lot of extenuating circumstances . . ."

"I'm sure there are, Paul, I'm sure there are. But we have to do that first."

"Then what?"

"Then we ask for a deportation hearing. She gets released pending the hearing, probably on bail."

"How long before we get a hearing?" Paul asked.

Ben stood up, indicating time was wasting. "That's what we have to ask them first."

Agent Dan Ellison and Acting Assistant District Director Fred Wilder sat listening to Ben Garza as Paul Foster and Anastacia Herrera sat on a couch in Wilder's office.

Garza was standing, enjoying playing the part of an attorney. "So I am hereby turning Miss Herrera over to your custody and as her representative, I request a deportation hearing at a time that will allow the proper investigation and gathering of evidence to show that she may indeed have legal status in the United States."

Wilder and Ellison exchanged glances of approval. Ellison spoke.

"Mr. Garza, in answer to your first question, yes, I think the INS will allow you to represent Miss Herrera, and from what I've heard of you, she has good counsel. But, on what grounds—what will be your case in pleading for her stay of deportation?"

"I don't have to answer that yet, Agent Ellison. She has a right to a hearing, a right to post bail and be free until that hearing."

"Of course," Ellison said, "Mr. Garza, we bend the rules as much as we can. We here at the immigration service are not the heavies in an inhuman drama. But after all returning illegal aliens to their place of origin *is our business.*"

"Your business is also being fair, Mr. Ellison. My client, Miss Herrera, by treaty with Mexico, has just about all the constitutional rights of a citizen. Including due process of law, etc."

"Yes, I know," Ellison said. "But you know she's already blown one possible legal loophole by not staying within the boundaries of the United States *continuously*. She went back to Mexico yesterday."

"You sent her back."

"Oh no we didn't," Ellison said, his voice rising. "She chose voluntary deportation as an alternative . . ."

"Under threat, coercion, of your people . . ." Garza was nearly shouting.

Wilder was slightly amused as he waved them silent. "Hey, hey," he said gently, "we're not hashing it out in front of the immigration judge yet. Let's get back to the point. Garza, you're going to ask for a hearing. That can be arranged. How long do you want?"

Garza looked at Foster, who had remained quiet up to now. Now Foster spoke. "If that last little exchange of legal doubletalk is any sample of what this courtroom battle is going to be, Ben, you'd better ask for enough time to prepare. Don't worry, you're covered financially."

Garza thought. "I think I'll be prepared, if there is a defense here, in . . . can you give me ten days?"

Wilder considered. "Yes, I think the immigration judge will go along with ten days. In fact . . . to avoid you coming back here then and asking for an extension, I'll try to make it three weeks. After all," he said in a tone that pleaded for understanding, "as Ellison said, sending illegal aliens back to Mexico is our *business*. We are not being paid to increase the population of the United States."

Attorneylike, Garza went on. "On the question of posting bail. As you see, Miss Herrera . . ."

Foster interrupted. "I'll post any bail . . ."

Garza silenced him with a quick, furious look. ". . . As you see, she came voluntarily to the INS, this time, anyway. She has means to support herself, which we can substantiate, she won't be a burden on anyone. She owns furniture, has a home . . ."

Ellison interrupted. "An apartment is hardly a home, Garza . . ."

Garza's voice was rising again. "An apartment is a home, Mr. Ellison . . ."

"Not if you're later going to claim equity as a factor in being granted a permanent stay of deportation . . ."

Again Wilder interrupted, avoiding unnecessary debate.

"Gentlemen, gentlemen, we're not at that stage yet. Mr. Garza hasn't stated on what ground he will try to obtain legal status. That argument is premature. Yes, I think we can waive posting of bond and release her on her own recognizance. She's not going to run away."

Garza looked extremely satisfied. "Okay, if that's all there is . . ."

Wilder got up, turning to Anastacia, "We can get the formalities over with now, I guess . . . Miss Herrera, will you come with us?"

For an instant, fear showed on her face and she looked at Garza as though for protection.

"We have to go through these motions, Tacha," Garza said reassuringly.

"Right," Wilder said. "We can at least give you some papers so if an agent stops you, you can tell him where to get off." He held the door open for her. The others waited in Wilder's office.

In the office of the hearing clerk Anastacia and Wilder waited for the documents to be prepared. It was a moment she had waited for.

"Mr. Wilder," she began somewhat uncertainly, "I have a very great favor to ask of you."

He looked at her and was taken by the depth of her imploring sincerity. He raised his eyebrows, not wanting to commit himself.

"You remember," she said, "the police wanted to talk to me about a man named Margarito Corrales?"

"Yes?"

"Mr. Wilder, I'm *begging*. Please, *please* have your people attempt to find him before the police do."

He hesitated, trying to find an answer.

"*Please*. He's done nothing wrong, I know. I've known him all my life. We grew up together. And I'm afraid if the police find him first he'll be killed."

Wilder still debated with himself. "For a wanted, illegal alien felon, suspected of murder, that's a very great possibility," he said gravely.

She hung her head as though she were about to cry, but suddenly straightened, blinking. "I know, if you really want to, you can have your men watching for him. Anything, just to improve his chances. I know you handle hundreds every day, but if you could only . . . just ask the large groups you take in if they know anything about him, perhaps you can find him. Before . . . *they* do."

"If he's going to resist the police, he'll probably resist us too."

"Yes, but your men won't shoot him just for fighting back, or running from them."

Wilder took a breath and nodded in agreement. "Yes, the police deal with felons every day, and subsequently their methods are . . . very different. They have to be . . ."

She shook her head. "You don't have to explain. Just try, *try* to locate him first. Once he's safe, I know something can be done for him. He told me all about what happened, and if he has a chance, maybe we can prove he didn't have anything to do with that killing . . ."

The clerk had the papers ready, and Wilder took them, handing her the ones she needed.

"I'll do everything I can, Miss Herrera. I think you may be right. Meantime, here's your copy of the order to show cause. If you're questioned, just show these. It proves we know you're here and are awaiting a hearing."

The two returned to Wilder's office.

Foster, Garza, and Anastacia left the Federal Building and were walking to the parking lot.

Anastacia looked at the papers she carried in her hand. The men watched her as she did. She glanced up at a car going by that bore a plate reading "U.S. GOVT." Two others went by that had lettering on the door reading U.S. IMMIGRATION AND NATURALIZATION SERVICE.

She looked at the drivers of the cars. Only one of them returned her gaze with mild interest, and she suddenly felt the power of the papers she held.

She noticed Garza and Foster observing her. "It's something new, not to be afraid."

Foster nodded. "You'll get used to it," he said.

She looked at him with a little condescending amusement. "How do you know," she said in a tone that was not interrogatory. He felt slightly uncomfortable.

"Well, Ben," he said, as they continued walking, "how does it look? Will you work on it? I'll give you five thousand dollars to make a case of it." Garza stopped dead in his tracks. They slowed while he caught up. Foster went on, "And a bonus if you can get her papers. And all expenses to carry out a full investigation."

She put her hand on Foster's arm as they walked. "Paul, I can't let you do this. There is no way I can pay you back. I'm not your responsibility."

They continued walking slowly, saying nothing. In this part of the city it seemed at least half of all the passersby looked of Latin American ancestry. All three noticed a sign on a food stand advertising kosher burritos.

Paul seemed to be studying the lines on the sidewalk as he said, "I'm not a great one for having a social conscience. I came up the easy way. I never worked for the things I have. All that was given to me. And I guess you two would have trouble believing something in me wants to pay a little on the bill I owe."

Anastacia and Garza glanced at each other. They walked in silence for a minute or so. Then she said, "Paul, nothing has really changed . . ."

He looked at her. "You going to embarrass me in front of my old college chum by publicly rejecting me? Don't do that," he said with a forced chuckle, "Ben still thinks I'm the irresistible young tycoon. Anyway, Ben, how about it?"

Ben thought. "I don't know. I'd like to work it out with my schoolwork. As far as she goes, there may be several ways to bring about legal residence, at least. Maybe something better than legal residence."

Paul looked at him. "What ideas do you have?"

"Well, there's the permanent stay of deportation. If the alien has been here a specified length of time, which I doubt in Tacha's case, and is of good moral character, has a job, and has equity and a few other qualifications, that person may be granted a permanent stay of deportation. The facts are laid before Congress and if no action to the contrary is taken within a certain time, it goes through."

"That's a complicated thing to go through," Paul commented.

"You ain't heard nothin' yet," Ben said authoritatively.

Foster nodded. "Any other possibilities in mind?"

"Preferential quota number," Ben explained. "Get on the

quota. They give twenty thousand a year on a first-come, first-serve basis. There's a six- or eight-year waiting list. But then the applicant can have preferential treatment, depending on his or her special skills, how badly the skills are needed here, whether it will deprive a U.S. citizen of a job, and so forth. Time-consuming and complicated. Then they're others, like U.S. Code 8, Section 1401 (a), paragraph 7. It states"—Ben closed his eyes, remembering. "I had to pass a test on it—'a person born outside the geographical limits of the United States and its outlying possessions, of parents one of whom is alien and the other a citizen of the United States who, prior to the birth of such person, was physically present in the United States or its outlying possessions for a period or periods totaling not less than ten years, at least five years of which were after attaining the age of fourteen years . . .' That's basically it."

The trio had stopped during the recitation and Foster and Anastacia were staring at Garza. He smiled.

"What in the world is all *that* gobbledegook?" Foster said.

"It's not really complicated. But it gives you an idea of the kind of thing we'll have to go through. And then there's no telling what the outcome will be."

They continued walking. "When will you give me an answer, Ben?" Foster asked as they arrived at the parking lot attended by furtive Latin-looking attendants.

Foster paid the parking fee for both vehicles.

"I don't know, Paul. I want to hear more about Anastacia's background and the circumstances of her stay here, etc. I wouldn't want to take your money and give you false hopes."

"Why don't you drive Tacha home now. I have some business. You can let her start filling you in and get back to me when you've made a decision."

When Foster's powerful sports car had roared away, Ben Garza held the door of his Volkswagen open for Anastacia. When she'd told him how to get to her apartment and they were getting on the freeway on ramp, he said, "Okay, Tacha, give it to me once more, with all the details."

By the time he was leaving her apartment he had a fairly good picture of the life of illegal alien Anastacia Herrera.

"Will you take the case?" she asked.

"I probably will," he said. "I don't know. I need to make

ANOTHER LAND

the decision carefully. It means a lot to me. And I need some expert advice first."

She turned to go and he saw she was hesitant, worried, and wanted to talk about something further, but she evidently decided now was not the time.

"I'll get back to you soon, Tacha," Ben assured her.

The next morning Ben sat in the middle of Echo Park lake, in the middle of Los Angeles. I'll think about it, he'd told Paul and Tacha, and that's exactly what he had been doing, to the exclusion of all other activity for the past eighteen hours. He'd known he'd end up here. All of his important decisions were made here.

A slight breeze ruffled the surface of the murky water, giving an appearance of freshness. The usuals were here. He got a kick out of the senior citizens fishing on the opposite bank. Safe and serene despite the sign behind them which said, "Fishing for Persons 16 years old and over is Prohibited." To his knowledge they'd never been hassled. The streets surrounding the lake were jammed with noisy traffic, but the lake was serene. The eye of the hurricane, or something like that.

First, to act out the ritual, he had approached the rickety boathouse which had a sign saying, "Fun Boats for Rent." The attendant greeted him with the same "So what's with you these days?" Once in a while Ben was able to take the time out to chew the fat with old Al, but not today. Ben had told him to put it on the tab for a half hour's worth of heavy, awkward old No. 17. He had long ago realized that no one else ever used it. He passed by the colorful small plastic boats with names like *Lusitania* and *Flying Dutchman* and looked at No. 17's half-peeled blue paint. The tin can lying in the bottom of the boat told the rest, although recently he hadn't had to bail. Maybe old Al had glued up the cracks.

Next he rowed madly round and round the lake until he was sweating and gasping for breath. Then he laid the paddles to rest, scooted to the bottom of No. 17, rested his head back on the seat cushion, pushed up his glasses, shut his eyes, and listened to the last drops of water falling from the paddles. The lake seemed to swallow each plop greedily, as though it needed every drop it could get in this drought year.

Underneath, Ben was a careful person. He had a system for

making decisions. He tried to levitate his mind—float it away about ten feet or so—then look at himself as a judge in a courtroom would look at the defendant. He would listen to the arguments from either side, then have a consideration period, finally make the judgment. Sometimes it required research, information-gathering. But there were only three weeks before the hearing.

Funny to hear from Paul again. Evidently he's really gone on this girl, Anastacia. Ben could see why. Too much. It'd be great if one of *us* had him by the balls for a change. He had had it made at school and in every other way since then Ben could think of. Tacha was not exactly what Ben had expected.

The sun was almost directly overhead. The boat floated without direction for several minutes. The abrupt wham against the rocky bank jarred Ben out of his lethargy. He knew what he had to do, and he had just enough time.

Ben rowed quickly to the dock, sprang across the narrow stretch of water, and tossed the line to the attendant. "See ya," he called over his shoulder, and walked to the car.

He drove to the Pasadena freeway and was headed through the tunnels, then maneuvered to the left lane to catch the Golden State north, relieved there was little traffic this time of day. A short stretch on the Glendale and 134 freeways brought him to the campus. He had a slight premonition coupled with a pang of regret as he looked at the Ad Building dome against the blue sky. Hell, it's been hard enough to get back into school here. Was he going to chuck it all?

Herbert H. Shaw stood a head taller than the students gathered around him. He had a perennial slight stoop so that his white head tilted toward his left shoulder. Compensation for the growing deafness.

The students were reluctant to let him go, and he always let them know it was mutual. Ben waited patiently. Finally the last student had his questions answered and Ben was able to say, "Can I buy you a coffee, Professor Shaw?"

"I'd like that, Garza. The cafeteria all right? I'll need to be back in my office."

Shaw found a table by the window. "I can never get accustomed to looking out at all this." He waved his hand, indicating the San Gabriel Mountains, which formed the backdrop for the foothills behind the campus. He chuckled,

"Columbia was never like this. New York City has a lot of advantages, but the scenery is not one of them."

"Something has come up, sir, and I need your advice," Ben said as they sipped coffee.

Shaw ran his hand through the thick white hair and focused intense blue eyes on Ben, in the amazing way he had of giving his all to the problem at hand. "Shoot," he said.

Ben cleared his throat and adjusted his glasses. Then he looked directly at Shaw.

"Your classes have been the greatest for me, sir. Shown me the direction I have to go. I knew I had to do something connected with—well, I know it sounds corny—but something to do with my . . . people."

Ben looked down and stirred his coffee. "Well, anyhow, a classmate of mine from UCLA days—haven't seen him for a few years—is offering me quite a proposition." He told of the adventure the previous day. "He seems to think if I try hard enough I can find some loophole to keep this girl here. He's willing to pay five thousand dollars if I can do it. Plus expenses."

Shaw raised his eyebrows. "That's a lot of money, Ben."

"Enough to allow me to go to school full time for my remaining term."

"Sounds like it might be right down your alley, too," Shaw said thoughtfully. "Why you?"

"Paul's a sharp dude—had things pretty much his own way all his life—I think he thinks anybody could do anything if *he* wants it that way. That and my ancestral genes," he grinned at Shaw.

"Take it, Ben. But I would advise you to give yourself completely to this job. If it's important enough for you to do you shouldn't be trying to study too. Go at it full tilt. There's a possibility the dean would see this as a project worthy of independent study credit."

Ben looked up sharply. "That would be too good to be true, sir. Okay, the other thing that really worries me is this: Are *you* going to be here next term?"

Shaw was pleased. "Ben, definitely yes. At least one more term. Columbia has allowed me as many terms of visiting professorship as I want." He shifted his gaze for a moment to the mountains. Then, as though having made a decision, he looked back at Ben with fresh enthusiasm. "I will help you in this, Ben, in any way I can. I have some influence, and my expertise, of course, is at your disposal. Now let's hear what you've run into."

Ben thought. "Really, Professor Shaw, I don't know where to begin."

"Why don't you tell me the bare facts of the case? Maybe I can see an inroad."

Ben told him sketchily the background of Anastacia and her family, including briefly how and where her parents had been raised.

Shaw was thinking seriously when he finished.

"Ben, the logical straw to grab at is right in front of you."

Ben looked puzzled. "How's that?"

"It's U.S. Code 8, Section 1401(a), paragraph 7. You're familiar with it. You had it last term."

Ben remembered. "Sure. In fact, I had occasion to recall it just the other day. But how is that pertinent . . ."

Shaw shook his head. "It's tricky. But you see, it says, 'a person born outside the geographical limits of the United States and its outlying possessions, of *parents* one of whom is an alien and *the other* . . .' and then those preconditions of an aggregate of ten years' residence, five years of which were after the age of fourteen, all that pertains to the *parent*. Don't you see? The *parent*. And from what you told me it looks like qualifying the parent is the real hope here. Forget the girl. And go reread paragraph 7 over and over until it sinks in!"

When Anastacia admitted Ben Garza at the door she felt his enthusiasm.

"You're taking the case," she guessed as she led him to the breakfast table and prepared coffee and warmed bearclaws.

"Right," he said emphatically, "but I've got to know more. I'm onto something promising in your case, but don't get your hopes up yet. I have to talk to your mother. She may be the key to this whole situation."

"You'll have to find her first, remember," she said absent-mindedly. She sat looking at the coffee cup in front of her for several moments. Finally she turned to look directly into his eyes. "But Ben," she said seriously, "I have to ask you a favor. Something I have no right to ask you. I'm desperate."

He felt misgivings. "I'll do everything I can . . ."

"This is something else. It's a man. An illegal alien also.

He's wanted for a murder he didn't commit. He's being hunted right now."

Ben's surprise was obvious. "But Tacha, I can't go into a murder investigation when Paul's hired me to work on your papers . . ."

"Then if you won't help with this, forget the whole thing!" She said it with quiet explosiveness, leaving no doubt as to the finality of her decision.

Oh, Jesus, he thought. All day he'd been thinking of the money he would earn. It meant a decent suit, getting the dents out of his car so he didn't look like a Chicano hillbilly, catching up on the rent, and eating out once a day. Aside from paying tuition.

He sighed. "If you want to tell me about it, at least I can tell you whether he can be helped. You know all the facts? Does Paul know about this? What's his name?"

"His name is Margarito Corrales. Yes, Paul knows about him. Margarito told me everything that happened regarding the murder . . ."

Eagerly, she related everything she could remember of Margarito's account of the night of the murder. When she finished, he went over certain points, then paced the room for several minutes while she looked at him anxiously.

"Okay, so he's never told anyone where he was the night of the murder? Except you?"

"He's never had anyone to talk to about it."

"Well, there is a chance we can establish his innocence. The coroner's report is a matter of public record. I'm very curious to see the established time of death. Then we'll know where we stand. I can do that later this week. I also have to work on finding your mother, you know. Any idea where she is?"

Anastacia's eyes took on a dreamy look. "I think I know," she said.

CHAPTER 20

Acting Assistant District Director Frederick Wilder of the U.S. Immigration and Naturalization Service picked up his ringing telephone.

"Wilder here."

"Fred, this is Ellison. You'd better come down to the processing room. I think we got the big fella wanted for murder."

Wilder thought a moment. "Okay. I have to make a call or two first. See you in a few minutes."

It's always the same, Wilder thought as he entered the processing room. Employees of the INS sat behind a dozen desks, interrogating aliens, filling out forms, informing them of their rights and liabilities.

Ellison was standing in front of the men's holding tank. From within, behind the glass windows, a dozen and a half men looked out, observing the goings-on, wondering what was going to happen to them and when. Wilder stood beside Ellison. Immediately Wilder's eyes fell on a man behind the glass who stood a head taller than the others.

"I bet a buck that's him," Ellison said. "Picked him up this morning in the Antelope Valley with a bunch of others picking lettuce. Claims he's Alejandro Díaz, from Guadalajara. No ID on him."

"Well, we'll soon find out," Wilder said, keeping his eyes on Margarito. "Did you spot him?"

"No. But we told everybody his description and that he'd probably be using a phony name. Every agent in the field was watching for a big handsome bruiser with bulging muscles. Not many match that description. One thing puzzles me, though. I thought you said the Herrera girl told us he spoke good English."

"That's what she said."

"Well, this guy doesn't understand a word."

Wilder eyed Ellison with skepticism. "Oh, he doesn't, eh? We'll see about that too. Who brought him in?"

"Clancy Stevens. He says he saw this group working in the field. Dozen or so. He was on his way to a big operation where there were a couple hundred, so he wasn't going to bother with them. Not enough manpower. But then he noticed this fella fit the description of the man you wanted us to find. Stevens was afraid if he singled out this guy for questioning, it would spook him and he'd think we were cops and he'd run or maybe put up a fight. So Stevens pulled it off like a regular raid, scooped up the whole bunch, and then notified me."

Wilder nodded, then glanced at his watch and looked toward the entrance of the processing room. He returned his attention to the glass window.

"Bring him out here," he told Ellison.

Wilder and Ellison sat on the edge of a desk, looking down on Margarito, seated in a chair.

Wilder spoke to him. "So you're Alejandro Díaz from Guadalajara."

"Sí."

"And you don't speak English?" Wilder asked in Spanish.

"Nada."

Wilder's voice took on a trace of good-natured sarcasm. "Tell me, Señor Díaz, what's the name of the main street in Guadalajara?"

Margarito fumbled for words. "Oh . . . I forget right now."

Wilder went on. "All right, then tell me the name of the big cathedral in downtown Guadalajara."

Margarito stammered. "Uh . . . well, you see, actually I'm from a little town outside Guadalajara. You probably never heard of it. I didn't get into the city much . . ."

"Well, then tell me the name of the little town. Believe me, Señor Díaz, I've dealt with tens of thousand of aliens. I am aware of every little village in that part of Mexico."

Margarito remained silent.

No one said anything for almost a minute as the two INS men regarded Margarito.

"I'll tell you what I think," Wilder said, breaking into English. "I think you're Margarito Corrales, of Ensenada, Baja California. I think you understand English perfectly, and you'd better listen to what I say." Margarito kept his eyes on Wilder with an expression that did not commit himself. Wilder continued. "You're a very lucky man, Margarito. Lucky we got to you before the police. Or before you went back to Ensenada . . ."

"Why am I lucky?" Margarito asked in English, conceding his identity.

Wilder glanced at his watch and at the doorway again and was about to answer when he saw what he was looking for. Anastacia stood there, looking around anxiously. Then she saw Wilder wave to her and saw that Margarito was there also. She hurried to them and burst into sobs as she embraced Margarito, burying her head in his chest.

"Tacha, baby, Tacha baby," he said gently, his arms encircling her. "What's going on here, anyway? How'd they know about me . . . ?"

She pushed herself away so she could look up at his face. "You big pendejo! I told them about you." She turned to Wilder. "Oh, thank you, Mr. Wilder. Thank you, thank you, thank you." She turned back to Margarito. "I was so afraid the police would find you. And you'd run or fight, and being wanted for murder, they'd have a perfect right to shoot you." She continued talking as fast as she could, as though she were afraid Margarito might disappear before she had a chance to tell him everything. "Oh, God! You don't know how I worried. I was afraid you might get back to Ensenada somehow. The new police chief there is waiting to shoot you. Rogelio Huerta worked that out," she embraced him again, still talking, "but now you're safe, thank God. And Mr. Wilder."

"Safe, hell," Margarito said defensively. "Now I have to stand trial for murder. Excuse me if I don't fall all over myself thanking you for getting me captured, Tacha."

"But Rito. You don't understand. I already have a private investigator working to clear you. And I'll see to it you have T. C. Segal to defend you. He's the best criminal lawyer in

ANOTHER LAND

the state. He'll get you off, Rito. I just couldn't stand it another day knowing the police were after you . . ."

A voice interrupted. "Excuse me, Mr. Wilder, but I believe you sent for me."

They all turned to look at the newcomer.

"What? Oh, yes, I did," Wilder said. He turned to the others. "This is Captain Glade of the Los Angeles Police Department, Homicide Division. Captain Glade, it's my duty to turn this man over to you. I believe you have a warrant for Margarito Corrales. This is he."

Glade regarded Margarito a moment. "Please, sir," Glade said with deadly politeness, "stand up and place your hands against the wall and spread your legs."

Margarito complied. Glade frisked him quickly.

"Now, sir, please put your hands behind your back." Margarito did so and Glade snapped on the handcuffs. He turned to Wilder. "I thank you very much for your cooperation, Wilder." He made a gesture as though he were touching a finger to a hat. Then to Margarito, "Now please walk ahead of me to the elevator."

Anastacia was fighting back tears but smiling. Margarito turned to her. His expression was pleasant. "You're really something, Tacha. Here I am being taken in to stand trial for murder, and you're happy about it."

She blinked back tears and wiped her streaked makeup. "Yes, I am," she said softly.

He gazed at her only a moment longer, then blinked both eyes, nodding slightly. "I understand, Tacha baby," he said quietly.

She wiped her eyes, still fighting back sobs of relief.

"Yes, I know you do, Rito," she said.

As they started toward the elevator she heard Glade saying in a monotone, "You have the right to remain silent. You have the right to have an attorney present . . ."

She turned suddenly to Wilder, still smiling. "And I have the right to give you a giant kiss," she said, and she did.

Ben Garza walked up the driveway to the Heath home feeling more than a little nervous. It was a tract home, but a nice one. The developers had left as many citrus trees as possible when the orange orchard had been converted to a residential development. It was a beige stucco home with red tile roof and large windows.

He rang the doorbell and waited. Within a minute it opened and he studied the woman who stood there.

"Are you Gretchen Heath?" Garza asked. She was a natural blonde, very pretty, in shorts and barefoot.

"Yes. Can I help you?"

"Yes, Mrs. Heath, you can," he said, and realized he was having difficulty in deciding how to get into it. "But I don't know if you will. I have something extremely important to talk to you about." He paused and she waited. "Something of a very personal nature."

She made a move indicating she was ready to close the door.

"I'm sorry, unless you can be a little more explicit, I'm afraid I don't have time for games, Mr. . . . ?"

"I'm Ben Garza, law student, currently doing some investigation work for a client, and like I said, I'm afraid you won't like what I have to ask you about."

She was still undecided. "Well, until you tell me what it is, we can't get on with it, can we?"

Garza realized he was stalling and that there was no easy way. "I have to talk to you about Margarito Corrales," he said.

She drew a sharp breath, putting her hand to her throat.

"Please come in," she said, stepping aside. Ben entered and turned to her. She went on, regaining her composure. "Can I fix us some coffee? We can talk in the kitchen."

"Yes, I'd like that," he said, following her. His appraisal of the shapely and tanned legs before him was automatic, but cut off almost immediately. He was here on business.

She put the pot on the burner and set two cups and saucers on the breakfast table, then turned to get the sugar, cream, and spoons. Garza watched her carefully.

"Well," she said nervously, "what do you want to know? I really know very little about him."

Garza could see she did not want to commit herself at this point, was unsure how much was known of the relationship.

"Did you know he's being held for murder?"

"No, I didn't know."

"You did know he was a fugitive?"

"Yes, I knew that."

ANOTHER LAND

Garza thought a moment. "Mrs. Heath, I'm afraid you're going to have to be completely honest with me if you want to save him. His life may be at stake. I have to know certain things if there's going to be a successful defense."

"What can I tell you?"

"Everything. How you met. Just what happened, when."

She sat down, pulled a cigarette from a pack on the table, and lit it. "All right," she said. "Margarito was a mariachi in a restaurant here. I used to go in and listen to the group rehearse in the afternoon. Before the place opened. He played the guitarrón, and I loved hearing them." The coffee started to boil and she put the cigarette in an ashtray while she rose and poured. Garza had heard the story from Margarito in jail, but was anxious to see if Gretchen Heath would embellish or delete. She did neither, and told it all, including the entire night they spent together while her husband was away, and how she dropped him at his truck in town at dawn.

"That's all," she said. "I came home. I slept and got up at noon. I flipped on the radio out of habit. Charles, my husband, had it fixed so that police calls come in when you turn it on. I was terrified to hear of a homicide at the Sloane place. I was afraid for him. I was afraid for myself. Without thinking I went down and told del Rio, thinking maybe he could warn Margarito or something. That's all I know. Maybe he did kill the old man. My husband's a policeman, you know."

"I know," Garza said. "That's how I was able to locate you. Margarito didn't know your last name."

"Anyway, I don't see how I can help. If this comes out, well, you don't know what will happen."

Ben's intuition picked up on an unspoken message.

"There's something you haven't said?"

She drew on her cigarette and looked away. "Only . . how Charles feels about . . . you people."

Enlightenment came to Garza. "You mean, he's a spic-hater." He smiled as he said it. She looked at him and saw that he didn't take offense personally.

"Yes, that's what I mean. And I know what you're thinking. That I did the worst kind of hurtful thing to him, deliberately."

"Sure sounds that way."

"I know that's what a psychiatrist would say. That me liking Mexican food, and music, and . . . men . . . is getting back at him for my frustrations and anger."

Ben thought a little. "Maybe, but we're getting off the track. I'm not here to analyze you, interesting as that might be. Now I'll tell you the news. I've gone over the scene of the crime. There's a possible witness, by the way. I'll come to that. Margarito's fingerprints were on the porcelain doorknob of the house, indicating he was the last one to leave the scene of the crime. That's the best evidence they have against him.

"However, I went over the coroner's report. And that's where you come in, Mrs. Heath. The medical examiner is prepared to testify old man Sloane was killed not later than three in the morning."

He stopped, taking a sip of coffee as he watched her reaction. She closed her eyes and slumped a little. It was a half minute before she spoke.

"I see. So I'm Margarito's alibi."

Garza nodded. "Looks that way, doesn't it?"

"And I suppose if you were a psychology major you'd say I got my secret wish, if I'm forced to tell in front of the world that I went to bed with what my husband hates most."

Garza smiled a little. "Like I said, I'm not here to analyze you. I'm here to save an innocent man."

"Anyway, yes, it's true. Margarito and I were in the bed right here in the next room, where I sleep with my husband, until about five in the morning. Then we got dressed and I drove him into town. The sun was coming up."

"Sunrise on that day was at 5:15 A.M.," Garza footnoted.

She smiled humorlessly. "You do your homework, don't you, Mr. Garza?"

"I sure do."

She thought a moment, lighting another cigarette.

"But . . . you said there was a possible witness."

"Yes, but that looks pretty hopeless. Sloane had allowed a man and his pregnant wife to live in the ranch house. There's a chance they saw, or at least heard, what happened."

"And you can't find them?"

Ben Garza sighed. "They were illegal aliens. Scared to death of authorities. If they knew what happened they would have split, knowing they'd be deported. We have no idea where they are now."

"Do you know their names?"

"Abel and Lida Carmona."

Gretchen Heath was quiet for a long while. Garza was trying to guess what was going through her mind.

"If his life depends on it, will you testify?" he prodded.

"Yes, I'll provide his alibi," she said. "But I may not have to."

"I don't understand . . ."

She looked at him with a little satisfied smile. "What you don't understand is just how strongly my husband feels about . . . you people . . . and just how good a detective he can be when he wants to."

Garza got up to go, knowing there was little purpose in staying longer. She followed him to the door.

"How can I get in touch with you?" she asked.

He took out a business card and wrote a number on it. "They'll contact me if you call this number."

She looked at it. "Mr. Benjamin Garza, you'll hear from me, or someone who can tell you where the Carmonas are, just as soon as possible."

Garza smiled gratefully, clasping her hand warmly.

"Thank you so much, Mrs. Heath. So much. I'll be waiting."

Charles Heath pulled around the house and drove the car into the carport. He entered the house through the kitchen entrance and, taking off his shoulder holster and gun, hung them in the corner of the front-room coat closet. He turned and saw his wife seated on the upholstered chair, a drink on the coffee table in front of her. She seemed tense.

He glanced casually at the drink. "Hi. Thought you didn't drink during the day."

She was looking directly at him. "I usually don't. But I needed this one because I have something to tell you."

He raised his brow slightly as he took a seat on the couch opposite her. "Oh? Now what?" He sat casually relaxed.

"There's no easy way," she began, then trailed off.

"Go ahead. I'm ready for anything."

She took a swallow of her drink and replaced it on the coffee table. "Do you know the facts about the Sloane killing?"

He wrinkled his brow. "Yeah. They caught the wetback

who did it. Took him off our sheets a day or so ago. What was his name. . . . ?"

"His name is Margarito Corrales."

His face showed a measure of surprise. "Right. Why?"

She took a deep breath and plunged ahead. "Margarito Corrales could not have killed old man Sloane, because the coroner's report shows Sloane died at three in the morning, and Margarito was in bed with me here in this house until five that morning. You were in San Diego." She closed her eyes and her head sagged a little.

Charles Heath's bland expression did not change as he sat digesting what he had just heard. After a minute or so he got up and unhurriedly went into the kitchen, got a soft-drink can, pulled the top, and returned to his seat opposite her.

"Go on," he said calmly.

"That's all there is."

He took a drink from the can, rose, and walked to her. His face was still bland. "You know what I could do to you right now?"

"Yes," she said quietly, "but you won't."

"Why won't I?"

"Because it'll get back to the department. If I suddenly have black eyes and a broken nose. Or worse."

He regarded her a moment, inscrutable. "You know me pretty well, don't you."

"I should."

"Well, go on. There's something you haven't told me yet."

She composed her thoughts. "I might not have to take the stand."

He looked at her sharply. "Why not?"

"There are possible witnesses."

"Who?"

"A couple who stayed in the Sloane ranch house."

"What are their names?"

"Lida and Abel Carmona. They disappeared."

"Why did Sloane let them stay in the house?"

"The woman was about to have a baby."

Heath paced the floor, glancing at her now and then.

"And they might have seen what happened?"

"They might have."

He continued to pace silently. Once or twice he stopped and stared at her, then resumed pacing. Soon he went to the closet, took out his shoulder holster, put it on, and donned his coat.

"Where are you going?" she asked, still frightened.

"I've got to find them, don't I? Or else have the world know my wife sleeps with every wetback who comes traipsing through the orchards."

She disregarded the slur. "How will you find them?"

He faced her. "I'm a cop. Remember? This woman is pregnant. Or was. It won't be hard. These people, you see, Gretchen, breed like rats. I guess you know. They come here smuggling themselves into the country, and what does our government do? If a bitch is knocked up, she can go to just about any hospital and have the kid free. They never turn them away. *We* pay for it. All of us. Anything they need. Well, if I can find out just about when this Carmona woman dropped her kid, I can probably find out where. And at least that's a start. I'll find them, Gretchen. Because if you take the stand for that wetback I'll kill you."

She looked at him directly and for the first time there was contempt on her face. "No you won't, Charles," she said quietly.

CHAPTER 21

With what seemed unbearable weariness, Ben Garza dragged himself aboard the 747 about to take off for Los Angeles. How many days, two? or three? before the immigration hearing on Anastacia's case. He had handled immigration hearings before, successfully and otherwise, but never had he dreaded one as he did this. Too much was at stake. In the few hours he had spent with Anastacia he had become completely enamored of her. But that was not all of it.

No. Professor Shaw had all but promised him academic credit for handling the case. That would be jeopardized if he hadn't done enough. Paul Foster had upped the ante considerably when he'd seen the case involved far more work and research than anyone had anticipated. This hearing could be the biggest feather ever in Garza's cap if he pulled it off successfully, but that was not all of it either.

He had a window seat, and now he looked out angrily at what he could see of the city of San Antonio. He had always liked the city, visited there many times, but now he hated it with a passion, because somewhere in its countless folds was a treasured secret he could not find. *It's there! It's right here in this city somewhere, the secret little document I'm looking for,* he said to himself bitterly.

But the city of San Antonio's secret had mocked him.

The rest of what he had needed—some of it, anyway—had been relatively easy.

Like finding her mother. Anastacia strongly suspected she was at a tiny crossroads far down the Baja peninsula, a place called La Tijera. That was, let's see, about fifteen days ago? He turned away from the window and rubbed an eye hard with each palm. His eyes were red and ached. In fact, he ached all over.

ANOTHER LAND

Where did I go wrong? he thought almost aloud as he waited for the plane to take off. Then he decided to relax back in his seat and go over the events of the past few weeks. Maybe he could discover where his relative inexperience had led him off course.

He'd driven to La Tijera as fast as he could. Time was important. He'd found Pilar working as a waitress-cook at the little cafe. Leonceo, Anastacia's father, was working as a mechanic there. God, how did those people make a living? Cars came by and stopped perhaps four or five times a day.

He chuckled, eyes still closed in his reclining position, as he recalled the utter amazement on Pilar's face when he told her what he was trying to establish.

They were seated—Garza, Leonceo, and Pilar—at a handhewn wooden table inside the tin-roofed, adobe-block cafe, the evaporator air cooler doing a fair if noisy job of keeping them comfortable.

Pilar spoke English almost fluently; Leonceo's English was not quite as good. But both spoke better English than he spoke Spanish, Garza had discovered.

He took a sip of his coffee and said, "You see, Señora Herrera, there is a very good chance that you and your daughter are legally citizens of the United States." And he had let that sink in.

Pilar thought she hadn't heard right and made him repeat his statement again and again.

"But you see, the problem is, if I'm to get Tacha out of trouble, I need lots of information about how and where you were born and where you traveled with your parents when you were growing up in the migrant workers' camps when you were little. And I need it as fast as possible."

Leonceo interrupted with a logical if somewhat self-centered question. "And if my wife is a U.S. citizen, does that make me one too?"

Garza grinned. "Almost, Leonceo, almost. What you'd have to go through for legal U.S. status would be mere formalities."

Leonceo had sat back, clapped his hand to his head, and whistled through his teeth. "And that would mean I could cross back and forth over the border all I want? Just like you can?"

Garza nodded and Pilar and Leonceo stared at each other a long moment. Then Garza took out his notebook.

"Now, Señora Herrera. . . ."

She cut him off, smiling. "Please, call me Pilar," and Garza saw that in her eyes and smile was a beauty only a shadow less than that of her daughter's.

"All right, Pilar, let's start with your early travels. We'll get to your birth, the most important part, after we've covered your travels. I want names of towns and what age you were. Names of schools and what grade you were in. Names of companies your father worked for and when."

Pilar concentrated a moment, fidgeting with her empty coffee cup. "Well, like I said, I was born on a train . . . but you said to get to that later, didn't you. I got to finish almost all of first grade at Smithbro Elementary in Texas. I remember because we had to learn to spell it . . ."

Garza came back to the present as a stewardess came down the aisle informing all to put their seats in the forward position and to fasten seat belts. Within minutes the plane was leveling off and a gentle chime sounded as the "Fasten Seat Belts" sign went off. He reached under his seat and brought out a handsome leather briefcase with an eagle holding a snake tooled on one side, a gift of Paul Foster's generous expense account. From it Garza took his fat notebook and turned to the page concerning Pilar's birth. He read:

> Pilar Constanza Batista
> Born Nov. 30, 1932, on train
> Baptized San Antonio Texas
> age 4, 5 days (or less)
> Father Francisco Jesús Batista
> Mother Angelina María Costa Batista

Pilar had a fairly good idea of the circumstances surrounding her birth, as it had been somewhat unusual, and thus the story had been repeated countless times in the evenings among her parents and their friends and relatives in the years when she was growing up.

A group of migrants had finished the crop picking and were

taken to a train, where they boarded and were being returned to Mexico. Shortly after boarding, Pilar's mother had gone into labor, and a midwife who happened to be among the passengers delivered Pilar. The train was ever so slow, stopping frequently to allow other trains to pass. It came to a stop a few days later and Pilar's father asked the conductor where they were. He was told this city was San Antonio. From the window a large Catholic church could be seen. Pilar's mother insisted her father, Francisco, take the baby to the church to see if she could possibly be baptized. Francisco asked the conductor if there was time. The conductor said if he hurried. Francisco hurried, after taking great pains to wrap the child warmly, as it was freezing outside. Snow could be seen completely covering a towering mountain in the background.

At the church Francisco encountered numerous obstacles which delayed him, but he managed to have the child baptized, and if it hadn't been for the kindness of a sympathetic conductor who held the train a quarter of an hour, the incident could well have been disastrous.

That was all Ben Garza had to go on.

He had found the rest of the work—verifying her requisite aggregate ten years inside the United States—relatively easy. Oh, it had been extremely hectic and time-consuming, but he had done it, and felt confident that the evidence he had gathered would stand up in court.

He had rented cars almost recklessly, driving to school districts and schools all over the Southwest, after spending three days on the telephone in a San Antonio hotel.

Then there had been a great stroke of luck. Code 8, Section 1401(a), paragraph 7 requires five years' U.S. residence after the age of fourteen, and he found that all in one lump at the hotel where she made beds from age fifteen through twenty. The aggregate probable years of U.S. residence he could verify prior to that age totaled almost seven years, so he was in good shape there.

But that goddamn elusive baptismal certificate that could cinch the whole thing. It just wasn't there. Finally, with time running out, he had hired a private detective to scour the records of every church standing in San Antonio in 1932, while Ben, through the notes he made from Pilar, located relatives across the border who gave him affidavits to the effect that they were present when the Batista family got off the train with Angelina carrying newborn Pilar in her arms.

That was the best he had been able to do. After all, looking at the bright side, the U.S. immigration people in a hearing were usually willing to settle for a *preponderance* of evidence when ruling on a citizenship case.

As the plane set down on the LAX runway, Ben felt a knot in his stomach. *Had* he returned with a preponderance of evidence? One minute he would think yes, he had it. The next minute he doubted.

Well, shit! he figured as he gave the cab driver the instructions for the twenty-dollar ride to his apartment (Paul's expense account again), he could do no more. Time had run out. It was late, he was dead tired, tomorrow he'd call Professor Shaw and invite him to the hearing (he wanted those extra credits), and then he'd just do his goddamnedest in front of the immigration judge.

Ben Garza could feel his heart beat as he stepped off the elevator on the eighth floor and proceeded toward the immigration hearing room of the Federal Building, actually a small courtroom. His new suit and shoes made him feel almost conspicuous, but he knew others who saw him would not know such attire was foreign to him. Sweat beaded his forehead as he entered the hearing room. He stopped. He recognized several students from his law classes. Paul Foster was seated next to Anastacia, and seated next to her was Meme de Beauclair. And there was Professor Shaw, his great white mane somehow making him look like a tamed lion sitting on a pedestal.

The attorney for the immigration service came toward him, extending a hand. "Garza? I'm Gerald Skinner, your opposition. We're about on schedule. You got Immigration Judge Conrad Rhine. As usual we're all jammed up. How long do you think you'll take?"

Garza set his briefcase down on the table. "Not long, Mr. Skinner. You've got copies of everything we have."

Skinner opened his folder and leafed through it with raised eyebrows indicating great doubt. "I'm afraid we're going to object to some of this, Garza. Rhine's known for bending over backward, but . . ."

As he turned away Ben again felt a cold knot in his stomach. What would Skinner object to? Where had he goofed? What exhibits were of no value? Trying to appear casual, he wiped the perspiration from his forehead with a handkerchief and then began setting the papers in the order in which he would present them.

There were only a dozen or so spectators in the small hearing room, and Garza felt the professor's eyes on him as he arranged the exhibits. Then he turned. Sure enough, the old scholar was looking at him. Anastacia was talking in a hushed voice to Meme de Beauclair and Paul Foster. Garza waited until she looked at him and then beckoned to her with a nod of the head. She rose, rubbing cold hands together, and came to sit at the table.

"Do I have to sit here?" she said in a whisper. "It would be better," he said, his eyes taking in her attire and general appearance.

At that moment Immigration Judge Conrad Rhine entered. He went unceremoniously to the judge's chair at one end of the table, nodding to Skinner. The room was suddenly quiet.

Judge Rhine looked at the papers before him. "The matter of the United States versus Anastacia Herrera," he said quietly. He looked up at Skinner. "Is the government ready?"

"We are, Your Honor," Skinner said.

Judge Rhine looked at Ben Garza. "And you are . . . ?"

"I'm Benjamin Garza, Your Honor," he said, standing. "I'm representing the respondent. I'm also with the Working People's Law Center in East Los Angeles."

Anticipating the question from the judge, Skinner spoke up. "We're accepting him to represent her, Your Honor. He's qualified."

Judge Rhine was looking over the papers. "All right, let's proceed."

Garza felt his pulse quicken even more. This was it. "Your Honor, we're claiming U.S. derivative citizenship for the respondent under United States Code 8, Section 1401(a), paragraph 7, stating a person born outside the geographical limits of the United States and its outlying possessions of parents one of whom is an alien and the other a citizen of the United States who, prior to the birth of such person, in this case the respondent Anastacia Herrera, was physically present in the United States or its outlying possessions for a period or periods totaling not less than ten years, at least five years of which were after attaining the age of fourteen years, is a citizen."

Judge Rhine was handling the evidence. "And these are your exhibits attesting to the aggregate of ten years' residency of her mother, establishing that five years of that were after her mother was fourteen years old. Is that right?"

Ben knew his face looked eager, and his nervousness had considerably subsided. "Yes, Your Honor. As you can see, there is a preponderance of evidence that the respondent's mother, Pilar Herrera, then Pilar Batista, was born on a train somewhere outside San Antonio, Texas, November 30, 1932. If you'll follow the exhibits, you'll see she was with her Aunt Alicia in Magdelena, Sonora, from 1933 to 1938. Then in 1938 she attended kindergarten in Pueblo, Colorado . . ."

"Yes, yes, I can see," Judge Rhine said with mild irritation, indicating he wanted Garza to let him look over the evidence without a running commentary.

The hearing room was quiet while he leafed through the papers. "You even have school class pictures of the respondent's mother as a girl," he said with approval. His eyes went from the picture to Anastacia at the table and then back to the pictures. "Miss Herrera," he said smiling, "your mother was a very attractive young lady also. There's a great family resemblance."

Appreciative chuckles went through those in the room. Judge Rhine looked up at Skinner. "Mr. Skinner, does the government object to these?"

"Not to the affidavits concerning confirmation of the required residency of the parent, Your Honor," he said, "but getting to the proof of birth . . ."

"Your Honor," Ben Garza cut in, "the respondent's mother, Pilar Batista, was born on a train carrying migrant workers. There was no doctor in attendance, hence there is no birth certificate. The railroad company does keep a record of births en route, but only for ten years. I went there. There is no way actually to prove U.S. birth. But as you can see before you, we have affidavits by disinterested persons who witnessed the family getting off the train that arrived nonstop from the United States with the respondent's mother aboard at the age of eight days. The persons signing the affidavits could possibly be here in person, but only at great expense and inconvenience . . ."

Now Skinner cut in, "Mr. Garza, they were *not* disinterested persons and their presence here would have no bearing on our accepting the evidence. They would no doubt testify to exactly what the affidavits say." He turned to Judge Rhine. "Your Honor, the government must object to these as proof of U.S. birth. We don't doubt those people saw the family get off the train with an eight-day-old infant, but that's all they can swear to."

Garza was angry. "We can establish the train did go nonstop from the border to Magdalena . . ."

"Even if you could, Mr. Garza, all those affidavits say is that these people saw a family get off the train with an eight-day-old infant."

"But . . ." Ben sputtered, "but . . . that's the only proof available. That together with the confirmed residency requirements is a preponderance of evidence . . ."

Now Skinner was becoming angry, "No, it is *not* a preponderance of evidence. Look, Mr. Garza, we bend over backward in accepting evidence that could be shaky. But there are probably tens of thousands of illegal aliens whose resident time in the United States qualifies them under 1401(a) 7. Now you're asking us to accept U.S. birth simply because some people saw a baby girl taken off a train in Mexico at the age of eight days. We object."

Garza fought to keep from trembling. "Then how else can we prove that this girl"—he pointed to Anastacia—"is a citizen under . . ."

Skinner raised his voice. "I don't know and it's none of our business how you prove it. The fact is you have not presented a preponderance of evidence concerning the citizenship of the respondent's mother!"

Judge Rhine leaned forward. "Gentlemen, gentlemen. No one likes a good, fair fight better than I, but we can do without the emotionality. Now, have you both presented your arguments to your own satisfaction?"

Garza was surprised to find himself glaring at Skinner, almost out of breath. Skinner glared back.

Garza looked at Judge Rhine. "That's all I have, Your Honor."

"And those are our objections," Skinner said, sitting down.

The room was quiet while Judge Rhine arranged papers. He looked up at Garza, and Ben felt the knot in his stomach tighten.

"On the basis of the evidence counsel for the respondent has submitted," Judge Rhine said, "I'm going to deny this. Mr. Garza, you've satisfactorily substantiated the residency requirements under Section 1401(a), but the main ingredient, proof of U.S. birth, is lacking."

Garza felt the accusing eyes of Anastacia, Professor Shaw, Paul Foster, and his classmates on his back. He felt nausea. He grasped desperately for some measure of composure. "Your Honor, could I have an extension? Another week? I'm sure I can come up with substantiation . . ."

"I suppose you can have another week, if you think it will help your client. But I'd advise you to come back with considerably more than you have. Extension granted. Now, Mr. Skinner, there are many others waiting to be heard. Let's get on with it."

Ben Garza entered his apartment, went to the refrigerator, got a bottle of beer, took it into the living room, and took a deep swallow. He took off his shoes. Previously, he had always worn pull-ons, and he mildly resented having to untie the stylish Florsheims before kicking them off. He hung his jacket on a hanger in the tiny broom closet. He resented that a little also. Until now he had always worn a sweater he could throw over any chair. He lay down on the sofa, intent on going over the details of his disastrous representation of Anastacia Herrera in the immigration hearing room four days ago. He had spent a precious three days rechecking the details of Pilar's story. Perhaps she'd been mistaken about the church's name, so he'd checked every other possible alternative. Negative. Maybe a St. Mark's Cathedral had burned down or been demolished. Again negative. There was a mistake somewhere, but had he made it, or had someone handing down the story of Pilar's birth? He looked at the calendar on the wall and a chill went through him. Three more days to the hearing, no fresh clues. He heard a knock at his door.

When he opened it he saw a man of medium build, short hair, in a nondescript business suit.

"Ben Garza?" the man asked.

"Yes. I'm Ben Garza."

The man handed him a slip of paper. "I understand you want this. It's the current address of Lida and Abel Carmona."

It didn't register with Ben, and the man sensed this. Still expressionless, he said to Ben, "They are the couple who are the possible witnesses in the Sloane murder up in Ventura County."

Then he remembered. "Oh! *Great.* Fine. Thanks a lot. How did you find them? Did you have trouble . . ." But the man was walking away, and then Garza knew who he was.

The next morning he was on the freeway heading out of Los Angeles, coaxing the little VW to the legal speed limit. He welcomed the diversion after the immigration hearing fiasco. It was only a little more than an hour's drive to the address where the Carmonas lived.

At the door he had a great deal of trouble convincing Carmona that he was no threat, and finally, once seated inside, he explained that Margarito Corrales' life was at stake unless Carmona and his wife testified.

"Yes, I saw who did it," Abel Carmona finally said. "We both saw. It wasn't Margarito. I saw the man through the partly open door, then I closed it when he started arguing in English with Sloane. I couldn't understand what they were saying. I heard them fight, and the man left. Then when we discovered the old man dead, we got away as quick as possible. But I can't go to the law. They'll send us back to Mexico, and I have a good job now. I've worked hard and managed to escape la migra ten years now in this country."

"I see," Ben said. "This house, are you buying it?"

"Yes."

"Señor Carmona, if I were to show you the American laws in Spanish that said you could stay legally in this country if you can prove you've been a good person here for seven years, you have a good job, and own property, would you say in a court of law that Margarito Corrales didn't kill Mr. Sloane?"

Carmona thought a moment, suspicious. "There is such a law?"

"Sí, señor. I know my business. Sometimes I represent people in the immigration court, and there is just such a law. I have the Spanish translation. I can show it to you."

Driving back to Los Angeles, Garza chuckled to himself. Things were getting more complicated. Now he not only had Anastacia and a murder investigation to deal with, he also had another immigration client.

But as he drove, inexorably his mind returned to the case of Anastacia's mother, Pilar. How close he had come. It almost came off. That damned baptismal certificate. St. Mark's. There was no such church in San Antonio. Never had been. Pilar's memory concerning what her mother said about her birth must be faulty. Where was there something he was overlooking? It had to be somewhere.

Well, he decided, it was a beautiful day and nothing could be accomplished right now by letting it lie heavily on his mind. He shook his head as though to cast aside the weighty load of his failure. A beautiful day. From where he was right now he could see the snowcapped summit of Mount Baldy glistening in the sun over the San Gabriel Mountains.

But that too brought Pilar's case to mind. She had remembered her mother telling her—he referred to the worn notebook as he drove, stealing fleeting glances to refresh his memory—"Your father got off the train. You were two days old, but we had to baptize you. In San Antonio it was freezing cold. As he walked toward the church I could see the snow down low on the huge mountain beyond the church . . ."

It struck him so suddenly his foot actually slammed down on the brake pedal. He brought the car to a stop on the shoulder of the freeway, looking at the mountain in the distance, while he mentally replayed Pilar's statement. There *were* no huge mountains around San Antonio.

". . . the snow down low on the huge mountain beyond the church . . ." *Of course!* He knew now. He put the car in gear and the back wheels spun as he headed for the nearest off ramp and then took the freeway toward downtown Los Angeles. He double parked in the parking lot at the public library and ran inside.

In the reference room he thumbed through the huge atlas until he found the town names. Yes, yes, he was right. More than right. There were about twenty San Antonios. He quickly eliminated most, such as San Antonio in Argentina and another in Pennsylvania. Then he was turning to the map of New Mexico. There it was. And the map indicated the railroad ran straight on down south. No wonder it never made sense trying to reconstruct the route the train carrying Pilar's family had taken from San Antonio, Texas, to Magdalena, Mexico.

He dashed to the checking counter. "Please," he said, thrusting a bill at the startled librarian, "give me some quarters. Hurry."

At the nearest phone booth he dropped a coin in and asked the operator for the area code of San Antonio, New Mexico. Then he dialed that area and the information number. "The train station in San Antonio, please," he said.

Soon he was talking to the station in San Antonio, New Mexico.

"No, I don't want ticket information. Just tell me, when you go outside of the station, is there a big mountain in sight?"

"Why, yes, there is," came the puzzled answer.

"Okay, now think hard. It's very important. Is there a St. Mark's Cathedral in the direction of the mountain?" And then he practically screamed, *"There is?!"*

And in another few minutes he was saying to a church official at St. Mark's Cathedral, "Now listen carefully. I will send you immediately a donation of two hundred dollars if you'll get a copy of that baptismal certificate in the special-delivery mail to me in Los Angeles today."

"It's not necessary but certainly appreciated, sir. Where do you want it sent?"

The next day when he opened the envelope and looked at the baptismal certificate, he was euphoric. He held it in both hands and thought he knew how Tom Sawyer-type kids must feel when they find a treasure map. He put it on top of the other documents of the Herrera case on the little coffee table in his apartment and looked at it again; the fading rococo design around the edges, a smear here and there (even though it was a Xerox copy), and the seemingly ancient signature of the priest all were beautiful. He picked up the telephone and called Meme de Beauclair.

"Thought I'd check with you. The hearing's at 10:00 A.M. tomorrow."

"Wouldn't miss it for the world, Ben. Best of luck."

Then he called Paul Foster. "By the way, Ben," Foster said, "T. C. Segal would like to see you and Tacha in his office on Wilshire Boulevard at seven tomorrow night. I gave him your file on everything you've done on Margarito Corrales and he's going to handle the case."

Ben's eyes went wide. "He is? Great. I'd like to see him in action. And you might tell him he's welcome to sit in on Tacha's immigration hearing tomorrow, if he'd like."

"I'll tell him, but I don't think he's interested. He knows absolutely nothing about immigration law."

Ben sighed. "Well, tell him he's welcome anyway."

Foster chuckled. "Say, you're pretty sure of this one, aren't you. Or you wouldn't be inviting everybody."

Ben forced himself to be realistic. "I think I'm sure. But after that last fiasco, I'll have doubts every time I'm ever in an immigration case right up till the judge gives his ruling."

He said good-bye and hung up. He picked up the file on Anastacia. Okay, he said to himself half aloud, I'm going to go over every single thing in this, so there's no chance of that happening again.

Now. One more thing and he'd be ready for the hearing tomorrow. He drove to the campus and found Dr. Shaw in his office. He gave him the file and sat silently while the old gentleman leafed through it. He thought about tomorrow. Ben had pictured a grand hearing room scene wherein he really rubbed the opposition's nose in it. He was somewhat disappointed when Professor Shaw responded to his new-found evidence with equanimity.

"You've done it, Ben," Shaw said mildly. "You've really got them this time. You won't have any fight up on that eighth floor."

Garza was still disappointed. "But . . . you don't think Skinner might challenge any of this?" He held up the whole folder.

Shaw shook his great white head. "They've already accepted the requisite residency time. Their only objection was you didn't have what you now have. This baptismal certificate. I know you'd like a good knock-down, drag-out fight now that you're fully prepared, but you won't get it."

Ben was still hopeful. "Maybe they'll challenge it. Claim it's fake."

Shaw again shook his head. "No. They'll know a simple phone call to St. Mark's will dispel any doubt."

"Maybe they'll think Pilar's not really the one named on the certificate."

"No. How else would the family have known about the certificate? Made out nearly forty years ago? You've got them, Ben. You've done a great job."

Shaw was right. In the hearing room Skinner, the opposition, glanced only briefly at the evidence and then Garza could hear him conferring with another attorney on a different case.

Judge Rhine was also rather casual about it.

"Nice job, Garza," he said, stapling the evidence together and signing an order to stop deportation proceedings. Rhine turned to Anastacia seated at Garza's side at the table.

"Welcome officially to the United States, Miss Herrera. It's always good to find a new citizen, or rather a newly found citizen. Yes. You're an American, and I think we're all better off for it. Papers will be issued forthwith for you to that effect. The clerk will take you to where you can pick them up. Congratulations to both of you." He turned away. "Next case!"

Meme de Beauclair and Paul Foster started forward to congratulate Ben and Anastacia.

"Please, Ben," Anastacia said quietly, "I'm in no mood for this," indicating those approaching. "Make an excuse, tell them we have to sign papers or something and we'll see them later."

Ben guessed the reason for her anxiety.

"Listen, Paul, Mrs. de Beauclair, we have a mountain of very important paperwork here. Can we get in touch later?"

"Of course, Paul," Meme said. "But we have one big celebration coming up."

Ben accepted the congratulations of Foster and Professor Shaw, and then he and Anastacia followed the INS man out of the hearing room.

As they walked onto the parking lot, Garza handed his ticket to one of the furtive dark men, who hurried out. The man quickly located Garza's keys on a board and scurried off to bring him his old Volkswagen.

"That," Garza said, indicating the towering Federal Building they had just left, "was rather anticlimactic, wouldn't you say?"

As he suspected, her mind was not on her brand-new status. "Ben," she said earnestly, "how can you dwell on that with the trial just about to start? Getting Margarito off is a thousand times more important to me than citizenship." Then she sensed his hurt. "Not that I don't appreciate it, Ben. I really don't think many people could have done what you did. Interview Mama in Baja. Track down her school records. Figure out where the certificate was. You did that because you care and that's what will make you a fine lawyer."

Garza smiled broadly. "Well, thanks, Tacha. But I really understand your preoccupation. And, yes. Time's running out. As you know, T. C. Segal is handling Margarito's case. He's . . ."

She cut in. "Is he really as big as they say?"

"As big? He's bigger than Ellery Queen and Perry Mason put together," the furtive lot attendant brought the car and Garza paid him, "and he wants us, you and me, to get together with him tonight. I'll take you home now and pick you up about six. Segal works nights as well as days."

Waving good-bye to Garza as he drove off, she went up to her apartment. She entered and closed the door behind her, then stood before the living-room mirror and looked at herself. She was an American citizen. She knew others expected her to be jubilant at this moment. But she wasn't. She had to analyze her feelings. She was glad to be a U.S. citizen. But was she *really* an *American?* No, not really. Nothing inside her had changed. Her historical heroes would always be Benito Juárez, Zapata, Pancho Villa, Father Hidalgo. To be proud to be an American would somehow be saying she had less pride in being Mexican. She took the citizenship papers from her purse and examined them. They were just words on paper with official seals and signatures. Yes, but they were also priceless—quite literally; they couldn't be bought. Not in this country, anyway.

She felt restless. Her thoughts turned to Margarito sitting in a cell a hundred miles north, waiting to go on trial, accused of killing an old man who had befriended him. She had been able to visit him once in jail, but now she longed to see him again, feel him, hear his voice, and laugh with him.

ANOTHER LAND

How would he react when he heard she was an American citizen?

Glancing at the clock, she realized Ben would be back in a few hours to take her to see the lawyer who would defend Margarito. Restless, she decided to go for a walk.

The neighborhood she lived in on the West Side of Los Angeles was a mixture of high-rise apartments, condominiums, and upper-middle-class homes. Trees and other greenery were abundant, and she enjoyed taking a leisurely walk through the area.

As she passed one house she saw a cactus garden next to a patio. She'd walked this way many times before but somehow had never noticed it. She stopped and studied it from the sidewalk.

She was familiar with most of the specimens. There was a barrel cactus. Plenty of them in Baja. A century plant. Also familiar. Several odd-shaped cactus she'd never seen. And a seguaro, as it was called here, which was either a cardon or a closely related species. These cacti were small, almost miniature, of course, but this seguaro lifting its arms skyward immediately made her think of the giant cardon at La Tijera, which she strangely identified with. A thought came to her: Cactus was very symbolic, perhaps not of Mexico, but certainly of Baja. She'd often heard Americans say they'd never seen abundant desert cactus growing right next to the ocean. Americans always thought that was odd, but she'd seen it all her life.

Cactus was symbolic because it grew, no, thrived, where nothing else would grow, like the people of the peninsula. It could grow strong and mature on less nutrient than any other plant. It had learned to survive in extreme adversity.

She idly wondered why the people who owned the home would have a cactus garden. Possibly because it required practically no attention once planted. She tried to pinpoint the source of irritation she suddenly felt. It was because those things that she grew up with, they were like animals in a zoo here in the cactus garden. Something unusual, for foreigners to gawk at. The way the families coming down the peninsula in their huge cars or recreational vehicles gawked at everything they came upon: the donkeys, the dilapidated cars of Baja, the barefoot, dusty children, the mud houses with cardboard or corrugated metal walls, the outdoor kitchens.

She realized she now felt very protective of those things that were symbols of her origins, and taking pride in her sudden U.S. citizenship made her feel that she was somehow abandoning all that as well as those who still lived there and daily fought poverty, desert drought, and primitive conditions.

Then suddenly the Baja boojum tree came to mind. It was a desert plant which would grow to a height of fifteen feet or so and then begin to bend over, forming a perfect arch until it touched the ground, and then what had been the top would take root, like some infinitely slow inchworm. Americans were always astounded at seeing this tree, and botanists frequently came to take pictures and study it.

She herself was also taking roots again at another point, wasn't she. She continued walking on a route that would take her back to her apartment.

That evening Anastacia and Ben rode a silent elevator nearly to the top of the Wilshire Boulevard skyscraper where Segal's office was located. When they stepped out there was practically no one about, due to the hour. A sign on a corridor wall indicated Segal's suite could be found to the left. The lettering on the door said only, "T. C. SEGAL Atty. at Law."

There was no one in the reception room as they entered. A battery of offices led from the room and within moments Segal appeared at the door of his private office.

"Garza? Anastacia?" he asked. They nodded and he strode toward them, trying, Garza thought, not to appear aggressive.

"I'm T. C. Segal." He shook hands with each vigorously and then led them toward his office. "I'm on a call right now, but please have a seat. It'll take only a minute."

As they sat waiting for him to finish his phone conversation, Garza tried to size him up. Like his office, everything about him said "expensive," but quietly. He wore a coat and vest and Ben tried to guess what the outfit cost. He settled on fifteen hundred. His hair was relatively short and he wore rimless glasses which were hardly noticeable. He was clean-shaven, even at this hour, and his jaw jutted out not with aggressiveness and determination but with strength. Garza guessed he stood no more than six feet, and his build was wiry and strong. At least forty, Garza thought, but he looked as though he swam and played tennis every day. As Segal talked his words were deft and his sentences economical. His voice was not unpleasant, but he gave the impression it was an effort to talk in a low-key tone. His office also said "expensive." Two Dong Kingman original watercolors hung on the walls, their brilliant colors helping to offset the almost solemn opulence of the decor. The only thing really ostentatious was the genuine South African krugerrand encased in clear plastic on his desk. Fleetingly, Garza wondered if using such an object as a paperweight was a contemptuous statement about the nation it came from. Amid the expensive new furniture and drapes in the office, an accent piece stood out in a corner: a French antique table. Anastacia saw him looking at it and silently mouthed the words "Louis XIV," then suppressed a chuckle.

Segal put the phone down and gave them his attention. "Now," he said pleasantly, "we'll get right to it. I know the rudiments of the case, but that's about all. From you," he indicated Anastacia, "I want everything you know about this man we're going to try to defend. How you met. Your relationship, all that happened in Ensenada leading to how you both got here. Everything." As he talked Garza noticed he took out two legal pads and placed them side by side. Garza strained his eyes and saw that he wrote in large capital letters in pencil "GAME PLAN" across one. He didn't title the other pad. "And from you, Garza, I want everything you've done on this and how you did it. For instance, I know you've located a couple of possible witnesses. Why weren't they willing to come forward before? Why are they willing now, etcetera. Okay?" He smiled at Anastacia as he poised his pencil. "Ladies first, if you please."

They each told all they could, and Segal showed varying degrees of interest at different points. He stopped the narrative during Anastacia's relating of the events in Ensenada concerning Huerta coming to great power through Police Chief Nachez, and wanted all the details he could get. Garza saw he was taking copious notes on the pad marked "GAME

PLAN" at this point. Segal murmured, "I have considerable contacts in Baja," and then continued writing.

When Garza told how he pressured Charles Heath, Gretchen's husband, into service, Segal again wanted to know more details than were offered.

"I don't know if you know what it's like to confront an out-and-out racist, Mr. Segal, but it's . . ."

Segal for the first time dropped his pencil and pushed his glasses up on his head.

"Wait a minute, wait a minute," he said. *"You're telling me, T. C. Segal,* that I don't know what *racism* is? Kid, the stories I could tell you about law school and business . . . well, another time. But we need this guy. We need to use his energy. You see, it takes a lot of energy to hate like that. You already used his energy once, Garza. But we're going to have to call on him for more help . . ."

Garza took the liberty of interrupting. "But I've already used him. I don't think he'll help us any more . . ."

"Oh, yes he will," Segal said. "We got him where they're short. He'll help." He kept adding to "GAME PLAN" as he talked. "A guy like that's got lots of energy we can use. You know, like a martial-arts man uses his enemies' strength against them. But in this case, we don't care if it's against him or not, just so it's for us. Okay, go on."

Finally they were through, and Garza saw that Segal had filled many pages on the unmarked pad and several on the game plan. My *God!* He moves fast, Garza thought.

Segal studied his game plan, crossed out some sentences, added others, as they all remained silent for some minutes.

"Okay, Garza, I think I can come up with something that'll work. I need you. In fact, I don't think I can pull this off without you. I'm going to have to send you back to Heath. And then you're going to have to find this Huerta guy. We'll have to flush him out, but that shouldn't be hard, once you find him. Oh, and I'm going to want you, for lots of reasons, to sit with me at the defense table."

Garza was aware his mouth dropped open. *"You?* Want *me* at the defense table?"

"Right."

"But . . . I still have a year of law school . . ."

"That's all right. I need you. Now, listen. Here's the most logical plan I can come up with right now. We may have to change it a little, depending on our luck, but this is what we'll try to pull off . . ."

Faintly, ever so faintly through his sleep, the words came through: "Rogelio! Rogelio! Wake up, cabrón. You hear me? It's an emergency!"

Then Huerta became aware of the pounding accompanying the voice outside his hotel door. No need to wonder who it could be. Even if he didn't recognize the voice, only one person in Ensenada called him cabrón.

Huerta sleepily got up and went to the door and opened it. A stern and worried-looking Police Chief Nachez stood there.

"What is it, hombre?" Huerta asked, still sleepy. "My God! It's only five in the morning."

"I know, I know," Nachez replied with little patience. "But it's an emergency. There's a federal committee in town looking around. It means financing for the town, political appointments, everything. But I want you out of town in half an hour."

Huerta snapped awake. "What? What do you mean? It's five o'clock."

Nachez, unaccustomed as he was to having his direct orders questioned, had already turned to go. Now he turned back and his voice was savage. "I said, cabrón, it's an emergency. I want you out of town, across the border, immediately. You can come back in a couple of days, but it's imperative you leave at once. I have my reasons. When you return I'll tell you more." And he whirled and was gone. Still bewildered, Huerta turned back into his room and began dressing.

Huerta sat listening to the radio in his car as he waited in line to cross the international border into the United States. Luckily, the line wasn't long. It would take perhaps eight or ten minutes. At this time of morning, only four of the two dozen or so checkbooths on the U.S. side were in operation. On weekends, particularly Sunday afternoons when thousands of American tourists were returning home, all lanes would be open and there would still be a three- or four-hour wait as border officials painstakingly checked each car, looking carefully at each occupant, asking questions which would force those crossing into the country to speak and say something which could not have been rehearsed. If an

American seemed too casual, his car would probably be searched. If it seemed an occupant of a car was Latin and had trouble answering questions as to where he'd been in Mexico and why, where he lived in the United States and his place of birth, he was in for further questioning, unless that Latin-looking person could present papers allowing him entry. Many of those in the cars at this hour were Mexicans with entry visas, such as himself, but even this early in the morning, the vast majority of cars lined up were returning American tourists.

Damn, they're slow! Huerta thought as he moved ahead another car length and then stopped again. He had his unlimited-entry papers in hand, and knew he would not be detained after presenting them at the checkbooth.

As he waited, he watched the border patrol people at their routine. After allowing one car to pass, an agent would frequently refer to something inside—either a TV screen with new instructions appearing, or a list of vehicles or persons to watch for for some reason. Frequently Americans bought large quantities of liquor at cheap prices in Mexico and tried to smuggle the booty across. Frequently those who sold it to them would immediately phone in to the Border Patrol the purchasers' description and license-plate number and thus be eligible for a handsome reward if their tip led to the arrest of the would-be smuggler at the border. They were given a reward of a certain percentage of the U.S. value of the contraband, and this percentage was often more than the tipster had charged for the merchandise originally. There were innumerable games played at the international border which were not really games at all, Huerta knew.

Finally, the driver being interrogated ahead of him was waved through and Huerta pulled up to the booth, papers extended out the window.

The agent took the credentials and examined them at some length, Huerta thought. Ordinarily they hardly did more than make sure his appearance coincided with the photo before handing back his visa and waving him through.

The agent still studied the credentials.

"You're Rogelio Huerta?" he asked.

Huerta refrained from becoming indignant.

"Yes, of course I am," he replied nonchalantly, but he was a little worried.

"Mr. Huerta," the agent said with remarkable indifference, "I wonder if you'd be good enough to park over there at the side and report to the office. Your visa will be waiting for you inside."

Huerta didn't panic. "Why . . . of course. Is something wrong?"

The agent shrugged with an indifferent smile. "I wouldn't think so," he said.

More than a little worried, Huerta parked and entered the office of the U.S. Immigration and Naturalization Service, Border Patrol Division.

He approached a man behind a counter.

"My name is Rogelio Huerta. They took my visa," he said, pointing.

The man nodded as though this were logical and went to a wire basket. Huerta could see as the man picked up a U.S. entry visa—his own, he supposed—studied it at some length, then went to a desk and took another paper. He read the paper, then referred back to the visa, repeated this a few times, then set both the visa and the paper down and returned to Huerta.

"Mr. Huerta, we're going to have to ask you to wait for a while. There are some questions. Take a seat in that room over there. I hope it won't be long."

Now Huerta became very apprehensive. "May I ask what the questions will be about and who wants to know the answers? I'm a very busy man and I'm in a hurry . . ."

The man behind the counter was equally polite. "Just take a seat in that room. I hope it won't be too long until someone's with you."

Huerta entered the little anteroom indicated. It had windows allowing a view of what was happening at the counter he'd just left, and only a few chairs. Undoubtedly it was some kind of preliminary interrogation room. His resentment at being detained was far overshadowed by his anxiety. He checked his wristwatch and saw it was six-thirty.

One hour later Huerta still sat in the chair, watching the goings-on at the counter. Some people came in to talk with the man at the counter. Others were escorted in under scrutiny. From where he was he could hear nothing but a faint buzz from the fluorescent lights overhead.

Another hour later Huerta still sat. No one had locked the

door to the room he was in; in fact, he could see no locking mechanism. Perhaps it locks automatically, he thought with some alarm. Casually, he got up and tried the door. It was unlocked. While he was up, he decided to take a chance. He approached the counter.

"Hi, I'm Huerta again. I thought you might have forgotten me . . ."

The man behind the counter spoke as politely as he had before, but this time his voice projected unmistakable authority. "No, you haven't been forgotten, Mr. Huerta. Just take a seat in that room. Someone will be with you before too long, I'm sure."

Huerta returned to his seat.

Forty-five minutes passed and Huerta saw a man enter and go to the counter. Something told Huerta the man was bad news. He was Anglo, wore a nondescript suit, hair fairly short, he was perhaps in his middle thirties, and his face was neither pleasant nor unpleasant, but completely expressionless. He conferred with the counterman a few minutes, glanced briefly in Huerta's direction, accepted what appeared to be a visa and something else, and then walked unhurriedly toward Huerta's anteroom. He entered and Huerta stood up.

"Hello," the man said and with automatic reflex produced his open wallet to show a badge. "I'm Sergeant Charles Heath, detective, of the Ventura County sheriff's office. Are you Rogelio Huerta?"

"Yes, I am," Huerta said with the beginning of a cordial smile as he started to extend his hand, but at that moment Heath sat down.

"Please have a seat, Mr. Huerta," Heath said, still expressionless. "I just have a few questions. Perhaps it won't take long."

"I hope not," Huerta said, smiling again.

Heath took a comfortable position, folding his arms across his chest. He regarded Huerta without expression. Huerta found himself feeling uncomfortable in the presence of this man, but he couldn't pinpoint why.

"Mr. Huerta," Heath began, "I'll get right to the point. We have reason to believe you were present at the scene of a crime ten miles east of Oxnard, Ventura County, on the evening of," he paused and quickly produced a notebook. As

ANOTHER LAND

if by magic, he flipped it open to the page he wanted. Huerta had the impression he needn't have bothered with the notebook. "August 17," Heath was continuing. "Yes, that was the date. We have witnesses, some not so reliable, perhaps" —he gave a little smile— "who place you there that evening. How about it?"

Huerta rubbed his forehead as though thinking hard.

"August 17? Ten miles east of Oxnard? I'm afraid you'll have to refresh my memory a little more."

Heath digested this a few moments, nodding ever so slightly. "All right. That night, some hours after witnesses place you at the scene, a rancher, Sloane, was killed and probably robbed. We are charging a man by the name of Margarito Corrales with the murder. In fact, he's on trial right now."

Huerta felt some measure of relief. He gestured, somewhat foolishly, he realized, and smiled weakly. "Then what do you need me for? If he's already being tried."

Heath again digested this a moment, nodded faintly, and continued. "All right. This man, Corrales, is an extremely dangerous man, I'm convinced. As I said, some of the witnesses in the case are, well" —again the faint smile— "not the best of witnesses. It is claimed you were present earlier. It would help our case immensely if you could corroborate that Corrales was there that night."

Huerta had his fingers to his lips. "Then . . . that's all you want from me? To verify I saw Corrales at the Sloane place that night?"

"That's about all," Heath said so casually that Huerta felt a pang of warning. He was beginning to fear Heath more and he still didn't know exactly why.

"You know," Heath went on, "this Corrales man, well, if he goes free, I think it would be almost a crime against society. No telling what he's liable to do. You do remember the evening now, don't you, Mr. Huerta?"

Huerta was picking up all kinds of bad vibes from Heath's deadpan and monotone. Did he know more than he was saying? He seemed to. Huerta suddenly wanted to do what Heath wanted, out of fear, he realized, but he still couldn't pinpoint the origin of that fear.

"Yes, Sergeant, I do remember that night now. In fact,

Corrales is so dangerous that for no reason, as anyone there will say, he broke my nose. Yes, if I can help put him in prison by saying he was there, I'll do it."

Heath seemed again to digest this for a moment.

"You know, Mr. Huerta, if my nose had been broken that night, I'd have remembered it right away."

Again Huerta found himself giving a foolish smile.

"Well, Sergeant, you know how it is. Perhaps I wasn't in the best position to volunteer information about the activities that night . . ."

Heath nodded faintly. "Well, if I were you, I certainly wouldn't worry about *that*," he said blandly, and again Huerta wondered about the exact meaning of his words.

"Sergeant, when do you want me to show up at the trial?"

Heath seemed a little preoccupied as he looked at Huerta but now he suddenly stood up. "Come on, we're going now."

Huerta got to his feet, starting to protest. "But Sergeant, I'm unprepared to leave this instant, I . . ."

Heath had put a very gentle hand on Huerta's back and edged him toward the door, and the deadly force Huerta felt just beneath that gentle hand gave him goose pimples.

"Oh, come on," Heath coaxed. "We have to hurry. That is, if you really want to help."

"I do, really I do," Huerta said as he felt himself being propelled through the door and toward the counter.

When they reached the counter, Heath stopped.

"Wait here," he said, and he pointed at the exact spot on the floor where Huerta stood. "I'll be only a second."

Huerta stood as though rooted.

Heath strode across the entry lobby to a rather impressive office suite. He entered and walked past the receptionist without a sideward glance. Through the windows Huerta could see someone who appeared to be a major official of the station rising to his feet as Heath entered. He couldn't hear but he watched the Border Patrol official shake hands vigorously with Heath, who looked like he was thanking the Border Patrol man. Then quickly Heath rejoined Huerta and again he felt that terrible, subtle pressure as Heath led him outside.

As they walked, Huerta said, "Sergeant, I believe you have my papers." He held out his hand.

Heath reacted as though he'd forgotten. "That's right, I do. Don't worry. I won't keep them."

Heath led Huerta to his car and held the door open on the passenger side, and in the bright morning sunlight Huerta for the first time got a good look at the cold steel-blue eyes of Heath. Huerta tried not to shudder.

"Sergeant, what about my car?" He pointed.

Heath was already slamming the door on the other side and engaging the starter as he answered, "Oh, if I were you I wouldn't be worried about *that.*"

Charles Heath spun the tires of the car as he pulled into the fast lane and accelerated far beyond the legal speed limit. And as mile after mile flew by and Heath said nothing, Huerta suddenly had the feeling he was riding with a homicidal maniac.

Judicial procedure was in abeyance in Ventura County Superior Court, in session regarding The People vs. Margarito Corrales, charged with the killing of Cyrus T. Sloane. The bench was empty. Two uniformed officers stood, arms folded, at each entrance to the courtroom, ever watchful. A bailiff, clerk, and a court recorder chatted before the empty bench. Abel and Lida Carmona sat, looking bored, next to a female translator in police uniform in the spectators' section. In a far corner, on instruction, sat Anastacia Herrera and Paul Foster. They conversed in low tones occasionally. At a table before the bench were Margarito Corrales, Ben Garza, and T. C. Segal.

Ben Garza glanced at his watch. "T.C.," he said carefully, "I think that judge is getting more and more pissed because of your requests for delays and recesses. If it were anybody else but you, he'd come down hard."

"I know, I know," Segal replied quietly. "We've pushed our luck to the limit. But one of the things you've got to learn in the business, kid, is that when you've got it you use it."

Garza felt a thrill at being in the confidence of a trial attorney of such renown. "You know," he said, "you've pretty much shown they really don't have much of a case against Margarito. Don't you think we might be better off if we didn't push it any more and asked for a dismissal?"

Segal shook his head. "No. I think they'd refuse. They

know they don't have much to prove Margarito did it, but they know we've got even less proving he didn't. He's the only suspect they have. Excuse the expression, kid, but it's a Mexican standoff right now. I know the prosecution would love to get me out of their lives, but I've got to hand them somebody else on a silver platter"—the door opening to the rear caught his eye—"and I think maybe we got the body. Is that Heath coming in now?"

Garza glanced briefly to the rear. "That's him."

Segal leaned toward Margarito. "Is that Huerta with him?"

Margarito was looking at Huerta as the two took seats in the front row of the spectator section. "That is Rogelio Huerta, Ensenada pimp and girl-beater."

"Okay, okay," Segal told him, "don't get emotional right now. Wait till you see the circus coming up."

Garza was observing Segal's courtroom conduct carefully, memorizing his antics, and now he saw the trial attorney nod almost surreptitiously to a court official. Garza knew a message would be relayed to the judge's chambers and the jury would reconvene.

Sure enough, within a few moments a soft buzzer sounded. The jury filed in. It was announced that the judge was returning to the bench but it was not necessary that everyone stand.

In a moment the judge was addressing Segal.

"Counselor," he said earnestly, "in all deference to your reputation, I do hope the trial can now proceed to whatever conclusion at the normal pace."

Segal stood. "It can, Your Honor," he said. "I don't think we'll need any more delays. I'd like to recall Abel Carmona to the stand."

The judge, noted for his informal approach to tradition, said, "I do hope we're not going to go over his good character and veracity again, counselor."

"That won't be necessary, Your Honor," Segal replied.

When Abel Carmona was installed on the witness stand, Segal proceeded: "Now, Mr. Carmona, you previously testified you are positive the defendant, Margarito Corrales, did not kill Mr. Sloane that night at the ranch."

The statement went through the translator and the reply came through her: "That's right. Sloane was alive and another man came in and fought with him and then I found him dead. This other man, he owns girls, if you know what I mean."

In the front spectator row Huerta's eyes slowly began widening as he saw what was taking place. He glanced back at the doorways and saw the uniformed officers standing at each. Then he looked at Heath next to him. Heath sat looking at Huerta, deadpan, saying nothing, and when Huerta read what was in those steely blue eyes he slumped down in his seat, defeated.

Segal continued the questioning: "Now, Mr. Carmona, is that other man, the one you saw fighting with Sloane just before you found him dead, is he here now? In this room?"

Again the reply came through the translator: "Yes. That's him in the brown suit in the first row sitting next to that blond man."

Segal dismissed Abel Carmona, and called his wife, Lida, but long before she finished corroborating her husband's testimony through the translator the prosecution was huddling quietly, paying scant attention.

When Lida Carmona stepped down the prosecution asked to approach the bench. When the prosecution returned to the table the announcement was simple: "Your Honor, the prosecution will accept a motion to dismiss charges against the defendant, Margarito Corrales, and simultaneously ask that the suspect indicated by the witnesses"—the prosecutor pointed to Huerta—"be charged with the crime." He sat down.

As the murmurs rippled through the courtroom Anastacia left her seat, made her way to the aisle, and was about to leave the spectators' area and come through the low, swinging doors. Margarito started to stand, grinning broadly, but T. C. Segal pushed him back into the chair, at the same time motioning Anastacia back to her seat. "Not yet! Not yet!" he whispered loudly. "It's not all over with."

The judge rapped his gavel once. "Motion granted. The jury is dismissed. Will the bailiff at the rear take the indicated man into . . ."

Then he stopped, because Charles Heath was standing, and he was the kind of man people stopped to listen to when he had something to say.

"Permission to address the court," Heath said matter-of-factly.

"State your name and business here," the judge said.

"Detective Sergeant Charles Heath, Ventura County sheriff's office. I want the court to record that the suspect next to me is here of his own free will. He crossed the border into the United States legally this morning, records will show. I met him at the Border Patrol station in San Ysidro and he willingly and without coercion or persuasion accompanied me to this courtroom. The deputies present"—he glanced over each shoulder, indicating the uniformed officers at each door "—will attest that he entered this room freely, with no persuasion or threat involved. Thank you." And Detective Sergeant Heath was striding out of the courtroom.

"What was that all about?" Margarito asked Segal.

Garza chose to answer. "So later he can't claim he was coerced, maybe even technically arrested illegally, and brought here."

"Thank you," the judge was saying to a departing Heath. A uniformed man was taking Huerta into custody. The man could be heard saying, "You have the right to remain silent . . ."

T. C. Segal signaled Garza to be quiet and the judge turned his attention to Margarito.

"Mr. Corrales," he said.

T. C. Segal leaned over to Margarito. "Stand up, dummy!" he whispered. Margarito stood, showing that whoever had picked his wardrobe for this appearance had misjudged his size.

The judge continued: "The court would like to apologize for the inconvenience caused you and tell you you're free to go. However, I can't quite do that. We do apologize, and you no longer face a charge of murder." The judge turned to the bailiff. "But I must ask that the bailiff take Mr. Corrales and remand him to the custody of the U.S. Immigration and Naturalization Service. I understand he faces a deportation hearing" —he turned back to Margarito— "which, believe me, Mr. Corrales, is a lot better charge to face than what you had here." The judge banged his gavel once and left.

It was then Anastacia came through the swinging doors to the defense table and she and Margarito embraced. Her head was buried in his chest, but it was apparent she was sobbing. Paul Foster sat in his seat in the spectators' section, pleased at what a fine thing a little money had wrought.

Garza tapped both members of the embracing couple on the shoulder, trying to get their attention, but saw that it was impossible to get through to them yet. T. C. Segal was carefully sorting notes and papers and arranging them in his Gucci briefcase. Garza looked to the seats and saw that Abel and Lida Carmona still sat there, trying not to look puzzled. Now that it was over, the translator had abandoned them and they were unaware of what had transpired. Ben started toward them but T. C. Segal was talking. Although he was still somewhat in awe of Segal, he liked trying to talk to him as a peer.

"Okay, kid. Round one is ours. We go to the second half and you're carrying the ball."

"What do you mean?" Garza asked, a little uncertain.

Segal indicated Margarito, still embracing Anastacia. "What are you gonna do? You gonna let 'em send Too-Tall Pancho here back to Mexico to make sandals and pick tomatoes the rest of his life? You did it for her, and when you do it for him I want to be sitting at your table watching you."

Ben gulped. "You want to sit at the table?"

"Right. I realized I don't know a thing about immigration law and . . . well . . . maybe I ought to. And I can learn a lot from you."

Garza was a little frightened at the prospect of having Segal sit and observe him before the immigration judge. "But . . . why? Why do you want to learn about immigration? I mean, as a criminal lawyer you make ten, a hundred times what an immigration lawyer makes."

Segal was through putting away papers. He closed his briefcase and regarded Margarito and Anastacia. A bailiff was beginning to tap Margarito carefully on the shoulder to remind him he was still in custody.

Segal went on. "Well . . . I won't get mushy but . . . my folks came from the old country. Didn't yours? How'd your people get here?"

"Well, as I understand, my grandparents just walked across the border. In those days it was an open border, anyone could cross . . ."

T. C. Segal nodded. "Some of you had it pretty easy. But my dad was just a half jump ahead of a bunch of animals in black uniforms with automatic pistols. He had a usable trade and somehow got admitted here. My mom was still over there. Some of you young kids think all you had to do in those days was tell immigration, 'Hey, if you don't let her in they're going to put her in an oven and turn it on high.' It wasn't like that at all. I realized when I found out what you did for her"—he indicated Anastacia—"and when you told me what you're trying to do for them"—he jerked his head in the direction of the still bewildered Abel and Lida Carmona—"that I don't know a damn thing about immigration law. I've always been where the big bucks are." He paused, briefcase at his side, ready to leave, but something kept him. "So I want to sit by you when you blow the opposition clean out of the hearing room representing the big fella."

He started to leave, but turned back one final time. "You know, kid," he said somberly, "I work late a lot in my office. At night some guys come in and scrub the toilets, replace the paper, do the floors. They're scared all the time, at first I didn't know what of, and they don't speak much English. Like my folks couldn't when they came here. If I learn a little about immigration, who knows? Maybe I can help one of them someday." Segal had stopped and was thinking. "Or his wife," he added as he turned and left the courtroom.

Finally, the embrace broken, the bailiff started to lead Margarito away as Anastacia looked tearfully after him.

"Officer! Officer!" Garza said somewhat authoritatively. The man stopped and turned, holding onto Margarito's arm.

"Yes, sir?"

Garza stepped to them. "May I speak to my client a moment?"

The bailiff shrugged and stepped aside. Margarito looked down on Garza.

All of a sudden Garza knew what he was going to do and how he was going to do it. "Listen, pal, don't despair," he told Margarito. "They're going to take you to downtown L.A., the Federal Building, and process you. Now, when they do, they'll ask you if you want a hearing, which if you lose may prevent you from ever again entering the United States legally, or if you will accept voluntary repatriation. Understand?"

Margarito nodded. "Sí."

"Okay," Garza went on, now the legal counsel in full charge, "at that point, tell them you want a hearing, reasonable bail, and you'll have representation. Got that? Then tell them you want five days, that's all. They'll be surprised you don't want two or three weeks to prepare your case, but you tell them you want five days. Got all that? If anything goes wrong, get ahold of me. If it goes right, get ahold of me. Okay?"

CHAPTER 22

Ben Garza walked into the crowded little hearing room on the eighth floor of the Federal Building only two minutes early. He now had almost a swagger about him, and he wore an expensive suit and polished shoes. He still carried the eagle-and-snake briefcase. He looked around.

Judge Rhine wasn't there yet, but his old enemy, Gerald Skinner, who'd beaten the pants off him once before, was there with another lawyer. Skinner looked at Garza with some annoyance and then looked at the clock on the wall. Garza saw old Professor Shaw among the dozen or so seated in the room. Anastacia, of course. Meme de Beauclair (he guessed she was footing some of the bill), a few classmates, Paul Foster, and T. C. Segal. Margarito was seated to the side next to a uniformed INS officer. Segal left his seat and approached. He shook hands with Garza, and Garza motioned him into a seat at the table he'd be using. Then Garza, with a minimum of flourish, indicated to the INS man that he should allow Margarito to join them at the petitioner's table.

As Margarito came toward them, Segal leaned toward Garza and said, "Your almost being late has your opposition table in a tizzy, kid, but I got an idea you know what you're doing."

"Thanks," Garza said, allowing himself a grin, "and now, thanks to my training with you, I know *how* to do it. In *style!*"

"Here he comes now, like a wet hen," Segal said.

Skinner approached Garza, just a little less than seething. "Mr. Garza," he complained, "I know the hearing is set for two. It's two now, but the least you could have done is give us your exhibits in advance. I mean, you throw us a curve *now*, and we can ask for time to study it."

Garza took an unlit Havana from his mouth and turned to

Skinner. "Really sorry, Skinner, but the exhibit I'm going to present has not been available until very, very recently." He opened his briefcase and at that moment Immigration Judge Conrad Rhine came in and unceremoniously took his seat.

Judge Rhine, ever mindful of the load all hearing judges were carrying from dawn to dusk, nodded at the concerned parties and said, "Okay, are we all ready?" He began leafing through the agenda.

Skinner was still standing and now Garza stood and handed him a paper. Then he handed another copy to Judge Rhine, who took it and began examining it. Skinner suddenly exploded, getting red in the face, but Judge Rhine waved him silent.

"Yes, your Honor," Garza said. "In this matter of the United States vs. Margarito Corrales, we're petitioning for a permanent stay of deportation and the right to apply for permanent residency, to be laid before Congress, etcetera, on the grounds that the petitioner, Margarito Corrales, is now married to a full-fledged citizen of the United States of America."

Garza sat down. Skinner had calmed down somewhat, but was dying to be heard. He waited. Judge Rhine continued to look at the marriage certificate a few moments and then peered over his glasses at Skinner.

"Mr. Skinner, does the government have anything to say at this time?"

Skinner stood, controlling his voice. "You bet we do, Your Honor. We're not going to allow this. It's obviously a marriage of convenience . . ."

Judge Rhine cut in. "What do you mean, *you're* not going to allow this? I'm the judge here and I'll make the decisions. No, Mr. Skinner, if you have something to object to, we'll all be glad to hear it."

Skinner forced himself even more under control.

"We do object, Your Honor. You'll notice the date on this marriage certificate. A day old. This is obviously a marriage of convenience, entered into for the purpose of circumventing the laws and regulations of the U.S. Immigration and Naturalization Service . . ."

Now Garza leaped to his feet, "Mr. Skinner, do you happen to have even a speaking acquaintance with either the respondent or the citizen he's married to?" he demanded.

Skinner paused. "Well, no . . . but it's obvious . . ."

Garza went on. "Then if I were you I would certainly reserve my opinion until someone a little more qualified than yourself ascertained whether this is a convenient marriage or one based on the usual sacred traditions which motivate most marriages."

The small room was hushed for a few moments as Judge Rhine considered. He looked at Margarito, then at Anastacia seated in the spectators' section.

"Very well," he said, "we'll see if we can determine whether it is a bona fide marriage or one entered into for convenience."

Garza was still standing. With quiet confidence he said, "Your Honor, I anticipated this and took the liberty of asking someone who is greatly experienced at determining marriages of convenience; that is, if the government is willing."

"Who do you have in mind?" Judge Rhine asked.

"I asked Acting Assistant District Director Frederick Wilder of the U.S. Immigration and Naturalization Service if he would make the determination. He's extremely busy, as you know, but he said he would make the determination this afternoon if the occasion arose."

Judge Rhine looked at Skinner. "Is that all right with you?" he asked.

Skinner glumly consented.

"All right," Judge Rhine said. He looked to the uniformed INS man present. "Would you be kind enough to take the petitioner and his . . . bride . . . over to Frederick Wilder's office?"

The man stepped forward and Anastacia and Margarito rose and accompanied him out of the hearing room.

Skinner busied himself with papers, as did Judge Rhine. Segal said in a low voice to Garza, "What's this all about?"

Garza was sitting with one arm over the back of his chair in an almost nonchalant position.

"Lots of times some dumb would-be immigration lawyer will marry off a client to a citizen, paying the citizen a small amount of money. That's a marriage of convenience. It won't stand up in a hearing if it can be determined."

Segal was still puzzled. "But . . . how can they determine if it's for convenience or because the couple loves each other?"

"Easy," Garza replied, "they simply get an expert in these matters, like this Wilder guy, and he questions the couple, separately. One at a time. 'Does hubby like his tortillas buttered every morning?' or, 'What's your wife's favorite, coffee or chocolate?' Any expert can tell in five minutes if the couple knew each other more than three days."

Segal was impressed. "What if the couple has rehearsed these answers?"

"Oh, they do," Garza replied, "but then the interrogator simply moves to a more intimate set of questions. At some point it will become obvious if they've just married to get citizenship for one."

Segal thought a moment. "This Wilder, is he good at making this determination?"

Garza looked at him coolly. "I hope so, but it doesn't matter. I happen to know he knows both Tacha and Margarito and knows they've had the hots for each other all their lives."

Segal chuckled and patted Garza on the shoulder.

"I knew you had it, kid. Pretty smart, getting him to agree to make the determination in advance."

Garza's attitude was still nonchalant. "If you've got it, use it."

Segal chuckled even more, then became serious.

"But what if this Skinner guy doesn't want to go along with Wilder's finding?"

Garza withheld his answer a moment, still aloof, then whispered, "Wilder is an acting assistant INS director. He's Skinner's boss."

The small room was startled as Segal guffawed heartily and slapped Garza on the back almost as hard as he could.

"By God, kid, you did learn something, didn't you!"

Soon Wilder came in with Anastacia and Margarito. In accordance with the relative informality of the hearing room, he simply addressed Judge Rhine, "Your Honor, I have interrogated both parties and believe me, if there was ever a marriage that was not of convenience, it is this one. Take my word for it. It is a bona fide marriage."

The spectators made sounds as though they wanted to applaud but were silenced by a stern look from Judge Rhine.

"Very well," Rhine said, "I'm going to allow the respondent Margarito Corrales to petition for stay of deportation and to apply for permanent resident status in accordance with the rules and regulations of the U.S. Immigration and Naturalization Service . . ."

Garza was aware of a previously unknown elation as he saw the glowering Skinner closing a folder. Garza suddenly heard Segal say in his ear, "Feels good, doesn't it, kid. It's only the beginning for you . . ."

Then Garza was on his feet, addressing Judge Rhine.

"Your Honor, you recall that the bride—the citizen in this case, Miss Herrera—was successful in establishing citizenship under Section 1401(a) 7."

"Yes, I recall, of course. Why?"

"Well, regarding the citizen's mother, whose established citizenship was a prerequisite, I'd like to set the wheels in motion to bring her here from Mexico to her native land . . ."

Judge Rhine smiled. "Of course. We'll issue the citizenship documents forthwith. Have her contact our consulate in Tijuana. No problem." He started to turn, but Garza persisted.

"And the . . . citizen's father, a Mexican national, I'd like to start proceedings . . ."

Judge Rhine was still smiling. "Counselor, the U.S. Immigration and Naturalization Service does not make a practice of keeping man and wife apart. You're well qualified to commence proceedings on his behalf to petition for permanent residence, and you know how to go about it." He said it with formal finality but then said in a confidential tone, "If you run into any technical snags, give me a buzz."

Anastacia was beside him, tears streaming. "Ben," she said in a choked voice, "I was going to ask you . . . I can pay you, I still have a good job . . ."

Ben faced her squarely, putting his hands on her shoulders. "Tacha, please. This one's on me. Maybe I want to pay a little on my bill too. Besides, I really did well on this one. And on top of that, I still need the practice." The little hearing room was filling with petitioners, defendants, and their counselors who would be taking part in the ensuing, unending hearings. "Come on," Garza said, pushing Margarito and Anastacia ahead of him through the crowd and into the teeming hall, "let's get the papers and get out of here."

Anastacia walked between Margarito and Ben to the

parking lot near the Federal Building. It had taken some time to get Margarito the papers verifying his pending status, and Ben was surprised to see several of those who had been sitting in the spectator chairs at the hearing now standing near the parking attendants' shack. As he approached them he saw Frederick Wilder parked in his official immigration service car at the curb, also waiting to congratulate him, no doubt.

Waiting there were Meme de Beauclair, Paul Foster, Professor Shaw, and T. C. Segal. Garza gestured to Wilder parked at the curb, indicating he would be with him in a few minutes.

"Hi," Garza greeted them. "Really a reception committee isn't necessary," he began a little self-consciously.

Foster cut him off. "We're not here to receive you, Ben. The parking attendants aren't around to give us our keys."

Garza looked around. "Oh. They're probably getting coffee. Anyway, I'm glad you had to wait. Quite a show, wasn't it?"

"It was great, kid," T. C. Segal said, stepping forward and offering his hand. "The minute you become a full-fledged attorney, come and see me. I got something to talk over with you."

Garza's mind reeled. Was he offering him a job? Maybe he wanted to start an immigration branch in his organization.

His speculation was cut short by Professor Shaw: "By the way, Ben, I'm recommending to the Independent Study Evaluation Committee that you receive ten units for the work you've performed."

Now Ben reeled visibly, hand to his forehead. "Ten units! Why . . . that puts me over the top! A whole term. I'm out of law school! Except for the final exam."

Shaw continued. "No, we're going to allow that your preparation for these cases and your research count as a final exam. It's unusual for the committee to do that, but not unheard of. You've earned it, Ben."

Garza actually leaped into the air, fists extended above his head. "I'm a lawyer!" he shouted.

"Not quite, kid," Segal put in, "you still got the bar exam to pass. Your professor can't fix that one for you. And it's a toughie. Like I say, when you pass it, come see me."

Anastacia was looking at an old Volkswagen parked in the

lot, with huge rear tires and camping equipment piled high on top. "Margarito, look," she said, pointing, "it's like our old car. Why . . . it's *Ben's* car . . ."

Margarito grinned. "It *was* Ben's. I bought it from him. I put the tires and rack on yesterday."

She looked at him almost misty-eyed, because she knew what he had in mind and where they were going.

Then she looked at Ben. "But . . . what'll you do for a car?"

Garza was lighting an expensive Havana. He pointed to a late-model Porsche nearby, glistening in the sunlight. "I bought that car. It's not new and it's not paid for, but I couldn't resist. Besides, I can still continue representing people in the immigration hearings before passing the bar, and my reputation must be spreading because I got clients pushing money at me to represent them."

Meme de Beauclair spoke up: "Tacha, dear, I know you two are off to Mexico. But promise me when you return you'll at least consider taking over my house. It's been a shambles since you left. You two could have the apartment over the garage . . ."

Anastacia cut her off. "I promise I'll consider it, Meme. I know what I owe you. I'll repay you somehow."

Foster spoke: "I don't see why you're going back to Mexico, Tacha. After all the trouble . . ."

She turned to him quickly, "Because, Paul, I have options now. *We* have options. I still have my apartment here. I have a home down in Baja. You see, we can cross the border any time we want, as often as we want. Just like you always could. None of you will ever really understand about that."

There was an almost awkward silence, finally broken by Segal. He cleared his throat. "Well, I wish those attendants would show up to give me the keys to the car. Where the hell are they?"

Garza looked around, and then suddenly it dawned on him. "Oh. Just a minute. I'll fix it."

He walked over to where Wilder was parked at the curb in the official government car with the emblem of the U.S. Immigration and Naturalization Service on the door.

"Good work, Ben!" Wilder shouted as he approached. "I just wanted to say fine job, and I know we'll be seeing more of you up on the eighth floor."

"You sure will." Ben smiled. "But now will you please get the hell out of here with this car so the rest of us can get our cars and go home?"

Wilder looked puzzled only for a moment, and then Garza heard him roar with laughter as the car pulled away.

Ben turned to join the others and as if by magic two smallish, dark men came scurrying toward them saying "Teekets? Geeve me teekets." Ben watched as they gathered the tickets and hurried to get the keys hanging on a board in the shack and then ran to bring the cars, wondering what their story would be and if he would ever hear it. He looked at Anastacia and Margarito. They too were observing the attendants seriously, and it was impossible to tell what they were thinking, whether they were happy or sad.

AZTEC

The National Bestseller by
GARY JENNINGS

"A blockbuster historical novel. . . . From the start of this epic, the reader is caught up in the sweep and grandeur, the richness and humanity of this fictive unfolding of life in Mexico before the Spanish conquest. . . . Anyone who lusts for adventure, or that book you can't put down, will glory in AZTEC!"
The Los Angeles Times

"A dazzling and hypnotic historical novel. . . . AZTEC has everything that makes a story appealing . . . both ecstasy and appalling tragedy . . . sex . . . violence . . . and the story is filled with revenge. . . . Mr. Jennings is an absolutely marvelous yarnspinner. . . . A book to get lost in!"
The New York Times

"Sumptuously detailed. . . . AZTEC falls into the same genre of historical novel as SHOGUN."
Chicago Tribune

"Unforgettable images. . . . Jennings is a master at graphic description. . . . The book is so vivid that this reviewer had the novel experience of dreaming of the Aztec world, in technicolor, for several nights in a row . . . so real that the tragedy of the Spanish conquest is truly felt."
Chicago Sun Times

AVON Paperback   55889 . . . $3.95

Available wherever paperbacks are sold, or directly from the publisher. Include 50¢ per copy for postage and handling; allow 6-8 weeks for delivery. Avon Books, Mail Order Dept., 224 West 57th St., N.Y., N.Y. 10019.

Aztec 1-82